D0204642

ALSO BY KIERAN KRAMER

THE HOUSE OF BRADY SERIES

Loving Lady Marcia
The Earl Is Mine
Say Yes to the Duke

THE IMPOSSIBLE BACHELOR SERIES

When Harry Met Molly
Dukes to the Left of Me, Princes to the Right
Cloudy with a Chance of Marriage
If You Give a Girl a Viscount

SWEET TALK
Me

KIERAN KRAMER

St. Martin's Paperbacks

This is a work of fiction. All of the characters, organizations, and events portrayed in this novel are either products of the author's imagination or are used fictitiously.

SWEET TALK ME

For information address St. Martin's Press, 175 Fifth Avenue, New York, NY 10010.

ISBN: 978-1-250-00991-3

Printed in the United States of America

St. Martin's Paperbacks edition / April 2014

St. Martin's Paperbacks are published by St. Martin's Press, 175 Fifth Avenue, New York, NY 10010.

10 9 8 7 6 5 4 3 2 1

To Devon Elizabeth Wray Hanahan
Much adored sister
Amazing teacher
Flawless reciter of *A Hard Day's Night*
and *This Is Spinal Tap*
With me through thick and thin

ACKNOWLEDGMENTS

Thank you so much to Jennifer Enderlin and Jenny Bent for being the fairy godmothers who got me to this place I've always longed to be. I'm so grateful you're in my life!

I'm also extremely indebted to the late Matthew Shear, who watched over all of us at St. Martin's Press with such joy, caring, and encouragement. Matthew, your light will shine always.

Thank you, as well, to the entire team at St. Martin's Press. What a delight it is to work with all of you!

Susan Adamé, a wonderful collage artist in California, gave me insight into her exciting world, and for that I'm grateful and inspired.

And as always, thank you to my dear family and friends, whose unflagging patience and support sustain me.

CHAPTER ONE

When country music superstar Harrison Gamble appeared on the sun-dappled sidewalk outside the hotel on Peachtree Street in Atlanta, the crowd roared its approval—everyone, that is, except True Maybank. She'd as soon scream as chase a pig around a mud pen. Maybanks didn't holler. They believed in decorum. Tradition. Using something until it wore out. Keeping up appearances even when the world had gone to hell in a handbasket.

"Well, I swanny," she murmured, her entire body filling with a prickly sensation. She'd never thought she'd see him again.

Behind her late great-aunt Honey's oversized Nina Ricci sunglasses, she watched Harrison take his fans' hysteria in stride, as if it had nothing to do with him, his smokin' hot body, that sparkling white smile, the bronzed skin, sexy stubble, and those sideburns, which were longer than they used to be—just long enough to qualify for serious bad-boy status.

Move on, *girl! You got a wedding dress to get home!*

She circled the heavily policed chaos, risking her life in the street for a few seconds, and quickly began walking again, uphill. With her mother's newly repaired vintage gown in her arms, it was as if Mama were walking with her, Mama with all her high expectations and impeccable standards. And here True merely hoped that the double-whammy dreamboat behind her—the first guy she'd slept with *and* her only one-night stand—wouldn't somehow recognize her.

At the corner, she couldn't resist a glance over her shoulder back down at the scene at the hotel. *What a collage that would make*. The thought crept up, wily and insistent, and she fought to dismiss it. But it was too wild, too alive . . .

It kept coming, the image, blossoming in her mind and taking over her body, making her fingertips buzz with the need to arrange. She would collage this memory. She would. It would be her best work yet.

And no one would ever see it.

Harrison signed an autograph and with a quick kiss to the crowd got into the back of a black Humvee. Two Taylor Swift look-alikes scooted inside as well. The car's dark-tinted windows slid up, its front tires angled toward the street, and True's arm began to sweat under the plastic bag.

Change, light, change!

Seconds later the Humvee whooshed past her. Two more scary-looking black SUVs followed behind.

Huh.

She took a deep breath. There. It was over. Harrison was the Big Bad Wolf to millions of captivated Red Riding Hoods, and once upon a time True had been one of them.

Admit it. You nearly got sucked in again today.

No. She wouldn't think of him anymore. It had been a crazy minute in an otherwise fairly sane week. All she had to do now was get to the parking garage, find her car, and drive the four hours back to Biscuit Creek. Back to

Weezie, her sister. To Carmela, her best friend. And to Dubose, the man she was to marry.

Back to the life that was finally falling into place.

A block later, a sporty aqua-blue coupe with darkened windows slowed to a crawl next to her, and the passenger-side window lowered a crack. "Get in, Miss Junior League," Harrison said, his voice ringing out loud and clear.

True's heart clanged like a fire station alarm bell, and she stopped walking.

She was seriously nonplussed. In Biscuit Creek, they'd say she was as nervous as a long-tailed cat in a room full of rocking chairs. But True favored words like *nonplussed*, probably because she was a big reader. She had a book stuffed up the right leg of her Spanx right now, a dog-eared Agatha Christie paperback that didn't fit into her pocketbook. That minimalist creation—a Target find, a faux yellow leather tote—was actually overflowing with three lipsticks of varying coral shades, a two-inch Velcro hair roller, travel hair spray, a pack of Kleenex, Juicy Fruit gum, her cell phone, a round hairbrush, a black Sharpie, her keys (which weighed a ton), a banana, a tube of Advil, a spare pair of sunglasses, and her ancient Cinderella wallet from Disney World, which had a rubber band around it to keep the cards and money from falling out.

"Well?" Harrison revved the engine. "You gonna get in here and tell me what you been up to all these years or stand there stiff as a poker and pretend you can't see me?"

True pivoted on a heel to face the car. "I see you, all right."

Daddy always said if you couldn't run with the big dogs, stay under the porch. True wasn't an under-the-porch sort of gal.

* * *

Harrison hid his amusement behind a cool stare, the one he dragged out when the higher-ups interfered too much with his creative vision or a fan overstepped her bounds, which was basically getting naked without asking him first.

That wasn't going to happen with True. She was a lady—at least on the surface. But those snapping blue eyes gave her away. Beneath that prissy exterior, a sexy damned hellion wanted out. He'd seen her. He wished he could forget her—he'd written songs trying to exorcise her from his brain—but sometimes he still dreamed her arms were wrapped around his neck and her sweet body was beneath his.

Now she leaned down to peer inside his passenger window, a bulky garment bag slung over her arm. She smelled good, like some kind of magical spring flower in a secret bower filled with singing chipmunks and tweety little bluebirds. "I can't ride home with you, even if I wanted to."

Implying that she didn't. Typical of her. She'd always been too proud for her own good.

"But we can talk," she added. "Lemme buy you a Coke."

Which meant any drink. Everything was a Coke in the South, especially in Atlanta.

"Not thirsty," Harrison said back. "Gimme your keys. I'll get my manager to drive your car all the way home." Harrison had always wanted to show Dan around his old stomping grounds anyway.

True shook her head. "The last thing I expect you to do is come back to Biscuit Creek."

No one expected him back. Ever. Which had always been fine with him. He went to LA. Aspen. Tropical islands.

"I don't have all day to argue," he said. "The paparazzi are hot on my trail. I gotta keep moving. So let's drop the polite chitchat and get down to business. Knowing you, you can't dillydally, either."

True never sat still.

"I might as well stop by and say hello to Gage," he added. "It's been a while since I've seen him." But he'd make the visit to his brother short. Harrison was due in the Hamptons at the beachfront home of an equally famous singer, a sexy, single woman who wasn't looking for a serious relationship but wouldn't mind the occasional fling and the publicity that went with it.

True hesitated. "There's a lady about to cross the street, and she has a tattoo of you with a guitar in your hand walking down her belly into her pants."

"My first album cover. People do all kinds of things with it."

True carefully laid her garment bag on his car roof, then dug through an enormous purse and managed to pull out a huge set of keys tethered to a pink rubber ball with pink rubber spikes all over it. "All right," she said. "I'll ride with you."

Score.

"That's the ugliest key chain I've ever seen," Harrison said to cover up how awesome he felt about her actually getting in his car.

"But I can see it, and feel it. It's gushy."

"*Gushy*?" Such a True word. He lowered the window farther.

She dropped the keys in his palm, but even so the tips of her fingers brushed his, and he had an instant memory of those fingers trailing over his naked back, curling into his hair. "Only you would want a gushy key chain."

She arched one eyebrow. "Lots of people like them."

"Is that so? How would you know?" Teasing her had always been his go-to diversion when wild sex fantasies intruded. Of course, now she had a big rock on her finger. A *really* big one.

"They have a huge barrel of them at Walmart."

Always the authority on things. She hadn't changed one bit. But when had she started shopping at Walmart? And who'd given her that ring?

"Was the barrel empty or full?" he asked her.

"Full. There were hundreds. Different colors, too."

"It would have been nearly empty if everyone liked 'em, though, right?"

"Maybe they just restocked." She sighed. "Look, Harrison, could you let me in? Preferably before the rest of the world figures out you've escaped your guards."

He unlocked the car door. "Like King Kong?"

"Something like that." She yanked the door open, grabbed her garment bag, and slid inside.

"Let me." He took the bag off her lap and laid it behind them. It was heavy and said CARR'S BRIDAL across the front.

Damn. She was getting married soon, from all appearances. Not that he'd ask.

"Thanks." She had two little spots of pink on her cheeks when she pulled her door shut.

The window on her side hummed upward and shut—his doing. "I'll drop the keys off with my team, and you and I will be on our way." He caught a glimpse of her tanned calves and tapered ankles. Bad idea. Heat flooded his belly. "What're you driving these days?"

"An Acura."

"Really? You're a loyal customer. Did you get a convertible this time?"

She gave him a sideways glance. "It's the same car I drove in high school."

Whoa. That surprised him. "Good for you, keeping it up so long. How many miles you got on it?"

She shrugged. "A hundred eighty thousand."

"Still got some juice, then." When his truck finally bit the dust, it had 245,000. "Nothing better than a reliable car."

"Honey taught me how to look after things."

He noticed that her hair was flipped out on the ends, the same way it used to be. "She still alive?"

True shook her head. "She passed on six years ago. Mama thought she was a liability, but that woman had game." She sang the song "Five Foot Two, Eyes of Blue" quietly in a husky-sweet voice:

Harrison could listen all day long.

"It was her favorite," True said. "That and 'S Wonderful.'"

"I'm really sorry." He was tempted to put a hand on hers, but he didn't, just in case she got all jumpy about it. "She was the coolest person in Biscuit Creek. She could work out a ukulele something fierce."

True chuckled. "Yes, she could." She looked down at her lap a moment, then back up. "You know how to get to I-40 from here?"

"I think I know my way around this part of the world." He grinned at her, and for a minute he was eighteen again. "Damn, True." He soaked her up, all that creamy skin, platinum-blond hair, wide blue eyes, and that pale mole near her mouth. "You're still gorgeous."

She fiddled with her sun visor. "You're not so bad yourself, as you well know. Although I'm not crazy about the hair gel."

He laughed and pulled out onto the street. "Me, either." He made a right turn and waited for the bodyguard to catch up with him so he could hand him True's keys. A few instructions later, and they were on their way. "My makeup girl insists on the gel. She was one of the women who got in the car with me today."

"You don't have to explain anything to me." True squirmed in her seat.

Damn, she was nervous.

"I know I don't," he said, and put on his blinker. It felt good to drive. "I'm just talking. Gotta break the ice somehow."

"Not really. We have no business talking to each other." Her voice was soft. Almost sad.

It was his turn to shrug. "How's everyone doing at Maybank Hall?"

"Ten years have gone by. Hasn't Gage kept you informed?"

"Of course not. He's too busy making crossword clues."

"That's a lot of catching up, don't you think?"

"Well, why not? We'll do it on the plane. Do you mind getting home a lot faster than you anticipated?"

Her eyes flew wide. "Please don't rent a jet for me."

"Rent-a-Jet. I like the sound of that." He grinned. "It's for me, not you, if that makes you feel any better. I gotta be in front of a TV before the Spurs game."

"So you can do that? Just get someone to fly you wherever you want to go for whatever reason?"

"It comes with the territory. Country music's been good to me."

She stared at him long and hard. "I'm glad for you, Harrison," she said quietly. "Mighty glad."

He snuck another peek at her. "Are you?"

She nodded. "Of course. Think how proud you've made Biscuit Creek. Why, you've put us on the map."

"Did I?"

"Most certainly. The water tower has your name on it."

"Did you see to that?"

She blushed again. "Of course not. It was the mayor."

"But you always were the civic-minded citizen," he reminded her.

"Oh, I still am." She looked straight ahead. Her earlobes had tiny pearl studs in them.

Harrison held back another grin. There was always something about True that put him in a good mood. Maybe it was how transparent she was. That was it. She wore her heart on her sleeve, and wary and practical as that heart was, it was a good one.

"Hey." He leaned over to her. "Do me a favor. At the airport, put on a hat." He pointed to the glove compartment.

She opened it, revealing a stack of sunglasses and two nylon baseball caps. "What?" A wrinkle formed on her brow. "Why?"

"A disguise, of course. Look out back. Someone's on to us. Probably the *National Enquirer.*"

She twisted her neck to look, and hell if he didn't enjoy seeing the swell of her breasts in that fuddy-duddy dress against the cream leather seat.

"How can you tell?" Her voice was a little breathy, and he felt a response in his jeans, which was wrong, considering who she was, but entirely understandable from a biological standpoint. So he wasn't going to lose any sleep over it.

"Easy." He sped up and switched lanes. "Watch what happens."

She kept her gaze behind them.

"Did a black Volvo follow us?" he asked.

"Well, I'll be," True murmured. "It most certainly did."

He switched lanes again, taking an odd satisfaction at hearing the wonder in her voice when she exclaimed that once again, the Volvo was keeping track of them, right on their bumper as a matter of fact.

Yep. Harrison really was famous. Although why he felt the need to make sure she knew, he had no idea.

"He should be ticketed!" she exclaimed. "Where are the police when you need them?"

"I don't know." It was fun playing a martyr, especially in a $160,000 sports car.

"It must be hell to be you," True said.

"I suppose it is." Harrison enjoyed her pity. "So you listen to my advice and wear that disguise, all right? Otherwise, my wife will be pissed when she sees a picture of us together."

True whipped around to face him. "Your *wife*?"

He laughed out loud at the drama he'd stirred up, then suddenly felt sheepish. "I was just kidding. There's no little missus. You ought to know better than to think there would be."

"Of course I knew better." True frowned at him. "Still, that wasn't very nice."

"Why?" He swung the car over to the airport exit. The black Volvo stayed with them. "What difference would it have made if I was married?"

There was a second of taut silence.

"It wouldn't have made any," True said. "It's just that friends don't tease friends."

"They don't? Who made that rule?" He followed a service road around to the back of a yellow Butler building, a hangar for a couple of Learjets. "You got a lot of rules, True. And the truth is, I don't recall us particularly being friends anymore."

What the hell. Let her feel a little embarrassed at dumping him. This was an opportunity he'd no idea he'd been seeking, but now that it was here, it felt good to get some things off his chest.

She pursed her lips. "I thought that by now—"

"I *am* over it," he said, and pulled the car into a parking space. "Which is why we can talk about it. You're never gonna leave Biscuit Creek, and I'm never going to tie myself down." He shut the engine off. "Got it."

"Harrison—"

He ignored her and opened his door. The photographer had already exited the Volvo, camera ready, the bag still on his shoulder. "Take a picture of me and my old friend together, Charlie, and I'm going to make sure my team puts you in the back row of every single press conference I give from here on out. And about the rock on her finger, it's not from me. I'm trying to get her home to her beloved, whoever the poor sap may be. Is that clear?"

"Got it, Mr. Gamble." Charlie didn't look the least bit fazed. He was a real pro.

"Dubose is not a poor sap!" True said from behind Harrison at the same time, right on cue. "And I resent you for saying so."

"You resent me? So what's new?" Harrison kept his eyes on Charlie and winked. "And you're kidding me about Dubose Waring, aren't you? He's a putz."

"No, he is *not*," she slammed.

He looked back at her in all her quivering, self-righteous glory. God, it turned him on. "When are y'all getting married?"

"None of your business!"

He pretended to be properly chastened, but from the withering look she sent him, she knew damned well he wasn't.

"How about a couple snaps of you alone, Mr. Gamble," Charlie interjected with a grin, "looking travel-weary. Is there a guitar in the backseat?"

"No." Harrison sighed. "But since you came all this way, you can grab a few shots when I get out—and then you leave." He glanced at True. She was clawing at her dress a little, wiping her palms on it.

It was odd, to say the least.

"Do you—do you have a paper bag?" she asked him in a squeaky voice.

"No," he said, wondering what was going on.

"Nothing?" Her pupils were dilated.

Uh-oh. Not a good sign. Was she taking drugs, his True?

Surely not.

"True, baby, what's wrong?" he asked her, his pulse speeding up.

She wasn't his baby and never had been. But for one night he'd pretended she was.

True shook her head and fumbled for the door handle, her hands shaking. "N-nothing." She got it open, stepped right on her giant purse, and jumped out, leaving the door wide open.

Harrison was already around the front of the car. "What is it?" When he caught up with her, she was shaking like a leaf, walking around in circles. And then a damned *book* fell out of her dress, a strange event he'd choose to ignore. He knew she liked to read, but this took the cake. "Are you diabetic?"

He held a finger up at Charlie. It meant, *Stand by. Just in case this is a real-ass emergency.*

Charlie didn't move. His camera dangled from his hand.

True swallowed, crouched on her haunches, and cupped her hands around her mouth. She breathed in, then out. In. Held it. Then out.

Harrison put an arm on her back. "I'm with you."

Her forehead was sweaty. Her spine curled, the muscles in her back trembling.

He pulled out his cell phone.

"No!" she cried.

"Yes." His tone was ugly. He'd never been able to remain cool in a crisis. "We can't mess around. You're pale. Shaking. Something's seriously wrong."

She shook her head. "Let me breathe into my hands," she said into her hands. Loud. So he could hear. Which was awfully considerate of her since he was now out of his mind with worry.

"Give me your camera bag," he yelled to Charlie.

Charlie came running with it and handed it directly to True.

She grabbed it and put her whole face inside.

"What the hell is happening, True?" Harrison's heart slammed against his chest.

"It's just a panic attack." Her face still in the bag, she fell back on her bottom. But it was a controlled fall, as if she was getting herself together again.

Harrison felt a slight—very slight—lessening of worry.

She lowered the bag. "I'm afraid of flying," she whispered and flinched once. Twice. Like a bird that had hit a glass window.

And then she burst into tears.

"Shit," he said. "Why didn't you tell me?" He sat next to her and pulled her close.

She put the bag back to her face. "I thought I could handle it."

Even muffled, her voice did something to him, especially those little hiccups. "You always think you can handle it."

She didn't say anything to that. Her arms looked so skinny, and her neck was just a twig, dammit.

"That's right," he said roughly. "It's about time you just shut up and breathed, Maybank. Let the world run without you for a few minutes."

Charlie backed away, his shoes making gritty sounds on the rocky asphalt.

Harrison rubbed his hand up and down True's arm, which was warming up a little, and waited. Waited for her to perk up. Waited to feel remorse that he'd reconnected with her.

But it didn't come.

Here he was comforting a woman who didn't think he was all that special. In fact, she was sure he was the opposite. She believed he—Harrison Gamble, number one right now on the iTunes country chart—had major flaws.

Who'da thunk it?

"Don't let my book get away," she ordered him from inside her camera bag house, then added, "Please."

But it was a feeble *please*. She was getting back to her old bossy self.

A jumbo jet coasted in for a landing above their heads, its wheels locked into the down position. *Welcome back to real*, Harrison thought, the smell of diesel in his nostrils. He might write and sing about the ordinary, the substantial—the stuff of life—but he'd been running from all that reality crap for a long time.

Funny how it managed to find him anyway here on a hot gravel parking lot with a mixed-up bookworm named True. He was sure after their effed-up good-bye ten years before that he'd be glad never to see her again. But he didn't want to leave her this time, either.

Damn, that surprised him.

Sort of.

He cast a sideways glance at Miss Priss with her knees hitched up, ankles touching, and eyelids closed. Her arm was tanned, her knuckles white as she gripped the camera bag. But her lashes lay thick on her cheek, like the old days, the really, *really* old days, when she'd join him on the trailer park dock and tilt her face up to the sun to bask in its warmth.

He remembered the first day she ever caught a crab on

that dock. She got so rattled, she tilted the net and the crab dropped out. It ran sideways, a little tap dancer, straight over her feet. "Ooohhhaaghh!" she'd shrieked, and fallen backward into the water.

In the Atlanta sunshine, he chuckled at the memory, threw a pebble, and watched it bounce. Nah. It didn't surprise him at all that he wanted to stay.

CHAPTER TWO

So True'd had a panic attack in front of Harrison. La-di-dah. She'd even cried for a minute, but those were tears of frustration. She never saw them coming, these unfortunate episodes—that's what her doctor called them. Each time she was sure she was going to die. She just wanted to breathe, to stay alive, and she always felt like such an idiot afterward . . .

But she refused to care this time.

As far as she was concerned, Harrison could see her do other embarrassing things, too, like wearing white shoes before Easter—or worse yet, adding dark meat to her mama's prizewinning chicken salad. She wouldn't even blush. And why should she? Right now he looked like a roughed-up Brad Pitt, weary from a honky-tonk brawl or a night of hot sex. Or both.

"Thanks for getting my book." She imagined him punching a drunk guy in the jaw and sending him sprawling across a table covered with beer mugs, poker chips, and playing cards.

"Not a problem." He spanked all the grit off the cover and handed it back to her with one brow quirked and the tiniest vertical line on his forehead, right above his nose.

True couldn't lie to herself anymore. She was secretly aghast that he'd seen her freak out—not the *Entertainment Weekly* A-Lister, but the guy who'd brought her to wild and utter completion on a beach when she was eighteen years old. It irked her that Harrison was the only person who'd ever witnessed her out of control.

Ever.

Yes, that meant the big O had never happened with Dubose. He didn't notice, and she didn't care. That was what a vibrator was for. It was a poor substitute for the real thing, but the real thing with Harrison had been a fluke. Right? An utter freak occurrence, like a 75 percent off sale on boots the same day your best pair gets chewed up by your dog.

"Are you sure you don't want a drink?" Harrison asked. "We could stop off for a quick beer—"

"No, thank you." After the barroom brawl, he'd probably kiss a girl up against a wall. Feel her up, too, while he was at it, his long, golden-brown hair hanging like a curtain to block the view.

"A Coke then?"

"I wish." A bead of sweat popped out on her brow, and she swiftly wiped it away. "But somebody'll recognize you in the drive-through. Chicken nuggets will go flying, and mothers will leave their children in the play area just to catch a glimpse of you. I'm fine, Harrison. Thank you."

"I hope so." He pulled out a pair of sunglasses and put them on.

Sickening. Truly sickening how good looking he was!

She picked up her book. "I really don't like the page corners getting bent." She didn't like her life getting bent, either, so he'd better not try.

"Then put it back in your dress," he said. "I don't care."

"Fine." She knew she sounded starchy. But not caring was her new theme. Especially now that she knew *he* didn't care. She looked pointedly at him and stuffed the musty paperback down her high scooped neckline.

Shoot. It wasn't very comfortable. It felt somewhat akin to a mammogram plate wedged between her breasts. But the book would warm up, she was sure.

A hand would feel better. A big, warm male hand.

"There." She hitched her shoulder and tried to think of Dubose. Washboard-ab and well-endowed-in-every-way Dubose—who had cold hands. But it wasn't his fault. He got it from his mother Penn's Puritan side of the family. "You can't be too careful with print books these days. Heck, this could be worth some money in a few years."

Harrison shook his head and held the passenger door of his car open.

True slipped inside and looked up at him. "Been in any fights lately?"

"*No*. Why?"

"No reason." She wouldn't dare ask him how many girls he'd kissed up against honky-tonk walls since he'd moved away from Biscuit Creek.

"I'll drive you home." He got in the cream leather driver's seat and put the car in reverse.

"Thanks," she said, feeling guilty. Then remembered it was *his* idea to take her home in the first place.

"Not a problem." He flicked on the radio. Then flicked it off immediately. His latest number one hit was playing: "Snack on This."

"That's a sexy song," she said.

"Yep."

"But people like it because it's funny, too." Like Harrison. He was flirty and fun. Real. Adorable, even—and she saved that word for special occasions. "The part about the Fig Newtons is cute."

"Yeah," he mumbled back.

She'd forgotten that he'd never taken compliments from her well. "How'd you come up with it?"

"You really want to know?"

"Of course."

He gave a little chuckle. "Late one night, I couldn't sleep. So I got up and had a handful of Oreos and some milk. I'd just drifted off when *pow*"—he made his fingers do a fireworks burst—"next thing you know, I was sitting up in bed singing, 'That damned tootin', Fig Newton, high-falutin girl of mine—"

"Junk food lover, undercover—" True sang.

"—I'm her Twinkie, and she's MoonPie fine." His velvety twang wrapped around True like a caress.

"Wow." She felt short of breath. "Straight from the horse's mouth."

He grinned. "It's your lucky day."

Her heart pounded like crazy. "I heard a bunch of kids singing it yesterday. Yelling it at the top of their lungs coming out of Sunday School."

Harrison stuffed a bunch of papers under his seat. His ear was red. "Some people might look at it as racy, but it's meant to be pure fun, okay? That's something you've never understood too well."

True felt her whole face heat up. "I do, too, get fun." Had he forgotten? She'd shimmied up and down his body like he was a stripper pole that night on the beach. She'd been so fun that it had scared her.

Harrison finished adjusting his mirror and looked over at her. "It comes off you in invisible waves. You and your mama both. Some sort of disapproval of the rest of the world."

"That's nonsense." She felt it again—the old gap between them. Nothing had changed after all these years, and it made her sad. "I'm as fun as they come, Harrison."

Or she wanted to be. Hadn't he seen long ago how her

life had been locked into place, and there was no room for maneuvering—except maybe once in a lifetime? That night on the dunes at the Isle of Palms had been her once. The cool sand, the full moon, the scudding clouds, his salt-spiked hair, her prom dress flung over a clutch of sea oats . . .

They'd had fun, all right.

"I like 'Snack on This,'" she said. "A *lot*. So does the whole world. You're the king of hick hop, and you're gonna win a CMA easy with that one."

"Thanks." He stared out his own side window for a long moment.

She could tell he heard compliments all the time. It must suck not to suck—at least at something. She prided herself on being hopeless at whistling. And making cookies. They always burned. And she was short-tempered in the worst way. That was a biggie—not that she was proud of it.

"Can you get me home by five?" she asked, hoping to distract him from the funk that seemed to settle over him.

"I'll have you there by quarter to four." He sounded a little peppier.

"But you can't—you'd have to—"

The sports car took off like a shot. It was a manual shift. No country boy worth his salt drove an automatic. They all learned to drive on tractors, as True had, as a matter of fact.

"I know a back way off the interstate," Harrison said. They'd returned to normal, whatever that was. "The paparazzi will never find us."

"Are you sure they're looking?"

"They're always looking."

A car was better than a plane, True reminded herself as they took a curve at a ridiculously high speed. And it was impossible to have two panic attacks in a row, wasn't it?

She sure hoped so.

"You okay?"

Her eyes popped open. "Sorry. Yes, I'm fine. There's a couples wedding shower for Dubose and me at seven in Charleston. So we have to leave by six, and if I factor in time to fix my hair—"

"I'll get you home in time, so stop worrying. I want you to tell me about what's going on in Biscuit Creek. But how about resting a few minutes first?"

"I don't need to."

"I'd rather you try." He flung her a quick look. "Whatever happened to you back there took a toll. Your voice is a little thin. Close your eyes again. Relax. We've got several hours to catch up."

"Okay," she said, "but only for a minute or two. I can't sleep in a car."

"That's fine."

She put her hand on the door rest, took a moment to be proud of the French-tip manicure she'd given herself— she hadn't had a real manicure in years—and closed her eyes.

CHAPTER THREE

Eighteen years earlier, True was on the porch with her father, which was her second favorite place to be. The honeysuckle bower at Sand Dollar Heaven with Harrison was her first. Harrison was her secret best friend. They'd met in front of Wyatt's Pharmacy under the awning. Mr. Wyatt never turned kids away, even the ones like Harrison who didn't always have money in his pocket to buy candy.

"Cumyeah, birthday girl," Miss Ada called to her in her Geechee accent. "Time for your favorite dinner."

Lunch was called *dinner*, and *supper* was the preferred name for the evening meal around these parts. True was excited about her pimiento cheese sandwich, sweet pickle, and potato chips.

"Give us another minute, Miss Ada?" Daddy asked their housekeeper. "I was just about to tell my girl something mighty impoh-tant. She's ten today, old enough to heah some things."

Daddy spoke with the same Lowcountry drawl as Miss Ada. So did Honey. They were white, and Miss Ada was black, but it didn't matter. Lowcountry born and bred—your words stretched like taffy, curled like smoke, and lingered . . . saltwater sounds. For True it was like listening to a fairy language. Her people said "boe-at," for *boat*. "Fohd," for *Ford*, "coat" for *court*. And don't ask them to say the letter *H*. "Ey-yuch" is what you'd get.

"Better make that birthday speech quick, Charlie Maybank." Miss Ada had known True's father since he was a baby. "True's got to ride her bike to choir practice."

"All righty, then." Daddy stood up from the bench they were sitting on, and beckoned True to follow him to the top of the house steps. True leapt up and raced to his side. Her father surveyed the property with a look of utter contentment. "You got yourself a special piece of the world right heah," he told her. "Better'n any birthday present your mothah's gonna buy you on Main Street."

"I know it, Daddy." True looked out over the sparkling wide body of water known as Biscuit Creek. The brown-green reeds of the marsh fronting it held all sorts of treasures: fiddler crabs, pluff mud, egrets, and tiny wrens. "My favorite part is the water. I love when the dolphins come."

"Me, too, sweetheart." He put his hand on her shoulder. "You know why it's called Biscuit Creek?"

"No, sir."

"A long time ago, an old Sewee woman lived up the creek. She made hardtack for the travelers going through."

Harrison said he was one-sixteenth Sewee. They played Sewee warrior and tribal princess all the time at Sand Dollar Heaven.

"And after a while," Daddy said, "the other women— the settlers—joined in with their own recipes. But that Sewee woman started it all. So eventually the creek was called Biscuit Creek in her honor."

"I love Honey's biscuits," True said.

"Don't we all." Daddy chuckled. "You know how she treasures her recipe? You have to do the same for this property. Don't you ever let it go. And make sure you keep the Maybank name prominent in these parts. I know you're gonna marry someday, but Maybank would make a helluva good first name, right?"

"Yes, sir, Daddy." True could tell he wished he'd had a boy. "I don't care what my husband says. I'm gonna be True Maybank forever."

"No, no, no," her father said. "You take your husband's name, like a good girl. Maybe you'll be True Maybank Waring. You marry Dubose, and bring our families together, then you'll have done your mother and me real proud."

She tried her best to look obedient. She felt sorry for Daddy. None of the women in his life listened to him. He called Honey his crazy spinster aunt, all because she refused to "settle down and behave," Mama's favorite phrase.

But Mama had misbehaved, too. Just last week, True heard Daddy and Mama fighting late at night after a party. Daddy found out that Mama had their new baby with another man's help. Daddy told Mama she hadn't behaved like a Maybank should. But Mama said he'd driven her to it by marrying her for her money and then slowly forgetting about her. Daddy cried. And Mama cried. And they both said they were sorry, and then Daddy pulled Mama onto the back porch and called her "Helen, my love." True didn't know what happened after that.

But she cried, too, from where she was sitting on the stairs. The next morning, she asked Ada what it was all about, and Ada said that all Daddy meant was that another man helped Mama pick Weezie up at the baby store. It was all in the past, Ada assured her, so it didn't matter. But True was ten, for goodness' sake. She knew babies didn't come from a store.

Her father looked down at her with a slight frown. "Warings and Maybanks are the two oldest families in Biscuit Creek. And we've never married."

"Why is that, Daddy?" True wasn't too crazy about Dubose. He was a tattletale. Once she stole a piece of ham off his mama's table before they were called in for Sunday brunch. And he told their cook. All because she'd sunk his battleship and beaten him at Go Fish.

"Rivalry," Daddy said. "And none of us have ever fallen in love with each other. No Romeo and Juliet stories. But these are harder times. We could lose everything our families have fought for and stood for these past two hundred yeahs. It's about time we unite, and you and Dubose would make a fine pair."

"But I'm only ten years old, Daddy. So is he."

"So?" He pulled out a cigar and lit it. "You just keep him in mind. You'll both be grown up before you know it."

"Yes, sir."

After that, True's father spoke to her on the porch every year on her birthday. When her twelfth one came along, she was wearing a bra even though she didn't need one, and she had a cheap lip gloss from Wyatt's hidden in the secret pocket of her purse. She was almost a woman, especially now that Harrison had kissed her—kissed her right on the lips—not three days ago. And it wasn't anything like that kiss they'd shared when they'd gotten married two years before in their fake Sewee marriage ceremony in the honeysuckle bower. She didn't know why things had changed between them. All she knew was that one day she was watching him, and his profile suddenly looked like the handsomest thing she'd ever seen. When he'd turned to smile at her, her heart had literally stopped in her chest and she couldn't breathe for a second.

She was madly in love. And as soon as she could escape, she was meeting him on the dock at Sand Dollar Heaven. He had a birthday present for her.

Now her daddy said, "The sheriff was over at Sand Dollar Heaven the other day."

"Oh?" True's heart sped up.

"He told me he saw you there." Daddy's voice was low.

"I-I go there sometimes to play." But True knew her mother wouldn't like it. Not one bit.

"You won't be going anymore. Heah? You're lucky your mama doesn't know."

"But Daddy—"

"Sheriff said you were hanging around the younger Gamble boy. That's gonna stop right now."

"Why?" True felt all trembly inside. Did the sheriff see them kiss? "Harrison's my best friend."

"Enough of that talk." Daddy's brow furrowed. "You got plenty of friends from good families. His daddy just got arrested for bootleggin'. He'll be locked up at least a couple years."

True got tears in her eyes. "R-really?"

"It's a sad story." Daddy shook his head. "He had a still out in the woods."

Was that what that collection of junk was—the one Harrison had always told her to ignore in the honeysuckle bower?

"If your mama ever finds out you been over at Sand Dollar Heaven, you'd be off to boarding school the next day," Daddy said in a scary voice. "She'd insist."

"I'm *not* going to boarding school." True could hardly fathom such a thing. Leave this house? Leave Biscuit Creek and all she held dear?

Never.

"I don't want you to go, either." Daddy spoke softer now. "But Weezie's a handful already. Honey's no easier. Your mama's stressin' about both of 'em. She can't take any more. I need your help, little lady, keeping the peace around here."

And she could tell Daddy really did. His eyes were troubled when he looked at her.

"Yessir." She was frightened seeing Daddy so worried. It shocked her that he thought a twelve-year-old girl could make things better. But maybe she could. She had to try.

In that moment, she grew up. A *lot*.

He patted her shoulder. "Good job, honey. Now you have fun today."

Behind a fake smile, True's heart broke. It was the worst birthday she'd ever had. But poor Harrison. He had it far worse. What was it like to know your daddy was in jail? And then for your best friend not to show up when you'd told her you had a gift for her?

But birthdays, True finally came to understand that day on the porch, weren't for herself. They were to remind her of her duty as a Maybank, which was why that night she wrote Harrison a note and told him she could never meet him at Sand Dollar Heaven again.

I hope you'll understand, she wrote at one point, tears rolling down her cheeks. *My family needs me to grow up.*

She added a few more lines, and then she folded the note into a tiny football and tried to shove it in his locker at school, but too many people were looking. So she found Gage at the high school track and told him to give it to his brother as soon as he got home—without delay. She made him promise over and over. It was all she could do.

CHAPTER FOUR

A few seconds later a bump and a rattle startled True, and she sat up. She'd forgotten where she was—

And then she looked over and saw Harrison and felt the book on her chest.

Wow. The whole Atlanta thing came rushing back.

"Feeling better?" His profile belonged on coins—a Sexy Man coin collection.

"Much better. Thanks." She'd contact the Franklin Mint right away, and next year *Parade* magazine would run the full-page ad, and she'd make tons of money . . .

Not that she needed to worry about money anymore. Thank God.

She sat up higher in her seat. "I can't believe I—" They passed under a familiar canopy of oak trees. "Wait a minute. We're here? In Biscuit Creek?"

"Yep." He wore a self-satisfied grin.

"I was asleep? For *three* hours?"

"You should've seen your mouth hanging open. You even snorted once or twice."

"Good Lord." She was a mess. She needed to get her act together, but she still had a book down her dress. So she pulled it out. It wasn't the most graceful action she'd ever taken.

Harrison gave a southern-boy chuckle, which bordered on a cackle.

"Redneck," she said.

"And proud of it." He shot her a wicked grin.

"Just drop me off on Main Street, and I'll walk home." No way was he going to see her house. "I never meant for you to take me all the way to Maybank Hall."

"You still there?"

"Uh-huh."

"Well, it's not much farther. By the way, what was that sign I just passed? U-pick tomatoes up ahead, two miles? That's y'all's place. I can't believe your mama would allow such a thing."

True lifted a shoulder and let it drop. "Community-sustained farming is in."

"I never thought the Maybanks cared about what was 'in.'"

"I'll tell you what I do care about—a big superstar showing up and scaring the customers, if we have any. Besides, Gage lives in the opposite direction."

"Yeah. You're a whole five minutes out of my way," Harrison said, "and we never got to catch up. I'm taking you home, and that's that. I'm gettin' me some sun-ripe tomatoes while I'm at it."

"You're used to having your own way, that's clear." True swallowed. "But I need to say something before we talk."

"Ruh-roh."

"Just remember the first song you ever wrote was about me. I think. And it made you a star."

"Are you saying I owe my success to you because a long time ago you told me to get lost and broke my teenage heart?"

"No." True paused. "Well, yes. Just a little. Right?"

"Wrong."

"It still wouldn't hurt you to do me a tiny favor."

Harrison whistled. "Pardon my French, but you got some balls, Miss Maybank. Isn't your world all sweet tea and Sunday chicken suppers served on china brought over by one of George Washington's generals during the Revolutionary War?"

She wouldn't disenfranchise him of that notion. "I thought that maybe since you're here you could . . . forgive and forget."

"Hey. It was high school. No big deal."

"Thanks." It had been a *very* big deal at the time, and if she still thought hard about it, she felt terrible about the drama that ensued post-prom. "So if we run into each other, you'll avoid bringing it up? Especially the part no one knows about?"

He lofted a brow. "Surely all of Biscuit Creek guessed we did more than walk on the beach that night. Damn, girl, I came to get you on a proverbial white horse the next day. Yeah, it was a blue Ford pickup truck, but hey, you use what you got when you're trying to be Prince Charming."

He turned onto the dirt driveway that led to Maybank Hall, past a sign of a giant painted tomato. Morning glory hung in gorgeous loops all around, lavender bubbles of color, the smell so sweet that True forgot for a moment that she was discombobulated.

Harrison would never be. The man did what he wanted. And he knew his own soul and somehow had a bead on everyone else's, too.

"Dubose doesn't know," True said. "He thinks . . . he thinks you just took me home from the prom, and I cried myself to sleep."

"He's not that naive."

"My mom confirmed the deets with his mom the next day."

"So your mom covered for you."

"She didn't want me to lose him." True didn't like remembering how desperate her mother had acted. "Dubose gets that he was a jerk. He doesn't blame me for leaving him that night. He's not mad at you, either."

"I don't care whether he is or not. And what does it really matter, all these years later?"

"It matters a lot to him."

"Why?"

"He has this thing about you. Can you blame him? No man wants his wife comparing him to a guy who's been named one of *People*'s One Hundred Most Beautiful People."

"He's got issues, your fiancé. It's not like I was named Sexiest Man Alive."

"*Yet.*" She let that sink in a second, but either he'd already considered the possibility or he was bored by the idea. His expression didn't change. "You're living in a dream world if you think your celebrity doesn't intimidate nine out of ten of the people you meet. All I'm asking for is some discretion. I don't need any paparazzi coming through Biscuit Creek stirring up trouble."

"As if I would ever talk about you. Real men don't gossip. We just do the things other people like to gossip about."

"That's my point. You and juicy stories go together like white on rice. You need to buy stock in the *National Enquirer.*"

Harrison parked the car on the gravel drive in front of the house, slung an arm over the steering wheel, and turned to her. "Always worried about what the neighbors will think. That should be the Maybank motto."

True's pulse ticked against her temples like bees against the inside of a Mason jar. "I don't care what the neighbors think—"

"Really?" His open collar revealed a tan neck. A smidgeon of dark golden hair. "That's a new development."

"No, it's not. If you'll look back with some objectivity, you'd see that the reason I didn't run off with you had to do with . . . common sense."

"Oh, yeah?"

She let out a gusty sigh. "I was eighteen and college-bound. Surely now you see what a disaster hightailing it to Nashville with you would have been for me. And for you, too."

"I see it, all right."

"I'm done going over this. It's old history."

"Believe you me, I'm not interested, either." He finally caught sight of the house, tilted his head, and squinted.

True's defenses came up, as naturally as breathing. "It's ten years older than last time you saw it," she reminded him.

"Yeah, but"—he hesitated—"it looks like hell, quite frankly."

"It's old. Almost two hundred years old." She pushed her hair off her face. "And we've been too busy to get it painted."

Harrison scoped out the surrounding fields, where nothing was happening other than two customers picking tomatoes down a row. "Look, a couple of those customers I could scare off."

"Don't you dare." Maybank Hall had two large fields dedicated to strawberries from late April to early June, blackberries and blueberries from late June to mid-July, tomatoes from mid-June to August, and from late September to late October, pumpkins.

"So y'all have been too busy to work on the house? For ten years?"

"I'll admit it's time to freshen the look. We will soon." After True married Dubose. It was his wedding present to her, to restore Maybank Hall to its former glory. He'd wanted to start last year, but she refused to let him. It didn't feel right when they weren't married yet. She wasn't taking a dime from him before they were married.

Harrison sent her a sharp look. "Is something not right in the Maybank world, after all? Your family isn't the type to let things slide. Or to let strangers hang around."

True shook her head. "Everything's just great."

She tried not to notice the new gleam of interest in his eyes.

"I don't know," he murmured. "You look a little desperate. That's what's new, what's different about you. And you had that . . . that weird thing happen at the airport."

"I *am* desperate." She swallowed. "I-I'm wondering whether I picked the right florist for the wedding." Let him think she was a nitpicky, shallow bride. The Bridezilla of Biscuit Creek.

He wasn't buying it. In fact, he was staring at her dress, Honey's vintage Lilly Pulitzer, which True had pulled out of an old trunk. It was timeless. Classic. In pristine condition. It most definitely did not shout *Hanging on by a thread.*

"You've been gone ten years," she said. "Please get that I-know-you-better-than-you-know-yourself look off your face. Nothing is wrong. I'm getting married to a wonderful man—"

"Yada, yada, yada." Harrison dropped his fist on the edge of the steering wheel. "I don't need to hear the Maybank party line. I asked you what's wrong—something *is*—and you're shutting me out. No surprise there." He shrugged, his eyes locked onto the house. "You were right. We really have no business talking to each other."

She was trying to hold on to her patience, her good manners, and her hard-earned indifference to him. But it was difficult. Harrison wasn't an easy man to ignore. Especially when he wanted to *know*—in the way that all ex-lovers were curious—how she was.

She wanted to know the same about him.

"We might as well talk." She wished he'd look at her and not the house. "You're here."

"I sure am." His eyes roamed Maybank Hall's buckled tin roof. Silver shone through the brick-red paint. And then there were the shutters, threadbare now, two of them hanging slightly askew on the second floor. "But I can't promise to act like we're BFFs if I see you around town."

"That's the last thing I want," True huffed, "you and me acting like BFFs."

His mouth quirked up. "I'm too rich and famous for that sort of thing. We celebrities tend to be hard-assed, if you want to know the truth. Sorry. "

Of course, their doomed little romance was nothing more than a blip on the time line of their lives, especially his. He'd done things. Really big things.

True opened her door a few inches. "Well, I'm not trying to curry your favor. So you can get that out of your head."

"Curry my *what*?"

"Your favor. Not everyone's an adoring fan."

"Uh-huh," he said slow, like molasses. "Thanks for the news flash, Miss Fancy Talk. I guess you can go now. Dan should be here in, oh, I'd say an hour. He drives like an old lady." He grabbed the dress from the backseat and placed it in her lap.

"Thank you for the ride," she said.

"My distinct pleasure." He had a voice that could make a girl think twice about turning away from the hot-pink-and-black lace thong in the Victoria's Secret sale bin.

A few moments passed, but she didn't move.

Neither did he.

The whine of a screen door swinging open broke the tension. Weezie came out on the front porch, followed by George, Ed, and Striker, their three Labs. Ed was a cinnamon color, Striker was pitch black, and George was pale yellow. Weezie's best friends. She lowered the open book in her hands, put a palm over her eyes, and stared at the little blue coupe.

"Aw, she's all grown up now," Harrison said. "But somehow she looks exactly the same."

"Yes, she does." Like Anne of Green Gables in the twenty-first century, True always thought. Weezie's coppery red hair was bound in a tight braid down her back. She wore a Mickey Mouse T-shirt over a white, ruffled mini skirt, and gray Oxford shoes.

"Mismatched as hell," Harrison murmured. "Geeky glasses. She'd fit in great in New York or San Francisco, but around here, maybe not so much."

"She's the epitome of the hipster. Not that she's trying to be, of course." The irony didn't amuse True. The world was a big, cold place. And Weezie wore her heart on her sleeve, making her vulnerable—to what, True wasn't sure. There were too many possibilities, which was why she could never rest easy.

"She's how old now?" Harrison asked.

"Eighteen. She loves TV talk shows. I mean, a *lot*."

"She always was a talker, so I'm not surprised." He gave a little laugh. "I think she recognizes me."

"Of course she does. The whole world does."

He shoved his sunglasses to the top of his head and lowered both windows. "Weezie Maybank? Is that you?"

"Harrison Gamble!" she shouted, her face breaking into a big grin. She dropped her book on their father's favorite old rocking chair, pushed up her glasses, and trotted down the three brick steps of the porch, the dogs hard at her heels. "It's been a long time, but I'm *so* happy to see you," she shouted as she approached him.

"You, too, Weezie, darlin'." She was a doll.

"Thanks." Even up close, she didn't turn down the volume. "Although the fact that you're sitting in a car with my sister doesn't bode well."

"Why is that?" Harrison asked.

"Weezie, please don't say anything you're going to regret," True told her.

Weezie halted for a split second, and True saw it on her face: the Back-Up, her sister's uncertain expression when she stopped for a second to think. Striker and Ed crashed into the back of her knees.

"Keep talking." Harrison put his elbow on the windowsill and waited. "I'm fine."

"You're not helping," True whispered.

"And you're being bossy," he murmured back.

"Well"—Weezie opened Harrison's door in a friendly hostess sort of way—"I can't help predicting conflict. The latest Gallup survey touts you as sex on a stick from the wrong side of the tracks—a womanizer, according to Joan Rivers and Katie Couric both. And True here's about to marry a conservative attorney with an antebellum home, friends in high places in the criminal justice system, and a barely concealed inferiority complex. This could make for some interesting gossip among the locals."

"*Weezie*." True's heart pounded, but she put as much threat into her tone as she possibly could when a body was leaning over a Maserati console and almost cheek-to-cheek with sex on a stick.

"Frankly," Weezie went on like a freight train to their guest, "if I didn't have my own selfish reasons for wanting to see you, I'd tell you to hightail it out of here before the proverbial shit hits the fan."

Harrison looked back at True. "Why am I thinking of Jerry Springer right now?" he said low, an amused gleam in his eye.

"Don't encourage her," True said faintly.

But she wasn't thinking much about her sister at the moment, or bad TV. She wasn't thinking at all, as a matter of fact. The song about the Twinkie and the MoonPie flooded her brain like a spring tide.

Snack on this, girlfriend. Harrison's mouth. His stubbly chin. His wide shoulders and sinfully flat belly. *You're not married yet.*

CHAPTER FIVE

Harrison had planned to leave Maybank Hall without getting out of the car. He couldn't hang out with old flames for long. He was too smart for that. Best to escape while he could.

But then Weezie showed up with that crazy speech of hers. And when she added, "Did True run you off all those years ago? I've always wondered, but she doesn't talk about you," he changed his mind.

True never talked about him? A flood of testosterone turned off his brain, and he got out of the car.

"I'll meet you inside," Weezie told him. "I'm making you a mystery drink. I was already working on one."

"No, Weezie," said True. "Harrison's leaving. I've got the couples shower in a few hours."

Couples shower? Damn, he was glad he was a bachelor. "Yep. I gotta go, too," he said. "The Spurs are on in twenty-eight minutes. Sorry, Weezie."

"It'll take me two seconds," Weezie insisted.

"No." True glared at her. "It's nice of you, but this is a bad time."

Weezie stalked back to the house, and the front screen door slammed behind her.

"She'll be all right." True fingered her pearls with her free hand.

"I hope so."

"She's just being a teenager. You're lucky you're the baby of your family. How old is Gage now—thirty-one?"

"Yes. I hear he has a girlfriend in her mid-forties. Maybe I'll get to meet her."

"Wow. I had no idea. Enjoy your time with him . . ."

True's words trailed off, and her mouth was like a candy heart, soft pink. If Harrison indulged his imagination enough, he could almost see the words BE MINE on it. She had no clue how sexy she was, which exponentially increased her va va-voom quotient to the nth degree.

He stuck his hand in his pockets and took a step back, toward the car. "I'll try. Gage doesn't seem too excited to see me when we get together. We golf every year at Cocoa Beach. Plan my whole schedule around it. Every once in a while, he'll say things like, '*Debit card* is an anagram of *bud credit*,' and then we go our separate ways."

"That's actually a pretty cool anagram." True grinned.

The tide was high, perfect for swimming. He felt an old stirring inside, a spark of nostalgia. "I'm heading out. How about meeting for breakfast tomorrow?" *Breakfast with a side order of happiness.* It came to him like a song lyric, which meant that someday it would be. "I'll be gone by tomorrow night."

It was a damn fool thing to say. To think. But what the hell. He had visions of her naked in his head. And why not let the fantasy last a little longer?

True blinked several times. "That's very nice of you. But . . ."

"But what?" Harrison hadn't heard *no* in years.

A crease formed in her brow. "I'm really sorry, but"—she plucked a leaf off a crape myrtle—"I just can't. You're nice to offer."

The sound of bees buzzing on a nearby azalea bush lent a laziness to the air. Everything was thick, sweet, slow. Laid out plain as day. But wrapped in comfort and ease. Even the word *no*. That was the South for you.

And he was a fool to forget it.

"Yeah, I can see that Dubose wouldn't like it," he said. "You're both Biscuit Creek royalty. Can't mess with that dynamic."

"Oh, please."

"I'll bet you've got him wrapped around your little finger."

"He's one of the best young attorneys in the state. He's not a wimp."

"Is that so? He sure took his time popping the question. Seems to me that if a man makes up his mind about a woman, he doesn't dawdle in that department." Harrison sure hadn't. It was her loss she'd told him no.

"I'm done talking about Dubose," she said with a glorious glare. She excelled at the old southern-belle put-you-in-your-place freeze-out, but he focused on her luscious lips instead.

"Whatever you say, *ma'am*." He put as much fake sincerity into the words as possible.

"Good-bye. And thank you again for stopping me in Atlanta to say hello. That was awfully kind of you to drive me home." She'd be polite to the devil if he ever showed up at her door.

"You're welcome," Harrison said lazily, but he was pissed. True brought out the redneck creek boy in him like no one else could.

The screen door opened again. "Get in here, Harrison!" Weezie yelled out to him. "Your drink's *done*."

But the Spurs were calling. And True was like the sun. Stay around her too long, and he was gonna burst into flames. "If I value my life, I think I'd better tell you I don't like mystery drinks," he called to Weezie, his eyes on True. "Thanks anyway."

"That's exactly why you need to drink one." Weezie was undeterred. "And while you do, I'm going to tell you all about what's gone on here the past ten years."

"He doesn't have time for that," True insisted. "He's leaving."

Aw, screw the Spurs. He'd get to Gage's by the end of the first quarter. The stubborn mule in him squinted at Weezie. "Are your parents home?"

"Yes," she shouted back. "You can pay your respects, drink your drink, and then you can be on your way."

"Excellent idea." After all, what did he really have to do tonight after the game? Talk to Gage? He'd like to, but they didn't have much to say to each other.

And face it. He loved messing with True. She looked as riled as he'd ever seen her. Plus, there was the mystery drink. Maybe he really *did* need to drink one. Nothing surprised him anymore.

"Get going, Harrison." True wasn't messing around now. All that southern cotton that padded her voice earlier was stripped clean away. "You can't see my parents."

"Oh, yeah?" He tapped into his onstage self when he breezed by her. If that meant he walked with a little strut, then so be it. He needed to feel all his oats to avoid falling under her spell. "What kind of man would I be not to say hello? They might not have thought I was worthy of you, but hey—I was great at cutting their hedges. Whoever they're using now needs a lesson in trimming."

He climbed the front steps, and she flew past him, straight to the front door, where she turned to face him.

"It's a bad time." She stretched her arms across the frame.

More than ever, he saw the desperation in her eyes.

"I'm going in" was all he said.

"No, you're not." Her eyes flashed fire. "Don't you remember what happened last time you brought me home?"

"Your daddy threatened to get out his shotgun and run me off the property."

"Exactly."

"I wasn't your prom date. And I brought you home eight hours late. He was a little upset. But I'm sure he's over it by now, don't you think?"

"Let him in," Weezie called from down the hallway.

"He's got to go." True's baby blues bored into him. "*You* drink that drink, Weezie. I suspect I know what it is. And he's not going to like it."

"She's wrong," Harrison said loudly, his eyes still on True. "I'm gonna love it."

Weezie's feet clomped down the hall toward him. "Well, if you don't get it soon, it's going to melt, and I *will* have to drink it."

"How come your parents aren't coming to the door?" he murmured to True.

Her pupils dilated. "They're occupied."

"A Maybank is never too occupied to greet a guest *or* run off a foe," he said softly. "I'm going to lift your arm. And then I'm going to walk into your house, invited by your sister. So no complaining about this being a home invasion. A man can only be unfairly accused of that once in his lifetime. Twice, and he just might not go running away. He might stick around and call some people out. Hear?"

"Over my dead body." True shut her eyes and pressed herself back against the door.

Weezie got to the screen. "Move," she told her sister.

"The mystery drink's melting." The three dogs whined around her legs, their claws clacking on the wooden floor.

All Harrison had to do was put his hands on True's exposed waist—it was slender and strong and his palms cupped it perfectly—and her arms came off the door frame in an instant.

"No!" she cried.

Releasing his hold on her body was hell on the primitive part of his brain. But he did what he had to do and was inside the house the next moment. It had the same smell: saltwater breezes, freshly ironed linen, and old wood. The slightly buckled wide-plank floors ran clear through the house to the back.

"Where are your parents?" he asked Weezie.

"Daddy's in the front room." Weezie snuck a sip out of one of the two red-and-white paper straws she'd stuck in a plastic Charleston River Dogs cup. "Mama's in the garden."

Harrison peeked at the drink. Ah. A strawberry milk shake. He took a sip, too. "Mmmm. That's good. You grow 'em here?"

"You betcha," said Weezie. "We have a whole freezer full."

"That's great." He walked the few feet to the living room door—the ceilings were fourteen feet high—and peeked inside. There was the old settee covered in butter-gold silk and littered with formal tasseled pillows. A low mahogany table with brass-tipped feet. On top, a blue-and-white china bowl filled with pink flowers. The deeply worn Oriental carpet, frayed at the edges. Old prints of southern aristocracy at play: Hunting. Dancing. Drinking tea. Riding horses. A watercolor of a rice field, a Low-country sunset casting golden rays across it.

But Mr. Maybank wasn't there, sitting in his usual chair, an overly plump brown leather one fronted by a needlepointed ottoman that displayed the crest of his Virginia boarding school, Woodberry Forest.

True came up just as Harrison turned around, prepared to go look in the library. Her face was white, and her small sheathed bosom heaved mightily.

"Stop right there," she said.

Stop imagining her perky breasts underneath that dress, or stop walking? "Your sister—"

"Is drinking your milk shake." She folded her arms, knowing full well he'd been eyeing her assets.

"I'll get over it. And I'll be out of your hair in a minute." He walked around her, past a blissful Weezie sucking on his milk shake in the hallway, and headed to the library.

"He's not there," Weezie called after him. "He's in the front parlor."

"No, he's not." Harrison kept his voice light. But something was wrong. Very wrong. He hadn't noticed at first, but the house was too quiet. Mrs. Maybank was always moving around, talking to Ada, who'd cooked, cleaned, and ironed for them for decades. And Mr. Maybank was usually on the phone making business deals or arranging a golf date with his buddies.

Ada was nowhere to be found.

"Maybe your daddy's out back." Mr. and Mrs. Maybank and Ada, all talking about the weather, the price of gas—or maybe they were helping the customers with their tomatoes. "Excuse me, ladies."

Why had the library looked so spare? Where was the old blue Oriental rug and the plaid couch that faced the fireplace? Why were there no papers on Mr. Maybank's desk?

"He's not out back." True's voice rang clear and commanding down the hall. "He's on the mantel in the front parlor. Inside the yacht club racing trophy."

Harrison stood stock-still in the hallway.

"And my mother's ashes are buried in the garden," True said, softer now, "below her favorite rosebush."

"What the hell?" He looked between the sisters.

Weezie had quit slurping the milk shake. "Mama and Daddy passed a long time ago," she said, "in a car crash on Highway 17." Her tone was somber. "But you never came to their funeral. Honey's, either. She died of natural causes not long after, but she told me just minutes before she went that she blamed Congress."

"She did?" Harrison's voice sounded hollow to his own ears.

Weezie nodded. "They frustrated her to death. She made us put that in her obituary. As a result, we got letters of condolence from both our US senators and the Speaker of the House."

Harrison's heart thumped slowly. "Nobody told me."

"You never asked," said True.

No, he hadn't, had he?

"I'm sorry." He couldn't believe it. He'd never approved of the Maybanks —as jovial as Mr. Maybank was— because they'd always kept True on such a leash. But the idea of them being gone . . .

It was awful.

"Where's Ada?" he asked.

"She's still here," True said, "in Biscuit Creek. She works for the Hanahans now."

But Ada was old. Even when he'd left, she'd been old. Why hadn't she simply retired? Hadn't the Maybanks left her set up with a retirement fund? He wanted to ask, but it wasn't his business. And he could see on True's face that she was on shaky ground, telling him this stuff. She hadn't wanted to, that was for sure.

"I miss Ada's fried chicken and Honey's biscuits," said Weezie. "And now I have to do all the silver polishing.

True makes me do it even though we don't use it any-more. She bought flatware from Target. It's night and day from Reed and Barton's 'Francis the First.'"

"We do, too, use the Francis the First," said True. "At Christmas and Thanksgiving. And we always will."

"She also got some Fiestaware at a garage sale," Weezie went on. "Pumpkin orange. Delightful in the au-tumn but so wrong for summer, according to Nate Berkus. Too bad his show got canceled . . ."

True at garage sales? *True using Fiestaware?*

What the hell was going on?

"Where's the library rug?" he asked Weezie. "And the couch?" He had a suspicion True would never tell him.

"Sold to the highest bidder," Weezie said glibly. "We needed start-up capital for the U-pick operation. We got rid of a lot of stuff. Whole rooms full. We were just about to advertise for boarders when Dubose proposed to True. Too bad. I was hoping a funny old lady would move in, someone like Honey. Now we're stuck with Dubose in-stead. He's dullsville."

"Weezie." True sounded genuinely pissed. "You know better."

"Whatever," Weezie flung back at her. "Because of you, I can't get a car until you get married. And if we'd taken in boarders, I could have had one by now."

"No, you couldn't have." True glared at her. "Every cent would have gone to the business."

"I hate that business." Weezie crossed her arms over her chest and looked at the ceiling. "I'm tired of strawber-ries and blueberries. I'm tired of everything we grow ex-cept for tomatoes. I'll never be tired of *them*."

Harrison almost laughed. Weezie was angry. But she'd never unleash her ire on a tomato, apparently.

"Good thing," said True—how did she keep a straight

face?—"as you're in charge the next couple of weeks, and we have a bumper crop."

Weezie's eyes filled with tears. "You expect me to juggle the tomatoes when I have your wedding coming up and school to get ready for?"

"You don't have anything to do to get ready for school," True said. "Now calm down. You're living at home, and everything will be fine."

"I'm not living at home," Weezie yelled. "I'm moving into an apartment in North Charleston with Jamie Rivers and Courtney Gadsden. And I'm going to work as a waitress to pay for it."

"No, you're not." True remained calm. "You're not ready for that yet."

Weezie stomped her foot. "You think I'm staying here with you and Dubose? *No way!*" And then she pushed past Harrison and ran up the stairs.

Good Golly, Miss Molly. There was nothing like a teenage girl in a tizzy to blow your hair back.

"So you've had hard times." Poor True. She was awfully young to play parent to Weezie.

She shrugged. "Nothing I can't handle."

Them were fighting Maybank words, he knew.

But they weren't enough to settle the strange, aching feeling hovering near his heart. Biscuit Creek was a story he carried with him wherever he went, against his will, like a song in his head that wouldn't stop playing. There were characters in this story, and they weren't allowed to change, much less die. Even his mama lived on, her tanned face taut with concentration as she crouched over an aluminum washtub and counted how many crabs he and Gage had caught for their supper.

Collier and Helen Maybank and their housekeeper Ada were supposed to be at Maybank Hall forever, the way the tide rolled in each day over the oyster beds in the creek and the locusts buzzed in the summer and the camellias bloomed by the front porch every winter.

And True was supposed to be the unreachable southern lady without a care in the world. That was what had sustained him all these years, and what had fueled his hard indifference to her, knowing she'd be all right, no matter what happened to him. He'd been able to forget her, to seal her up in a ziplock bag of old memories and toss her aside.

"I'm sorry about your parents," he told her. "They were a fine couple. And Honey was a grand old lady."

"I don't cry about them anymore," she said. "I don't have time." Her gaze met his full-on, but her mouth . . . ah, that mouth. It told him all he needed to know. She'd never had a chance to recover. She must have hit the ground running . . .

Had she ever gone to her beloved Chapel Hill?

"That's a good thing, you not crying anymore," he told her. "Your parents and Honey would want you to be happy again." He paused half a-second. "I hope you will be."

And he really did.

"Thank you," True said quietly, and stepped aside so he could leave.

When he crossed the threshold onto the porch, he ached for her and Weezie both. And it ran through him then, like a translucent shrimp streaking across the surface of Biscuit Creek, how no one had ever told him they were sorry for all that *he'd* lost over the years. He'd give away his whole fortune and start over again as a newbie in Nashville to hear that.

Just one time.

But like a flash that thought disappeared, sinking deep into the briny darkness where Harrison never went.

CHAPTER SIX

Embarrassment warred with wounded pride when True ran to the living room window and hid behind the curtain so she could watch Harrison walk to his car. She had a one-inch crack to peer through, which drove her nuts. She fumbled with her cell phone and, barely looking down, texted Carmela: *Harrison's back.*

You're kidding! The response was instant.

Carmela was a tall Italian bombshell from the Bronx with curly dark brown hair twisted in a knot and a Sophia Loren mouth.

I'm totally serious, True texted back and wondered if she was a disloyal fiancée talking about an old love affair. *He gave me a ride home. I ran into him when I was picking up my gown. No big deal.*

OMG, Carmela answered her. *It's not every day you run into an international star, much less one you relinquished your V-card to. It's definitely a big deal.*

True's heart sank. She was trying so hard to make sure it wasn't!

Can you come in? Carmela wrote. *I'm doing inventory. I want all the details.*

She owned a gift shop on Main Street called Southern Loot.

I'm late for the couples shower in Charleston, True wrote. That was what mattered—her marriage to Dubose and the life that awaited them. *I'll tell you tomorrow. XOXO*

You'd better! But being the good sport that she was, Carmela added: *Have fun!*

True would try. She wasn't crazy about the downtown Charleston crowd. She knew them all from cotillion, which Mama had always insisted upon, but they were a little fast for her taste. Dubose, however, fit right in and told her she only felt that way because she was insecure.

"You're a Maybank," he always said. "You have nothing to apologize for."

True hated hearing that she was a Maybank, as if that made her any more special than anyone else. "Big deal" is what she always said back to Dubose.

But he didn't get it.

She could hear Harrison talking with the dogs, taking his sweet time, but he finally walked through the gap in the curtain. Her pulse quickened and she dared to push the curtain back just a little bit more.

He knew.

Finally.

She could see in his eyes on his way out the door that he'd figured out the gist of things: Her family had come down in the world. Big-time.

True had never finished her degree at Chapel Hill. She'd come home in the middle of her sophomore year when her parents had died to help seventy-eight-year-old Honey raise Weezie. But she'd also had to figure out a way to bring in money. Co-op farming was a big trend, so she came up with the idea of starting a U-pick business from the berry patch Mama used to tend to amuse herself. She'd called in favors from farmers who'd hunted deer and quail with Daddy on the far reaches of the property and coaxed them into putting in two big fields. Gifts from her father's collection of bourbon, baskets of Honey's fried chicken and biscuits, and permission to continue hunting had sweetened the deal and brought the men back occasionally to teach True how to get real use from the ancient tractor in their barn. They taught her how to tend her crops without having to hire help.

But her first year's harvest was so abundant, she'd had no choice. Luckily, she'd found some hardworking teens who wanted a little extra cash, so whenever she was over-whelmed, she'd give them a call. They were worth their weight in gold.

True and Honey had sold every valuable piece of fur-niture they owned, save for the pieces in the front parlor, but Honey had made True swear she'd never sell off any of the family land or the china and silver. True's great-aunt had been a pragmatist by nature, but even she drew the line there. "All of that's got to be passed down, dar-lin'," she'd said in her strong Geechee accent, "as you well know. Otherwise, we lose the Maybank mojo."

True had been tempted many a time since Honey's death to defy her wishes, but she'd restrained herself. She didn't want to be the Maybank who let the family down. She was saving more than herself, Weezie, and Maybank Hall. She was saving the family history that went back all the way to 1703 when the first Collier Maybank had taken up residence on this spit of land on the curving tidal creek near the mighty Atlantic.

Harrison finally took off in the Maserati. He'd put the top down, and his golden brown hair streamed out behind him. Had the shocking revelation about her parents roused pity in his heart? True dreaded that it would. She didn't want him feeling sorry for her.

It was the last thing she wanted.

"Shootfire," she whispered.

Dubose's black Mercedes came into view and approached Harrison's car on the gravel drive. The vehicles stopped, side by side.

Dubose lowered his window.

Harrison slung his arm over the Maserati door.

What was Dubose doing here an hour early? He should have called. True wasn't anywhere near ready, and the last thing she needed was for her fiancé to show up at the house in a sulk about Harrison. Tonight was a big night for them. A romantic night.

"When two bulls meet—" said Weezie from behind her.

True nearly jumped out of her skin. "Don't sneak up on me like that, please."

"—only one survives," Weezie finished with a dramatic flourish of the red kitchen towel she held in her hand.

"Neither Harrison nor Dubose is a bull." True yanked the heavy linen window drapery back to its proper place. "And they're both going to survive each other's company just fine. Harrison's leaving tomorrow anyway."

She glanced at the lighthouse clock on the mantel, ticking slowly, serenely away next to her father's ashes in the shiny silver trophy. "Please tell Dubose I'm in the shower and will be downstairs in half an hour. I didn't expect him this early, and I'll get ready as fast as I can."

She wasn't ready to see him yet. She needed to disentangle herself from the events of the day and come back to center.

"You're going to have a hard time thinking about Dubose now that you've seen Harrison." Weezie had an uncanny way of saying exactly what she was thinking. "I will, too. So please don't expect me to entertain Dubose, Sister."

Weezie often called her Sister when she was overexcited.

True stopped. "I don't expect you to entertain him. But promise me you'll make him feel welcome. And if you do start talking with him, don't go on and on about Harrison, okay?"

"I don't like Dubose," said Weezie. "And I never will."

"You know what?" Usually True was patient—Weezie took a while to get used to change—but it had been a long day already. "You'd better start liking him soon. He cares about you a lot, and he's going to be your brother-in-law."

"He's not yet." Weezie followed her into the hallway. "And now the man who took you right out of his arms at the senior prom and didn't deliver you home until the next morning—"

"Please stop channeling Wendy Williams."

"—is back in town for the first time since that eventful day."

"Thanks a lot for bringing it up," True said.

"You're welcome."

"I wasn't *really* thanking you. It doesn't matter anymore anyway."

"Yes, it does. Harrison's hot and single. And Dubose dumped you in college when Mama and Daddy died." Weezie was thrilled with the drama of it all.

"Don't hold that against him. It was a really tough time. I needed to pay attention to what was going on here, and he needed to get through college. We got back together eventually, didn't we?"

"Only when he moved back here, and you were right under his nose."

"We got back together when he could make a commitment," True told her firmly. "Law school's hard. And he had to pass the bar." Her whole body hummed with anxiety. "Now please behave yourself."

"Me?" Weezie pointed a thumb at her chest. "I'm not the fickle one who doesn't know her own heart."

"Please, Weezie!" True seldom got into real arguments with her sister. "Don't you understand how much it hurts me to look back at that time?"

Weezie stared at her. "No."

That was the problem. Weezie had deep feelings herself, but she didn't always recognize the depth of other people's.

"Well, listen closely," True said more softly. "It does hurt. It hurts me the same way it hurts you to think about stray dogs and cats."

Weezie winced.

"Or when Will Ferrell's wife divorced him in *Talladega Nights* and married his best friend."

"God, that broke my heart."

"Exactly." True was glad she was getting through. "So I'd rather forget what happened ten years ago. I want to move *on*."

Weezie bit her index fingernail. "All right," she murmured around it.

"Thank you." True let out a big sigh. "See you in a few. Will you check on the customers, too, please? Give them all some extra tomatoes."

"Sure."

Which reminded her, Harrison never got his.

Oh, well. That was probably a good thing. She might have pelted him with a few just because he got under her skin. Around him, she always questioned the status quo. It had reversed itself since they'd last seen each other. He was the one now who was surrounded by shiny stuff while she—former high school homecoming queen and sorority girl—was happy with her dirt-stained shorts and blunt fingernails she could never grow long, not if she was going to continue farming.

And she was. The community relied on her now, and she liked being outdoors and working hard. She especially liked the money. It was just enough that she and Weezie could remain independent.

While her sister headed outside, Truc took the main stairs two at a time. But she was too late. Her future husband's familiar, confident tread sounded on the front porch. She paused and straightened her shoulders. It was time to act like a grown-up and remember what she had—an amazing fiancé. In fact, if she were an answer in one of Gage's crossword puzzles, the clue would be *lucky woman*. And if *Dubose Waring* was an anagram . . .

Who knew? She'd ask Gage—just for fun—next time she saw him.

CHAPTER SEVEN

"Hey there, beautiful!" It was Dubose's usual greeting, but his voice had a wary edge.

True composed herself and turned around with a smile on her face. She felt like an adulteress. And she hadn't even done anything wrong.

"Hi, sweetheart," she said.

In the doorway stood the high school and college boyfriend who'd come back into her life at her lowest point—five years after her parents' death, when her trials kept coming and coming—and told her she'd never be scared and alone again.

For that, she'd always be grateful.

He was nearly as handsome as Harrison, but in a totally different way—a more refined way. He was a gentleman, scholar, and athlete (he'd been second-string quarterback at the University of Virginia), and his hair was parted perfectly, the short sideburns and crew cut neat as a pin. He had the square jaw all the Waring men had and a broad forehead over groomed blond eyebrows, evenly spaced hazel eyes, a handsome nose, and strong cheekbones. In his smartly cut suit from Berlin's on King Street in Charleston and his Hermès tie, he was a poster boy for eligible southern bachelors.

"So the great Harrison Gamble is back in town." He gazed up at True with a confident grin that was still a walking advertisement for Biscuit Creek's only orthodontist, his uncle, Dr. Waring. His own father, who'd died two years earlier, had been a well-established attorney, and his mother, Penn, was a general surgeon. "He told me all about taking you home from Atlanta."

He would, thought True. Harrison loved to make trouble.

With her heart in her throat, she came down to the bottom stair and wrapped a hand around the elaborate carved finial. "He took me by such surprise. I'd have felt churlish saying no. It's been ten years, after all."

Why did she feel so nervous? She'd done nothing wrong. She had nothing to hide.

They shared a perfunctory kiss. Dubose was obviously as distracted by Harrison's presence as she was. "I guess he's come a long way from the Sand Dollar Heaven trailer park."

"Trash talk's not really necessary, is it?"

He picked up her free hand and kissed her knuckles. "I love how noble you are. If a bit naive."

She backed up a step. He climbed one. They were now eye-to-eye.

"Harrison worked hard to get where he is," she said. "And you work hard, too. There's no need to drag him down. *Or* make fun of me. I'm not naive in the least."

Dubose laughed. "You go, honey."

"*Dubose*—"

He put his hands around her back and pulled her close. "Don't you see all this is about you? Not Gamble's money. Not his fame. You're *my* girl. Not his."

Normally, True would have felt flattered. Cherished. Right now she felt a bit owned, although that was a strong word. Dubose respected her. She knew he did. He was being something of an ass at the moment about Harrison, but he had strong provocation. What man wanted an old rival for his fiancée to show up right before their wedding?

She pushed a lock of hair off his brow. "You don't need to worry. He's leaving tomorrow, okay?"

"Good. I don't want him around when I'm gone. He's a troublemaker."

"Wait." Her pulse quickened. "What do you mean, when you're gone?"

He frowned. "I'm going to New York."

"You are?" she whispered.

"Tomorrow morning." Dubose never apologized about work requirements. "I have to get a couple of depositions and attend a big trial. It's going to seriously impact one of our cases."

"When are you coming back?"

He paused. "Not until two days before the wedding. Just in time for my bachelor party."

"You're kidding." She'd begged him, *begged* him to clear his travel calendar the two weeks before the ceremony. "They can't get someone else?"

"Ned's back went out. He's getting surgery next week. He was the only one who could've taken my place." He caressed his thumbs over her shoulders. "This is the price I have to pay if I want to be partner someday. Remember?"

"I know." It didn't make any difference, though. It still felt as if everything were unraveling somehow. She never should have gone to Atlanta. She should have had her dress repaired in Charleston. Maybe the effects of that panic attack were still lingering . . .

"You can hold down the fort," Dubose said. "What's there left to do anyway?"

A lot. Although there was no point in complaining. He

was going. "We have a couple more pre-wedding parties," she said, "one at the Sawyers' and one at your godmother's." Special celebrations in their honor. It was going to be awful going without him.

"Lola will understand, and so will the Sawyers. Ben's an attorney. Anything else?"

True swallowed. "Your fraternity brothers need a beach house since your mother's is already being used."

"Really? She told me she was saving it for them."

"Well, she forgot." True couldn't believe Penn had been so careless. Then again, she had a lot going on. She was a busy surgeon, in and out of Charleston all the time. "She's already given it to a few girlfriends of hers from college."

"That sucks. Call Island Realty. They'll hook us up."

"Can't your friends just stay in a hotel or find their own beach house?"

"True, we made them a promise. We have to make it right since it didn't work out. I know Mom got us into this mess, but she's got an important job. We can't ask her to help." He pulled her close. "Besides, it would mean so much to me if you found a house for them. I can't just hand them a number to a hotel. These guys are my best friends."

"I know."

"Hey." He spoke softly. "Who's always there for you?"

"You are." True tried to smile, but it was hard. "We were going to talk to the band about the songs, too, remember?"

"You can text me when you're there, and I'll chime in with a few favorites. At least we both know how to dance." He'd gone to cotillion in Charleston, too.

"Yes, but—what about finalizing things with the caterer and photographer? And the restaurant for the rehearsal dinner?"

"I thought we'd already worked all that out."

"We have, basically. But there are a few little details—"

"True." He cupped her face between his hands. "You've got this."

She closed her eyes and sighed. "Of course I do. Although"—she opened her eyes and couldn't help feeling a bit lost—"you were going with me and Weezie to Trident Technical College's open house." They'd both agreed that even though it was a week before the wedding, they'd attend. It would be an ideal time for Dubose to bond with Weezie.

His gaze became distant, as if he were Superman looking over his city. He did this in the courtroom, too. Whenever he felt as if he needed to think. To connect the dots. To put something into words. "I know how important that is to you," he said slowly. It was the closest he'd come to apologizing, she knew. "Of course, you two girls will still go. Weezie won't mind my being gone."

No, she wouldn't. But True was glad he showed some misgivings about missing their special night with her.

"All right." She gave him a wobbly smile. It really wasn't his fault he had to go. And as for Weezie, she'd change her mind about him. Just as soon as she realized True wasn't going to stop loving her just because she was getting married.

"Life's not fair, sugar." Dubose chucked her on the chin. "Once you learn that, you'll do less fretting and more enjoying."

All her focus on being stoic and gracious dissolved. She turned from him and began walking up the stairs. *Damned man.* Wait. *Damned men.* She'd include Harrison in that observation, too.

"Don't condescend to me, all right?" she said over her shoulder. "I already know life's not fair."

"Duly noted." Dubose caught up with her, took her by the hand, and pulled her to the top of the stairs. "I'm just trying to get you happy again, is all." He bestowed a slow kiss on her temple. He always smelled like Polo cologne, starch, and cotton.

His sexy intentions came through loud and clear. But he was kidding, right?

Of course he wasn't kidding. He was a guy.

"Well, you went about it the wrong way." She knew she sounded sulky, but it hurt when he didn't take her seriously.

"Let me make it up to you," he said immediately, in a serious, mature-man voice.

But then he laid an entirely outrageous kiss on her. Good Lord! Did he really think having sex right now would make her feel better?

She gave him a tight smile. "I've got to take that shower. Sorry."

"I need one, too. I left my bag in the car. I'll be right back."

He still didn't get it. "Weezie's due inside any minute. We have a few people picking tomatoes."

"Oh." The syllable couldn't have fallen any flatter. "I thought she was out somewhere."

"Nope." True sighed, and a beat of awkward silence went by. His irritation was palpable. She decided to try to get cheerful again for both their sakes. "But we'll have fun tonight in Charleston, won't we?"

"Yeah. I guess."

She'd try a little harder. "Come on, Dubose. It's a party for *us*. And it's on the Battery in a house overlooking the harbor with a lot of good friends." Well, *his* good friends. "We'll have a great time."

He eyed his watch. "I was really looking forward to some alone time with you."

"Me, too," she lied. She actually hadn't had much time to do anything but think of wedding details.

"Especially now. After the party, I have to go straight home and pack." He frowned, and she could see it in his eyes—he was trying to calculate if he had time to see her in the morning for a quickie before he left.

She folded her arms over her chest. "What a shame I have to be up and out early tomorrow to get ready for the ladies from St. George's. They're coming over at eight to pick enough tomatoes to can a hundred jars of spaghetti sauce for the church bazaar."

Feeling guilty, she stood on tiptoe and kissed him quickly on the lips—nothing special, as she obviously wasn't following through. "Maybe this is a good thing. We can wait for our honeymoon."

"That's too long—"

She took his hand. "I think we should wait. Why not? We have a whole lifetime after the wedding to enjoy each other."

He looked none too happy about that. "Is this really necessary?"

"It's romantic." She squeezed his hand. "Please?"

"All right," he muttered.

"Thanks. That means a lot to me." And it did. There had been only one time in her life when she'd made love because the craving had been as relentless and intense as a swift summer storm—when she'd been with Harrison that night at the Isle of Palms.

She'd put it behind her, but today it had all come roaring back in vivid color.

Snack on this . . .

Maybe after she married Dubose and all this stress about staying afloat was behind her, they'd have the same sort of relationship.

He lifted her hair and placed a kiss on her neck, and

his lips were hot and dry, like a man with a fever. "Now hurry up out of that shower. And you'd better lock the door. I'll watch ESPN in the meanwhile."

"And maybe talk to Weezie when she comes in?"

"Sure."

So all was well. A little glitch here, a blip there . . . that was what real relationships were like. And when True got herself ready for the party, she reminded herself that she had only two weeks to go before the wedding. Surely she could manage that.

But all night long in Charleston, while she sipped champagne with Dubose's arm around her, she couldn't help wishing that she'd said yes to breakfast with Harrison.

It was a good thing he was leaving.

CHAPTER EIGHT

From Maybank Hall, Harrison headed to a mobile home park called Sand Dollar Heaven, his childhood home. There weren't any sand dollars. You needed a beach for that. But they had fiddler crabs, pluff mud, and Biscuit Creek, which were way better. And it sure wasn't heaven, at least for the grown-ups. If it was between May and December, some of them, like his father did in the old days, got up before dawn to drive their pickups down a skinny two-lane road to get to the wharf and the trawlers to work the shrimp trade. Sometimes they didn't come back for days.

And then there were the ones who worked at the restaurants, at the dry cleaners, or at keeping people's houses clean and making 'em dinner, like his mother used to. Most of the adults came back way after dark, when the locusts were buzzing hard.

"You sure you don't want me to stop and get something to eat?" he asked Gage on his cell. He really wanted to turn around, take True out instead, and catch up on what had happened to her since she'd been on her own.

"I've got a mess of crabs," Gage replied in his sand-paper southern drawl.

Harrison would like to kiss True again, too, to see if

the old spark was there. Strip her clothes off and make love to her. Sing her a good song afterward. And maybe before, too, because she was always his best audience.

In your dreams, boy.

"Got beer?" he asked Gage.

"Michelob. And crackers."

"I'll bet you're working on a puzzle."

"Yep. A Tuesday one for the *Times*."

"Got a theme?"

"James Bond Disco."

"I can only imagine what that's about." Harrison felt like an idiot when it came to crossword puzzles. Although he did have a gift with rhyme and song lyrics. So somewhere back in their gene pool was a writer or poet. "See you in a few minutes."

He clicked off and pretended, as usual, that the short conversation with Gage was just the way guys talked.

The trailer park still had the old painted plywood arch over the entrance. It was so faded, the giant sand dollar had lost all its details and looked like a faceless moon. The rutted dirt road snaked between tall yellow pines, and Harrison could swear each pothole was in the same place. He evaded them without thought, like Luke navigating the Death Star.

On the well-tended lots, sturdy mobile homes with attached porches nestled discreetly between old oaks. A thriving vegetable garden or a bright new swing set advertised a happy family inside, or at least one that got outdoors to enjoy the abundant Carolina sunshine.

Other lots looked as if a zombie apocalypse had swept through and wreaked havoc: old cars strewn everywhere, storage sheds falling down, tires in piles beneath trees. Gage's lot was one of these minus the flotsam.

Harrison got out of the car in front of their parents'

ancient trailer and slammed the door. Hell and damnation. His brother had lied. He'd said years ago he'd gotten
a new mobile home.

The same old latticework at the bottom that Harrison
remembered as a kid was still there, warped and broken
in places. God knows what was lurking underneath. A
familiar dent above the kitchen window reminded him
that he'd had once thrown a football wildly off target after he'd consumed too many beers with a friend in high
school.

He knocked. Just to be safe. Wouldn't want to offend
Gage, who was particular about having everything in its
place. There was the whine and scrabble of dogs charging
toward the door. Everyone around here kept dogs, and
that was one thing Harrison really missed. His old mutts
Private and Sergeant were buried out back.

The door finally opened, and two hairy canine faces
about a foot off the floor pushed out and snorted and
snuffed around his legs, getting particularly enthusiastic
when they picked up the scent of Weezie's dogs. They
looked like some sort of combination of boxer and Jack
Russell with a little bit of Pikachu, a Japanese anime
character, thrown in.

Gage stood frowning above the dogs with a pair of
reading glasses on the tip of his nose. He looked like Ke-
anu Reeves might if he were a college professor. They'd
had a beautiful blond mother, but their father had in him
a trace of Sewee, a Native American tribe that had lived
in these parts long before the white man came. Gage was
a throwback—short ebony hair swept off his forehead,
dark brows and coal-brown eyes, wide cheekbones. He
was in his usual white buttondown, Levi's, brown leather
belt, and Sperrys.

"*Entrez.*" A Lowcountry accent and French didn't mix
too well, but Gage was always dropping short foreign

words and phrases. He probably dreamed them all the time, those and the names of rivers, countries, rare breeds of animals, ancient leaders, and whatever other words a crossword constructor couldn't escape in his profession.

"Hey." Harrison reached out and slapped his shoulder. Hard as a rock. The military training had stuck with him. "Glad to see me? You wouldn't know it from that zombie stare. Your ear gonna drop off next?"

"*Ergo?*" Gage's tone was dry as he lifted a hand to touch his left ear.

Ear go. Harrison grinned. "Damn, you're clever." *If a bit odd*, he didn't add. But that was Gage for you.

Gage's mouth tilted up on one side, as if he had a stomachache, his version of a welcoming smile. He turned and went back inside, the marble-pattern vinyl floor protesting loudly beneath his feet.

Harrison followed after him, uninvited, into the main living space, and was instantly depressed. The trailer was neat as a pin. But almost everything inside was from another era.

To his left was a sitting area with an ancient TV with a channel dial, a banged-up black metal desk, a file cabinet, a vinyl couch—puke green—a nubby red-and-orange plaid armchair, and cheap canned track lighting above an Ikea bookshelf with sagging shelves. On his right was the kitchen—vintage '80s with faux wood cabinets, faded red-flowered curtains with ruffles up top, and a laminate counter of indeterminate color with the edges worn away.

The walls were a dreary beige. Gray-black water stains loomed on the ceiling like threatening storm clouds. And in the corner by the TV, a piece of plywood stuck out from under Mama's oval rag rug.

"What's that?" Harrison asked, his heart beating a fast tattoo against his rib cage.

"A piece of plywood."

"No shit." Harrison glared at his brother. "What's it for?"

"A hole in the floor."

"You gotta be kidding me." *You trusted him. You stupid, dadgum fool.* He scratched his ear to buy himself some temper-cool-down time. "I believed you when you told me you got a new trailer."

Dammit, he should have put the concerts and studio time aside and come back to check on Gage in his own space. He shouldn't have made up all those excuses, that Gage was a grown man, that he pulled in seventy-five thousand dollars a year with his puzzles. He'd seen the world with the navy, and he could cook and clean and didn't have any dangerous vices that Harrison knew of.

So what? He obviously needed a friend.

Or a brother.

When Harrison felt guilty, he was like a pacing lion in a cage at the zoo. Ready to roar and shake something to pieces. Anything but focus on the guilt.

Gage shrugged. "I knew you'd be worried. So why not stop that from happening?" He walked into the kitchen. "Now, what would the famous country music singer from South Carolina like? Coffee or a beer?"

"Darius Rucker's not here. Is that the best clue you can come up with for me?" Harrison sauntered into the kitchen, looking for further evidence of his brother's overwhelming aversion to change. "Speaking of which, why haven't you put me in any of your puzzles? Or at least one of my song titles?"

Gage held up a K-Cup, his face smooth and untroubled. "This?"

Harrison knocked it out of his hands. "I'm pissed."

The little plastic cup rolled across the floor until it came to a slight depression and got trapped. He'd been angry for years—his whole life—because he was confused. And worried. He hated being either one. But around Gage, he was always one or the other or both.

"I didn't know you had a fragile ego," Gage said without any heat. "I haven't put you or one of your song titles in a puzzle because neither your name nor those song titles have ever come up during the construction process."

Harrison ran both his hands down his face. "I don't care about *the goddamned puzzles.* I know you see them in your head—not the whole thing at once, but corners. And you use those mental images as inspiration."

"Exactly." Gage opened the refrigerator. "So what's the problem?"

"This place, man." Harrison lifted his hands and let them drop like heavy weights against his thighs. "Sorry I went all cyborg on you. But I can't believe you've been living here. Except for college, and a couple years on a ship, you've been in this trailer your entire life. It's time to move on." He walked a few steps—*squeak! squeak!* went the floor—bent over, scooped up the K-Cup, and stuck it on the counter.

"I have new things, too. Like that Keurig machine." Gage angled his head at the compact machine on the counter.

"Am I supposed to be impressed?" Harrison tried not to inject too much scorn into his voice. "I wouldn't let my worst enemy live here."

"It's Mom and Dad's trailer." Gage took a beer out of the fridge, pried off the cap with the old-fashioned bottle-cap remover screwed under a cabinet, and shoved the bottle in Harrison's hand. "I'm fine here."

Harrison took a long swig. "Change is hard for you, I know. But this place should have been condemned when I left it. I sold it to the owner of the park for fifty bucks, did you know that?"

"No."

"He said he'd use it as his man cave. Emphasis on *cave*."

"He made a profit then. I bought it back from him for a hundred dollars." Gage, unperturbed, as always, went back out to the sitting area. "The couch still pulls out."

"Oh, God. I can't even imagine what the mattress must be like. Let me see the rest."

If his old bedspread was still there—

Yes. It was. Red ribbed cotton from Sears. Mom had bought it at Goodwill. The other twin had a blue quilt with little moons all over it. That had been Gage's.

"Don't tell me you kept Mama's floral bedspread." Harrison stalked to the bigger bedroom where their parents had slept. Yep, nothing—nothing—had changed. Except for the fact that half the rear wall of the trailer, not visible from the driveway, was covered in a plastic tarp and duct-taped down.

He turned. "You really have to move."

Gage looked unfazed. Then again, he always did. "I sleep in our old room. I don't come in here."

"The place is clean, I'll grant you that," said Harrison. "But it's uninhabitable."

"That's a relative term. If we were on *Survivor* right now and ran across this trailer in the jungle, we'd be celebrating our great find. We'd move in out of the elements and win the competition."

"We're not in a jungle. You could own a home, a nice one, and you could invite people over. No one's gonna want to visit. You definitely can't bring your girlfriend here."

"She's moved away, and she wasn't a girlfriend. She lived next door, and we were friends with benefits."

"The benefits obviously took place at her house."

"Yeah, so?"

"What about other friends? Don't you need some?"

"I have plenty. I see them every year at the National American Crossword competition and I talk to them online every day."

"That's awesome. But what about having people over? An honest-to-goodness girlfriend, maybe? You can't do that here."

It was the first time since he'd crossed the threshold into the trailer that Gage's face showed some change in expression. His mouth opened a fraction, and he got crinkles around his eyes. It was a genuine wince.

"See?" Harrison got closer, in his face. "*See?* You know you want a girl around here. Someone you can cook a romantic dinner for."

Gage's mouth thinned. "I have little chance of that. Biscuit Creek's population is minuscule, and single women, ages twenty-five to forty, number less than fifty."

"Oho." Harrison chuckled. "So you keep track."

"Of course. I'm a bachelor. I try to stay attuned to the social scene."

"That's staying attuned? I call it sitting back and missing out. You need to join in."

"How?"

How? Did he ask *how?* Harrison took a subtle breath. "By getting your ass out of this trailer," he said in a tight voice, his arms crossed over his chest. "You're moving out, Gage. And I'm not giving you a choice."

There went his long weekend in the Hamptons. He'd have to stick around here a few days and help Gage find a new place.

"*No.* I'm staying." Gage walked ramrod-straight back into the sitting room. The TV came on. ESPN. His second favorite love was baseball.

Harrison was desperate for something to kick. His brother was so smart—a genius—yet the simplest things just went right over his head.

His phone chirped. "What?"

It was Dan. "I drove this woman's piece-of-crap car all the way back from Atlanta." His Boston accent was thick. "The AC doesn't even work. She could've warned me."

"Sorry. Google Maps got you to the right place?"

"As far as the sign with the giant tomato. After that, I was on my own. I was worried some southern people might come out of the woods with their hunting rifles and shoot me for trespassing. Or offer me lemonade. I wasn't sure which. They do both down here, right?"

"You're an idiot. *Some southern people.* As if we're from another planet."

"Well, you kinda are. A girl named Weezie met me out front. She didn't even know me, but she talked my ear off, quite frankly. She wanted to know what the worst part of my job was. And the best. And then she asked me who I'd have to dinner if I could invite five people over, living or dead."

"Did she try to give you a strawberry milk shake?"

"No."

"You missed out." Harrison paused a beat. "Did you meet her sister?"

"Yes, and her fiancé, too. They were running out the door to a party, so we only exchanged hellos. She didn't look too happy, to tell you the truth. She was smiling, but I could sense some tension."

A deep, secret part of Harrison reveled at this news. But he put the lid on the feeling quickly. "You? Mr. Insensitive Clod?" he said easily.

Dan chuckled. "Yeah, well, I had some help. The talkative sister told me the fiancé's leaving tomorrow and won't be back until two days before their wedding."

"For real? That would suck pretty bad, I guess, if you're a girl." Poor True . . . although Harrison didn't want to feel sorry for her when she was marrying such an ass.

"He's a smart cookie, getting away from all the craziness." Dan released a big sigh. "Hey, I can see why you drove her home. She's a looker. But the guy made it very clear she's taken."

"Sheesh. I know that. What's it to you anyway?"

"I need you to focus."

A black cloud in Harrison's head started pouring buckets over his imaginary parade, which was already limping along pretty poorly. "Any particular reason you're bringing this up now?"

"You betcha," said Dan with sickening good cheer.

Harrison dreaded the answer. He knew the answer, but he'd pretend he didn't. Why not buy himself a few more seconds of denial? "Yeah, well, maybe we can talk later. I'm kinda busy right now—"

"The studio called," Dan interrupted him. "*Again*. They want to know when they can expect the first batch of songs."

Right. Songs. They needed more. *Now*. So why wasn't Harrison writing any? He didn't know. Which pissed him off. "I told them." He jetted a breath. "*Soon*."

"Soon isn't good enough anymore," Dan shot back. "You've been saying that for a year. You're gonna lose momentum if you keep this up. Think of all the people who rely on you, buddy. We need product."

Harrison's bristles went up. "You know how hard I work," he said quietly. "I don't need you tightening the screws. Leave that to the studio. And if you ever call my songs *product* again, I'll be forced to kick your ass."

"Desperation drove me to it," Dan protested. "I just don't know how much longer I can hold them off."

"It's what I'm paying you to do."

The sound of crackling paper came over the line. "You and I both know I'm the best in the business"—Dan was obviously eating a Big Mac or something like it—"but there's a limit to my talent. Okay? I'm admitting that. Help me out here, Harrison, please—if you don't want me to say the other *P*-word again."

Product.

Harrison hated that designation. But it was true—he couldn't keep playing the same songs forever, even if they were number one hits on the country charts and climbing the pop ones, too. "Okay," he said. "I get it."

"Stay here in Biscuit Creek." More crackling.

"I was already going to stay a couple extra days. Help my brother find a new place to live."

"That's good—good. But stay longer."

"No." Harrison stared at the duct-taped wall. "That's crazy."

"No, it's not. You need to get out of your regular life. Biscuit Creek is where you wrote your first hit song."

"Wrong. I wrote that in a Motel 8 in Atlanta after I left home." Brokenhearted and depressed. Thinking his life was over. That was what real country songs were about. Country singers might be crossing over into the pop realm, and now into the rap world with hick hop, but beneath a real country anthem there was always a broken heart.

"Still. You got your inspiration in Biscuit Creek. Right?" Dan was persistent.

"Yeah, I guess I did." From True. From his mama's eyes. And from the salty brown-green waters of Biscuit Creek itself.

"Well, see if you can get it back. You been workin' too hard, bro. Your soul is tired."

Harrison shut his eyes. Dan had hit the nail on the head. It was the main reason Harrison put up with him. "I'll stay maybe a week."

"Come on, man. I'm willing to fend the studio off another month."

"I'll think about it." No way was he staying a month.

"The music will come. It will." Dan sounded serious but calm. "And from now on, I'm going to watch out for you better. We got caught up in the hype, the fun. But you need time and space to breathe." Dan tried to sing the chorus of Faith Hill's big hit, "Breathe."

"Your jokes suck." Harrison was still looking for something to kick or punch. "And you can't even sing."

"Hey," Dan said, all peppy and annoying, "it was a hit for a reason. And so are your songs. See you later. I'm not gonna call you. You call me if you need anything. But I swear, if I hear from you before the month is up—"

"What? What'll you do?"

"I'll kick *your* ass."

"You couldn't kick my little pinkie."

Dan chuckled. "Just don't get into trouble, okay? I'll need you back fresh."

"Right." Harrison threw the phone against the wall. But not before Dan disconnected first. The loser. They refused to say bye to each other on the phone. Just like in the movies. Dan could have at least let Harrison hang up on *him*. He was paying the guy enough to get that one little thrill.

He fell back on the bed and stared at the ugliest ceiling he'd ever seen. God, he was pathetic. He had no excuse, either. Except that when you were on the road with the same old people all the time, you developed little ways to entertain yourself because there was nothing else to do away from the spotlight.

Except write songs.

Idiot.

But apart from that . . . hanging out in a local pub was out. So was going to the movies. So was visiting a museum or eating out at a restaurant—not unless you wanted a lot of hassle from fans seeking autographs and the occasional picture while they were groping your butt, trying to jump in your lap, or kissing you.

All he could do was spend money. He'd written lots of big checks to charities he had no personal connection to and had a closetful of cowboy boots, leather jackets, and sunglasses. He'd accrued three houses—in Nashville, Vail, and LA—and five collector cars and was looking at a sixth in England. An old Studebaker owned by Elton John. But even buying cars was getting boring. Who'd he have to show them off to? Dan?

There was no escape from the same old same old. None. Not even in Biscuit Creek, where just this morning a girl caught a glimpse of him at the stoplight between Black Oak and Main and fell onto the street crying and screaming, "Harrison Gamble! Is that you?"

The same old same old was really bad here in Mom and Dad's trailer with a brother who couldn't seem to live in the present. What were they gonna have to do? Carry the old TV with them wherever he forced Gage to move? Rip down those kitchen curtains and hang 'em up in the new place?

"Shyeah," Harrison said, in the worst funk of his life since he'd last left Biscuit Creek—maybe this place was bad luck, huh?—then stood up from the edge of his parents' bed and had a couple of brilliant ideas despite himself.

CHAPTER NINE

The next day, a few hours after the ladies of St. George's left Maybank Hall with a pickup truck bed filled with baskets of tomatoes, True was at the Starfish Grill, reading a Dick Francis book behind a menu in the back booth, away from prying eyes. She felt prickly. Upset. Worried. The opposite of what the brides in the magazines looked like.

But she made sure you'd never know it, looking at her. She was dressed for lunch, in a crisp blue-and-white-striped Brooks Brothers blouse and red pencil skirt with navy pumps, all cobbled together from her college wardrobe and the Junior League shop in Charleston. She'd spent extra time fixing her hair, flat-ironing it so that it curled demurely on the bottom.

And her makeup—Revlon, all of it—she'd applied sparingly, except for the classic red lipstick she'd used on her lips. Mama's pearl necklace and earrings almost completed the ensemble. But the final touch was the classic Coach messenger bag in navy blue, a 1970s find in Honey's trunk that True had restored with oil and a great deal of love.

She was southern-girl chic, and no one was going to figure out that she was all manner of bridal crazy, least of all Penn, her future mother-in-law.

Carmela, curvaceous and sexy in a pink leather dress with a heart-shaped neckline, slid into the other side of the booth and grinned. "I've got exactly ten minutes before I have to get back to the shop," she said. "How was the shower?"

True thought hard. "Nice?"

"That's the world's worst word. May no one ever remember me as Nice Carmela."

"But you *are* nice."

"I know." Carmela sighed. "But I want to be remembered as Bold Carmela. Or Talented Carmela. Or even Bad Carmela."

"Yeah, well, I'm Lightweight True." She'd felt so out of place at the mansion on the Battery, not because the owners were crazy rich but because she didn't really know anyone. "I overdid it with the champagne to have a little fun with Dubose and to forget he's leaving. But it didn't work."

Carmela lifted a dark Italian brow. "Did you think about anyone else while you were at the shower? Someone whose name begins with *H*?"

"Of course." True was mortified to admit it, but she couldn't lie to Carmela. "I wondered why he pops up at the weirdest times, like an unlucky genie. But I'm glad he's gone."

Carmela leaned in close. "You're a bad liar," she whispered.

"I'm not lying," True insisted.

Carmela narrowed her eyes.

"All right, I *am*." True put her face in her hands. "But who cares? I'm getting married. This isn't high school anymore. This is real life."

"Tell me how Dubose was last night."

"Distracted, checking his BlackBerry." True had felt embarrassed, too. For a smart lawyer, he could be woefully lacking in good manners. "The only time he really paid attention to the party was when the hostess started talking about a recently married couple they all knew from college who'd already filed for divorce and were fighting over property."

"Ugh. Real nice topic for a wedding shower."

True had thought the same thing. "I did my best to act interested. But I wasn't. I wished I were with you instead." She grabbed Carmela's fingers and squeezed. "We've hardly seen each other."

Carmela squeezed back. "I know. You're busy being a farm girl. And I'm running a dying business." She stretched out her long legs, the better for them both to admire her new platform heels, and eyed the restaurant entrance. The walls were covered in black-and-white photos of old shipwrecks. "You think Prince Charming is out there looking for me?"

"Of course," True said right away. Somewhere out there was a man who'd appreciate Carmela's truth speaking and huge heart even more than her fantastic body and sultry looks.

Carmela's cat-eyes were hopeful. "I'll get Roger to bring over some water with lemon." Roger was the seventy-three-year-old busboy at the Starfish. "And I hope you and Penn have a fabulous lunch, even if she won't buy anything from my store. Maybe you can work on her."

"You mean, drug her," True said drily. "It would be the only way I could get her in there. General Sherman burned down her ancestral home during the Civil War. Your last name is Sherman, you're from New York, and your store is called Southern Loot. She doesn't have a sense of humor. At all. Plus, there's a store selling southern-themed items on every street corner in Charleston County."

"Those are pretty good reasons," said Carmela. "But she's the queen bee around here. If she comes in, so will everyone else. Maybe she'll want one of my Mississippi Mud Pie kits. I got in a whole case."

Carmela was nothing if not an optimist.

When True was alone again, she inhaled a cleansing breath and focused on being happy.

Happy.

She tapped her foot.

Happy . . .

Shoot. She was still miserable. Maybe it was because she was always a little afraid to talk to Penn—although the woman was going to be her mother-in-law, so she needed to get over that. Right then, as a matter of fact. Penn was at the door, dressed to the nines, as always, in a cream-colored suit with gold buttons True had seen in a window in at the St. John store in Charleston. She could buy a small used tractor for the price of that suit. Or a hundred yards of new fencing for the back field where the deer feasted on her strawberries.

Carmela stayed with Penn on her way to the table and held her own. She always did. She winked at True. "You guys have fun."

You guys. True closed her eyes for a second. She'd told Carmela never, ever to call Penn a guy. Penn simply didn't get it.

Carmela suddenly realized her mistake. "Oh, and if you ever get a *hankering*," she went on nervously, "for some delicious southern treats or treasures, I *reckon* you can visit my shop, Dr. Waring."

Penn sent her an eat-shit-and-die look. Kind of well deserved, actually, so True let it go. Carmela slunk off, defeated. True would comfort her later. Meanwhile, she leapt up to pull out Penn's chair as her way of apologizing for her friend's wretched attempt at using local vernacular.

"Thank you, Gertrude," Penn murmured in her refined

Charleston accent—Geechee with a twist of old, old money.

True's jaw clenched. Her name was True. Not Gertrude. She'd told Penn a thousand times, but apparently she didn't believe her. Once again, she was tempted to call her fiancé's mother Pennsylvania, but wisely, she refrained.

Roger brought them two menus, but Penn flicked hers away with a beautifully manicured hand. "I already know what I want. A Caesar salad, balsamic vinaigrette on the side, topped with grilled salmon. And a Diet Coke. No ice, with lemon."

"I'm not one of your operating room nurses, Penn Waring. I don't take orders." Roger looked down his nose at her. This was his forty-fifth year at the Starfish as a busboy. "I went to school with your older brother. I remember when you were a mealymouthed brat tootling down the Battery wall on your tricycle."

"Well," said Penn, and opened her mouth to say more.

"Don't you dare bless my heart, either," he interrupted her. "I'll send your waitress over if your attitude improves."

Penn inclined her head. "What do you do here, Roger? You're certainly obstreperous."

"You know very well what I do," he replied. "I get water or tea"—sweet and always a free refill—"when I like someone. And I take away everyone's dishes, whether I like 'em or not." He softened his glare and looked at True. "You doin' all right, young Miss Maybank?"

True smiled. "You bet, Roger."

He sent her a meaningful look—*Good luck; you'll need it*—and walked away.

Her heart sank. Her armpits were sweating. She was a wimp, and she was afraid of Dubose's mother. Even imagining her on a tricycle didn't help.

"So." Penn unfurled her napkin with a snap and placed

it on her lap. "Let's cut to the chase, shall we? I have some
bad news. The wedding caterer quit, and she's taken the
reception place with her."

It was like a bomb went off in True's eardrums. But it
turned out only to be her heart almost exploding out of
her chest in shock. "*What?*"

"I'm afraid so."

"I need to call her right now and get her back!" True's
fingers trembled as she reached for her phone.

"Don't bother," said Penn. "I already tried. It seems
there was a huge mix-up. She thought the wedding was the
following weekend. She's already booked for your weekend."

True felt the fingers of a panic attack brush against
her throat. "If it's her fault, can't we force her to make it
right?"

"She doesn't have the resources. She knows this opens
her up to a lawsuit, but she has no option but to cancel."

Of course, Penn was cool. She was a surgeon. True
wouldn't take it personally—but she did. It hurt that Penn
wasn't freaking out with her. "Why were *you* dealing with
the caterer?"

"I'm paying for the wedding." Penn sounded slightly
offended. "Did Bosey not tell you?"

Her nickname for Dubose always rankled. So did not
knowing that Penn was in control of their wedding. "No."
True swallowed hard. "He didn't. I'm sorry. I just assumed—"

"If you want to be an attorney's wife, you can't crack
under pressure." Penn's eyes bored into hers. "As you
know, my son likes to do things in grand style. He loves
tradition. Pomp. Elegance. The best champagnes, a string
quartet, and of course he just bought his five-thousand-
dollar custom-made tuxedo from Savile Row when he
was on his last trip to London. If you don't want to disap-

point him, you'll find a way to make the big wedding happen."

"Of—of course, I'll do my best. Surely with your connections, we can get someone else. I know it's last-minute—"

"I won't be here," said Penn.

"*What?*"

"I'm going to England to a medical conference. I told Bosey. He must have forgotten to mention it."

True gulped. "He never did."

"You simply can't tell him any of this when he's trying so hard to do a good job in New York," Penn said. "You'll have to handle this on your own."

True blinked. "Maybe . . . maybe we can elope."

Penn drew in her chin. "How disappointing that would be for all your wedding guests, some of whom are Dubose's clients. The partners will be there, too."

"Dubose won't blame me. He'll blame the caterer."

Their waitress brought their meals—not that True could eat anything now without becoming ill.

"Perhaps he *will* blame the caterer," Penn said. "But he'll be disappointed in you all the same. He'll want to know why his future wife couldn't make lemonade out of lemons. He'll be hurt that you didn't think of his business interests. Or his personal preferences."

She opened her purse, put a discreet fifty-dollar bill on the table, and stood. "I think it's best that I go and let you mull this over. I've got to pack. But listen to me, True. If you manage to repair this problem, imagine how impressed Dubose will be with you. Let's face facts. He wants to marry you because you're reliable. Dutiful. And you're easy on the eyes. But he pulls the most weight in this relationship, doesn't he? You owe him one."

Oh, God. She owed him one!

When Penn left the restaurant, True pushed her platter

of flounder, new baby potatoes, and green beans aside. She pulled the Dick Francis title over, and laid her head down. It was warm and stuffy inside her arms, and pitch black, and she could smell the pages of the book. She never wanted to leave this little cave. Ever.

Penn had hit on her greatest fear—that she brought nothing to the table with Dubose. She ran a two-bit U-pick operation. Her house was falling down about her ears. She read novels instead of going back to school. Every day, she asked herself the question: Why was he with *her* and not one of those fabulously successful Charleston girls?

A few seconds ticked by. Silverware clinked against plates, laughter rang out, and talking continued. And then she sensed rather than saw a presence looming over her.

"Go away, please, Roger. I'll give you this booth back in a minute. I swear."

"It's not Roger, Miss Priss."

Her eyes popped open. But she didn't lift her head. "No," she said in a thin voice. He was still here. Her unlucky genie. The one who always showed up at the wrong time.

She felt the table shake as Harrison slid into the opposite seat.

"You can quit your crying over my imminent departure," he said. "I'm sticking around, after all."

CHAPTER TEN

True raised her head, and if her eyes could have shot deadly gamma rays at Harrison, they would have. "I'm not crying about you. I'm not even crying."

"Oh, yeah? What's the deal then?"

Whatever happened, she was all worked up. In fact, even in that schoolteacher blouse, she was prettier and sexier than a half-dressed Kitana from *Mortal Kombat*. Not that he played video games. Much. He was way too busy and important.

And you just keep lying to yourself, Earthrealm warrior.

True tucked in her chin. "It's a long story."

"I got all day, in between a bunch of phone calls." In fact, his phone was vibrating right now. He lifted it to his ear and held up an index finger. True scowled in his general direction.

"Vince?" he said into the receiver, then put his hand over it. "Move Dick Francis, and eat that flounder," he said to True. "You look like you need some fuel."

She shoved the book in her purse and pulled the platter over. Without a word, she picked up a piece of fish with her hand, stuffed it into her mouth, and began chewing slowly.

He got back to Vince. "I'm here."

"Your manager woke me up, you know that?" Vince was the best architect in LA. He was also a cross-dresser with a fondness for Donna Karan.

"Good. I need you on the first flight outta LAX. You'll have to connect in Atlanta, then Charleston."

"Damn, Harrison."

"I'm making it worth your while." Vince had done a great job renovating Harrison's Venice Beach surfer shack and transforming it into a sleek, minimalist bachelor pad. The photo spread had recently landed in *Architectural Digest*.

"Dan told me about it." Vince sounded a little nicer now. And he should. He was being paid out the wazoo to get his butt over to South Carolina. "What's this about building a house in a couple of weeks? Are you on drugs? Or just your average demanding celebrity?"

"The latter." True was eating a baby potato now. It looked like a big acorn stuck in her cheek. "You interested?"

"Of course, I am," Vince said hastily. "I'll make it even cooler than your place. I've got connections in Atlanta and Miami. How soon do you need a construction crew?"

"I'd say three or four days."

"That's easy. And we can have the whole project done in three weeks."

"Good."

"But it's going to mean throwing around major money."

"I've already begun. I bought myself a trailer park this morning. They weren't going to allow the house to go up, but that's where Gage wants to stay. I convinced him he deserves the primo lot facing the creek and the elements—too close for comfort in a trailer but just fine for a solid house, a breezy Charleston style, by the way—"

"With a piazza on both floors and twelve-foot ceilings," clarified Vince. "Yeah, I got your number."

"I hired a bushwhacker to clear out the undergrowth," Harrison went on without missing a beat, "but he'll have lots of oaks. Which reminds me, you'll have to raise the first-floor height. We get hurricanes over here, and we're in a flood zone."

"Done. Who is this Gage guy?"

"My brother. And he's gonna hate this. He wants his trailer back. But I'm padlocking the doors and getting it hauled away."

"Don't do it yet. I'll use it as my office while I'm on site. If it's habitable."

"It's clean as a whistle. Just about to fall down, and the decor will burn your eyeballs. Vintage early 'eighties with a southern sensibility."

"Oh, okay. Does that mean there's an Elvis rug on the wall?"

"Sadly, no. Just a couple of mounted deer heads and a Creedence Clearwater Revival poster." True was staring at him wide-eyed, so he winked. She fluttered her lashes, as if the wink had disturbed her zoning out. At least half her flounder was gone. "Good girl," he told her. "Keep going."

She picked up a wilted string bean and began chewing, and she was so cute and unintentionally provocative a jolt of lust hit him hard.

"Are you there, you crazy southern coot?" Vince barked down the line.

"I'm here." Good thing he was sitting down. Otherwise, he'd embarrass himself in public.

"I'll see you late this afternoon," Vince said. "Where am I staying? And don't tell me that trailer. I don't want to live *Duck Dynasty* twenty-four hours a day."

Harrison resisted the urge to play footsie with True.

She'd probably choke if he tried. "I booked a block of rooms at the Francis Marion in Charleston for everyone involved in the project, and I'll have a fleet of limos for transport. Someone will meet you at the airport. I told the limo company to look for a guy in a dress. He'll have lumberjack legs, so he'll be hard to miss."

"Wow, I'm impressed." Vince chuckled. "I didn't know big, handsome stars like you were capable of doing anything but looking good and singing."

"Surprise," said Harrison, and hung up grinning.

True was still chewing her string bean. She looked so forlorn, Harrison stood up and went to the bar, where he ordered her a straight shot of Firefly Sweet Tea Vodka. It was local and damned good.

While he was waiting, Carmela walked in ready to fight someone, apparently. Her hands were clutched into fists, and her cheeks wore red flags. She went straight to see True, but a few seconds later she was back with Harrison at the bar. "What's happened to her? She called me and then she didn't say a word. So I ran back here . . . in case she was choking, which she's not, thank God."

"I have no idea what's going on with her. I'll bet you wondered if she was kidnapped, too, huh? Imagined she was on her way to the ladies' room and some guy put a revolver in her back?"

"How did you know?" Carmela crossed herself. "She's okay but a little odd acting."

The bartender, a twenty-something guy with a big Adam's apple, was freaking out, looking blindly around him for a shot glass.

"Do I know you?" Harrison asked him.

"Paul Westfall," he squeaked. "I was a year behind you in school."

"Cool." Harrison grinned. He remembered the guy now. Total geek. Chess player. He often taught class for their usually hung-over chemistry teacher, who'd sleep at his desk.

"It had to have been Penn who shook her up." When Carmela bit her lip, she looked just like Brigitte Bardot. "They had lunch. Penn would make a scary mother-in-law for anyone, but especially True. She's down on herself because she's been stuck at Maybank Hall all these years, and Penn's so accomplished. I told her, look at me! I'm running a business with no customers."

Harrison flipped through his wallet and tossed down ten hundred-dollar bills, along with his business card, for Paul. "Keep the change, buddy. And get yourself back in school. You need to be mixing things in labs, not at a bar. If you need an interest-free loan, call me. I also give scholarships."

Now he did, that is.

He picked up the shot—a gorgeous amber color—and turned away before Paul had a stroke or something. "Isn't Gage in your store now?" he asked Carmela.

"Yes, God bless him. He's practically my only customer. He loves to straighten my shelves." She stood on tiptoe to get a better look at True. "Roger told True they needed her booth because the line's out the door and down the block, thanks to you being here. She told him over her dead body. And now she looks like Dracula's wife, all pale and bloodless and cold."

"I'll work on her." Harrison would like nothing better than to warm her up. He remembered that night on the Isle of Palms. Jiffy Pop had nothing on that girl. But that girl also had a ring on her finger and a wedding coming up. And he was a country music star with a career that stayed in the fast lane because that was where he wanted it.

Carmela gave him a knowing look. "She's getting married, you know. Please remember your boundaries, or you'll have me to deal with, Mr. Gamble. I love her too much to see her dreams get pulverized in the blender of your celebrity, all right? She's been through a lot."

"Nice metaphor," he told her. "And nice Sunday meetin' biker dress." He gave her a nanosecond's once-over.

Carmela blushed. "Thank you."

"I'll be good. And call me Harrison." He winked at her and took off with True's vodka shot. At the booth, he slid the glass across the table to land right in front of her—in the early days, he'd done his share of bartending himself— and sat down next to her. "I need to ask you a favor." He enjoyed their physical proximity, which was a nice way to say she made him randier than a bull surrounded by a herd of cows in heat.

"Oh?"

"Maybe you should down that first and tell me what happened." He indicated the vodka.

"This is a bad time for me, Harrison."

"Go ahead."

She lifted the glass to her mouth and drained it, then gasped for air. "Thanks," she said. "That was really good. But I need to get busy. You sound busy, too. You're building Gage a house?"

"Uh-huh. Exciting times."

She actually seemed to break out of her haze a little. "That's really nice." She looked him straight in the eye. Hers seemed so sad. But flippin' gorgeous, too. He could get lost in those eyes for a long, long time.

"Hey." He heard the huskiness in his voice. She always got to him, even in her prim southern-lady outfit that she needed to dump in favor of something less uptight. "You all right? Anything I can help you with?"

She shook her head. "No, this is something I have to handle myself." She took another sip of vodka. "You said you had a favor to ask me. Ask away. I'll have to say no, though, whatever it is. I'm too busy to help anyone right now."

She didn't look very busy. But he wouldn't tell her that.

"All right." He slung an arm behind her.

She scooted away. "You can't do that."

"Do what?"

"You know." She angled her head at his arm, which was still on the back of the seat. "*That*."

"Okay," he said. "Maybe we should talk while we're walking, then. You wanna come with me and find Gage? He's straightening shelves at Southern Loot."

"All the shopkeepers look forward to his visits."

"He's OCD, I guess. He even told me he's figured out he has this so-called Asperger's syndrome. You ever heard of it?"

"Sure. But he's really just Gage."

"Exactly." Harrison leaned close. "He can stack boxes *and* think out of the box, all at the same time."

"Yes, he can." True's smile was serene. "And Weezie is just Weezie. Our doctor said she's an Aspie, too. But they're both bigger than any label."

Yes. It was as if a Zen bell rang in Harrison's head. *This woman. This one. Right here.*

Their faces were so close. He wanted to lean in, lay his forehead on hers, close his eyes, and be. Just be. And maybe wind up kissing. And running a hand over her sweet little breasts and wrapping a leg around hers, which looked mighty fine in that skirt. Yes, they were in a restaurant and everybody was probably staring at him, but they should be looking at her. She was the fascinating one—

"Harrison?" She pushed on his chest. She was acting alert now, and the zoning out had somehow been transferred to him. "I'll walk with you a little and say hi to Gage. But then I really do have to go."

He mentally cleared his head. "Right."

He stood up, watched her slide out of the seat, enjoying every moment of looking down the pucker in her blouse, and extended a hand. She took it—ah, sweet Jesus, those fingers felt good—and he pulled her up. Right into his face. Or beneath his face. But close enough.

"Who are you marrying again?" he asked her, low in his throat.

She looked blankly at him, then said, "Dubose," in the next instant.

"Too late," he replied, much satisfied.

"It's that vodka," she said. "And if you expect a favor when you tease me like that, you'd better think again."

"You already said you're too busy to help."

"I did say that, but since you're an old friend, I'll do it. As long as it won't take very long."

"It won't. All you need to do is say yes. I can handle the rest. You can just sit back and watch."

"Really?"

"Scout's honor."

"Okay, then."

"Fantastic."

They were walking side by side through the restaurant, Harrison nodding at everyone he made eye contact with. Which was everybody. He was good at sweeping a room. Didn't want anyone to feel left out. He was also a master at acknowledging questions, comments, and good wishes without actually stopping.

"Thank you so much," he said to a sweet young couple, then, "I know, crazy, huh?" to someone else. When a snarky old guy turned around and told him that he obviously approved of spray tans for men, he said, "You betcha!" even though he'd never had a spray tan in his life. Always better to kill 'em with kindness.

Oh, but that was Roger-the-busboy asking about the

tan. Damn. Harrison would've flipped him off had there been no ladies present. All in fun, of course.

"Your name's on the water tower!" cried Mrs. Bloomfield, his old third-grade teacher. "How many people can say that?"

Aw, hell. He had to stop to see *her*. He leaned over her table and took her tiny, withered hand. "I hope you're well, Mrs. Bloomfield."

"Except for a weak bladder, I'm fine." She smiled demurely.

"Mama." The woman with her put a finger to Mrs. Bloomfield's lips, then looked at Harrison. "Sorry. She says anything she wants these days."

"Not a problem," Harrison replied.

"You look so handsome," Mrs. Bloomfield said behind her daughter's finger, "in your tight trousers."

Awwk-ward . . . He glanced at the daughter, who just rolled her eyes and put away her finger. "Uh, thank you, ma'am."

"You must be rich as Croesus." Mrs. Bloomfield fondled her dyed macaroni necklace, probably made by one of her own students.

"I never met the guy," Harrison replied with a smile that had won him millions of female fans, "so I wouldn't know."

She laughed. "Is this your girlfriend? Or wife?"

True's eyes widened. "No, Mrs. Bloomfield. It's me, True. You were my third-grade teacher, too."

"True?" Mrs. Bloomfield squinted at her. "Oh, for a minute I could swear you were your mother in that outfit." Ooh. Sucker punch from an innocent old lady. "Aren't you marrying Dubose Waring?"

True nodded. Poor kid.

"Then what are you doing with Harrison?" Mrs. Bloomfield said, right into a lull in general conversation in the dining room.

True looked at him.

He'd let her handle this one.

"We're just friends," she said into the silence. "Old friends."

"That's right," Harrison told Mrs. Bloomfield. "True here's putting up me and my brother Gage—and his two mutts—at Maybank Hall while his house is undergoing renovations. A few weeks tops, and then we'll be out of her hair."

"What?" True's eyes flew wide.

"He said you're letting him and Gage and his two mutts stay at Maybank Hall," Mrs. Bloomfield repeated to her as if True were deaf.

Which meant the whole dining room stopped chewing so they could hear True's answer. She smiled like an angel, but Harrison could tell she was seething.

"I heard every word," she told Mrs. Bloomfield. "I'm just not sure he got that right."

"Sure, I did," he said easily. "I've got Gage's pickup truck out front on Main Street now. The dogs are kenneled up in the back. Oh, and we needed to bring his old TV set along. A chair, too, and a few other little things. I hope you won't mind."

"Of course she won't," said Mrs. Bloomfield. "Who wouldn't want to help out Biscuit Creek's two biggest stars? I'm not sure we appreciated the extent of you Gamble boys' talent when you were growing up. We should flog ourselves for being so obtuse. Or at the least bend over backward to make it up to you now."

Yeah, that pretty much summed things up.

"Isn't that right, everyone?" Mrs. Bloomfield said.

"Hell to the yeah," crowed a guy in a Simpsons T-shirt, his mouth full of okra gumbo and corn bread. Touching— but a little gross.

"Good golly, yes!" Paul the bartender, who was still a

geek, piped up from the back. Good ol' Paul. Rather, *Dr.* Paul. At least someday.

"Anyone who likes Twinkies is a friend of mine," one elderly woman at a table of church ladies said.

"I prefer MoonPies," another church lady averred.

A vigorous discussion of the merits of MoonPies versus Twinkies broke out across the entire dining room, with Harrison trapped right in the middle. True pointed at an invisible watch on her wrist. Crowd control.

Good call.

He wished he had his bodyguards, but he didn't. It looked like he'd have to do this Biscuit Creek style. So he put his fingers between his lips and whistled.

Like magic, the hubbub ceased. If only the rest of the world would shush at a whistle.

"Hey, everyone." Harrison took True's arm, and when she met his gaze, her eyes were snapping blue fire. "As you know, I can't stay in Charleston. I'd be stalked by the paparazzi. And Gage isn't fond of hotels. I know here in Biscuit Creek among our own, Gage can work on his crosswords without distraction. And I need a few good weeks of peace so I can write another hit song." He gazed around the dining room. "If we can both manage to accomplish what we have to do, I'm gonna update the Biscuit Creek library as a thank-you, so it's in everyone's best interests not to call in *Entertainment Tonight*."

"He needs to write that hit song!" Mrs. Bloomfield clutched True's arm. "And Gage needs to construct his crosswords! Help Harrison, True. Help him help *us*. I want more Darynda Jones and Nora Roberts novels in the fiction section. And my son-in-law can't live without his Gage Gamble Sunday puzzles in *The New York Times*."

"Help Harrison help us help the *library*!" a man in a bow tie and suspenders exclaimed.

"That should be the town's temporary top-secret slogan," a second man in a bow tie and suspenders said.

Anything was better than BISCUIT CREEK: YOU WERE HERE!—which was painted on a bullet-ridden sign at the turnoff from Highway 17.

Everyone started chatting loudly about the library and all that Harrison's money would do for it. One man pulled out a harmonica and started playing a little ditty—for the sheer heck of it. Because some moments were just too exciting *not* to play the harmonica.

Aw, small-town life. Harrison had forgotten how downright heartwarming yet peculiar it could be. "True?" he whispered in her ear. "Remember I said you just have to say yes?"

"All right," she murmured back, "but only if you and Gage help Weezie run the U-pick operation while I attend to wedding matters. And take care that Skeeter and Boo behave as nicely as our three hairy hooligans, which isn't saying much."

"Piece of cake," Harrison said. "Deal?"

True bit her lip. "Deal."

"Who's getting married again?" Mrs. Bloomfield asked above the harmonica playing.

Good Lord. Someone was playing spoons now.

"Dubose and I," said True. "You're invited. Everyone here is."

"Oh." Mrs. Bloomfield's face fell even farther than it already had due to her preponderance of wrinkles. "I guess I'll come. Although . . . are you sure? Harrison here is *very* handsome."

"*Mama*," her daughter chided her above the merriment.

But Mrs. Bloomfield would not—could not—be stopped. "They'd make a fine couple. In fact, I seem to remember a story about Harrison crashing a fuddy-duddy party after the prom and making some idiot look the fool."

Dubose, of course.

Harrison coughed into his fist. He had to stay on True's good side. "We've really got to go, Mrs. Bloomfield."

"I hope to see you at the wedding," True said, her smile tight. "Bye, now."

Mrs. Bloomfield blew her a kiss. "Good-bye, dear. Live it up while you still can." She looked pointedly at Harrison then back at True. "For me if not for you."

"I-I'll do my best." True took off, her gorgeous behind swishing like nobody's business between the seats, in time to the beat of the spoons.

Harrison had a feeling she wasn't even aware of it. He kissed the back of the old lady's hand and went after his new landlord, who had damned good rhythm.

"My, he's a hottie," he heard a third church lady say. "But no *Entertainment Tonight* reporter will ever hear those words from *my* lips."

Good, Harrison thought. At the door he found Carmela trying to soothe True by offering her a stick of Fruit Stripe gum. Lord, this really *was* a small town.

"We'll go get Gage," he said to Carmela—no way was he going to look at True, but he could hear her, groaning and whimpering under her breath while she worked that stick of gum—"if he's still at your store."

It was time to move into Maybank Hall.

CHAPTER ELEVEN

Lord, have mercy on my soul, thought True, borrowing one of Ada's favorite sayings. She had one goal: to keep her sanity long enough to marry Dubose. But with Harrison and Gage moving into the house, the bumper tomato crop, and all that she had to do to keep her wedding from turning into a shambles, she didn't know that she'd make it. She really wanted to get to her studio. Playing with her canvases always calmed her down. But since she couldn't, she had to be content with getting the men settled in, the rules established, and Weezie cooperating.

When Harrison and Gage arrived at the house, the first thing they did was let the mutts, Skeeter and Boo, out of their kennels to be welcomed by the Maybank Labs. That was a chaotic scene. And then everyone worked together to unload a few things from the trailer and put them upstairs in Gage's temporary quarters: an old rag rug, a dented desk, a hideous plaid armchair, an ancient tacky bedspread.

The vintage TV set they left downstairs in the front parlor.

Weezie was in awe of it. "Is it really from 1979?" she asked Gage. "What's that dial? Where are all the channels? Why is it so big? What's that giant antenna for?"

She couldn't have cared less that an international

country superstar was temporarily moving in, or that his brother the crossword constructor would be creating marvelous puzzles for the most widely read newspaper in the world. She had to watch her talk shows on that TV.

"Sorry," said Gage. "It won't get any of the networks."

"Jumpin' Jehosephat," Weezie exclaimed. "What good is it then?"

Whereupon her love of the vintage appliance ceased forthwith.

In between herding dogs and testing the antenna's reception on the TV, Harrison grabbed Weezie around the shoulders and squeezed. "So you finally got your boarders. How do you like it?"

And with that, she suddenly seemed to see him for the first time again. "Oh, Harrison!" She wrapped her arms around his waist. "I'm so glad you're here. It's not fun with just True." An awkward beat went by. "Is Gage nice?" she asked right in front of him.

Without waiting for Harrison's answer—maybe she never really wanted one— she sat down next to his brother and watched him flip through Daddy's old fishing encyclopedia, which Gage had picked up from the coffee table. "Hey, what's your favorite color?"

He made brief eye contact. "Gray."

"That sucks," Weezie said. "No one says gray."

"I do." Gage kept reading.

She leaned over his shoulder. "What do you think St. Peter will say when you show up at the Pearly Gates?"

He shrugged. "I have no idea. You'd have to ask him."

"But I can't." Weezie was getting flustered. "It's a joke. You're supposed to go along with it. Don't you know who James Lipton is?" She put her palm over the page he was on.

"Of course I do." He pushed her hand off. "But I don't like jokes. Not unless they're clever. Some crossword clues could be called jokes. There's a twist, an *aha* moment. What's the *aha* moment about St. Peter?"

"I don't know," said Weezie, worriedly. "I don't even know what we're talking about."

"Me, either," said Gage, and he went back to reading.

Weezie flung herself out of her chair and stared at him, her thumbnail in her mouth. "Someday, Gage," she said with utter sincerity, "someday I'm going to get this interview with you. And it's going to be a shocker. Secrets unveiled. Assumptions blown out of the water."

Gage turned a page. "I had no idea the lowly bristlemouth was the most common fish in the world," he murmured to no one in particular.

True exchanged a glance with Harrison.

"They're like two ships that pass in the night—and need to keep on going," he murmured in her ear.

She almost giggled. But it wasn't funny. Or shouldn't be. Yet somehow it was.

"Guys," Harrison said good-naturedly to Weezie and Gage. "Be polite. Weezie, thanks so much for having us in your home. Gage, Skeeter, Boo, and I will try to stay out of your hair. Gage, I know you're old enough by Weezie terms to be mummified. But if she's trying to engage you in conversation, it wouldn't hurt you to pay attention. We're guests here."

Weezie sent a cool glance Gage's way. "You're boring."

Gage didn't react beyond glancing up at her and then getting back into his book. Harrison threw True a look— *I'm sorry I brought this on you*—and put his hands in his pockets. He strolled over to Daddy's bookshelf and pretended to peruse the pictures there. Or maybe he really was. He held one up to the light—it was of True in a hideous dance costume. She was a young teen and had just won a first-place ribbon. That was the era in which she'd wanted to please Mama and Daddy at all costs—an era that was still upon her, she supposed.

"Weezie," said True. "*Apologize*."

"No," she said. "It's the truth. Gage is boring."

"Listen closely to me, Weezie." True was firm but calm. "If you *ever* want to hold down a job or build relationships, sometimes you're going to have to hold back. If there's one thing you'll take from this house—along with the fact that you are loved—it will be that other people's feelings matter."

Weezie blinked. She wore the wistful, almost frightened expression she got when she realized she'd messed up.

It was only the ten thousandth time True had told her to think before she spoke. Sometimes it was frustrating. Sometimes she wondered if Weezie would ever learn. But on those days when True really did despair, she made herself look back long-term and saw that Weezie, indeed, *was* advancing. Every year, she learned more and more about how to behave properly.

"But I was trying to find out what interested him." Weezie sounded on the verge of tears.

"You have to take your time." True softened her tone. "You could see that Gage was reading. That meant he wasn't ready to be interviewed."

"Come on, man," Harrison chided his brother. "You should have been paying attention to Weezie. Not a book."

Gage seemed to come out of his trance. He put the book down, his face registering a flash of resentment that he had to talk to a teenage girl with whom he had nothing in common. But then, catching Harrison's irritated gaze, he seemed to pull himself together. "Sorry, Weezie."

"It's all right." Weezie dropped her eyes.

Gage scratched his temple and sighed. "My brother's right. I should have put the book down. I-I get caught up in things sometimes. I love learning new facts."

"About fish?" Weezie looked up, her face alight.

True's heart turned over. It was so easy to make her sister happy. She just needed company.

"About everything." Gage's mouth went up at the corner. "For my crosswords. You can interview me sometime, okay?"

"Okay." Weezie sounded good again.

Gage went back to reading.

True had to wonder if this gap in understanding between them would crop up again. It seemed all too likely. Maybe it was no big deal. But she'd like to keep it that way.

"Can I talk to you?" she asked Harrison pointedly.

"Sure."

They walked into the kitchen, where she'd already put on a pot of water to boil for pasta. They had home-canned tomato sauce—jars and jars of it—and right now the contents of two were simmering in a deep frying pan. She'd fried up a pack of ground sirloin and some onions in a third pan for the meat lovers among them, and in a fourth pan chunks of tofu for Weezie. The chopped salad was ready, Mama's homemade vinaigrette mixed, and a crusty loaf of whole-grain bread from the Publix bakery was warming in the oven. True peeked into the water pot and saw it bubbling.

She was glad to stay busy around Harrison. In this house, especially, her own territory, he felt dangerously close. He was handsome, funny, and smart. And he knew something of what she was going through with Weezie.

He leaned on the counter a few feet away. "So," he said—and even that sounded sexy—"what's on your mind?"

She took a swift glance at him and could instantly tell what was on his. The guy was the poster boy for Insatiable Hot Male. A flush spread through her entire body. *Big*

Bad Wolf, she reminded herself. *Be afraid. Be* very *afraid.*

She cleared her throat. "Well, apart from their big intellects, Gage and Weezie have only one thing in common: They both tend to be clueless about social cues other people are giving them, right? And they don't know how to put out the right communications signals themselves. He's like a monk who's taken a vow of silence. She's a Mack truck."

"Bingo."

True ripped open a box of penne pasta and poured it into the water. "They know the meaning of the words *finesse* and *tact*. But they have a hard time implementing them."

"Exactly." Harrison watched her stir. "And the irony is that neither one appreciates their connection. Gage could be a great big brother to Weezie. And he could use a little sister to jolt him out of his tendency to stay on one track."

Gosh, it felt good to talk to someone else about this! The water came to a boil again, and True set the timer on the stove. "If I were diagnosed with Asperger's, I think I'd want to meet other people with similar issues. Share strategies for coping with it. Stuff like that."

Harrison was so *close*. So she retreated to the fridge. "Want some wine? It being Italian night and all." She didn't want him to get any romantic implications from the offer. "I've already got a bottle of white open."

"Sure." He slung himself into a chair at the kitchen table.

She pulled two stemless wineglasses from the cupboard and poured them both a glass of Sauvignon Blanc. "We can open a Shiraz with dinner."

When she handed him his, he wrapped his tanned fingers around the globe and took a sip. "Mmmm. Good."

Her toes curled at his intimate tone. "One of Daddy's

from his wine cellar." She sat across the table from him and vowed to keep her distance.

"Mr. Maybank always had good taste."

"He did, actually." True paused, sad that Harrison wouldn't be able to tell her father that for himself. And then she thought of Daddy and how happy he'd be knowing she was marrying Dubose.

"Back to Weezie and Gage not sharing coping strategies . . ." Harrison swirled the wine around his glass. "Maybe it's only the people who don't show Asperger's traits who want to 'fix' it because it doesn't fit standard norms of behavior. Gage and Weezie seem pretty darned happy."

"Except when they come up against those norms," True reminded him. "Gage, a college graduate with a fabulous job, in an ancient trailer and with all his old stuff . . . that just doesn't compute among the upwardly mobile. And Weezie genuinely wants to understand people, but she annoys or embarrasses them—or even insults them—when they don't respond the way she wants them to."

"It would be damned freeing not to care." Harrison drained his glass and stood. "To say what you wanted, when you wanted to—without worry about the consequences." He went to the back door, flicked the white eyelet curtain aside, and trapped it with his right hand. His profile was unyielding—taut, almost cold—as he gazed out the window.

"But I thought you could do anything you wanted." True sensed some tension in his back, in the way the muscles of his raised upper right arm bunched and strained against his shirt. "You're rich. You've got influence."

"Hah." He turned back around, and the delicate curtain fell behind him, accentuating how ridiculously manly he was. "Every move I make I have to consider the consequences to a whole lot of folks. Not just my business contacts and the people I work with on a daily basis on the road, but my fans. All those young guys out there who look up to me. The women who want me to represent the perfect man. The down-and-outers who want me to bolster their spirits, and the songwriter musicians who expect me to uphold country traditions yet also leave my unique mark on the genre."

"Dang," said True.

He poured himself another glass of wine. "You?" He held up the bottle.

"No, thanks." Just this one glass was loosening her up enough that she was starting to get a little hot and bothered. Which was awful of her, she knew. She was spoken for. And the man she was going to marry was exactly the type of man she needed: someone secure, predictable. Someone who knew what it was like to have the weight of a whole family lineage on your back.

She set her glass down and went to stir the pasta. "Almost done." The cheerful Girl Scout cooking a simple pasta supper, that was who she was—a woman who had values and was a proper southern lady.

Harrison was a leaner. Now he'd braced himself against the doorjamb leading to the hallway, his wineglass in his hand. "You don't have to worry about me, True."

A shock went through her body, and she stirred the pot slower. "Oh?" she said over her shoulder.

"I know you're getting married. I didn't come here to cause any problems. And I really appreciate your hospitality. To be able to have Gage feel comfortable means the world to me."

Inside, she felt a combination of so many things . . . guilt, fear, understanding, and what she dreaded most— attraction. She put the spoon down and turned to face him. "You're welcome, and I'm glad to do it. You sure did spring it on me, though, at the Starfish."

"Yeah." He pulled at his collar, and she could read embarrassment in the movement. "Sometimes I'm a little impulsive. Some might say hotheaded."

She gave a short laugh. "You? Hotheaded?"

"What about you? We both know what you're made of, Miss Moonlight Dancer." His eyes told the story. That night on the Isle of Palms. Her wildness. Her demands.

"You're pushing your luck," she said.

And he really was.

"Uh-oh." He was as scared of her as he was of a kitten. "The prickly Maybank side of you is showing."

"No, it is *not*."

He laughed.

"Stop laughing." But she was smiling, too.

"I'll go check on the others," he said. "Let 'em know dinner will be ready shortly. And True?"

"Yes?"

"I brought Gage's paddleboards over. He's got two. His old neighbor left hers behind when she moved to a land-locked city in New Mexico. Maybe we can try them later, huh?"

"In your wildest dreams. I'm too busy to have fun."

"Fun's exactly what you were made for, woman." He turned around and got himself out of sight—fast.

She couldn't help it. She was grinning broadly, and she felt happy, for some reason, happy in a way she hadn't felt in a long time.

She was mistress here at Maybank Hall, and she had guests to whom she was serving a fine if unsophisticated meal. Her business was thriving, if not very profitable, and she was getting married in a few weeks.

She'd come through it. The hard times. And she'd survived.

So had Weezie.

She closed her eyes and counted her blessings.
Harrison was one. But he was very, very bad.
Oh, Lord. What had she done letting him stay here?
She closed her eyes, took a sip of wine, and tried not to feel so damned good.

CHAPTER TWELVE

As comfortable as Honey's old feather-tick mattress was, Harrison knew he was going to sleep like hell on his first-ever overnight stay at Maybank Hall.

The problem was that when True was stirring the penne for dinner, he'd caught a glimpse of her bra strap. He hadn't been able to forget it all night long, throughout the meal (which was delicious) and afterward when they'd all taken a walk with the dogs and then come home to watch an episode of a reality show singing competition.

That bra strap had been lacy and French looking. True might buy her flatware at Target, but she didn't skimp on her lingerie. He couldn't help imagining her slipping off that dadgum bra along with the rest of her clothes before donning a nightie to get ready for bed. In fact, he paused the daydream at the naked part. Maybe she slept in the buff.

He knew the real True. And she knew he knew. It was enough to drive a man crazy to have to pretend that he didn't, especially when he was told to use her private bathroom and stumbled upon a mysterious package in the drawer she told him to put his razor. The label said NIPPLE PETALS, and they looked like flower-shaped Band-Aids.

What the hell?

But they were kinda cute. He wouldn't mind seeing them on her.

They were still on his mind when True decreed it was bedtime and went into mistress-of-the-house mode. She first settled Skeeter and Boo, who were desperate to stay with the Labs in the kitchen. Gage spent five minutes trying to convince her they really needed to be in his room on the old rag rug.

"They're fine," True told him firmly. "They're on vacation. When you're on vacation, you change things up, right?"

She had this way of instilling confidence in people while at the same time getting them to shut the hell up. It was quite a gift. Gage succumbed to her charm after a puny fight.

Everyone who wanted water by their bed got some. Then True laid out her schedule for the next day. She planned to be gone all morning, at least until she tied up some loose ends for the wedding. Weezie was in charge of the U-pick customers.

"Gage, what are your plans?" True asked nicely.

"Constructing a crossword, mainly. But I'm also running in the morning."

"Good," she said. "Can Weezie call you on your cell if she needs help?"

"Of course."

"And you, Harrison?"

She was such a little general.

"I'll be over at Sand Dollar Heaven meeting the crew."

"I really wish you hadn't done this," Gage told him.

Chill, Harrison told him with his expression.

"I was perfectly all right—"

"Gage," True said, interrupting him equally, "a successful man like you shouldn't live in a trailer that's ready to be condemned. That goes beyond stubbornness. That's outright lack of common sense. Do you want to be known as that weird dude who can't see the forest for the trees? Would that make your mother proud?"

Gage just stood there for a minute. "No," he said.

"Then stop complaining that your brother is kicking you right out of the rut you were in. Maybe show a little appreciation."

Whoa. Harrison was a little scared. And flattered. And turned on. He sensed that Gage was rattled. His brother didn't say a word, but he was clearly pondering.

"She's always like this," Weezie said helpfully—or not—to Gage, and slid down the hallway in her socks to her room.

True went over to Gage and took his hand. Harrison knew his brother was uncomfortable with that, but to his credit he didn't flinch.

"I'm only talking harshly to you because I care," she said. "If I'd known you were living the way you were, I would have come over long ago to coax you out, too." She smiled at Gage, and then the next second she was back at her bedroom door, all tension forgotten. "Good night, everyone!"

"G'night!" Weezie called from her room.

Harrison wanted to scoop True up and kiss her all over her face. And her body. But that wasn't allowed. So he said his manly good nights, and then everyone shut their doors. Skeeter barked a couple of times, and one of True's dogs answered. But other than that, the house was quiet.

Here he was, near midnight back in Biscuit Creek, among ghosts and very real people who still meant something to him, even though he hadn't been here in ten years. The wind blew low over the fields from the marsh and creek beyond. The windows rattled softly, and the house beams creaked.

There was no place like home. He still couldn't believe he was back. Sometime after two, Honey's feather-tick mattress finally lulled him to sleep.

The next morning, Gage had to get up at six forty-five and follow his damned schedule to the letter, so Harrison gave up on trying to get more shut-eye and threw off the covers. After a short perusal of Honey's hats on a shelf, accompanied by much yawning, he decided that the purple one with the polka-dotted band and the enormous flower was his favorite.

In the shower, he noticed that he was actually excited to wake up and start the day—for the first time in ages. He needed to get over to Sand Dollar Heaven. That was going to be fun. But the best thing was that he'd get to see True at breakfast.

He'd better hurry.

In the kitchen, True was stirring another pot while she read a book propped up on the counter on a funny portable shelf. She looked up, and his heart quickened its pace. She was damned beautiful, even in her straitlaced clothes. Today she wore a dress that looked like a pipe sleeve and totally disguised her figure. It went straight down and had a large blue, black, red, and white geometric pattern.

"I've seen that before," he said, "in Austin Powers or something."

She smiled. "It was one of Honey's favorites. Luckily, this style's back in now. I hope you like oatmeal."

"Love it." Hated it.

"If you're lying, you'll change your mind when you try it the way I make it." Her eyes twinkled. She saw right through him.

"You run the roost around here, don't you? And you're mighty proud of it, too."

"I do, and I am." Except when she was around Dr. Penn Waring, according to Carmela. "Why don't you get yourself some coffee? Weezie's out back, feeding the chickens. And Gage is out on his run."

Harrison gladly obeyed and poured himself a cup of the steaming black brew.

"Let's go together," he said while he watched her ladle out two bowls of oatmeal.

"Where?"

"On our errands."

"I don't think so." She opened a jar of dark chocolate peanut butter—cool; was it like a Reese's?—and scooped a spoonful into each bowl. "I have a lot to do. I'll be in Charleston. You're going to the construction site."

"I won't be long. Maybe an hour, tops. And then I'll check back late this afternoon. I can drive you around. A bride-to-be needs to be pampered." Why he was torturing himself by bringing *that* up, he didn't know.

"I thought you were here on the down-low." She picked up her own mug from the counter and took a healthy swallow. Nothing like a girl who could drink scalding coffee without flinching. Then she reached into the fridge and pulled out some fresh raspberries. She rinsed them under the sink in a little mesh colander, shook it, and then slung the berries into the oatmeal like an old pro.

"Sit," she said, "and stir it up."

Damned if he didn't sit at her command and pick up his spoon. "Real men don't like raspberries."

"Yes, they do."

"Just don't tell *GQ* I ate some." He stirred. "I'll wait in the car, and if you're very long, I'll wear my big sunglasses and Indiana Jones hat and venture forth. I've got to stop somewhere anyway."

He took a tentative bite.

She looked very concerned as he swallowed. "Are you a big sugar person?"

"No. I'm a rough, tough man who refuses to succumb

to the siren call of sweet." Unless it was her lips, of course. Or apple pie. He was a sucker for that, too.

Her face lit up. "Then you like the oatmeal?"

"Yeah. I do." And he really did.

"I was going to say we could add some brown sugar to yours if you want . . ."

"Nope. It's perfect just like this." Like this moment. He wasn't used to shooting the breeze and having a happy little breakfast with a friend he'd never been able to forget. Especially a sexy friend he'd like to kiss.

They ate for a minute in silence, but he could tell how much she was enjoying her breakfast. She made a little moany sound at one point and then caught herself.

"I love raspberries," she explained.

Lord, if she was that passionate about breakfast . . .

"I always keep an overnight bag in the car," he said, "so I'm good for today. But I'll need to pick up a couple weeks' worth of shower things and clothes."

"What about borrowing Gage's clothes?"

"Have you seen Gage lately? He wears a white button-down and Levi's *every day*. We'll look like the Hardy boys without a mystery to solve. As for the toiletries, I need my super-fancy ones. I'm a spoiled country music star, so I'm heading to Ben Silver. They'll have what I need. And I can count on their discretion."

"You *are* spoiled. You can get your clothes there, too. Be the Charleston man-about-town."

"Local boy makes good, and local boy is gonna live it up." He scraped the bottom of his bowl with his spoon. "Although I still have a thing for Goodwill. That place got me through high school."

True put her chin in her hand. "You *have* come a long way."

"So have you."

They looked at each other a beat too long.

"Yes, well—" She stood up and made a fuss over gathering the dishes.

"You need some help? You don't want to mess up that dress."

She went to the sink and dropped everything into already sudsy water. "I usually wear an apron." She turned around. "But no way was I going to wear one around *you*."

"Why?" He approached her, and she leaned back on the sink. He'd love to wrap his arms around her and kiss her. "Do you think I'd tease you? Modern woman wearing her grandmother's apron, and all that kind of thing?"

She grinned. "I like Honey's aprons. And I wear them a lot. They're functional, you know?" She turned back to the sink and started wiping down a bowl. "But I also love them because she wore them first. I have so many good memories of her cooking in them, and—well, I know you're in the big leagues now. I saw those girls with you in Atlanta. They wouldn't be caught dead in an apron. It's too homey. Too small-town."

He watched her hands in the water, mesmerized by their grace. "I wouldn't have laughed." Her back looked so delicate. "Did you ever get to Chapel Hill?" He didn't want to hurt her by asking. But he wanted to know.

"Yes." She lifted a sudsy spoon out of the water and rinsed it under the tap. "I was there three semesters. And then I had to come home."

Hell and damnation. He felt so bad for her. "I'm really sorry. I know how much it meant to you to go."

She shook her head and smiled at him over her shoulder. "It's okay. I survived. I never thought I would, but I did. I thought life would be incomplete without having the quote unquote college experience right after high school. Another Maybank truism that isn't true." Her sadness was coupled with a steely bravery. "Although I'd like to go back to school someday. I'm thinking about the College of Charleston."

"Good," he said, probably too fast. He didn't want her to think he pitied her for her lack of diploma. Hell, he didn't have one, either.

"How about you?" She pulled the plug in the sink and dried her hands off on a dish towel. "Was there a big bend in your road anytime during the last ten years? Apart from the abrupt fame? Your rise was pretty meteoric."

"Wow, that sound good. Meteoric." He grinned, but he was embarrassed. Sometimes he still couldn't believe all the crazy things that had happened to him.

"It's the truth."

He had to look away for a second because it was the first time someone he'd truly cared about before he was famous said something so . . . supportive. And it felt good. Why had he stayed away so long? What had he been so afraid of?

"It was a case of be careful what you ask for," he said. "Fame and fortune came at a steep price. I'd always heard they would. But I thought I'd be the one who didn't have to pay it."

"What kind of price?"

He didn't want to tell her. And he didn't even have to make something up because Weezie came flying through the back door with a basket of eggs.

"Phred almost got me this time." She put the eggs on the table and took a couple of deep breaths.

"He's our rooster," True said. "*P-h-r-e-d*. And he's as crazy as his name. He likes to chase us with his spurs out and send us on our way, preferably screaming."

The dogs started barking, which meant that Gage was back from his run.

Sure enough, he showed up in the kitchen, a sheen of sweat on his face. "True, I didn't see the paper outside."

She winced. "I had to cancel our subscription a long time ago. We get our news on the Internet. Did you have a good run?"

"Yes."

But Harrison could tell Gage was a little uncomfortable with the lack of paper. "Don't you read *The Wall Street Journal* online anyway?"

"Yes, but I always read *The Post and Courier* first."

"You get by without it when you come to see me, or when we meet in Cocoa Beach."

"I read it online when I do that."

"Well, read it online today," Harrison said, getting mighty annoyed.

"When I know it's available as a paper, I'd rather read it that way." Gage's face, still red from his run, was lined with tension.

"Geez, buddy—" Harrison couldn't believe his ears.

"We'll bring you one back when we go on our errands," True said. "Problem solved."

"But I don't read the paper in the afternoon." Gage made an attempt at a smile. "Don't worry about it, True."

"Damned right, we're not going to worry about it," Harrison snapped. "Ever heard of something called flexibility? You need it."

"He's trying!" Weezie cried out. "Don't be so mean to him, Harrison. I read once that you got pepperoni pizza in the green room instead of sausage, and so you threw the pizza out the window like a Frisbee."

"That's not true," Harrison said. "The tabloids make that stuff up to sell papers."

But he could see the wheels in Weezie's head still spinning. "Oprah asked you if you ever wrote songs on the road," she said in a smart-alecky manner, "and you said no, absolutely not, that you had to be alone in your hotel room. Not on a bus with all your roadies."

"Well, that *is* true."

There was a beat of taut silence.

"See?" Weezie's tone was righteous. "You're not flexible, either."

"Yeah." He paused, hating to admit he was a big, fat hypocrite. "I see, all right."

Weezie glowered in his general direction, but he could tell she was also secretly pleased she'd wrangled a confession out of him. Maybe she *would* make a good talk show host.

True opened the cupboard. "You want some coffee, Gage?"

"Sure. Thanks." Gage stood awkwardly in the middle of the kitchen, the worst houseguest ever.

Or maybe Harrison was the worst houseguest ever. He ran a hand through his hair and let it drop. "All right. Ready to go?" He looked at True.

"As soon as I get Gage settled," she said, all prim with him now. She clearly disapproved of his behavior.

Well, shit. A guy couldn't win around here.

Weezie came up and hugged him tight around the waist. "I still like you," she said into his armpit.

"Do you now," he said, striving to hold on to his bad mood.

She looked up at him. "Yes. You always talked to me when you were watering Mama's flowers." She turned to Gage. "Harrison loves you, even though you're a pain in the ass sometimes. We all are. Even True."

Dang, this was getting awkward. And funny. But Harrison didn't dare laugh.

Gage stood there like a wooden post. Harrison had to admit he felt like one, too. That was rare for him. True's mouth was half open. She definitely wanted to say something. Or laugh. But maybe she felt mentally Tasered by Weezie's unfettered truth telling, too.

"Shall we go?" she asked him in a voice pitched a tad higher than usual.

Harrison pulled his keys out of his pocket. "I'm ready if you are."

Yes, her eyes told him. She grabbed her purse off a hook on the wall.

Weezie blithely ladled herself out some oatmeal. "I'm starved," she said as if she were Oliver Twist. "Gage, you want some?"

"Uh, sure," he said, "although I usually have eggs—"

"I can make those," Weezie offered.

"No." He moved toward the stove carefully, as if he were approaching a sleeping lion. "Oatmeal's all right."

True sent Harrison a sideways glance, and this time it was openly amused. And hopeful.

"Shall we, Miss Maybank?" He grinned and held out his arm.

She took it with alacrity, and he tried not to be too flattered. It was high time to get out of the kitchen.

Off they went: a guy and a girl in a Maserati on a sunny day. Life didn't get no better'n that.

CHAPTER THIRTEEN

Back in high school, when True was at the height of her own popularity, Harrison had been on the fringe, not quite a loner, but not someone who sought out friends, either. He wore his hair much longer than the average southern boy, down past his shoulders in a golden-brown wave, and he favored jeans and graphic T-shirts from Goodwill.

At lunch, he was always on the far edge of the courtyard strumming a guitar.

People came to him, and he'd stop playing and talk. Occasionally, True heard him laugh, and whoever was with him would laugh, too. But he was generally above the fray, not interested in who was dating whom or whether the football team was winning—which irritated the boys in True's crowd.

"He's a redneck," Dubose always used to say whenever he saw Harrison not giving a damn. Dubose was the ultimate prepster, high school quarterback, and True's boyfriend. "His daddy died in a riot a month after he got to jail. The apple won't fall far from the tree, I can promise you that."

"Stop it," True would say. "That's so mean." And she'd

fight with Dubose and not talk to him for the rest of the day.

But after school, he'd always come back and say he was sorry. She'd forgive him because he'd admit he was jealous. He knew Harrison and True had been friends as kids, and he didn't like that. She always convinced herself that Dubose's confession was romantic.

Even so, she wished she could talk to Harrison again, the way they used to when they were friends together at Sand Dollar Heaven.

Hey, she wanted to say softly whenever he walked by. *Don't you remember all those days I'd sneak over to play at the trailer park? How about the lazy afternoons on the dock—and our secret marriage ceremony in the honeysuckle bower? You were the Sewee warrior. I was your princess.*

But she never did.

He didn't even look at her anymore.

But there was that one lunchtime he wasn't at his usual hangout spot. He was cutting class, someone said, for the rest of the day. He'd been doing that a lot lately, and no one knew why.

True was worried. And so she forged her mother's name on a fake note about a doctor's appointment and left school. They all knew her so well in the office, no one questioned her.

She found him on the dock at Sand Dollar Heaven and sat down next to him.

"What are you doing here?" He wouldn't even look at her.

She said a little prayer and focused on an old life ring hanging on a piling at the end of the dock. "I'm so sorry about your dad. I tried to tell you, but you never let me."

"That was three years ago. I'm over it."

"He was a bootlegger," she said. "He didn't deserve to *die*."

"I know that. He wasn't rich like your dad. He did what he had to do to help the family. Crewing on the *Miss Mary* wasn't enough."

Miss Mary was a shrimping trawler, and those people worked long, hard hours. Sometimes they didn't come back for a week. And still they were poor.

True swallowed, her face flaming with shame at how easy her life was compared with his. "It might seem like a cop-out to you after all the fun we used to have . . . my being a well-dressed, prissy girl who doesn't speak out or do anything different or get all A's when I know I can. But if I don't want to be ostracized by my friends, punished by my parents, and made to feel guilty by the townsfolk who expect Maybanks to be a certain way, I have to act the way I act. And it gets even more twisted. That's in public. At home in private, I have to carry a lot of the weight around the house. Mama gets easily overwhelmed by Weezie. Daddy retreats. Honey's old. I'm not really different. Not deep inside. I'm still the bossy, smart girl you knew. The brave one you climbed trees with."

"That's such bullshit." He lay back on the dock, slung his arm over his eyes, and sighed.

And when he did that, her heart felt as if it literally broke into a million pieces. Where was he, the boy who used to care for her?

Pinpricks of tears sprung up. "What's wrong?" she asked. "Are you on drugs or something?"

"No," he snapped.

"Why are you cutting school?"

"None of your goddamned business."

He hated her. She didn't blame him. Really, she didn't. He thought she was a weakling. And acted stupid. She was fifteen. Most of the time she felt grown up, but part of her was still scared about how to handle the world. Part of her wanted to run to her bed and get under the covers and let Mama take over. In her daydreams, Mama would bring her chicken soup and a candy bar and a good magazine . . . in real life, that had never happened. But True liked to imagine it that way.

"I feel sorry for Weezie," she said, even though Harrison was ignoring her. "But I feel guilty, too, because I'm glad I'm not her, always getting into trouble. How many kids get sent home from kindergarten for three days for acting out? I have to be the good girl—to help Mama and Daddy. I'm doing the best I know how."

Harrison lifted his arm and stared at her. "So you came looking for me to talk about yourself? Get some sympathy?"

Her pulse raced. "No, that's not it at all. I-I only told you all that so you'd understand, so you wouldn't think I didn't like you. Because I do. And . . . I'm worried. I hope you're all right."

He got up and walked to the end of the dock, stared out over the water. "Are you finished?"

"No."

He gave a short laugh. "You're a piece of work."

She heard the scorn. But she'd tell him anyway. "Hanging out with you for three years changed me. Opened up my eyes. I know we were young, but it did."

Those were halcyon years, between nine and twelve. They played on the dock and in the woods, or rowed around in a borrowed johnboat. She'd collect leaves and moss and flakes of oyster shells with Harrison and hide them in a cigar box in their honeysuckle bower. Her own special treasure in their own special place. He'd bring her things, too: Pieces of a broken bowl from his mama's kitchen. A swatch of purple silk he'd found outside the

Lutheran church, just lying on a bench. Coke-bottle caps. She'd throw these into her box, too, and all jumbled up, they spelled her hopes and her dreams and her happiness.

"After I stopped coming over," she told him, "I still collected things. And now I put them together. I make collages in my bedroom using cardboard as the backing—or sometimes scrap wood from the storage shed—and a hot-glue gun."

She hid the resulting artwork in her closet. It wasn't pretty and neat. Or predictable. It was odd, almost ugly in a way, reflecting the way she felt inside sometimes: guilty, disloyal, angry.

"Am I supposed to be impressed?" Harrison turned to face her.

She wished she could confide in him that she'd been born into a world that had defined her before she could ever define herself. She was only trying to survive, to figure it out, to understand why she only received love when she behaved the way other people wanted her to.

She couldn't win.

She'd had to choose.

Yet she'd *had* no choice.

She was trapped.

She was a Maybank.

"No, I guess not," she said. "My artwork isn't very good. But I like doing it. It reminds me of us."

"Go away, True." His voice was cold. But beneath his stoic gaze, she recognized hurt.

"We were only kids," she pleaded with him. "Why are you taking this so hard? Friends come and go, especially when you're young."

"Everyone comes and goes," Harrison said. "I know that. I don't need you apologizing about that fact. Now get back to school before you get in trouble."

"I'm sorry." She started to cry. "Do you need money?

Because Daddy's looking for a new boy to mow and trim the hedges. If you call him 'sir' a lot, and tell him you admire how well he did in last year's Rockville Regatta, he'll hire you. I know it. You can find him on Saturday afternoons at the hardware store."

Harrison walked past her, and she reached out her hand to touch his arm. But he yanked it away before she could. And then he walked off the dock, never once turning around.

She found out the next day at school that Mrs. Gamble had been recently diagnosed with breast cancer. She died four months later.

CHAPTER FOURTEEN

Sand Dollar Heaven. Good Lord, did this take True back! She really had thought it was heaven when she was young. She'd never cared about the run-down state of some of the lots. She came for adventure, for freedom. She wasn't a Maybank here. She was a Native American princess from the Sewee tribe. And sometimes she was a mermaid.

Today she was only a boring grown-up. One with responsibilities and worries. She stood among trees that had become bigger, taller—like herself—and mobile homes that had acquired the patina of age. She had, too. Her dewy eyed days were long over.

Yet the waterway hadn't changed at all. Neither had the dock.

"It's the same one," she told Harrison when she got out of the car. He was there, holding the door, which made her feel a little self-conscious. It was such a chivalrous thing to do. Dubose hadn't done it in a long time.

He stared at the dock through his designer sunglasses. "It needs an update, that's for sure."

But he didn't offer to walk out on it with her.

So many mixed feelings surged. She'd been happy on that dock, and, at one time, despairing. She'd also been in love. Sure, it had been puppy love. But that didn't mean it wasn't special.

"Maybe some other time." She felt super awkward for some reason and adjusted her purse on her shoulder. "I really have to get to Charleston as soon as you're done here." She most definitely didn't need to be reliving any old emotions she'd felt over him.

While they walked the hundred yards to the construction site, she checked her phone for a text from Dubose. None yet. He wasn't always very accessible when he was in New York. She tended to let him call her. She didn't want to interrupt a meeting.

"These loose ends you have to tie up giving you fits?" Harrison said.

She put away her phone. "Yes, as a matter of fact."

"What do you have going on?"

She was embarrassed to tell him. But there was no way to pussyfoot around it. "I need to find a new caterer. And a new reception site."

He stopped in his tracks and turned to stare at her. "Less than two weeks before the wedding?"

She nodded. "I know." The emotion of it hit her hard again. "We have two hundred fifty people coming. How will I ever figure this out?" Her knees began to feel shaky.

"Come on." He took her by the elbow. "Sit over here. We can take ten minutes to talk, and we'll both still get done what we need to get done."

There was a swing beneath a massive old oak tree nearby. It hadn't been there when they were kids. She looked up into the oak's branches and wondered who had climbed up there to attach the swing's ropes.

"You aren't tying up loose ends," he said. "It sounds like you're trying to save your wedding from being a total disaster. How did it happen?"

She told him the story. "And Penn's overseas. So I'm handling it myself."

"Do you want her to be your mother-in-law?"

"She's kind of scary," True said.

"But you obviously want Dubose."

"Right," she said, and felt embarrassed for some reason.

Harrison gave her a little push from behind, and her feet left the ground. The swing had a long, low arc, and for a second all her cares dissolved.

"Why do you want him?" he asked. "And you can't tell me because your parents wanted the match. This isn't the olden days. Modern women just say no to arranged marriages."

Swinging through space was giving her some sort of courage. "I was alone," she said, remembering the misery she felt for so long, "and he showed up and gave me hope again."

Harrison gave her another push. This one was big, and she went soaring. "What else?" he called up to her. "I'm not letting you down until you tell me everything."

"I'll just jump."

"You wouldn't."

"Sure I would." She laughed and pulled some hair out of her mouth. "But I'm not ready to stop swinging. I'll think about talking if you keep going."

"How did you get control of the situation so fast? You'd make a great publicist. Or dictator of a small country." He pushed her so high, the swing went over his head, and he had to run out from under it in front of her.

Wow. The feeling of flying so high was awesome. And he was strong. She tried not to notice how tight his T-shirt was over his upper arms. He stood there watching her, his sunglasses hiding his eyes.

She couldn't tell what he was thinking, and it made her

nervous. So she decided to talk. "After Mama and Daddy died, I finally figured out that all those old, stuffy rules they taught me about the importance of tradition and being a Maybank and never quitting were to get me through life's hard times. Dubose was brought up the same way. We understand each other."

"The way Charles and Diana understood each other."

"That's mean."

"But it's the same idea. Same stratosphere of society. Same rules."

"You do the same thing in Nashville. How come you never date a woman not in the business? It's always another celebrity."

"Hey, you're the one trapped on the swing, not me. I don't have to answer any hard questions."

Her feet came within a foot of him, and he made a pretend grab. She pulled her shoes in and laughed, realizing that she'd really needed a silly, carefree moment like this for a long time. She swung up close to him again.

What you really need is some good loving.

Damn. She wished she could leave the sexy thought hanging in the ether while she swooped backward, but it came with her, stuck on hard to her brain with invisible sex superglue.

She knew very well it wasn't Dubose but Harrison who'd inspired that notion. He looked like he was posing for an album cover wherever he was—leaning on her kitchen counter, driving his car, or standing there with his thumbs hooked into his jeans pockets and staring at her as if—

As if he wanted to give her some good loving, too.

Good Lord, she needed to jump.

"Get out of the way," she called in a take-no-prisoners voice.

"No." He grinned. "We can't have the dictator—I mean, the bride—breaking her ankle before the big day."

She kind of liked when he called her a dictator. But a secret part of her hated when he called her a bride. Was he making fun of her? Was he glad she was going to be off the market soon?

She was swinging low enough now that she could scrape her feet on the grass and stop herself.

"Aww." He sounded truly disappointed.

She was, too. "I wonder who put this swing up?"

"I did."

She was shocked. "But you haven't been back—"

"I did it before Mom died. She used it a few months. Swinging always made her happier than anything else."

True's heart nearly broke at that. "I'm so sorry."

They'd never talked about it. When she died, True told him she was sorry on the blacktop at lunch. He'd shrugged and said, "Thanks." There'd been no funeral, or she would have gone to it. When he'd come over to mow the grass a week later, she'd tried to give him a basket of cookies, but he wouldn't turn off the mower—he indicated she could leave them on the porch, which she did.

And then they'd never talked again, not until prom night—

Best not to think of that night right now.

He looked at his watch. "Yeah, well, shit happens. You know about that."

"I sure do." She looked down at her feet as the swing ropes dangled.

"Ready to go meet the construction team?" he asked.

"Sure."

He pulled her out of the swing, and she landed against his chest. A heavy tension hung between them.

Must control, her head told her. *Must control*. She pushed away from him. "Ten minutes be enough time?"

"That should do it."

They strode—not walked—toward the construction site, not saying a word to each other. Someone had moved Gage's trailer from its original site to the new one.

"It's Vince's office for now," Harrison said, "and when he's done, it's going to the Great Mobile Home Park in the Sky. By the way, Vince—the guy drawing up the house plans—is a dude in a dress. He's tried working in guy's clothes, but he's not nearly as inspired."

"Whatever it takes," True said.

Harrison threw her a sideways glance. "Spoken like an artist. You still doing your collages?"

She shook her head. "That was . . . a phase."

"Oh." He didn't sound disappointed or curious to hear why, maybe because Vince came out of the trailer.

True guessed he was somewhere in his mid-forties, and he looked like a runner: whip-thin and tanned. His hair was a bit wild—sandy brown and unkempt, as if he'd just finished jogging across a bridge. He wore a gray paisley-print short-sleeved shift dress that looked like something from the Athleta catalog, the belt smartly wrapped around his trim waist, and black gladiator-meets-huarache leather sandals. If the guy was going to wear a dress, at least this one seemed to complement his athletic build and the way he moved, with lithe confidence.

He came toward her, a look of utter fascination on his face. "Oh my God, is that an Yves Saint Laurent? The Mondrian-inspired dress from the 'sixties that made the cover of *Vogue*?"

True smiled. "Yes. It belonged to my great-aunt."

He came over for a better look, then noticed Harrison. "Everything's under control, Mr. Country. I just need to show you a few sample house photos before I start getting really serious about the blueprints."

"Good," Harrison said. "Trip uneventful?"

"It's never uneventful," he replied. "TSAs love me." Like a laser, his gaze returned to True. "Now back to *you*. Do you have any idea how much that dress is worth?"

"No idea. But I love it. And I didn't want it to waste away in a closet."

"You are one lucky girl." Vince cocked his head to one side. "Pretty, too."

"Thank you." She liked him. He had energy, and he was himself.

The way Weezie is herself.

It wasn't lost upon True that she spent a lot of her waking hours trying to make Weezie like everyone else so she wouldn't get hurt. So she'd be able to find a job someday and live independently. And let's face it—so she'd toe the Maybank line. But it was that very same line that had kept True afloat the past ten years. So she didn't feel guilty.

Even so, Vince intrigued her.

Harrison made the introductions. When they were inside the trailer—which looked like Andy Griffith's backwoods cousin's man cave—True hung back and watched the two guys get into discussing the house plans. They were debating whether the media room should go on the first or second floor when she finally got a text from Duhose.

These NYC DAs run a mile a minute, Dubose wrote. *Early mornings and late nights every day. Now I know why they call it the city that never sleeps. I'm loving the work, but it doesn't leave any time for myself. And that makes me feel bad for you, sweetcakes.*

Ugh. Sweetcakes. The old-timey term of affection made

her feel like Betty Boop with no brain. But she wouldn't nag him about it. Not now.

Don't worry about me! Her thumbs flew across her iPhone's surface. *You just do what you have to do. I miss you, but I'm staying busy, too. I'm going to get everything done before you get home.*

She wouldn't dare tell him that she needed to find a new caterer and reception site.

Great, he said. *I hear Mom is going to England. You sure you can handle any last-minute wedding details alone?*

Of course. Her heart was pounding.

I'm so proud of you, he wrote back immediately. *Okay, back to work.*

Love you she texted.

XOXO, Dubose texted back.

Harrison looked up at her from the blueprints Vince was beginning to assemble on the kitchen table and smiled at her like Harrison-the-kid used to. True felt suddenly ill.

His eyes clouded. "What is it?"

"Nothing." She stuffed her phone into her purse. "I need to make a phone call." She got outside and inhaled a deep breath of pine-scented air.

Harrison came right after her. "I knew you didn't have to make a call. You went pale as a ghost in there. Is it happening again? The airport thing?"

"No." She swallowed. "I just accidentally forgot to breathe. I was thinking about not having a caterer."

Not really. She didn't know what she'd been thinking about. One second, she'd been texting Dubose that she loved him, and then she felt as if she were a being sucked into a giant whirlpool.

"I can get you a caterer," Harrison said. "We can fly someone in if we have to."

True shook her head. "Thanks a lot, but I have to do this myself. My mother-in-law is testing me, I think. I have to prove to her that I'm capable."

"You already know you are."

"I know. But I have to prove to *her*."

"Why?"

"Because if she thinks I'm not, she'll tell Dubose, and—"

"And what? If he believes her over you, then he's a fool. Was that him you were texting?"

"Yes. Why?"

"Nothing." His lips thinned and his eyes narrowed slightly.

"It's not nothing." Nothing felt like nothing around Harrison. Life was big and Technicolor, and she was never bored, and he needed to leave town. He needed to leave soon. Before the wedding. And she was stupid to come with him today, but he was a giant magnet and she was a paper clip wearing a very old dress. "I can tell you're dying to say something."

"Fine." He was casual. "Just that I'd never text the woman I love. It's a phone call or nothing."

True's face went hot all over. "What's that supposed to mean? What if you're in a meeting and you can't talk on the phone, but you need to tell your wife that you're going to be late? You wouldn't text her?"

"I'd get up and say, *Meeting over. I can't be late to see my wife.*"

"What if the meeting was really important and you couldn't leave?"

"I'd say, *Shut up, everyone. I need to call my wife and tell her I'll be late.*"

"You don't live in the real world," said True. "You're in your Famous Man world, where women and doughnuts appear like magic, and your bathroom contains little gold statues. Besides, there's nothing wrong with texting."

"Oh, yeah, there is. It's not romantic. It says, *We're buddies, not lovers.*"

"You're the only person in the entire world I've ever heard say that."

He shrugged. "I'm ahead of my time."

"Or maybe twenty years behind it. What do you know about romance anyway? Have you ever had to woo a woman, Harrison? Or do they all fall into your lap, one Taylor Swift look-alike after the other?"

His eyes looked dangerously black. "My love life really isn't your business anymore. You gave up rights to me a long time ago."

"I never had them." Her heart knocked against her ribs.

"You damned well did—" He paused, raked her up and down with a searing gaze. "—and you know it."

Her entire body vibrated with heat and misery. And there was lust and longing in the mix, too, especially when he turned his back on her and walked back toward the trailer, his jeans sagging just the right amount, his shoulders flexing in that ridiculous white T-shirt that lent him a combination of James Dean and Danny Zuko charm.

But she'd never let him know.

"Harrison?" It was Vince, poking his head out the door. "I think I've got a preliminary sketch of both floors. Sorry, True. We need five more minutes."

She forced herself to smile brightly. "No problem, Vince. I'll go look at the dock."

Harrison turned, and she caught a glimpse of something raw and hurt in the way he stood, his hands loose and open, and in his gaze, which projected no judgment of her at all. Only vulnerability. Suddenly he was that boy she knew, the one whose daddy died in prison, whose overworked mother succumbed to cancer, and whose big brother had issues that weighed heavily on his heart and still did, obviously.

But the impression was gone the next second.

The clamoring need to get to Charleston to talk to some caterers could be held at bay awhile longer. It was important, yes, but so was Gage's house. So was the price of gas and world peace, for that matter. Who was she to get so worked up about something she knew she could fix if she'd only keep anxiety at arm's length?

"Hey, why don't you come, too?" Vince called after her. "I'd love your opinion."

"Sure," she said. "Thanks." She'd see the dock another time.

At the trailer, Harrison held the door open for her and walked in behind her. Guilt made her tense. She'd been really rude with that Taylor Swift comment. But it was only because he'd hurt her, too, by implying that Dubose wasn't romantic because he'd texted her.

He's not *romantic*, a small inner voice said. Dubose did all the right things—sending her roses on Valentine's Day and taking her out to fancy dinners—but real romance was unpredictable. Not forced. Sometimes it didn't make sense to anyone else but the two people involved.

And it seemed like a lot of it had its foundations in a childhood filled with random moments of beauty and rapture: Weeds picked by the side of the road for a loving mother. A cake with really gooey frosting baked for a best friend's birthday. A song plucked out on a fiddle for a family gathered around a table.

Unsolicited advice from a rascally boy telling you how to catch a blue crab on a rickety dock.

Surprises. Symbols of love. Spontaneous and heartfelt. A wistful smile tugged at True's lips as she thought about Harrison's outrageous texting comment. Whoever he wound up with eventually—if that day ever came— would be a lucky woman. She'd never tell him so. It would go straight to his head. But she believed it with all her heart.

CHAPTER FIFTEEN

House building under way for Gage—check.

Beautiful ex-lover in need of friendly support in car—check.

Song written for new album—

The big fat buzzer of loserdom went off in Harrison's head. He had to get a move on when it came to the song-writing, but it was hard when True was sitting next to him. He took a quick glance at her serene face looking straight ahead on Highway 17. Damn, she was hot, but she also had a good head on her shoulders. She'd suggested to him and Vince that Gage's house have an outdoor kitchen facing the water to attract chicks. He could cook for them on cool autumn days or early-spring ones. Hell, he could cook for them in the dead of winter, too.

"Anything to get him socializing," she'd said. "He could use a hot tub, of course. And the media center should have theater-style seating and a popcorn machine."

Harrison was truly grateful for her input.

Vince was, too, because he'd raised her hand to his mouth and kissed it. "You're a special girl," he'd said, and threw a distinct what-the-hell-are-you-waiting-for look at Harrison.

"Thank you." True had smiled shyly. "I like you, too, Vince."

Harrison put his arm around her. "She's going to make a beautiful bride in just a couple of weeks when she marries a guy we both knew in high school."

"Oh," said Vince, his face falling.

Harrison's mood fell, too, at the very thought of Dubose wedding True, but it was none of his beeswax. Guitars, jets, hot dates with no strings attached, concert stages, and multimillion-dollar-making careers were his thing.

And so the visit to the construction site had ended on kind of an awkward note. But Harrison was pleased about the house plans. Vince had everything well under control, and the Sexy *Leave It to Beaver* House, as Vince called it, was going to be a spectacular place for Gage to live.

"Hey, are you sure you don't want me to go in with you to say hello to any of the caterers?" Harrison asked True in the Maserati. They were coming up on Charleston. "Dubose's mother doesn't have to know you used me to get somewhere with them."

True shifted in her seat. "I'm sure. They'll tell her everything because she's paying. And then she'll think I'm useless, and she'll tell Dubose you helped get his wedding back on track. He'll hate that. Plus, he really wouldn't approve of our hanging out together on general principle."

"The whole town knows I'm at your house. He's bound to find out."

She sighed. "I know. I need to just tell him what's going on." She took out her purse. "I'm texting him right now."

"Uh-oh."

So she did. She wrote him a big, long note with her spindly girl fingers. Harrison was dying to ask her what was in it. Within thirty seconds, she got a text back.

"What does it say?" Harrison was on pins and needles.

She smiled. "It says, *Gamble's obviously put you in a no-win situation in front of the whole town. It's up to Maybanks and Warings to make the sacrifices that make a difference, though, so if this will improve the condition of our library, then I'm okay with it. As long as that bastard keeps his hands off you. You tell him I said so, and that his ass is grass if he so much as looks at you sideways.*"

"He's always liked me," Harrison said.

True laughed. "I'm glad I did that."

They drove along in what he thought was damned happy silence for a few minutes.

"We still can't risk you being seen by anyone," she said. "That text to Dubose reminded me that you do need to write yourself at least one amazing song ASAP, and you need peace and quiet. Going with me on wedding errands is busywork. It isn't going to help your cause, especially if some paparazzi land on your trail."

"I'm an evil genius when it comes to evading the paparazzi."

"I don't care. I'm not going to be the reason they descend upon you. Besides, I can do this alone."

"I know you can," he said. "But are you sure you don't want me to call an out-of-town caterer? Or celebrity chef? They can handle southern cuisine, if that's your sticking point. And then this mess will be behind you and you can do all that fun bride stuff like painting your toenails or whatever it is brides do."

"No, thanks." She flipped her hair out for no reason at all, which he loved. "This sounds snobby, but getting a caterer or celebrity chef from 'off' would be considered tacky. And I'm still without a location. I need a big room overlooking the water. Something grand that'll suit a string quartet, and then it needs a stage for the band."

"What'll they play?"

"Mainly old standards. Dubose's law partners will be there. So will Penn's friends. They never do anything with the Waring stamp on it that's not entirely tasteful."

"Thank God for the classy among us," Harrison said drily, "saving us from our own worst selves."

"What about you and your songwriting? How will you go about that?"

"Well, I can't just sit down and say to the gods of country music, *Hit me*. I don't know how it works. It seems that the more I try to come up with something, the worse my output is. Maybe my subconscious mind is working on a song right now."

About a hot girl named True in a funky little dress.

"Is there anything I can do to help?" True asked.

"I don't think so," he lied.

God, yes. He hadn't had sex like he'd had with her since he saw her last. He'd written his first hit song over the next two days. Was there a connection?

Yes.

No.

Hell if he knew. Even if there wasn't, his body insisted on pretending there was. Any excuse to get that girl back in his bed. And sure, he'd steal her away from Dubose and not feel a smidgeon of guilt if that were the right thing to do. But he knew it wasn't. She deserved top billing in someone's life, but apart from his lifelong devotion to Gage, that slot would always go to his career. Besides, True wasn't cut out to be a groupie, tagging along with him all over the world. She belonged in Biscuit Creek.

Keeping her at arm's length was the order of the day. But so was being a friend to her. He could manage both if he took a cold shower every night and imagined his mother and all the angels floating right above him, watching his every move.

No, *X* out the part about his mother and the angels. He'd stick with the cold shower. And maybe punishing himself with the Shopping Network channel if his thoughts strayed to the sexy.

"You can't do a thing to help." Harrison put a further lid on his raging libido by reminding himself that he'd been able to write twenty-four additional Top Ten country hits without having access to True's sexual favors. "Being around a songwriter is like watching a squirrel reaching for an acorn on the other side of a window. Painful. Pitiful. And in the end, you're mad at the squirrel for wasting your time, and you start to think he's pretty dumb."

Thank God they were getting close to town. Harrison needed out of the car. True smelled like flowers again, and her lips were all plump and ready for kissing. It was too much for a man to tolerate in a small, enclosed space without wanting to reach his hand across and grab her thigh and give it a good rub up and down.

He'd turn on the radio, but it would only remind him that he still had music to write. So instead, he asked True all about the politics of the city now. Who was mayor of Charleston? Was it still Joe Riley? Who ran the school board? How were they handling the tourism trade? What was happening with the port?

She knew everything about everything and loved to talk about it, which made him wonder if she was as relieved as he was not to think about sex. Or maybe it was the opposite—sex wasn't on her mind at all. And this talking of hers was just what she wanted to do anyway.

Thank God the Ravenel Bridge loomed ahead, and the city was on the other side. Last time he'd been here was when he'd worked a couple of nights a week as a busboy at Carolina's the second semester of his senior year in high school.

"I'd never think of you as a squirrel," she said out of the blue.

"Um . . . thanks?"

She sent him a sideways look of semi-amusement.

"What animal do I remind you of?" He was dying to know. "And don't you dare say a jackass. That's too easy."

"All right." She feigned disappointment. "If I had to choose something else, you'd be a . . . lion."

"Really? Or are you just saying that to make me feel good?"

"Why would I do that?"

"Oh. Right. Why would you? Our history pretty much sucks, except for those halcyon days when we were tweens, and then—"

"Don't say it," she said, but she wasn't angry. She simply didn't want to talk about that spectacular night they'd gotten together.

"Why am I like a lion, then?" he asked. "I've got a massive ego. I need to know so I can get my secretary to write it in my gold-plated journal."

"Because you watch after Gage. And you have great hair. You've also got a temper."

"Is that all?"

She made a face. "Okay, you're sexy and you know it. Lions know they're hot. Feel better now?" She scrunched down in her seat. "As if you don't already have the whole world lying at your feet," she muttered.

"And *you*," he said grandly, "remind me of Lady in *Lady and the Tramp*, tough and smart but always elegant. Perhaps a little demanding, too?" He was driving down King Street, where Charlestonians did most of their shopping. "Lady's my favorite girl Disney character. She beats out all the princesses."

"So I'm a dog," True said. "I notice you didn't use the word."

"I'm not an idiot, that's why. Although who doesn't love dogs? I miss having them."

"You can't?"

"Not really. They'd be ignored most of the time. I don't want to do that to an animal—or a person." He pulled over into a parking space. "My life has enough space for one—me."

There. The lines were clearly drawn between them, which meant he could have more fun now. Not that he wasn't already.

"You were born lucky," True said. "I can never get parking down here by Bits of Lace. And look! They're having their annual sale!" She obviously didn't give a crap that his life had space only for one. "I still need a few things for my honeymoon."

Did she now.

"I'm going to run in there first," she said in that breathless way women did when they saw a good sale, "and then can we check back via text in an hour? All three caterers are either on King or Wentworth."

"Sounds like a plan."

"Oh, and Ben Silver is up the street near the city market."

"Good."

"While you're there, would you mind looking at what they might have for groomsmen gifts? Dubose didn't have time to work on that."

"Not a problem." He scratched the back of his neck. Damn Dubose.

She smiled. "Thank you, Harrison. Really."

They were both searching for quarters to put in the meter when his phone chirped. He didn't recognize the number, but it was a New York area code. Curiosity made him pick up, just in case it was someone from the studio.

"Hey, you." Bad timing. It was Valerie Wren, the hottest single female country singer in Nashville. Her voice was like sweet bourbon going down slow.

True held up two quarters. "Not enough," she mouthed.

"Hey, Valerie," he said, and pointed at the glove compartment.

True got the message.

"How are ya?" Valerie purred.

"Great, great." She was a sex kitten. No doubt about it.

True opened the glove compartment, and a pair of pink, polka-dotted panties fell out.

Damn. Those were actually brand new, never worn, and Dan had given them to him to give to Valerie. Dan liked to live vicariously, the sicko, all while pretending to help Harrison out with his lady friends, the way a thoughtful concierge would. Harrison had literally stuck them on Dan's head, and this was Dan's puny revenge—hiding them in his car.

True sent him the laser look of death and kept looking for quarters.

Harrison shrugged and tried to look like a choirboy.

"I was thinking about coming to visit you since you can't come up here," Valerie said. "These Yankees know how to throw some parties."

"You're sweet," he said, "but I'm kinda busy, Val."

"Too busy for me?" Valerie practically meowed.

True slammed the glove compartment shut and started rummaging through the little recess beneath the radio and then beneath her seat. Finally, she took out her purse and pulled everything out. No quarters.

"I'm too busy for everyone," Harrison said into his cell. "I have some songs to write. But let's catch up soon, huh? Maybe we'll do a duet at the CMAs. They should be calling soon, don't you think, with this year's lineup?"

"I have no idea." Valerie was pouting through the phone. "I'm busy, too, you know."

Harrison pulled out his wallet and handed it to True. Then he pointed at a store. "Change," he mouthed.

She glared at him, opened the wallet, pulled out a twenty—and a condom fell out between them.

God, no.

True stared at it then, without looking at him, tried to get out of the car.

"Hey, Val, I hate to go but I really need to." True was practically yanking off the door handle. "You're sweet to call."

"Whatever." Valerie hung up.

Harrison reached across True—the prettiest fire-breathing dragon he ever saw—and opened the door. She got out without a word and strode into the store.

The car felt lonely without her. With a sigh he reached into the back and pulled out his Indiana Jones hat. He already had his uncool sunglasses on, the ones he'd gotten at Bob's Fireworks Palace on I-95. A bike rickshaw almost hit him when he got out of the car. He could see it now: *Famous Country Singer Killed While Wearing Dorky Disguise*. He pulled his hat brim down, leaned against the meter, and waited. He was in deep kimchee, and he knew it. Of course, he shouldn't be—he and True didn't have anything going on—but he was anyway.

And he liked it.

When True returned, she handed him a sheaf of bills.

Plunk, went the meter when she dropped in the first quarter. *Plunk, plunk, plunk, plunk, plunk.*

She didn't look at him the entire time. It was too cute for words.

"Hey," he said, "sorry about the panties and the condom."

"That's your business," she said. "I'll text you in an hour."

And walked away, nearly bumping into a sweet old man in a seersucker suit in her haste to be gone.

Harrison couldn't help smiling after her. Damn that girl for making him happy.

CHAPTER SIXTEEN

True was so bummed. Not about Harrison and his lady
friend. That was *his* business. If he wanted to go off all
cockeyed and date someone as ditzy as Valerie Wren, he
could go right ahead and look the fool! True had his number. Sex and PR—good, bad, or indifferent—were probably his top two priorities. Was she ever glad she was
through with *him*.

No. She was mad about the caterers. Not one of them
gave her the time of day. Less than two weeks? She had
to be kidding! They had no interest in speaking to her beyond saying no.

When she met Harrison back at the car, he was carrying
six shopping bags from Ben Silver.

"What did you get?" she asked, in a terrible mood.

He threw them in the backseat. "A bunch of clothes and
toiletries. Plus Dubose's groomsmen's gifts."

"You did?" Her mood brightened ever so slightly.

He came around and opened her door. "It was my pleasure to help."

Her mood sank again. What was he doing being so willing to help her marry another man? An ex had a certain
amount of pride to maintain, right?

Which was why when she slid past him to get into the

car, she didn't make eye contact. She felt very feminine and sexually needy, although she hoped he didn't guess the latter part. "I wish you'd have called me to let me know. I would have told you if the gifts are appropriate or not."

"They are," he said, and shut her door.

It irked her that he didn't notice her bad mood. It bothered her that he was so confident and incredibly good-looking even in that ridiculous hat and pair of weird-for-a-guy sunglasses. It riled her just as much that she hadn't been able to find a single thing at Bits of Lace. She'd walked in and seen a million pieces of slippery satin and delicate cotton lingerie, but when it came time to try them on, she just wasn't in the mood. She'd have to come back before the wedding or find something closer by.

"So what did you pick out for the guys?" she asked as he slid out into traffic.

"Bow ties." He tossed his hat in the seat behind him, yanked off his ugly sunglasses, and put on his cool shades. "With little frogs."

She sat in shocked silence. "Frogs?"

He nodded. "They're killer."

A beat of silence went by.

"But I picked up something else, too, just in case Dubose doesn't like 'em," he added as he maneuvered the car around a horse-and-carriage.

"What else?"

He sat up straighter. "Cuff links. Sterling silver."

True was relieved. "That sounds good."

"With little pigs on them."

Oh, Lord. "Really?"

He nodded. "They rock."

She looked out the window. It was hard to hold on to a bad mood around him. "We'll pay you back. But did you save the receipts? In case Dubose wants something else?"

Harrison looked shocked. "Why would he?"

She tried not to laugh. "Well, not everyone likes frogs and pigs."

"Guys do," Harrison said. "And I mean all guys, just in case Dubose has a groomsman who's gay. I've never met a man who doesn't like frogs and pigs."

"Okaaay . . . thanks for doing that."

"It was fun," he said.

"Did anyone recognize you?"

He nodded. "One of the clerks figured it out as soon as I walked in. I thought my disguise was pretty good, but he's a die-hard fan. He said my chin gave me away. Go figure."

She understood. He had a sexy chin. "Did he give you any trouble?"

"No, they were great about it. One of them had a Moon-Pie and asked me to sign the wrapper with a Sharpie. It was the least I could do, considering they tried to comp me the bow ties and the cuff links. And they were 'spensive, too."

True's mouth dropped open. "How expensive?"

"Five groomsmen, right? So the bow ties added up to eight hundred dollars. The cufflinks were three thousand."

"Oh, my God." True was mortified. "You shouldn't use your celebrity status to get free stuff. Don't you get enough freebies when you go to the Grammys and CMAs?"

"Sure." Harrison put on his blinker.

"I mean, I appreciate your doing that for Dubose, but no, we can't take free things—"

"I didn't," Harrison said. "I put 'em on my card."

"Oh, thank God." True exhaled in relief. "But . . . I can't believe Dubose would want to pay that much for groomsmen gifts. Although he did buy himself a five-thousand-dollar tux for the wedding."

"He did?"

"Yes. But still. We need to go back. I'm going to return all that stuff and start over."

"I got them to write me a phony receipt for half that price for Dubose. Just in case he objected."

"But that means you're paying the other half!"

"As if my bank account would even notice . . ."

"It's not right."

Harrison sighed. "If we go back, then the owner will be miffed. He's a big guy. Dapper as hell, but if he took off the blazer, he could be a bouncer at any hole-in-the-wall he wanted to patronize. Do you really want to mess with a man in a bow tie who could kick Arnold's ass?"

"Why would he be so upset?"

"They had a Miracle League fund-raising poster in the window. I wrote them a check for that first. And then when I went to buy my clothes and stuff, he tried to comp me the groomsmen's gifts as a thank-you. His son plays in the Miracle League. It took me a long time to convince him I couldn't accept those items comped and for him to take my card instead. By the end of it, we were bros. I can't diss my new bro. Besides, he won't want back those frogs and pigs. They'd been sitting around awhile—"

"I told you no one wanted frogs and pigs!"

"Let me finish." He eyed her askance. "They'd been sitting around awhile because some fella by the name of the duke of Argyll ordered them for his hunting buddies at his castle in Scotland."

"No way."

"Way. The duke wound up ordering too many, so the store had some left over. No one bought them because the owner was saving them for—get this—Channing Tatum and his posse. They're coming through to play golf at the Ocean Course on Kiawah Island next week. But I rate higher, being a local boy, so I got 'em."

"Wow." And she meant it. "How much was that check you wrote to the Miracle League?"

He gave her a sideways glance. "You don't want to know. High enough to keep you in silk lingerie from Bits of Lace for ten lifetimes."

"Oh." She was still a little in shock.

"And I don't want you to tell Dubose how much those groomsmen's gifts really cost," he said. "I didn't do it for him." He looked at her. "I did it for you."

True's heart beat hard with totally inappropriate feelings. And the rest of her body wasn't far behind. But luckily, her cell phone rang. It was the Realtor, confirming their appointment. They were going to see three beach houses and decide which one they'd choose for Dubose's fraternity friends.

"I'll meet you there, but I can't stay long," the Realtor said, "so if you don't mind, I'll give you the keys to the second and third houses while we're in the first. They're friends of mine and are okay with that. You can just drop them off at the office when you leave."

"Great," said True. It was getting to be lunchtime, and she was hungry. She put her phone away and looked at Harrison, driving as if he hadn't a care in the world. "Are you hungry?"

"Always."

The way he said it left her short of breath. But that was her fault, not his. He couldn't help being hot, and it was up to her not to notice that he was.

"Then let's get the first house out of the way and then walk up the beach to the Windjammer," she said. "It's only a few blocks—if you can get away with it."

"Have hat, will travel," he murmured. "Just wish I'd remembered my Speedo." He looked at her with a naughty-boy smirk.

Merciful heaven, it just wasn't fair how many man genes he was given when God passed them out.

"You mean a ding-a-ling sling?" She folded her arms over her chest, shocked at her daring. He wasn't the only one who could dish it out.

He let out a whoop of laughter.

She looked out her side window. How dare she have so much illicit fun without Dubose? Suddenly she felt stuck up in the worst way. "I'm ready to get out of this car."

"Hey, you can't turn all schoolteacher on me now."

"I most certainly can." She pressed her lips together and felt quivery inside. Upset. Stupid. Like she wanted to cry. "The house is up ahead on the left. It's got a sailboat mailbox."

Focus on Dubose. Focus on the wedding.

Harrison got very quiet as they glided down the street. And when he pulled over onto the sandy berm behind another car that read ISLAND REALTY on the back window, he said, "I'm sorry. I never should've mentioned the Speedo."

True lifted one shoulder and let it drop. She still wouldn't look at him. "I shouldn't have said what I said, either."

The car's engine ticked in the silence, and a big garbage truck went roaring by. "We're old friends," he said gently. "So you don't need to be shaken up by a little friendly banter. You're not being disloyal to Dubose."

She inhaled a deep breath and finally turned to face him. "Well, I feel that way. Here I am with another man, and we're talking about . . . pickle pinchers."

She couldn't help herself.

Harrison's brows flew up. "What?"

"That's another name for a Speedo." What was wrong with her? But she had to laugh. It was funny.

He laughed, too. And when they were both recovered, his face got serious and he pulled a piece of hair off her cheek. "You got nothing to worry about. We go way back, and this is how friends talk—silly, fun—especially right before a wedding. An important event like that causes a lot of nerves to flare, and it's good to laugh. It's better than having a panic attack, isn't it?"

She nodded, and he rubbed a thumb across her cheek.

"Thanks for understanding," she whispered.

"I get you, True Maybank."

He really did. She couldn't tear her eyes off his. But was this how one felt toward an old friend? Really?

Luckily, she didn't have to answer that question because he dropped his hand and unbuckled his seat belt. "Looks like a great place to stay for a wedding." Yeah. There he went helping her with her wedding again. He was definitely in the old-friend category. "So how many guys are staying here?"

"Five." She told herself she was relieved to be on solid ground again. "Three are bringing their wives. Two are single."

"All righty then. Let's check it out." His thigh muscle strained against his jeans as he levered himself out of the car.

Great golly, he was a wicked temptation. Was he supposed to be some cosmic test? She waited as he came around to open her door, as if they'd been in the habit for years.

Just what are you doing, True Maybank? It was as if she were upside down in a swimming pool. She needed her bearings. *You'd better follow the bubbles*, she told herself when he yanked her up by the hand.

They'd lead straight to Dubose.

CHAPTER SEVENTEEN

As True walked side by side with Harrison up the impressive front steps of the house, she wondered how Dubose was doing at that moment and tried to stay focused on how happy he'd be when she got his friends a good place to stay.

At the door the agent didn't recognize Harrison and treated him with semi-cool professionalism. "And you're . . . ?"

"A wayward cousin," Harrison said. "But I vow not to disrupt the wedding. *This* time."

The woman's eyes widened. "Oh."

True smiled. He really was a troublemaker. "Let's take a look, shall we?"

"Of course." The agent's back was straight and her expression dignified as she showed them about the house. Not once did she look back at Harrison, and she directed all her comments to True.

True decided that she needed to treat Harrison the same way, politely yet with indifference. Yes, they were old friends. But they'd been lovers, too, however briefly. As much as she wanted to forget that night, for her sake and Dubose's, she shouldn't. She needed to be wary. And if she were feeling vulnerable before the wedding, she'd talk to Carmela. Or Weezie. Or she'd go to her attic studio.

That was what she really needed to do. If she stayed away too long from her studio, she got antsy. Emotional. A little restless.

How she felt *now.*

The house was stunning. A vacationer's paradise. And when she found out it was the cheapest of the three, she said, "We don't even need to bother with the others. This one will do well."

"I still think you should see at least the one that's a block over," the agent suggested. "It's only three hundred more for the week—split among five parties, that's not much more. And it's truly spectacular." She held the keys out to True. "Your guests will be impressed by this one but blown away by the other. I promise."

True hesitated. Impressed was good enough for her. But for Dubose's sake, she took the keys. "All right."

The agent beamed. "I've already turned off the alarms over there. So just lock up when you're done, run the keys by the office, and we'll sign the papers."

She walked them out onto the back porch overlooking the Atlantic and shook True's hand firmly. "Have a wonderful wedding weekend."

"Thanks." True smiled politely.

Harrison held out his hand, too, but the agent pretended not to see him and trotted down the stairs.

He looked back at True. "Ouch."

"It's *your* fault."

"I kinda like her," he said, gazing after her as she rounded the corner of the house.

"Maybe lunch at the Windjammer will take your mind off the fact that she doesn't like *you.*"

"I don't know," he said with the sigh of a man who

knew full well that if he'd wanted to charm that woman, he could have. Blindfolded and with his hands tied behind his back.

They walked down the private boardwalk to the dunes and took off their shoes. The wind was strong, blowing their hair back from their faces as they walked south toward the Windjammer. The sand felt good between True's toes, and the enormity of the ocean helped relieve her of the twisty, strange feelings she'd had all morning. Feelings related to Harrison.

"So," she said, "when was the last time you've been to the Windjammer?"

He squinted at the water. "I was a senior in high school, using a fake ID. There was a band I wanted to see. The Hoodlums. Do you remember them?"

She squinted into the sun. "I think so. They weren't country, though."

"Right. They were alternative. But they could play guitar and harmonize really well. I stayed late and helped them break down their equipment. I got to ask them what it was like being on the road. And I told them it was what I wanted to do."

"Were they nice?"

"Yep. They confirmed for me exactly what I thought— that being on the road and playing music was like being in heaven. It didn't matter if the place was a dump or the Taj Mahal. When you love music, you do it."

They didn't talk for a minute or two. There was no need. They had the sand. The warm rays of the sun. Breathing that matched the sound of the waves and steps in perfect sync . . . like the V-formation of pelicans steering themselves on the breeze. Harrison's feet were wide and tan. Feet that had gone barefoot a lot during the growing-up years.

It was the most glorious, peaceful, happy couple of

minutes True had had in a long time. "I believe you're meant to be where you are right now," she said eventually. "Your success wasn't an accident."

"I was determined to get out of Sand Dollar Heaven," he said, "much as I liked it when I was little."

She wanted to take his hand and squeeze it, but she didn't dare. "I'm sorry I wasn't there for you in high school."

He shook his head. "I'd rather not talk about the old days. I like to stay here in the present."

"Is that why you never came back to Biscuit Creek?"

"You got it."

She looked to her right and saw a sand dollar and picked it up. It was still perfect. "Here," she said, handing it to him. "A memento. But you'll break it in your luggage. Maybe you can leave it with Gage."

"Thanks." He tucked it in his shirt pocket. They didn't say anything else. The Windjammer loomed in the distance. True saw a couple of kids playing on the makeshift volleyball court and remembered when she, Harrison, his friends, and Gage had tried to play volleyball without a net at Sand Dollar Heaven.

Inside the bar, it was cool and dark. But the salt air rushed through, smelling of fun times and laughter. Flirting and Coppertone. They both ordered burgers and cold beers.

True poured her beer into a frosty mug. "I wish you could take off your hat and sunglasses."

Harrison shrugged. "You get used to it."

"But it must be hard. It's almost like you're in a cage." She felt instantly sorry for saying that. "Sorry."

"It's all right." He wiped the beer mustache off her lips with his thumb, then licked the thumb. She supposed she should be annoyed or grossed out, but instead her insides heated up like a steel bar being blowtorched. "I think of it this way—everyone else can have an average day if they don't recognize me."

"But most people don't want an average day," True replied. "If they see you, they'll have a special day."

Their burgers came, and she peeled off her pickles and put them on her plate.

He took a swig of beer. "The most special days in the world are average ones. You don't realize it until you don't have them anymore." He clinked his bottle to her mug. "Here's to a really average day. Thanks for it."

"Cheers," she responded, a lump in her throat. It was a weird compliment, but she got it. She was glad she helped him have an average day. She remembered average days with her parents and Honey. How she wished she could have those days back.

A few minutes later, both their plates were clean. Maybe all that walking had worked up their appetites. "You ready to walk some more?" she asked him.

"You bet," he said, and left three twenties on the table.

They both thanked the server and bartender for a great meal.

"And thank you for lunch," she told Harrison outside.

"Hey, you're covering dinner. It's the least I can do. What *is* for dinner, by the way?"

"Shrimp and grits."

"Mmmm."

They found their shoes outside and walked back up the beach, past the first house, talking about the development of the island since he'd last been home.

"It's changed," he said.

"There are a few houses pre-Hugo. But not many. Look at that one." She pointed to a modest-sized, old-fashioned house on stilts.

"Ah, that's a real beach house."

"I'll bet it has cedar-paneled walls," she said. "And a bright little kitchen."

Harrison scanned the seemingly endless line of vacation rentals on either side of it. "These other ones look like hotels. They're not meant for a family."

"Corporations build them and lend them out to their executives for retreats, or they rent them out for family reunions or weddings, like mine and Dubose's."

The wedding. It was really happening. And soon.

They watched a black dog leap through the waves with his owner. And talked about the turtles that laid eggs in the dunes. And then they arrived at the other beach house recommended by the agent. The pool was gorgeous, with pale-pink-and-gray shell tiles lining silver-gray pool walls. A volleyball net was strung across the middle, and at one end was a separate, in-ground hot tub.

They dropped their shoes on the pavement near the hot tub, rinsed off their feet, and entered a luxurious great room.

"Whoa," Harrison said. "It's Hamptons style. Done up by a fancy designer, and too perfect to be real. The other house was, too, but this one goes even farther."

He was right. There wasn't a family picture in sight. The house was definitely corporate-owned. But as they walked through the impeccably decorated rooms downstairs, True knew that Dubose would really like it for his friends. It had every luxury they'd need: a big ice maker, a pool table, a movie theater, and beneath the house, a Ping-Pong table with a cool tiki bar. Of course, the outdoor pool area was a huge draw, too, heated in the colder months.

"Let's check out the bedrooms," Harrison said, "starting on the third floor."

They were cute, perfect for kids, teens, maids, housekeeping staff. In the middle was a gathering area with a huge flat-screen TV and a game system. The French doors led out to a breathtaking view of the Atlantic and a wide porch perfect for sunbathing.

The second floor was more luxurious. The first four bedrooms, two with twins, two with queen-sized beds, looked as if they came out of *House Beautiful*. Harrison was studying a line of books on a shelf in one of the twin rooms facing the street when True moved on to the master bedroom on the ocean side. It was spectacular, with a big fireplace, a king-sized bed stacked with European pillows, and a bathroom larger than True's bedroom back home.

"Come look," she called to him as she marveled at the gigantic marble tub and glassed-in shower with multiple jets on the walls. Her voice echoed in the quiet. Only the sound of the sea, like an endlessly fizzy Coke, broke the silence.

She exited the bathroom and stood by the four-poster bed, her hand exploring the carving of a rice sheaf on one of the posts. It was beautiful. "Harrison?" she called again. "Come see this. Rice is such a huge part of Charleston's history."

When she looked up, he was in the doorway. And for some reason—maybe it was the oblong block of sunshine illuminating the bed covers, or the sudden gust of wind that made the deck chairs rattle on the porch outside—his curious gaze gave way to something knowing and deep.

Unbidden thoughts surged in True. There was the quiet, the kind that lulls you into submission. Privacy, made more exotic if the doors are open to the sun, wind, and sea. An expansive bed to make love on—no one the wiser.

She felt bewitched by the ephemeral silence that stretched between them. The fact that they were alone together made her dizzy with longing, her legs and arms heavy weights. She looked down at the hardwood floor, red-hot shame turning her mute.

She wanted him.

"I'll see you outside," he said.

He knew. She could tell by his serious tone. Maybe he pitied her.

She closed her eyes and tried to pick up the sound of his bare feet on the stairs, but she couldn't. The house was too sturdy. Untried. With all its temporary occupants, it didn't absorb anything and maybe never would.

Whereas she was broken. Scarred. A permanent home for worry and loss.

A small hiccuping sigh escaped her. She clutched the bedpost with both hands and laid her forehead on it. "Harrison," she whispered aloud to break the silence, to mend her guilty conscience, to find her way.

Not *Dubose*.

Just *Harrison*.

CHAPTER EIGHTEEN

When True walked slowly out of the beach house, she remembered that there was only one time in her life she'd felt beautiful the way she was meant to be beautiful, through her skin and down to her bones and even deeper, to the place where her secret heart's desires lay.

It was the night Harrison took her to the very same beach they'd walked on today. That time, too, they'd left their shoes at the public path and walked on the shore—but holding hands, an illicit couple . . .

He'd stolen her away from Dubose at the prom.

They'd known what people were saying. Who was he to do such a thing? She was the homecoming queen. He was the loner. They never *talked*. They never even looked at each other when they passed in the school hallway.

Good Lord, he was her daddy's lawn boy, and Dubose was quarterback on the football team!

At the time, all True could think was, Why? Why had it taken her six long years to come to her right mind? No wonder she'd been miserable through junior high and high school. Harrison had been off limits. Her *best friend* had been living right alongside her but leading an entirely separate life.

She'd let the hem of her gown drag through the sand.

They'd talked about school, about the old days in Sand Dollar Heaven. He'd asked her how she was doing with her parents. She'd wanted to know where he was going after graduation.

At one point they stopped near a sand dune, and he ran his hands up and down her arms. "I'm heading to Nashville," he said with gravitas. But with excitement, too.

"Wow." Her heart twisted. She didn't want to lose him right after she'd found him. "That's such a huge step. You're so brave." And she'd reached up on tiptoe and kissed him.

He pulled her close and kissed her, telling her over and over without speaking how much he cared. She'd never felt this way with Dubose. Ever. Kissing him had been an exercise in trying to learn how to feel something she really didn't.

Finally, they pulled apart. Just a few inches.

He turned her by the shoulders to face the ocean. "The moon's behind a cloud, so we might be able to see the bioluminescence."

"What's that?"

"Tiny marine organisms that emit light. It's like seeing a million little stars in the water."

She leaned back against him, and they watched a few waves crash . . . and glow.

"Oh, my gosh!" She pulled forward.

"Isn't it amazing?" He laughed and brought her back.

She nestled in his arms. *Happy*, she thought. *So very, very happy*.

"What's really fun is swimming in it," he said. "Gage and I did that once. Mama took us to the beach one night."

"She sounds like she was a wonderful mother."

"She was."

"Let's swim—" she said.

"Wanna jump in?" he said at the same time.

She laughed and turned in his arms. He kissed her again, and it was hot and sexy. So sexy that she was scared.

He pushed her hair out of her eyes. "Don't be afraid. It's just me."

" 'Kay," she whispered.

"I might look tough," he said low, "but the truth is, I don't have much experience with girls. I've kissed a few waitresses after work, but it was all in fun. Nothing serious."

She couldn't take her eyes off his. "Are you—are you a virgin?"

"Yeah." He sent her a crooked grin. "I know I look like I get around. But I never wanted to. Not if"—he paused—"not if it wasn't with you."

She kissed his chest, right where his shirt opened. And then she laid her ear over his heart and listened. "Me, too," she whispered, then looked up at him. "Dubose was hoping to get lucky tonight. It was why he was ignoring me at the dance. I told him I wasn't interested."

Harrison kissed the top of her head. "He's a spoiled brat."

"I don't know why it took me so long to see that. Maybe someday he'll grow up and make some girl a nice husband. But right now, he's all about himself."

"Most guys are. I think it's because they haven't met the right girl. When you do, that changes everything."

"You've changed everything for me—in a night." She grabbed his hand and held it tight. "I knew you were working at a restaurant in Charleston. But I had no idea you were at Carolina's."

"I've been there six months." He gave a short laugh. "Dubose knew. He's been there with his family."

"Are you kidding me?"

"No."

She sighed. "Coming in tonight with him and those

other couples, seeing you there taking away our plates while I was dressed for a big night out with a guy I didn't care about—it was torture."

"For me, too. I finally came to my senses. Dubose doesn't deserve you. Why do you think I crashed the prom?"

They kissed again, and this time he ran a hand over her right breast, and the wonder of it—so different from when she was with Dubose—made her knees weak.

"So are we swimming?" He kissed her behind her ear. "If so, I don't advise you going in like that."

"Yes, we're swimming." She laughed because his mouth tickled. "Don't you have to bring that uniform back to work?"

"I do." His palms made slow circles on her belly. "They dry clean 'em for us. They'll be upset if I bring it back stiff and dry from being soaked in salt water."

"We're taking an awfully long time to explain that we have to go in naked," she said with a grin.

"You can wear your panties and bra. And I can wear my boxers."

"Not briefs?" She stepped away a few feet. She was feeling playful. Not scared about this part.

"Nope." He lunged for her and caught her. "I'm a boxers kind of guy. The tackier the better. I've got shamrocks and beer mugs all over this pair."

"Aha," she said. "I don't know about you, but I don't want to have to explain to my mother why my bra and underwear are wet. So I'm going in naked. And I don't want to be naked alone."

"I'm in." He began work on his bow tie, then his shirt.

Mercy. She had a hard time not standing there and ogling him. So she busied herself shimmying out of her gown. "I've never skinny dipped," she admitted.

"It's the best way to swim." He stepped out of his

pants. In the moonglow she saw his flesh and the shadowy area of his groin, but not for long. Next thing she knew, he was down at the water, whooping. She laughed and ran after him, naked as a jaybird.

'S wonderful! 'S marvelous! Honey's favorite song came to her.

She was free.

When she caught up with him, she was out of breath. They stayed apart except for clasping hands. Then together, without speaking, they half walked, half ran into the water, which wasn't cold enough to shock True but cold enough to get her heart pumping and her skin tingling.

"Look," Harrison said, striding through the briny water.

True lost her breath. It was heaven. All around them, jewels of light sparkled, glowed.

"I don't feel like I'm on earth anymore," she said. "We're on another planet, someplace new."

"And we're the first explorers," he said.

They lowered themselves into the surf and basked in the miracle of being together.

He pulled her close, their naked chests pressed together, and clasped her bottom. She wrapped her legs around his. His erection butted against her thigh.

"I love you," he murmured.

"I love you, too." And she knew then it was true. "I always have."

They kissed while the waves foamed around them, knocked them sideways, sluiced between the small gaps where they were separate. And then he picked her up in his arms, bent low to suckle her breast while she kneaded his hair, and walked seamlessly through the surf back to shore.

"Here," she said, and he stopped.

He let her down—she was loose, like a rag doll—and

they continued their declaration of love without words. Side by side on the gritty sand—slippery knees, bellies, chests touching.

"Tonight," she murmured between kisses. "For both of us."

"I didn't bring anything. I didn't know." He ran his hand to the V between her thighs, and she shuddered when his fingers probed her with no reticence.

She was his. He was hers.

She thought quickly of her calendar and of Mr. Grover the science teacher, who'd been so disapproving when he saw Harrison—and not the golden god Dubose—leaving the prom with her. He'd be upset to know that he was helping them tonight, but he'd inadvertently taught her how not to get pregnant when he'd explained ovulation.

"It's okay," she assured Harrison. "It's not the right time."

They kissed again, their hands everywhere, exploring. She reveled in the hard, strong length of him. He was Poseidon, washed up on the shore.

"Someday," he murmured on her belly, "I want to make a baby with you."

"You do?"

"Of course." This was the solitary boy on the parking lot at school speaking. The one who looked like he cared only about his guitar.

When he kissed her between her legs, she was the wind. And the sea. Of the earth and sand. He was her moon. And when he loomed above her, their bodies joined, she was a starfish on the beach, set aglow by his light.

CHAPTER NINETEEN

Harrison spent most of his free time the day after shopping in Charleston with True helping out with the tomato-picking operation. In his spare time, he played his travel guitar on the porch, surrounded by dogs either scratching fleas, laid flat out on their sides, or staring at him as if they were in love. Gage and Weezie were watching vintage *Star Trek* on his crappy old TV in the front parlor. They'd reached a new level of amicability since the rotten tomato fight they'd had with Carmela yesterday when True and Harrison were gone.

Carmela came by on the way to True's party—it was in honor of her and Dubose—and brought them a peach pie, for which Harrison thanked her profusely. Gage barely said a word.

"You're just mad I beat you in the tomato fight," Carmela teased him.

"I'm not mad." Gage's ears turned red.

Carmela laughed. "Are you sure? I smashed three tomatoes onto your naked torso yesterday. Good thing you took your shirt off because you never would have gotten the stains out."

"Yes, I'm sure," Gage replied. "Did you know that an

old term for 'tomato' is *love apple*? I've used it as a cross-word clue. The tomato's also a heckler's weapon."

Harrison wanted to slap him. His brother had no idea how to flirt. He had washboard abs, and from the look in Carmela's eyes, she'd noticed.

"I learn a lot from talking to you, Gage," she said sweetly. "Don't you want to go to the party with us?"

"No."

Carmela put the pie on the kitchen counter. "Okay, then. Enjoy the pie."

"We will." Harrison glared at Gage. Was he blind? The girl *liked* him!

"Thanks," Gage finally said.

"You're welcome," Carmela answered him brightly then left with Truc.

Harrison hated to see them go. True had made all kinds of noise in the morning about him and Gage going to the party, too. Gage had obviously meant it when he said he wouldn't. The guy didn't lie. Ever. But she'd persisted in asking Harrison. He could tell she was putting on to be polite, so he'd just as politely declined. She was the consummate hostess, but beneath that act, he was positive she wasn't interested in hanging out with him too much after their awkward moment at the beach house.

He knew damned well what she'd been thinking about in that second-floor bedroom: hot, raw sex. With him. He'd thought about the same—with her. But it was incumbent upon him as a gentleman not to take advantage of a lady on the verge of marriage to someone else when he had no intention of following through with any commitment to her on his part.

He'd had to pretend to be oblivious. It was difficult, as he'd been seriously aroused by seeing her cling to that bedpost, but he made a quick 180 and beat feet out of the house. Good thing she never caught on that he'd guessed the sexy, forbidden, and entirely flattering direction of her thoughts. It meant he could continue on at Maybank Hall as a nerdy guy just visiting an old friend—and not someone who knew that she'd been tempted to cheat on Dubose with him . . . and had gotten subtly turned down in the process.

Maybe she felt guilty about what happened, maybe not. But that wasn't Harrison's worry. If his presence was testing her allegiance to Dubose, then so be it. If she was meant to be Mrs. Dubose Waring, then it would happen. She had a few more days to make sure she really wanted it to.

Harrison himself didn't mind being constantly tempted by her. It was good for him to get all shook up. He wrote better songs that way. Or so he thought. After she left for the party, he had no luck sitting on the front porch. All he did was wish like hell he could jump her bones.

A couple of hours later, her car drove up, and his heart skipped a beat.

"Hey," he said when she walked slowly up on the front porch. She was a knockout in a classy red dress with a plunging V-neck and straight skirt. There must have been a lot of Spandex in the fabric. It clung to her curves.

"Hey," she said back, and sat down on the swinging bench.

He was on the rocker opposite it. He tried not to look at her thighs when her skirt rode up, but it was difficult. He focused on her face, on her smoky, glamorous eyes. He was on stage all the time, and he recognized false eyelashes. They turned him on. "Wasn't it any fun?" he asked her, and wished more than ever that Dubose Waring would never come back from New York.

"I guess it was sort of fun." She put her folded hands between her knees and splayed her ankles out, like a little girl. Skeeter came over and nuzzled one of her spiky black heels. "But it's pretty lame when your fiancé isn't there. I know we couldn't avoid this, and I should probably get used to it . . ."

Harrison played a riff on his guitar. "Dubose work a lot?"

She nodded. "I can't fault him for that. He's good at what he does."

"I'm sure he is."

"*You* work all the time."

"Pretty much." He fiddled with a chord or two, and thought about a sad girl in pearls coming home from a party. That would make a depressing song—the true country artist in him responded to that. But he also knew that when he was calculated in his approach to songwriting, he produced dreck. Dan didn't get that. He'd texted him that morning and asked him how it was going.

It's not, Harrison had written back.

She inclined her head and watched him strum a few light chords. "Will you come to the next party? Everyone's dying for you to show up."

Not her, though. Her tone was light, but he could read her like a book, too.

"I don't know," he said. "If it's not all Biscuit Creek people, I could run into some trouble. I'm surprised someone hasn't spilled the beans already. I was sure the paps would show up by now."

"Goes to show you how much the people here want that library rebooted. And maybe how much they like you, too."

"Aw, they don't like me."

"Sure they do." She got her swing going gently. "You weren't part of the gang, but you never caused any trouble around town. You worked hard. And you were nice to anyone at school who spoke to you nicely."

"I'll agree with that assessment." His palm rested flat on the guitar's surface. "But I don't belong here. Never did, never will. I know how the rich folk talked about my parents. We were trailer trash. Money and fame don't change that perception. The only difference now is that I'm an object of fascination. I can entertain your friends, but I'll never win their respect."

He played a complicated riff to blow off steam—and maybe to impress her a little bit.

She grinned. "Show-off."

He grinned back. "You caught me."

The crickets chirped, and the wind off the marsh blew True's hair back from her face.

"What you said does hold true for some people," she said. "But you'd find their type anywhere you go in this world. They're mean because they're scared of anything different. That shouldn't hold you back from socializing here. Heck. Your name's on the water tower. Of course, you belong."

"You have a point. But I'm still not interested, thanks. If anyone asks, chalk it up to my need for time away."

"All right." She sounded genuinely disappointed. He was a little confused. He'd thought she didn't want him to go anywhere with her. Too much temptation and all that.

Maybe she'd gotten her lust for him under control already.

Too bad.

He went back to making love to his guitar. It was a poor substitute for what he really wanted to do with the woman in the red dress, but it was something.

"Well, if you won't go with me to the next party," she said, "will you come with me to Weezie's open house at Trident Tech tomorrow night? Dubose really wanted to be there. She's still talking about wanting to get an apartment. I know it'll come up a lot. It would be nice to have some moral support, but there's the matter of your disguise. I don't know how you can get away with wearing an Indiana Jones hat and those weird sunglasses all night."

"I've got it covered." He smiled at her the way a brother would, kind of sickly and forced.

But she didn't notice. "Good." She jumped up from the swing, all happy. "And boy, am I glad tonight's over. A couple people asked me about the wedding plans. I couldn't tell anyone that I don't have a venue yet or a caterer."

"Time's a wastin'," he said. "I can get someone here tomorrow to take over. I guarantee you my friend in LA will find you a place that'll rock. And the food will be incredible."

"No, thank you." She was at the door now, and the light did amazing things to highlight her figure.

"You're stubborn," he said.

"No more than you."

"Interesting that Carmela brought by a peach pie."

"She baked it for you and Gage. She never brings us pie. I guess that *is* interesting." She grinned.

"Not as interesting as this: You and I are gonna paddleboard soon."

"No, we're not. I don't have time."

"Sure you do. You got nothing to do without a caterer and a place for the party."

She made a face at him and let the screen door swing shut behind her.

"Don't take the last piece of that pie!" he called after her. "I need it for inspiration!"

And solace—since he couldn't throw her down and have his way with her. And he had mush for brains when it came to writing new songs. And *Star Trek* was probably over.

Yep, peach pie was the answer to his woes. At least for right now.

He grabbed his guitar by the neck, stepped over the dogs, and followed True into the house. Maybe he could watch *her* eat some peach pie.

But she wasn't even in the kitchen. Gage was, and he was eating pie—not nearly as gratifying a picture. Thank God there were a few pieces left.

Harrison took one and joined him at the table. "Good, huh?"

"The best," Gage said, slicing off a flaky bite with his fork.

"True says Carmela made it for us."

"For *you*, maybe. You're the star."

"So are you. You've got geniuses from Harvard and Stanford sending you fan mail—and big-time celebrities like Jon Stewart and Ben Affleck. Carmela barely spoke to me when she came inside. She was all about you and tomatoes. She didn't say a word about country music."

Gage said nothing. But there was something pained on his face, and Harrison couldn't figure it out. He didn't think his big brother was jealous of him. "Are you all right, man? Is it the house? I really do think you're gonna love it. It'll be worth all this inconvenience you're going through having to move out of the trailer."

Gage put his fork down. "It isn't inconvenient coming here. We're lucky."

Harrison looked around him, at the homey kitchen. "You're right." They'd had a lot of fun eating meals with their two hostesses right here at this table. "'Fess up, then. It's the house."

"You already know how I feel about it. As if I'm stupid. Needing assistance. I don't like things being done for me. I'm a grown man—I'm your big brother. But—"

"But what?"

"But I also know that sometimes I get these blind

spots. And I—" He hesitated. "—I appreciate having you call me on them."

Whoa. Harrison's heart just kinda turned over or exploded or melted or whatever it was that happened to chicks all the time. But in a guy way. Most definitely a guy way.

"Hey," he said. "I get those blind spots, too." He grabbed Gage's neck and squeezed for a split second before dropping his hand. "I'm glad you're my brother."

It was true. But the moment felt a little awkward, naturally. Gage did the right thing, picking up his plate and heading to the sink.

"I'm sorry about stepping on your toes." Too late Harrison regretted that he'd come barreling in and set off a bunch of fireworks—totally oblivious to Gage's dislike of change. It was because he'd panicked at the sight of that trailer. And maybe he'd been disconcerted already, seeing True. Being back in Biscuit Creek.

Gage opened the fridge and poured himself a huge glass of milk. "Want one?"

"Sure."

Gage brought two glasses over to the table.

Each picked his up and drained it. Gage set his glass on the table half a second before Harrison.

"I forgot we used to do that," Harrison said. They'd race. Mom would yell at them to stop it. But she really liked it because they were drinking milk.

"I always won," Gage said matter-of-factly.

"That's because you have a mouth like a bass," Harrison said back.

Gage's eyes gleamed with amusement.

Harrison shook his head. "Look. I really don't want to stop building this house. Can you give it a chance?" He paused for half a beat. "If you don't like it, we can sell it—"

"We're not going to sell it." Gage was emphatic.

"Sure we could."

"*No.*"

There was another awkward silence. Harrison wondered what the girls were up to. Were they listening in? He kinda hoped not. It was embarrassing for anyone else to see friction within a family. You felt like a failure, in a way. Or maybe it was more that you felt it never happened to anyone else. All his life, Harrison knew that other people were aware his family had issues. It had been like walking around naked. It hurt. It was tough.

And where was the good in it? Had it made him a better person? He didn't see where it had. It had simply been part of who he was, this uneasiness between him and Gage. His father's incarceration and futile death. His poor mama's getting let go from her housekeeping jobs by people who didn't trust her anymore because of his dad—and then dying of cancer. There was pain. And it made him tired in a very deep place that he wanted to forget even existed.

"I wouldn't have any other place to go," Gage said. "I don't want to keep doing this, moving out, starting over. It's . . . hard."

"Okay." Harrison felt for the guy. He could hear it in his voice, the discomfort. He hated being uncomfortable himself, and here he'd gone and made his brother unhappy. *Way to go, big ol'* dumb *country music star*! "I understand. I hope it's making it a little easier to navigate the transition with me here, even though I'm the one"—*who was the dumbass who screwed you*—"who initiated it."

"It's fine. You're spending a lot of money. At least let me pay what I can. I've got enough saved to cover a house. Maybe not the fees of the Hollywood guy who came in, or the expedited construction, but I can make a substantial contribution."

"If you want to."

"Of course I do."

"Well, all right." Harrison grinned at his brother. Thank God, it was settled. Or was it? Gage was never relaxed, really—at least not the way Harrison relaxed. So he couldn't tell if things were actually cool between them or not. "Anything else on your mind? I won't be here much longer. And who knows when we'll see each other next."

Gage looked down at the table. "Yeah, there's one thing."

Harrison leaned forward, excited that Gage was confiding in him. Nervous, too. In a big way. "What is it?"

Gage looked up at him. "Carmela."

Carmela! "Um, do you like her?"

"Yes. A lot."

Inside, Harrison wanted to hoot and holler. Yes. *Yes!* Gage was into Carmela, and she obviously had the hots for him. And no wonder. Once you got past his reticence, the guy was chill. Brilliant. Witty in his own weird way. Good looking and healthy. Strong as an ox. Cut like a marine. Made a good living. What more could a girl want?

"You like her?" He kept his runaway thoughts in check by using a calm voice.

"Of course."

"Shoot." He slapped his brother's shoulder. "You'd never know it by the way you treated her tonight."

"What do you mean?"

"You ignored her. She was flirting with you."

"She was?"

"Yes."

"I had no idea."

Harrison pointed to his eye. "Right here. Look and see if a girl's eyes are twinklin' or sparkin' when she talks to you. If they are, she's flirting. Same with if she says your name a lot. 'Gage, this. Gage, that.'"

"Huh." Gage cocked his head. "Are you sure?"

"Positive." Harrison leaned back in his chair. "She looked real pretty in that pink dress the other day. Tonight, too, in her party dress."

Gage gave a short laugh. "You should have seen her in the tomato fight. She was hot, even covered in pulp."

"She has a great personality, too," Harrison threw in to class up the conversation.

As Gage's wingman, he should have mentioned that first, but guys tended to go straight to the looks category. It didn't mean the rest was small beans. Hell, he'd dated plenty of gorgeous women who turned out to have no heart, no humor, and nothing substantial going on upstairs. The great face and perfect bod could only take one so far.

"She's the nicest person I know," Gage said.

"How long you liked her?"

"Ever since I first saw her. Over a year ago. I've been going in every week to, uh, shop in her store."

"You mean straighten the shelves."

"Yeah, whatever. I buy things, too."

"Is that why you had a whole row of southern dip mixes and salsas in your kitchen? And how many Rainbow Row coasters can a man have?"

"I've got crab and shrimp ones, too. And palmettos. But I'm there to see *her*."

"So what happens?"

"I hardly speak to her. I just can't figure out what to say. But she'll talk. And I listen."

"We can work on that. You talk about how pretty she looks. What the weather's like. What's on the news that day. Has she done anything fun lately. If you have to, memorize those things."

"I already have. I have to pretend, in a way, that I'm in a movie, and this is my script. So it doesn't come off naturally, the way it does with you. I'm a bad actor."

"Who cares if it's natural or not? As long as you do it. That gets the ball rolling, and you'll get better the more you practice. You haven't asked her out yet?"

"No. I'm always about to, and then—I cop out."

Harrison shook his head. "You just gotta do it, man. She's gonna say yes. But on the off chance she doesn't, at least you know you've tried."

Gage sighed. "I know."

"Hey, she made you a pie."

Gage raised a brow. "We don't know that. You're here. Come on."

"All right, maybe, *maybe* she made it for both of us. We're nice brothers. We look like we need pie. But you were in this tomato fight with her yesterday, and it's so freaking obvious she noticed you. I saw her looking at you with *interest*."

"Really?"

"Yes. Dude, she saw your abs. She even mentioned them tonight. You're hot and you don't even know it."

"Yeah, right."

"For real. You know how hard that is for a brother to say that? I'm gagging as I speak."

Gage gave a short laugh. "I guess so."

"Hey, if you don't believe me, how about this: Did you act any different yesterday?"

"I talked a little more. And I laughed."

"Well, shoot. That's it, too. She saw your abs, and then she also something *inside* you that you hadn't shown her before."

"Maybe." Gage paused. "I wish I could get into another tomato fight with her, if that's what it takes."

"That's *not* what it takes," Harrison said. "You can win her over at her store, too. And then you'll take her out. To the movies, to dinner."

"I hope so."

A good twenty seconds went by, while overhead, footsteps made the ceiling groan. That was True's room. Harrison had to resist imagining her getting naked and ready to slide into bed.

"What about you?" Gage eventually said. "How's your love life?"

"Hah." Harrison slid lower in his seat. "It ain't happenin.' I'm on the road too much. I think I'm gonna have to be the crazy uncle. So settle down and get married, okay? I wouldn't mind having some nieces and nephews."

Gage stared at him a second too long.

"What?" Harrison felt nervous all of a sudden.

"I wasn't here when you left town the day after prom," Gage said, "but when I came back, I heard plenty. I know how you showed up at Dubose's house and tried to whisk True away to Nashville."

Harrison waved a hand. "That was a long time ago. I was a dumb kid."

"Sure you don't still have feelings for her?"

Harrison spoke low. "If I did, there's nothing I can do. She's getting married. And I'm in no position to take on a serious relationship."

What could anyone say to that? Especially someone as quiet as Gage? Harrison stood, picked up his glass and plate. He was going back out on the porch. He didn't dare go upstairs and bump into True. He'd taken to waiting downstairs until he was sure she was in bed.

But Gage wasn't done with him. "Why are you writing all these songs about love?"

Harrison didn't know what to say. "It's actually a good question. I can't write for shit these days."

"Maybe because you're a fake." Gage stood, too, his expression neutral.

He never got when he was insulting. Or if he did, it didn't register that the other person might be miffed.

"What the hell is that supposed to mean?" Harrison was irritated despite himself. "You've got to realize that sometimes you say some pretty harsh stuff. Pay attention to how you phrase things."

"I *am* paying attention," said Gage. "Country music's supposed to be about real life. But you live in a bubble. Maybe *you* should pay attention to how you're phrasing things. Could be that's what's holding you up with your songwriting."

Well, shit. Harrison felt the old steam come roaring out of his ears. "Let's not talk anymore about me and my issues, okay? By the way, you live in a bubble, too. You're supposed to be so worldly wise—you know geography. Pop culture. You've got passing knowledge on just about every subject in the world. But you were hiding in that trailer. Hiding behind your OCD, too, letting it run your life."

Gage stood silent for a minute. "Mom and Dad wouldn't be happy with either of us, I guess. Let's face it. We're going to be old bachelors. And maybe it's best that way."

"That's nuts."

"Dad going to jail and getting killed there made us both scared of life."

"What?"

"I've had a long time to think about it," Gage said. "And that's what I believe. We never learned what it was like to be a man from him. You're hiding. I'm hiding. The Gamble brothers don't gamble at all."

Harrison cocked his head. "For a major geek, you're pretty astute sometimes."

"Thanks."

"Though not in this case." Harrison glared at him. "You're watching too much Dr. Phil with Weezie. From now on, speak for yourself. Not me. I've gambled plenty in my life. And on the big things, I've lost."

He stalked out of the kitchen and headed to the porch.

"Good night," Gage called to his back. "By your logic if it's not too late for me to be an average guy, then it's also not too late for you."

Didn't he get it? Harrison was mad at him! *Shut the hell up* was what he wanted to say. "G'night," he said instead. He didn't turn around, either. Guilt and frustration made him mutter the word like a coward.

Damned brother.

But on the porch, he wrote his first song in months. It came quickly. Cleanly. And it was good.

CHAPTER TWENTY

True had had no sleep. No sleep at all. She was going to look like a zombie at her own wedding. It was ridiculous how little time she had left to find a caterer and a venue. She actually had *no* time. No sane business would take her with mere days to go before the ceremony. It was too late to pretend that a disaster hadn't happened.

"What have I been thinking?" she asked Carmela on the phone in bed after the party. "I should have told everyone there."

"You need to call Dubose."

"I will, as soon as I hang up with you."

"Did the guys like the pie?" Carmela asked.

"Oh, yeah." True managed to smile into the phone. "They did. That was very nice. Thanks."

"No problem. What guy doesn't like pie, right? And Gage has been so good, straightening my shelves for over a year."

"You mean it wasn't for Harrison, too?"

"Oh, sure. Harrison. He's welcome to it. But you know, Gage has been displaced. I was thinking maybe a little TLC wouldn't hurt." Carmela paused. "So whatever. It's only pie."

"Right, well, it was a huge hit."

"Good. And don't you dare feel guilty about eating some. Too many brides lose weight before the wedding. You want to have a vibrant glow. You can't do that when you're starving. And don't feel guilty about calling Dubose, either."

True sighed. "I won't. In fact, it's a good thing Penn's on the other side of the Atlantic. I'm furious with her for abandoning me so totally. I don't know why it's taken me so long to work myself up to that point."

"Harrison, maybe? He's quite the distraction."

God, yes, he is. True curled a lock of hair around her finger. "That can't be it." There was a second's silence. "Although he's very charming. But you know that."

"Uh-oh," Carmela said.

"No, no, no. Nothing to worry about."

"Right," said Carmela, not very convincingly, which did nothing to help True feel less anxious about his presence in her house.

She could hear him playing chords on the front porch. "Um, talk to you tomorrow?"

"Sure. Maybe I'll run over after work with another pie. Or just help Weezie out with any U-pick customers. Sounds like you girls could use some support."

"Thanks, but Harrison and I are taking Weezie to Trident Tech for the open house. Only Gage will be here after five."

"Oh?" Carmela sounded a little out of breath. "Well, I'll bring over some dinner then. My famous lasagna. I'll just drop it off."

"That would be nice. Thanks, Carmela."

She dialed Dubose's number next. This news called for talking, of course. Not texting. It was far too important.

"Hey, honey." Dubose's familiar drawl instantly made tears come to her eyes. She'd been crazy to think she could handle this wedding calamity alone.

"Hi." She wished she could see him. "Where are you?" It was eleven PM. Maybe she'd called too late.

"Just getting into bed," he said. "It's been another helluva day. I'm beat."

Shoot. She couldn't send him to bed depressed and worried. She'd wait one more day. Catch him while he was alert. Or better yet, she'd go out tomorrow and she would *solve* this problem! She'd give it one last shot. "I wanted to say good night, is all, and I miss you."

"Damn, I miss you, too. Everything going well there?"

"Yes," she lied. It literally pained her to say that. "I went to one of our parties tonight. Everyone missed you."

"That's nice."

"*I* missed you." She could hear the TV on in the background—a crowd yelling. Baseball, no doubt. "But guess what? I got your friends their beach house."

"That's good." She could tell he was watching a game.

"It's beautiful. Upstairs, it's got a—"

"I'm sure it's fine, honey. I really have to go now."

"Oh, right. Sorry. Good night. I-I love you." And she did, she was sure of it. Just because she was attracted to Harrison didn't mean she didn't love Dubose. She heard married people didn't stop being attracted to other people—they learned how to deal with it. It was human nature. It was in everyone's genes to be hardwired for sexual attraction to anyone who was good looking. She'd simply ignore the siren song because she was civilized, not a cave girl, and she had a lot to lose—the love of a very good man.

"You sleep tight," he replied. "Bye."

"Bye," she whispered.

Fudge. She clicked off and stared at the ceiling. Harrison was done playing the guitar now. She wondered where he was. She couldn't hear a thing from Weezie's or Gage's rooms. Was Harrison in the bathroom brushing his teeth? Or maybe he was getting ready to take a shower. The pipes here were in miserable shape. He'd told her he'd take his shower at night so they wouldn't have to fight over hot water in the morning.

Her imagination switched on like a movie projector and produced an unwelcome image of her walking into the bathroom and slipping into the shower stall with him.

Stop.

She turned over to face the wall, shut her eyes, and tried to be thankful that Dubose was going to fix those same water pipes next year. He was thoughtful. And thorough. He'd make an excellent husband.

But she couldn't sleep. The wedding was on her mind. Weezie and school. Harrison and his sexiness. Carmela and her store that would have to close soon. Her own U-pick business. Gage and his new house. The dogs and going to the vet for their shots. Dubose and all the work he was doing in New York.

Harrison, asleep next door.

Dubose's mother drinking tea in England.

Dubose and the shock he'd feel when he came home and the wedding was in shambles.

An hour passed. Two.

Was Harrison asleep? Or was he tossing and turning like her? Who could she talk to? Who?

It was all too much.

Go, something inside her whispered. It was her studio voice, the one that took over at the most inconvenient times.

She slid out of bed, crept down the hall, and opened a skinny door that looked like a linen closet. But it led to the attic, to Honey's old music room—with an electronic keyboard, Honey's ukulele, her old vinyl 1940s albums, and a turntable. True had converted it into a studio. When she got to the top of the stairs, she flipped on the light and breathed in deeply.

Ah, the smell up here—paint, canvas, fabric, varnish, wood, and old memories—always revived her. Gave her new ideas. Hope.

She walked carefully, knowing exactly where the creaking floorboards were, and spent two hours sifting through her canvases and then sketching a new idea for a collage—the one of Harrison with all his fans in Atlanta.

She got on her knees with her notepad and sketched another possible scene on the floor in a beam of moonlight. This one was of the dogs and Gage watching TV together in the front parlor.

Yes. Yes, yes, yes.

And then she was done for the night. She laid her pencil aside and felt the peace and strength seep into her bones. Her body was ready to rest. Her mind was calm, clear. The house, dignified and quiet, reminded her of her purpose. It was the house that Dubose was going to help her save. It would become their family home. Her children would sleep, eat, run, and dream here.

Tomorrow, she told herself. Tomorrow, she would fix this wedding problem once and for all, and she'd do it for her future husband. He'd done so much for her.

She treaded carefully down the stairs and closed the attic door behind her. When she got to her room, she saw Harrison's closed door. Unbelievable, to think that he was here. He made a great subject for a canvas. He was the quintessential country music star—a fantasy man, not husband material. He could wave his magic wand (magic guitar?) and he'd make all her wedding problems go away.

But she wouldn't use his help.

She was a magic woman.

When she remembered to be.

When True woke up the next morning, she knew instantly what she had to do. She must go see Penn's best friend,

Lila Dunworth. She lived on the water in a big mansion next to Rosewood, the Waring estate. Before anyone came downstairs—even Gage, who was an early riser—she slipped out the back door and walked quietly to her car. She knew Lila would be awake. Penn always said she exercised at six in the morning then went straight to her garden. She was a renowned botanical specialist. But she was known also as a supreme hostess. Once she'd even appeared on NPR to talk about the art of throwing a good party. She'd written a book on the subject, too. So she would definitely know every caterer in the area.

"How are you this morning?" Lila asked her when she showed up in her backyard flower garden. True had texted her to make sure it was all right that she came over.

"Worried." True followed behind her into a small glassed-in porch at the back of the house. Lila indicated a chair, and she sank into it. "Thanks so much for seeing me."

"My pleasure." Lila was always the lady but never particularly warm. She wore casual L.L. Bean–style clothes—ironed jeans and a floral cotton blouse with a pair of English garden clogs—and tons of gold jewelry. Her white-blond hair was swept up in a chignon and sprayed into place.

"Did you talk to Penn about the wedding before she went to England?" True asked her.

"No." Lila had a soft, elegant voice. "I was in Augusta teaching a workshop on how to serve lunch to the press before the Masters. I missed her. Is something going on? You don't look too well, to tell the truth."

True smiled weakly. "I'm not getting much sleep, that's why." She proceeded to tell Lila what had happened with the caterer and venue. "I wondered if there's anything you can do, please, to help me get them back?"

Lila sighed. "If Penn can't, then I can't, either."

"Can you help me get someone else then, please? You

know everyone. I looked through your entertaining book this morning, and it's marvelous how extensive your network of connections is."

Lila smiled, but it didn't reach her eyes. "No one will help you this late in the game. They have reputations to protect. How can any caterer put forth his or her best effort if the wedding date is so close?"

"But wouldn't that prove how good they are? Wouldn't word spread like wildfire that they're amazing under pressure?"

Lila shook her head. "It's the busy season. No one can afford to take that risk. Not only that, they don't need to. They have too many clients as it is."

True inhaled deeply. "So . . . you can't help me?"

Lila walked to a small desk, wrote something on a piece of paper, and handed it to her. "These two women are gardening friends of mine from Augusta who've moved out to Seabrook Island. I'll call them and see if they can have lunch with you. But I wouldn't count on anything. They sometimes help me put together parties for large crowds. On a lark. They're premier hostesses in their own right."

"Thank you." Any lead was a good thing.

Lila came back a few minutes later. "They'll meet you at Magnolia's in downtown Charleston at eleven thirty."

"Perfect. Thank you, Lila!" True wanted to hug her, but she wouldn't dare. She noticed there'd been no tut-tutting about the absolute awfulness of the situation. Nothing warm or sympathetic in Lila's manner. But their families had known each other forever. Didn't she have any sense of nostalgia and desire to help based on that alone?

She's like Penn, True thought. And had the horrible feeling that neither one of them liked her. How could she have not noticed before? But she comforted herself with the thought that Mama had come across as a cold fish, too, yet she'd loved True. She'd simply been unable to show it very well.

True to form, Lila merely stood in the doorway of her home and watched True drive away with a standard polite smile on her face.

At lunch, the two women greeted her warmly. One was silver-haired and wore smart designer eyeglasses and wide pants, like Katharine Hepburn. The other was probably mid-thirties, with curly auburn hair and a '50s kitsch appeal about her. Maybe it was her pale yellow pencil skirt, formfitting white blouse, and matching plaid hair band. They asked question after question about what True was looking for.

"Elegant finger food," she told them. Southerners generally didn't have sit-down dinners at their wedding receptions. "Open bar. The best of everything. For two hundred fifty people. And I'll need a spectacular place, one to showcase a string quartet and a band. Of course, we'll need a dance floor, too."

They didn't seem fazed by any of her desires. She felt hope. Huge hope. And then over coffee at the conclusion of the meal, the silver-haired one said, "I'm afraid we can't help you."

The other one nodded in agreement.

True's eyes widened in shock. "Are . . . are you sure?" She looked back and forth between them. Sunlight streamed through the large bay window facing East Bay Street and sparkled off the older woman's glasses. "You seemed so interested. And you didn't even confer with each other before saying no. What happened?"

"We really wanted to try Magnolia's since it's been re-styled," said the younger one.

"What?" True stared at her in disbelief.

The older one patted True's hand. "And offer you our sympathy."

"Of course," said the younger one. "I meant that, too."

"Thanks," True said. *For nothing.*

"You poor bride," the Katharine Hepburn one murmured. "There's no way you'll be able to pull off what you're looking for in the amount of time you have."

"Perhaps you should change direction." The younger one languidly stirred a little cream into her coffee. "We think you should elope."

"It'll be the only way to save face," said the older one. "People will find it charming and stylish if you do it right. And you have no other option as far as I can see."

"But how will she get the word out in time?" Her copper-haired friend leaned on her fist and looked suitably curious.

"She'll need to start now," the bespectacled one said. "It will require a quickly drawn-up card at the stationery store. And then a mass mailing."

"Not Paperless Post?" said the younger one.

"Not in Charleston, honey." The older one lowered her spectacles and chuckled. "We should buy stock in all the stationery stores around here. They'll never go out of business. We can go with her right now and help her pick out a card." She looked expectantly at True. "You don't have a moment to waste, dear."

True picked up her pocketbook, her fingers trembling, and pulled out thirty dollars to cover her portion of the meal and tip. She placed it on the table. "No, thank you. I don't know what to say, other than good-bye." She turned and walked away, almost colliding with a waiter.

"Good-bye," the older woman called after her.

"And good luck," the younger one chimed in.

Of all the nerve!

It took True the full thirty-five-minute drive back to Biscuit Creek to calm down.

She was utterly miserable all afternoon and hid at the

public library. She couldn't go home and face Harrison. She knew he'd have too many questions. And she also didn't want to talk to Carmela. True didn't want to bother her at work. She also dreaded hearing what her best friend would say. What if she agreed with those women that eloping was the best thing?

Perhaps it was. She'd already mentioned that as a possibility to Penn. She didn't mind for herself. But she knew that Penn would think she'd failed. And Dubose . . . well, he'd be seriously disappointed.

But what could she do?

Nothing.

She needed to call him ASAP. So she gathered her courage and did just that. But all afternoon, his phone went to voice mail.

"Call me when you can," she told his mailbox recording. "We need to talk about the wedding." She tried not to inject any panic into her tone.

She couldn't hide forever from Harrison. Late that afternoon they got ready to drive Weezie to Trident Tech's evening open house.

"I forgot to tell you," said Weezie. "You meet all the teachers and tour the place, and then there's some kind of barbecue afterward."

"Good," True said. "We won't have to worry about dinner." She looked at Gage. "Carmela said she's coming by with her special lasagna."

"She is?" Gage's brows shot up.

"That's mighty nice of her," Harrison said.

It really was. If True didn't know any better, she'd think Carmela was trying to impress Gage. First a pie, and now a lasagna? She stole a swift glance at Harrison's brother. He *was* really handsome. But from all accounts, he barely spoke to Carmela at the store. And Carmela had never mentioned him before yesterday. Maybe she had a thing for Harrison and just didn't want to say so.

"I'm meeting my friends after the tour at the barbecue," Weezie said. "The people I want to room with. Remember?"

"You're not rooming with anyone," True reminded her. "You're staying with me and Dubose at his mother's guesthouse while Maybank Hall undergoes some renovations. Then you'll come back here to live with us."

"No, I won't," said Weezie, a stubborn light in her eyes. "If I have to, I'll work to make my rent. And I'll also pay my tuition if you won't. I'm not your daughter. And Dubose isn't my father. He's *your* problem, not mine." She flipped her hair over her shoulder. "That's my final say for today."

That last part was her latest talk show sign-off. A few weeks ago, it had been: *We got this, Biscuit Creek,* followed by a wink.

True refrained from rolling her eyes. "Can we talk about this later? I was ready to go, but I've just now decided I need to wear something a little snazzier to match Harrison."

He looked justifiably proud. "You do that. But I'm a stickler for being on time. It's the one OCD trait Gage and I share. So no dawdling. You'd look gorgeous in a paper bag anyway."

True tried to let her annoyance at his bossiness outweigh the fluttery, flattered sensation she felt at his outrageous compliment, but it was a struggle. When she got back downstairs exactly four minutes and twenty seconds later, Gage was busy straightening the dogs on the porch. They'd been lying in a heap, but now their wet noses— mostly black, although Ed's looked like a red rubber eraser—were all lined up in a pretty row.

"Whoa," Harrison said. "You look great."

"Thanks." True tried her best not to blush, but she felt the heat creep up her neck.

"Shall we?" He held out his arms—one to each woman—and escorted them to the Maserati.

True didn't know why she felt as if this were a date. It definitely wasn't, especially with Weezie in the mix. But she was ready for someone else to take charge for a little while so she could stew in her misery.

Weezie wanted to do something similar. She sat in the backseat with her iPod turned up too high and her ear-buds firmly plugged into her ears, her expression a combination of resentment and nerves. Slowly, True noticed in the visor mirror, it gave way to absorption in her music. Thank God. She didn't know what she was going to do with that girl.

"No way she can live on her own," she said to Harrison in low tones.

"You think not?" In the confined space of the car he was bursting with more than his usual masculine appeal—which was already huge—in his navy blazer, collared white silk shirt (which he wore open one-button-too-many), chunky cuff links at his wrists, khaki pants, tasseled loafers, and very subtle cologne. It was the southern man's uniform. Ben Silver had done him right. But that dangerous extra button he'd undone, along with his long hair and new stubble, added an insouciance that proclaimed him his own man.

"I think it would be disastrous," she said. "Hey, what about your disguise?"

"I *am* disguised," he said, and pulled a pair of John Lennon wireframes out of his jacket pocket and put them on. "I'm Terence Jones, a man who looks a lot like Harrison Gamble. It's my out-in-the-open disguise. Risky, but sometimes necessary when large hats and dark sunglasses won't fly. Terence is gay. So keep that in mind if you try to have your way with me in a broom closet at the open house. It'll be an epic fail."

"Aw, shucks," she said sarcastically, but inside she was still mortified about how obvious she'd been at the beach house, yearning after him like a desperate fan.

He chuckled.

"Well, I hope Terence Jones works for you." She kept her tone airy so he wouldn't guess that inside she was still a seething cauldron of feelings for him. "We'll need to get Weezie in on the act."

"I already have. When you ran upstairs to change outfits, I talked to her about not giving you a hard time tonight. I also said that if she wants to live on her own, she needs to prove her trustworthiness to you. She totally agreed."

"Oh?" True could handle Weezie herself. But as she'd asked Harrison to accompany them tonight for moral support, she couldn't very well complain when he butted in, now, could she? Nevertheless, she was slightly irritated. "By the bye," she said testily, "your hair looks better than mine."

"I disagree. Yours is a marvel, all shiny and swingy with that little flip on the end."

Once more she refused to be flattered, but that silly feeling came back anyway, the one that craved him noticing everything about her—then kissing her senseless.

What was her problem?

"But I'll pass on the compliment to Biscuit Creek's own barber, Henry Carter, anyway," Harrison went on. "He's never heard the term *hair product* in his life. Which reminds me, I've had a good day with the locals. When it comes down to it, not a one of 'em thinks I'm a big deal. And I love it. Old Mrs. Finch, who has enough medical issues to warrant opening a hospital in her honor, made me carry her empty basket while she picked out her ripe tomatoes one by one. Now, that was a good time. I know more about the perils of improper digestion than I ever thought possible. You need to buy more food with fiber, by the way. I did a quick rundown of your cupboards."

"Fiber's not my problem." True sighed. "I still haven't heard back from Dubose. We've got to talk." And she told Harrison all about Lila and her two friends from Seabrook Island.

"Whoa," he said. "They should have brought popcorn and candy if they were just coming into town to be entertained by you."

"I know. But they reminded me of an idea I already had. Dubose and I can elope."

Harrison frowned. "Is that what you really want to do?"

"I honestly don't care. This big wedding—that was more for Penn and Dubose than me."

"But don't you want your friends there? I hope I'm invited."

She closed her eyes a second. "Of course, you're not invited. No offense."

He made another face. "Why not? I'm in town. I'm not going to cause any trouble."

"Harrison"—True laid her hand on his arm—"I'm sorry, but Dubose doesn't like you. You know that."

"But if *you* do, I should be able to come. Or are you letting him call all the shots?"

"People will talk."

"Oh, really?"

"Yes, really."

"I don't know why. It's not as if we had a big relationship or anything."

She met his eyes. Behind the John Lennon frames, they were glinting with humor. But there was something else there, too. It would always be there between them, that night at the Isle of Palms. She remembered the insistent beckoning of his rebel's body to her very proper one, a primal drumbeat she couldn't resist, calling her to carnal revolution.

She'd become a soldier of love, all right. But the next day, she'd deserted him.

The old pain welled up, and she looked out her passenger-side window, not willing to see even his profile. Not wanting to be ashamed again of her betrayal.

But she'd been so young. So very young. And he'd asked so much, *too* much, as if she were this larger-than-life person who didn't live in the real world. As if she didn't have to listen to any rules but those governing her own heart. He'd treated her . . .

As if she were a painter in the attic who made wild canvases and needed to show them to the world.

She leaned her forehead against her window and watched the asphalt roadway pass on by.

CHAPTER TWENTY-ONE

"Hi, Terence Jones," Harrison said as he shook the hand of the provost at Trident Technical College. *Watch out*, he wanted to tell her, *you have a firecracker on your hands. And we expect her to have every opportunity to excel while she's with you.*

The woman was a looker in her fifties, he guessed. A swirl of blond hair framed sharp eyes and a confident mouth outlined in deep burgundy lipstick. "Don't worry, Mr. Jones. Your daughter—"

"Goddaughter," he lied equably.

"Your *god*daughter"—the provost kept the handshake going—"is going to love Trident Technical College."

"She's got big plans," he said. "Two years of general ed courses here, and then on to the University of South Carolina's broadcasting school. We're hoping the Trident experience will give her the wings she needs to succeed there."

The provost nodded. "She'll gain all sorts of know-how and confidence in the program here and blow them away at USC. They love our students. And you tell your goddaughter that if she ever has a problem, she can come straight to my office."

"Thank you for that." His knees were almost weak with relief.

"I mean it sincerely." She angled her head. "Has anyone ever told you . . . ?"

"Yes, ma'am." He almost winked, but he was still a little rattled from how incredibly emotional he was about Weezie, her plans—hell, her growing up. "I've never met the guy, but supposedly we're distant cousins. On the Jones side. The Aiken branch of the family."

"No fooling." She finally let his hand go and leaned close. "Don't worry, Mr. Gamble," she murmured. "Your secret is safe with me."

Shit.

But then he realized he was actually glad that she was so damned on the ball.

"Thanks," he whispered. He felt really good about this place. He moved on down the line behind Weezie and Truc, repeating the same Terence Jones story to anyone who asked. There were a few who didn't—always a relief.

"Terence?" True inquired politely. She reminded him of a daffodil in her pale yellow dress, formfitting until you got to the puffy skirt that ended mid-thigh. Sexy as hell.

"Yeeesss?" he drawled with a little more color than he usually did. Might as well play Terence up, do the fictitious man proud.

"Mrs. Bangor, the head of the culinary department, would like to talk to you." True smiled prettily at him, but her eyes signaled that she was upset, which meant that she was either secretly begging him to cooperate—or secretly begging him *not* to cooperate.

It was a conundrum for the ages, so he'd go on instinct.

Mrs. Bangor, who was short, round, and fond of large floral prints, grinned broadly at him. "Young man, you're the spittin' image of Harrison Gamble."

He gave her the spiel.

"I don't care who you really are, Mr. Jones," she said.

"We're doing a foodie calendar to raise money for the school. Would you be Mr. January? That's a high honor. We'd want you to pose with some of our students' desserts. They make a credible homemade MoonPie *and* Twinkie."

He feigned confusion. "MoonPies and Twinkies?"

"You know," she said, "there's a song called 'Snack on This.' Harrison Gamble sings it. About people's favorite snacks. MoonPies and Twinkies are mentioned."

Harrison scratched his temple. "That's the connection?" He shrugged. "I'm a fan of opera and baroque music. So I wouldn't know. But sure, I'll be glad to pose. I assume you mean discreetly unclothed."

Mrs. Bangor's face turned red. "No. No, indeed. You'd wear clothes." She paused. "But maybe we should reconsider that."

He winked at her. "You just let me know what you decide, Mrs. Bangor. I'll be prepared either way. My goddaughter Weezie Maybank can serve as my contact."

Mrs. Bangor beamed. "Excellent."

True tugged on his sleeve after they moved past Mrs. Bangor. "What if you're not here?" she whispered in his ear.

"I'll fly back in," he whispered back. "I've always wanted to be Mr. January."

True's pretty mouth puckered. "Are you ever serious about anything?"

"Not lately," he said. "Are you ever *not* serious about anything?"

She frowned at him. "This is Weezie's future we're talking about."

"And I just won her major points with the school."

"With Mrs. Bangor, maybe. But what's going to happen to Weezie when everyone figures out you really are Harrison Gamble? Because they will eventually."

He shrugged. "How could that hurt her?"

True blinked. "They won't treat her like Weezie any-more. She'll be known as Harrison Gamble's goddaugh-ter. You're a celebrity. Whoever hangs out with you is always going to be in your shadow."

He stared at her a second. "So basically, I'm a liabil-ity."

She paused. "No, not that exactly."

"A dark cloud?"

"No. Well, sort of. But that sounds so mean."

"You ever heard of projection?" he asked her.

"Of course."

"I think maybe you're worried about *you*, not Weezie. You're not stepping out into the sunshine for whatever reason—maybe Dubose or his mother is casting you in the shade. And it's easier to pick on me and the horrible effects I could have on everyone else's chances to shine than to look at your own issues. I'm calling bullshit, how-ever. There's no way that people won't recognize Weez-ie's awesomeness on her own terms. She won't let that happen."

True's already petite chest seemed to cave in a little.

A minute later, they finished the line.

Weezie was waiting for them, her whole body shim-mering with joy at being there. "Terence! True!" she said. "This is so great. Only a month to go. I really need to start apartment—"

Harrison waggled his eyebrows to jolt her memory.

It was their secret signal. She clamped her mouth shut. He'd told her they'd discuss it later. *Not* today. If she stayed within the bounds of socially acceptable behavior her entire first semester, he'd buy her a car.

All because when True was upstairs changing outfits, he and Weezie had had quite a productive discussion.

"You know what those socially acceptable boundaries are," he'd said to her. "I know all about having a stage persona, too. But I leave it there in the concert hall. You're going to make a great talk show host someday. But one thing you haven't figured out is that you're bigger than your work passion. You have family and friends, and they matter even more. If you had to choose between True and being a talk show host, which would you choose?"

"True," Weezie had said instantly.

"See? And if someone told me to choose between a hit single and Gage, I'd choose Gage." He'd choose True, too, but he wasn't going to go there. With Weezie *or* himself.

Weezie seemed to be getting it.

"This means you're going to save your tell-all interviews for a studio set," he'd advised her. "When you're at home or at school, be Weezie, the sister, the friend, the intellectual, the *Star Trek* fan. That girl is a joy to be around. You always made my day brighter when I'd come over and water your mother's plants all those years ago. Am I making sense to you?"

"Yes. I really, *really* get it." She'd hugged him to prove her point.

He'd hugged her back. He'd seen it in her eyes—she was soaking it up.

"And to help you remember that your talk show side is only part of who you are," he'd said, "I'm going to buy a car for Weezie, the friend."

"Really?"

"As a little girl, you liked the color blue more than anything else. And you constantly showed me the sky because you wanted me to enjoy it along with you."

"I remember, too."

"So if True says it's all right—because we can't go forgetting she's your sister and really cares about you—I'm getting you a blue car. And it's gonna have a personalized plate that says THING ONE, because that was my nickname for you back then. Are you on board with that?"

She'd jumped into his arms. "Yessirree, Thing Two!"

Now Thing One—Weezie—was doing her best to appear docile in the large, drafty multipurpose room at Trident Tech, her hands folded in front of her, a not-so-believable Mona Lisa smile on her lips. That girl was dying to walk around the room and play Oprah. Or Kelly. Or Rachael Ray. God bless her for trying just to be Weezie.

True didn't seem to notice her sister's subdued attitude. She looked around the room with her left eyebrow raised a fraction of an inch. Not all the students looked particularly wholesome. There was the biker chick. A guy who looked a little like Charles Manson. And an older man wearing a *Rugrats* shirt. The usual suspects you'd find at a community college: good people who needed a break, some of whom needed advice about making a positive first impression.

"All right," Harrison said sweetly, "why don't we check out all the buildings? And we'll head on over to the barbecue after that?"

"Fine," said True. She was barely listening.

Weezie flipped her hair off her shoulders and walked proudly in front of them.

He squeezed True's elbow. "A little pep from you would go a long way. There's nothing to be afraid of. You've brought her up right. She's got a good head on her shoulders. She's gonna do great."

"How do you know she will?" True murmured.

"Because the provost has it going on. And that's Weezie's nature—to thrive. Why don't you trust in the universe a little bit more?"

"I did. And it took my parents before their time."

He sighed inwardly. He couldn't make True believe anything she didn't want to. And for all he knew, Weezie would forget everything they'd talked about. All he could do was try to help. The same way he'd tried to help

Gage. If they blew him off, then there was nothing he could do.

It was frustrating to see people he cared about suffer. But he'd learned to live with it by packing his bag and leaving.

Nothing like becoming a country music star because you have a God complex and no one else will play along with you. He'd had to create his own little kingdom where he was ruler, and it was working out pretty good. Except for the studio always breathing down his neck. And the total lack of privacy.

And the loneliness.

As the evening progressed, True did all the right things with Weezie: Expressing admiration for the beautiful new library. Wondering along with her if all her teachers were going to be friendly. Reassuring Weezie that no matter what, she'd survive as long as she put her studies first. After they'd explored everywhere they could—including locating the parking lot for students—they headed to the large reception area, where a bunch of serving tables were set up with the smell of hickory-smoked barbecue strong in the air.

"Mmm, that smells good," he said to the ladies.

Weezie followed him and True to join the line. "I hope they have barbecued tofu."

Harrison kind of doubted it. But then, wonder of wonders, there was tofu spinach salad for the vegetarians among them.

They found seats across from the buffet at a section of tables decorated with red-and-white-checkered throwaway plastic tablecloths. The centerpieces were made of silk sunflowers stuck into a ribbon-wrapped foam base with a little scarecrow stuck on the side. The decorations were cute but not over-the-top, striking just the right note with parents who'd rather the school spend its money on teacher salaries and student resources anyway.

A disc jockey was setting up. Harrison looked for a dance floor and saw one in a dim corner, a couple of barn-style lanterns glowing overhead.

"It's not even fall yet," said Weezie, poking at the centerpiece. "But they know we all want it to be."

Her enthusiasm made mush out of Harrison's heart. He shared a glance with True. She felt it, too. Here her sister was so proud and excited to go to college, to figure out her future.

He remembered when he was Weezie's age—depressed and starving. But he knew he'd been on the right track, too, heartache or no, so it had all been worth it.

"Do you remember feeling the way she does now?" he asked True.

"Yes," she said. "I do."

He heard a little sadness in her tone. "It's not too late to do what you want to do. It's never too late." He bit into a huge barbecue sandwich loaded with pickles, so he wouldn't look like a know-it-all.

She pushed some barbecue around her plate and seemed to be thinking of what to say back when another family joined them.

When everyone introduced themselves, no one questioned his Terence Jones persona. Their student was a skinny young man with a farmer's tan coming from Berkeley County, where he'd been working construction.

"But I want to be a radiological technician," he told Weezie. "Medicine is a surefire way to stay employed. And I like big machines that can see right through your body."

"Cool," said Weezie. "I want to be a talk show host."

The boy's mother chuckled. "That's an interesting job. Not many of those around."

"You might as well just run off to Hollywood," the father said. "What's the point of school?"

"It takes more than natural talent," Weezie replied. "It takes connections in the business and technical expertise. I can't get those by waiting tables in Hollywood and waiting for my big break. I need to be in school."

Damn, Harrison was proud of her. She didn't get annoyed with the naysayers, and her answer made such good sense. She had what it took. He sensed it, having entered a profession himself where doubters proliferated.

"If anyone can become a talk show host"—True laid her hand over her sister's—"Weezie can."

His two girls—he knew he shouldn't call them that, but he couldn't help himself—shared a special look, and Harrison, who was a geek at heart, mentally high-fived himself.

As the meal wound down, the disc jockey introduced himself, the lights dimmed, and the music began. "Play That Funky Music" got some of the crowd up on their feet and over to the dance floor. Their tablemates stood and said good-bye—they couldn't stay. The boy had to get up at four AM to go to work on a new road.

After they'd left, Weezie gazed over the room. "I'm glad I'm coming here. I like it, and I don't care that it's not New York or Atlanta. I'll get to those markets someday."

Markets. Harrison shared another secret look with True. Weezie had a clear vision of what she wanted to do. It was cute. And impressive.

"Good," True told her sister. "There's no need to rush into total independence at one fell swoop. Take it one step at a time. That's sensible."

Weezie looked down at her plate. "I really wanted to"—she looked up at Harrison, and he could tell she was fighting a mighty war within herself—"I really wanted to thank you for taking me here tonight. And showing me such support."

True put her hand on her heart. "Weezie, we love you." True looked at him. "Harrison believes, just like I do"— *Yes, you're on the right track*—"that you're going to succeed at whatever you put your mind to do. I want you to be independent. And if things go well for you this first semester, we can think about letting you get an apartment after Christmas."

"Really?"

True nodded and smiled, her mouth showing signs of strain but maybe some excitement, too. "I know you said you'd go ahead and rent your own apartment now. But if you could be patient just one semester, I'll be able to help you with the rent. You're brave to take on the expense on your own, but wouldn't it be nice if you could work because you want to, not because you have to? That's a lot of stress."

Weezie nodded. "That makes sense. But I'm going to be stressed living with you and Dubose in his mother's guesthouse. You're going to be on one long honeymoon. I don't relish being a third wheel. And you know I don't even *like* him. That'll make it worse."

Harrison wisely said nothing.

"It's not going to be like that," True promised her. "I don't want you ever to feel uncomfortable in your living space. And Dubose won't want you to feel that way, either." She grabbed Weezie's hand again. "Please give him a chance."

Harrison felt a little guilty for enjoying True's discomfiture. But not too guilty.

Weezie looked down at the table. "All right," she muttered, and won points with him for responding within the bounds of socially acceptable behavior. "I see Jamie, one of my friends I want to get an apartment with. I'm going to dance." She pushed her chair back.

"All right," True said. "Will you bring her over later to say hello?"

"It's a guy," Weezie said.

"A *guy*?" True called after her, then looked at Harrison. "Over my dead body."

"What do you mean? What if it's a three- or four-bedroom apartment? It would be nice to have a guy around to change lightbulbs and take out the garbage. Plus, maybe a guy's presence would fend off would-be intruders."

True's expression was so bereft, Harrison took pity on her. He put his hand on the back of her neck. "Hey," he said, "she's a Maybank. She's made of tough stuff."

"Actually, she's not a Maybank, at least by blood," True said quietly. "Mama got pregnant by another man. I don't know who he was, though."

"You're kidding me."

True shook her head. She wasn't looking at him—her eyes were on the dance floor. "I found out when I was little. I was eavesdropping on the stairs and heard Mama and Daddy fighting. Not that it matters. We're sisters, and she was raised to fight, not roll over. Mama and Daddy may have stifled us in many ways, but they did endow us with the sense that we don't quit when the going gets rough."

"Exactly." He caressed her back, and barely even realized it. He'd comfort anyone this way. "She'll do great."

He was looking at the dance floor, too. Weezie was having the time of her life dancing with a guy wearing a black-and-white-striped scarf and tight black jeans. His hair was dyed orange. But she was also dancing with a girl dressed in a nondescript dress and comfortable shoes. She appeared not to have a lot of money to spend on fashion. Or maybe she just didn't care.

"Look at her," he murmured. The kids were all laughing together. "She's holding her own."

"Yes," True said.

"I hope knowing your mother's secret wasn't a big burden on you all these years."

She sighed. "No, not really. But it did make me somewhat afraid."

"Of what?"

"Of being bad. Rebelling. Daddy was so very sad and upset . . ."

"But that was between them," he said. "It shouldn't affect your choices."

"I know. But there was Honey, too, punished her whole life for being herself."

"She still managed to have a heckuva good time. She didn't let it bother her. Maybe you care too much what other people think." He sat quietly a few seconds and hoped his point sank in. "Will you ever tell Weezie about her origins?"

True tugged at her paper napkin. "I think she has the right to know who her father is. But until we find out, I'm not even considering it."

"Are you actively trying to figure out who he is?"

She shook her head. "I don't see the point. I'm afraid it would shake her up badly. And she's doing so well right now."

"I agree." He stood and reached out his hand. "Come on. Let's go dance. We need to celebrate. Not stress. Weezie's on her way."

True laughed. "She is, isn't she? The world had better watch out."

"Amen." He drew her up and wrapped her hand in his arm. A lot of people looked their way, so he exuded the worldly opera lover Terence Jones as best he could. Surely they were admiring True and not wondering if he was

Harrison Gamble. She was breathtaking whatever she wore, but tonight she was a real stunner.

They made sure to steer clear of Weezie when they got out on the dance floor. A current pop hit was playing, but they caught only the tail end, just long enough for Harrison to make a fool of himself, folding his arms behind his head and rolling his belly.

"Stop!" True was laughing so hard that when the song ended, she leaned on his chest to catch her breath. "You're an idiot sometimes."

"I'm Terence Jones," he said, not cracking a smile.

"See you at the table." She grinned and pushed off his chest, not giving him the time of day anymore. She used to do that when they were kids, too. She'd be all played out and want to go home. But he always managed to get her back.

"Crazy," by Patsy Cline, started playing, and Harrison grabbed her hand. "You're not escaping. This song's too good to sit down to."

She pursed her lips a little.

"It sure is refreshing to be rebuffed so openly." He paused a beat. "*Not.*"

"Do all country music superstars have such fragile egos?" Reluctantly, she lifted her arms around his neck.

Yowza, was all he could think. True Maybank's arms were around his neck for the first time in ten years. And it felt better then he ever thought it would.

"Yes," he said, "it's a prerequisite for the job. It's the only way we can feel tortured enough to write our music."

"You weren't tortured when you wrote 'Snack on This.' That's a happy little song."

He thought back to when he'd written it. He'd been on autopilot—no particular challenges, nothing special going on in his personal or work life. "It's a fun song," he said. "But I wrote it when I was missing you and the boys and Sand Dollar Heaven and all the fun we had in the old days. When we could get happy just buying a candy bar at the pharmacy."

Wyatt's. It was such a great place with its spinning leather stools and that big counter to lean on. A boy felt like a man there. You could buy hot dogs, ice cream, soda, and candy with the loose change in your pocket. All you had to do was turn in all the Cheerwine and Coke cans and bottles you found on the side of the road, and in a week or two, you'd have enough to treat yourself. And best of all, if you didn't have any money, Mr. Wyatt never chased you away if you hung out underneath the striped awning with the other broke kids.

As Patsy sang her heart out, True smiled a little dreamily. "I remember. The first time I ever talked to you was outside Wyatt's. I was walking into the store with Mama. Gage said something funny."

"The boys and I were talking about car engines. But then out of the blue Gage said, 'Take the *D* off the front of Dunkin' Donuts and put it at the end, and it's Unkind Donuts."

They both laughed at the memory.

True pulled back and looked up at him, her eyes twinkling the same way they had that long-ago afternoon. "I remember I said, 'I didn't know you had such a funny brother, Harrison Gamble.' And then Mama dragged me into the store."

God, he remembered that, too. It was like a lightning bolt had gone straight through his body.

"And that was that." He pulled her under his chin again. "We became best friends. Crabbing, swimming, playing in the woods."

She sighed. "The simple pleasures of life are always the best."

Yeah, like holding you, Harrison wanted to say. A sense

of nostalgia gripped him, so strong he had to close his eyes. Not just for their childhood, but for that special night at the beach.

Their night—

That had slipped through their fingers.

Had they been crazy to let it go?

True leaned her head carefully on his chest. He burrowed his chin into her hair—God, the feel of her against him!—and let the music take them back to the last time he was happy.

But Patsy's voice eventually drifted away. People around them began to pull apart. The disc jockey got on the microphone and promised that a door prize would be picked soon.

In the midst of the laughter and chatter, True's eyes shone with something that made Harrison feel whole. What was it? And why did he want it so badly?

"Harrison?" she whispered like a question.

He was an inch away from kissing her when one of his older hits began to play: "Truckload of Promises." He wrote it two years after he'd last seen her. He'd been hungry for success. It muffled the heartache. She'd made her choice, and it hadn't been him.

> *Riding high on the seat,*
> *Your laughter's low and sweet*
> *And you swear you'll be faithful till the end,*
> *But we know, me and you,*
> *That your promises ain't true.*
> *They won't last till we drive around the bend . . .*

As he heard his own voice singing, he thought, *My career.*

My music.

True's lips parted.

Her wedding.

And he pulled back. But just barely.

"We should sit down." He barely got out the words.

"Okay," she murmured back.

And they wended their way back to the table, separate but close, the bright lights away from the dance floor making Harrison squint behind his John Lennon glasses.

At the table, True put her chin in her hand—her eyes not on him but on Weezie, still on the dance floor—and sang along with the chorus:

> *Truckload a' promises don't take me very fur,*
> *Hard work, not lies, will see me through.*
> *I got a world to see while strummin' my guitar,*
> *Truckload a' promises won't do . . .*

The irony struck him deep. Did she have any idea the song was about her? 'Cause it was.

But tonight he'd figured something else out, and it wasn't pretty.

It was about him, too.

CHAPTER TWENTY-TWO

On their way home from the open house, True signaled to Weezie in her visor mirror to take out her earbuds. Weezie looked extra content, probably because her night had gone really well, unlike True's.

There was no way she could pretend this time there wasn't something sizzling just below the surface between her and Harrison. If it hadn't been for him and his restraint, she'd have kissed him on the dance floor. That was bad on her part. Very bad. She refused to blame him for any of it. It was *her* problem.

"What's up?" Weezie leaned forward between the two front seats.

"I know what I'm going to do for the wedding," True announced.

"Oh, yeah?" Harrison was being a little removed, as he should be.

And it was lucky for her that he was, because in that gap True had done some hard thinking and come up with a plan. A multifaceted one.

"We're still going to have the big wedding," she said. "But I got the number of the guy who catered tonight's event at Trident Tech, and we're going to have a barbecue picnic instead of a fancy finger food reception."

"You *are*?"

That was from Harrison. Was he happy for her? Or simply shocked that she'd made such a bold decision?

She was amazed herself. "He's going to get his wife to make up more of her tofu strawberry spinach salad for Weezie and whoever else doesn't like barbecue." Penn and her lofty expectations didn't matter anymore. Nor did Dubose's. Their wedding was on the line.

"I love you, Sister," Weezie said, which made True grin. "Where's the picnic going to happen?"

"At home." True felt so good saying that. "At Maybank Hall. Outside, beneath the two big oak trees."

"Hallelujah!" yelled Weezie. "Right, Harrison?" She held up her hand to high-five his.

He twisted his right hand around backward to complete the move. "This is big," he said, sounding über-serious.

Which scared True. It *was* a big deal. But if she was going to carry it off, she had to act like she could handle it. So she laughed. "I know. Right? It was staring me in the face the whole time. And tonight . . . it just all came together."

Thanks in large part to Harrison. What he'd said about the simple pleasures of life resonated. As did his suggesting that she cared too much what other people thought. What kind of example was she setting for Weezie, who needed to know that being herself was okay?

However, she wouldn't thank him specifically for influencing her. She couldn't afford to open those doors to close friendship again. Some people, she knew now, you simply can't be close to.

So instead she said, "Thank you both for your support," then smiled tentatively around the car, like a shy political candidate. She didn't think those existed. But if one did, he or she would look just the way she did right now.

"You're very welcome," Harrison said formally.

He got it, too, the fact that they had to back off from each other. She appreciated his diplomacy. And hated it at the same time.

Maybe he's acting cool because he's not happy about this wedding news, a secret part of her heart whispered. *Maybe he doesn't want you to marry Dubose.*

Wrong, wrong, wrong. He was plenty happy to see her settled. If he weren't, he'd have kissed her when he'd had the chance.

"I am *so* glad you've made this decision," Weezie told her. "Except for Dubose being there."

Harrison looked back in the rearview mirror. "I think your sister gets it, Weezie. You don't have to keep rubbing it in."

"All right." Weezie wore an abashed smile. "I'm just sayin'."

"I know you love True and want what's best for her." Harrison was acting so *mature* at the moment. It was quite unsettling. "But she's an adult. She makes her own decisions."

Yes, she did, although his saying so reminded her of some choices she'd made that she still had regrets about.

"Let me tell you about the cake," she said. Cake was always a happy topic.

"What about it?" Weezie hopped once on her seat.

"I talked to Mrs. Bangor, the head of the culinary department." True was excited at her own daring. "The students are going to make us cupcakes. Three hundred of them."

"Cupcakes!" Weezie squealed with delight. "So much better than a big ol' wedding cake! And from Trident Tech, too!"

"How about the music?" Harrison kept his eyes on the road.

"I'm canceling the string quartet." True felt no pangs of remorse. "It was supposed to play while everyone has a cocktail and some nibbles as they're waiting for us to finish up the wedding pictures." She loved baroque music, but this was a celebration. She wanted something more upbeat, from start to finish. *She* wanted. Not Dubose or Penn. "I'd like to find some fiddlers to play instead. I'm releasing the other band, too. I'm working on getting Booty Call."

"*Booty Call*?" Harrison inclined a brow.

True felt an unwelcome but wildly strong attraction hearing him say such a sexy phrase.

"You've been gone too long," Weezie told him. "They're a great cover band."

"Yes, they are." True tried to pretend it was Roger, the elderly busboy at Starfish, driving the car to provide relief from her incessant need to glance at Harrison, but it didn't work. "I checked their schedule on my phone, and that day they're free. Let's hope it's not for personal reasons. I already sent them an email, but I'll call them tomorrow. They'll get everyone going on the dance floor, for sure."

Weezie clapped her hands.

Harrison sent True a sideways glance. "Penn's just gonna love that."

"It's her fault if she has a bad time." *Let's get this show on the road* was True's new motto. She wanted past the uncertainty and straight to the wedding band on her finger. "This reception's going to be fun. I'm really hoping Booty Call will come through."

"What about Dubose?" asked Weezie.

True looked back at her sister. "He'll love it."

"Or else." Harrison chuckled rather wickedly.

Weezie cackled in the backseat.

True let them laugh. Harrison wasn't far wrong. If Dubose gave her grief about trying to save their wedding reception any way she possibly could, then they had a bigger problem to work on. "I'm calling the tent company tomorrow. Hopefully, they'll have tables, chairs, and a dance floor. If not, I'll find 'em somewhere."

"You done good," Weezie said.

"You've certainly figured things out," echoed Harrison politely.

"Thanks." True had a reluctant vision of a younger Harrison reaching across the front seat of his pickup truck and taking her hand, squeezing it hard, their fingers locked for miles and miles . . .

Her contentment.

Their bliss.

"I have an idea about the fiddlers," Harrison spoke up.

Which brought her down to earth again. Once again, he was helping her pull together her wedding to another man. "What is it?"

"We should talk to Cornelius Dearing," he said. "He lives up the creek on Pee Dee Island. I remember hanging out with him and his friends in high school. Great bunch of guys. One of 'em plays bass. They play washboard, too. I'll bet he's available. He's not big on paying gigs, but it's worth a shot."

"Thanks. I'll call him tomorrow."

"He probably doesn't have a phone. He lives pretty primitive. And that's a long way around by car. Forty minutes. But by kayak, it's only ten."

"Go by kayak," Weezie suggested. "Explore the pristine waters of Biscuit Creek. Reveal their secrets."

True sent her the proverbial stink eye. "Not everything and everybody has secrets to reveal."

"But the creek does for sure." Harrison sounded firm about that. "Tell you what, let's go on the paddleboards. Remember I said we'd use 'em?"

"Yes, but I really don't want to. Thanks." She wouldn't tell him in front of Weezie that he had to move out the next morning. Gage had issues with transition, and she was happy to have him, his TV, rug, and chair stay. Harrison could not. He could hole up in a hotel somewhere, and he'd be just fine. "I'll go by car. And—and you really don't have to come. You have those songs to write."

"It's no trouble. I can't miss visiting Cornelius after all these years. Especially as I'm not coming to the wedding."

"What do you mean, you're not coming to the wedding?" Weezie sounded as if she'd inhaled helium.

True braced herself. Let Harrison explain. She wasn't sure she could pull it off without making Dubose look bad. There was no need to upset Weezie, and Harrison was a whiz at spin.

"Dubose doesn't like me," he said into the silence. "So your sister says I'm not allowed to come."

True gasped. "Wait a minute."

"Are you kidding me?" Weezie screeched. "If you're not going, *I'm* not going. And that's no lie."

True twisted in her seat to look at her. "You're coming, sister o' mine. I don't know why *he*"—she tilted her head toward the offending party —"is trying to stir up trouble. It's perfectly natural to leave certain people off the invitation list."

"Like who?" Weezie demanded to know. Her expression was glacial.

"Like—" Shoot. She was getting herself into trouble. "—like, you know. Old, um, friends you haven't seen in years."

"Nuh-uh." Weezie's eyes narrowed. "People invite old friends all the time. Do you mean old boyfriends? Because Harrison was never your boyfriend. I remember Daddy getting down the shotgun. He said no debutante daughter of his was going to stay out all night with any boy, but especially with the boy who mowed our lawn."

True's face flamed red. "I told you to forget about that."

Weezie's eyes widened. "Wait. Did you two . . . *do* it? I was so young then. I didn't get it. But now I do. I know all about one-night stands and the wretched heartache that often follows. Not to mention secret babies."

Geez. If she only knew *she* was one of those.

Harrison didn't say a word. But he had an extremely smug look on his face. True wanted to put him in a room with nothing but a bowl of cold oatmeal. He was a Wild Thing, and she couldn't believe his audacity in using her sister as leverage to get invited to the wedding.

"This is one of those times when you're supposed to keep quiet," she told Weezie in steely tones. "You don't ask other people about their private lives."

"But you're my sister. And you're trying to exclude one of my very best friends from the wedding."

Harrison turned the wheel to the right, and they were heading up the dirt road leading to home.

True seethed inside. "I call the shots." She hoped Weezie was listening. "Harrison doesn't mind not going."

"Is that true?" Weezie asked him. "You won't be able to see me in my bridesmaid dress."

Harrison cleared his throat. "It's an unfortunate turn of events over which I have no control." He stole a sideways glance at True.

Such a martyr was the look she threw back at him. He was eating this up.

"You can be a wedding crasher," Weezie said. "Like those guys in the movie."

"I could." He put the car in park in front of the house. "But then your sister would never talk to me again. And I don't want that to happen. I'm glad I've renewed my friendship with the Maybank girls."

What a wholesome thing to say. Was he for real? Or was he trying to make her feel guilty?

Because she already did. Tomorrow she was going to tell him to get lost. But he deserved it. He *was* a trouble-maker, as Dubose warned her the day Harrison came back.

Before she knew it, he'd walked around the front of the car, opened her door for her, and held out his hand.

She took it, for the last time. "Thanks," she mumbled. Touching him still rocked her to her core. He definitely needed to go.

He waited to help Weezie out, too.

Damn him.

Harrison was, as much as True hated to admit it, a genuine gentleman. He was a thoughtful, mischievous one who made her laugh and would no doubt give her as much pleasure in bed now as he had that night on the sand at the Isle of Palms. He was rich. Successful in his field. He knew Brad Paisley and Tim McGraw. He and Tina Fey, of all people, were pals. George Clooney had invited him to his house on Lake Como in Italy, and he'd gone. The queen of England liked his music and invited him to her house for tea.

His eyes were golden brown, and when True looked into them she forgot all that was wrong with her world.

Why are you marrying Dubose again?

She walked quickly up the front porch steps to escape that wicked question.

Inside Gage was in the kitchen wiping down counters with a sponge. "Hi," he said, looking oddly disheveled. His hair . . . it was a mess. And his shirt was tucked in only on one side.

"Hi." True stared a second too long. "Are you okay?"

He stopping wiping. "I'm fine." But his face registered some kind of stress.

Harrison and Weezie came tumbling in, loudly discussing whether or not the *Today* show was better than *Good Morning America*.

"I've been interviewed on both." Harrison's sexy, smooth voice echoed around the hall. "And I have to say it's like comparing peanut butter and jelly to grilled cheese. They're both your favorite."

"I like fried baloney sandwiches myself," Weezie said to him, then breezed into the kitchen past True. "It smells good in here. Like an Italian restaurant."

Harrison stopped at the door, his brows lifted at Gage. "Hey."

Gage turned his serious gaze to him. "Welcome back."

Weezie opened the fridge. "Yum, garlic bread and lasagna. Salad, too."

"How was supper?" Harrison crossed the kitchen floor, his steps slow and sure.

"Excellent." Gage kept going with the sponge.

True pulled out a chair and was immediately surrounded by dogs sniffing her shirt and shoes. "Did Carmela stay and eat with you?"

Gage nodded. And went back to wiping the counters.

True shared a look with Harrison. *Something's up*, his eyes said. She had to agree.

"Anything on your mind?" Harrison leaned lazily against the counter, smack dab in Gage's way.

Gage stopped moving the sponge around. "Besides wanting my trailer back? No."

"You look like you been doing tai chi or something." Harrison refused to rise to the bait.

"You can blame the dogs," his brother said. "We were roughhousing. *You* look like you need some serious fashion intervention. Granny glasses are culturally obsolete."

"I'm bringing 'em back," said Harrison.

"You could, too." Weezie high-fived him again.

Gage lobbed the sponge at his brother's head. "Geek" was all he said.

True was pleasantly surprised. But maybe she shouldn't

be. Gage had been in that tomato fight with Weezie and Carmela, after all. Maybe that had loosened him up.

The sponge skittered off Harrison's temple to hit the floor, and Skeeter rushed to pick it up. But Harrison got there first and threw the sponge like a Frisbee. It ricocheted off Gage's abs and landed next to the sink, where it belonged. "Stick with tomatoes, old man. I got sponges covered." He chuckled triumphantly.

"Pure luck." Gage looked a bit happier now.

When True stood, she couldn't help smiling. "I'm going upstairs. See everyone tomorrow."

"Good night." Weezie poured herself a glass of milk.

Gage waved at her, then folded a crumpled dish towel and hung it precisely over the oven door.

"Sweet dreams," Harrison said.

It was weird. True felt happy. And sad. Tomorrow night would be different. Harrison would be gone. And who knew? Maybe Gage would feel the need to leave with him. But this ordinary moment felt . . . like family.

All her life she'd wanted that feeling. It meant you were comfortable. You could be yourself. She'd loved her parents, but the atmosphere had always been slightly strained in the house. The only time she got relief from it was when she visited Harrison at Sand Dollar Heaven. Or hung out with Honey in her attic studio.

When it was just True and Weezie after their parents and Honey died, the tension was still there, mainly because she never quite knew if her decisions were good ones. She felt alone, cast adrift. And even when she'd started dating Dubose again, she felt on edge. She could ask him for advice, but she never wanted to rely on him too much. She was the leader of this family. She had to stay alert.

Harrison squatted down and let the dogs love all over him. "You're jealous of Boo," he told George. "No need to be."

Tails wagged, canine tongues lolled. Show-off Labrador snorting made True laugh. "Good night," she said again and, without looking back, sauntered down the hall and up the stairs.

Somehow this old house—this very, very old house—had become more than a relic of her family's long history in Biscuit Creek. It had shifted from dignity to softness and become a safe harbor, her home.

She didn't want to think of why. She *mustn't* think of why.

CHAPTER TWENTY-THREE

When True shut her bedroom door behind her, she sank onto the edge of her bed. Tomorrow was going to be a long day. There was a lot to get done—all doable, however, so she wasn't going to stress. But she couldn't go to sleep without checking in with Carmela.

She texted her: *What happened? Gage was a little cagey. More than usual, I think.*

I don't want to talk about it, Carmela texted back. *Ever. So please don't ask.*

Uh-oh. *Okay*, True wrote. *I'm worried about you.*

Don't be. I'm a big girl. I've got a store to run. Men are stupid. I'd be done with them if they weren't at the top of my C&N list.

Which is?

Cute and needy. They're first, followed by kittens, puppies, and baby dolphins.

I'd laugh, True wrote, *but you're upset.*

I'll get over it. Maybe.

Poor Carmela. *Well, when you're ready, call. I have big news.*

That's not fair. Now I'm going to have to call you!

True chuckled. *You don't have to. I'll tell you right now. The wedding's going to be here at Maybank Hall.*

OMG! That's great!!!!! came back, and then the phone rang.

"I think I can pull it off," True said instantly without even looking at the screen.

"Gertrude?" The word was staticky.

True's stomach dropped. "*Penn*?" Yikes.

"I'm in London. Did you think I wouldn't touch base with you? You've got a lot on your plate."

"No, no . . . I wasn't sure— Isn't it late over there?"

"Four in the morning. My body clock hasn't adjusted. How are the wedding plans going?"

True shook her head. "Fine, um, just fine."

"Everything under control?"

"Yes," True said softly, scared again. She shut her eyes— *Don't be! You're the bride!*—and opened them again.

"I can't hear you!"

"Everything's *fine*," True said louder.

"Excellent. Who's catering?"

"William Parnell." Of Billy Bob's Pig Pickin' Emporium in Moncks Corner.

"Never heard of him."

"He's . . . highly selective." *Not*. Unless you counted the fact that he didn't take credit cards. Only cash.

"I see," said Penn. "Good for you. What about the venue?"

"It's a surprise," True said right away.

There was a pause. "I don't *like* surprises."

It's not your wedding, True wanted to say back. But refrained—for Dubose's sake, she told herself. But she knew she was still a little bit afraid of Penn . . . because she was Penn.

"Surprises are good for you," True said. "They keep the brain cells young. According to Dr. Oz." Say something was approved by Dr. Oz and you were golden.

"Dr. Oz is a quack."

Oh. True looked up at the ceiling. "Um, it's still a surprise. So you have something to look forward to when you get home. Did your conference go well?"

"No," Penn said in clipped tones.

"What a shame." True swallowed. "I'm sorry."

"I don't need your pity."

"Right." True bit her lip. "Okay, I guess we'll talk soon then."

"Have you heard from Dubose?"

As a matter of fact, she hadn't in a while. But she'd been so busy, she'd hardly noticed. "He's super busy. We talk when we can."

"All right." Penn was clearly annoyed. Or maybe she was sleep-deprived. "Just remember what I said."

"I remember. Waring women are strong and unflappable. I'd like to add that they need to be creative when it comes to problem solving."

"That's what personal assistants are for."

"But I don't have one. And you're between assistants." None stayed long.

"I've got Bosey."

"You do." That nickname again.

"And he has you."

"Aw. Thanks, Penn." It seemed a rather sentimental thing to say.

"Which means that essentially *you're* my assistant. So don't disappoint me. Just don't."

And then she hung up.

Ouch. True should have known better than to think Penn would get all warm and fuzzy with her. When she married Dubose, things would smooth out. She'd have more clout, as Dubose's wife. And he'd stand up for her, she was sure. He'd better. Because if he didn't, True would have to. She didn't relish the thought.

There was no way she could sleep now. She called Carmela back and told her Penn called.

"Forget about her," Carmela said. "Let's talk only about the wedding plans. Are you stressed or excited?"

"Neither," True said. "Honestly. I don't know why except I just want to get it behind me. It's only a wedding. The important part comes after."

Carmela sighed. "You're so wise. I, on the other hand, am an idiot."

True sat cross-legged and pulled a pillow to her stomach. "Why?"

"I slept with Gage."

"I suspected shenanigans. I wasn't sure of the extent. But wow."

"I know," Carmela said, "but it was great. And then he ruined it. He said he wouldn't text me or call me. He'd read modern women need their space. And he gave me the opportunity to go home. So I did."

"I'm so sorry," True said. "But we both know he's different. He didn't mean to hurt you. He's awkward, you know?"

"I know."

"Do you really like him?"

"Yes. I can't believe it, but I do." She sighed a most unhappy sigh. "Getting in that tomato fight changed everything. He laughed. He took his shirt off. He was a primo specimen of manhood, and I couldn't believe that I hadn't noticed all those times he came in the store."

True liked him, too. "So what that he's kind of clueless sometimes? What guy isn't? He's smart and good looking. And I can't believe that he'd be the type of guy who'd use a girl. He's too sweet for that."

"That's what I thought, too. He was adorably shy. And . . . the sex. It was incredible."

"Really?" True was reluctant to admit to herself that she was jealous, but she was.

"I'm not exaggerating. I'll remember it forever. Even if the rest of the night sucked."

"Oh, boy." True could so relate. She'd never forgotten her night with Harrison, either. "So what's next?"

"Nothing. I'm not going to chase him."

"But he might need help understanding how to be in a relationship."

"Maybe so. But do I want to be the woman who teaches him how—only to be dumped by him later so he can use all the great things I taught him on someone else?" Carmela was getting worked up.

"No, Carmela," True said softly. "You can't let your old boyfriend in New York make you bitter. Stop right now."

"Okay." Carmela hiccupped a little. "I'll try. But I'm tired of losing men I love."

"You didn't love him."

"But I loved my dad. And he was taken way too soon."

"He was a hero. Cling to that."

"I do," Carmela whispered.

"He wouldn't want you to give up hope."

"I know."

True could hear the guys and Weezie coming upstairs.

"In 1941, German scientists accidentally created a polyurethane with bubbles in it," Gage was saying.

"Enough about sponges," Weezie said next. "Did you know that Ireland's *The Late Late Show* is the world's longest-running talk show?"

"So?" Gage said. "In 1954, the first commercial production of foamed polyurethane began. From there, our modern kitchen sponges evolved."

"La-di-effin'-da to both of you," said Harrison. "I just want to know who won the Braves–Yankees game and what the weather's gonna be like tomorrow morning."

True knew why. For their paddleboarding expedition that wasn't going to happen.

"I almost kissed Harrison," she confessed to Carmela.

"Damn those Gamble boys."

They both started to laugh—but stopped at the same time.

"We'll be okay," True whispered, her eyes stinging just a little. "We don't need to analyze it to death. We just need to move forward. Both of us."

"Yeah," Carmela answered back, sniffling. "Take each day as it comes." A few seconds went by. "Good night."

"Good night." True hung up, crept to her bedroom door as if she were deathly ill—because she felt weak and depressed now—and turned off her light.

When she crawled back into bed, she stared into the darkness a long time, wondering why Dubose hadn't called or texted—and why she hadn't tried, either.

CHAPTER TWENTY-FOUR

Harrison might have his flaws, but one thing he'd never done was lie to himself. He had feelings for True that had never gone away. He'd been sure he had it all under control, but he didn't. Last night at the dance had been a close call.

He had to leave town, or stop the wedding.

All night long he thought about what he would do. Cursed a blue streak in his head. Tossed and turned. But when the sun came up, the plain and simple truth came clear. He had to go. Stopping the wedding was a dumb idea. He'd only bring True heartache if he tore her away from Dubose a second time. She wasn't the innocent girl she was on prom night. She was a survivor—a smart woman making her own choices. Who was he to interfere with that?

And the kicker was that even if he did stop the damned wedding, he wouldn't know what to do with her once she was free. He had feelings for her, yes. But that wasn't enough. She needed tending, like a beautiful, prized rose. He'd be the gardener from hell, leaving her to find sunshine and rain where she could.

So he was going to leave. But before he did, he'd help her pull off this wedding. She didn't have a father to walk her down the aisle. He sure didn't feel fatherly toward her, but she deserved to have a man in her corner who cared about her, supported her, and was willing—in the end—to let her go where she truly wanted to be.

And if that was with Dubose, he had no right to object.

Especially when he was Mr. Hotshot Country Music Star with a huge career and a manager and a studio waiting for him to pay attention to the *Billboard* charts again. He wasn't that young boy on the dock anymore, catching blue crabs in a net. Now he was scooping up CMA awards and Grammys. It was nice coming back and checking on the home place, seeing all the people he used to know, but he didn't belong. He wasn't sure that he ever had.

Dan called while he was in the shower. He wrapped a towel around his middle, stuck the phone to his ear, opened the bathroom door to go to his room, and met True in the hall.

"Hi," she said, her face pale as a sheet.

"Hey," he said, only a little embarrassed. Because she was in a pair of tiny pink polka-dotted shorts and one of those flimsy tees that clung to her boobs.

Damn, he thought, and stretched it out to two syllables, too—the ultimate expression of male appreciation of the feminine form. Then decided he'd better channel Terence Jones. Terence Jones wouldn't give a shit about her boobs.

"You there?" Dan shouted down the line.

"Yeah, hang on a minute." Harrison put the phone on his chest and grinned down at True. "Tide's up. Will you be ready to get on the paddleboards in half an hour?"

"I told you I'm driving." She stood tippy-toe on one foot and then the other. Classic True balking. She'd done it on the dock at Sand Dollar Heaven all the time when she didn't want to jump into the creek. She had a thing about encountering crabs if her foot touched the pluff mud. High

tide was the preferred time to swim. It meant she was
"safe." But on a really hot day, if it was only mid-tide, she'd
do the toe dance.

"Come on," he said. "You need some color before the
wedding. You're looking mighty pale."

"I *want* to be pale. Like Nicole Kidman."

"But her kind of pale's different. You look a little off.
You need some sunglow. And face it, you need to get on
the water. When was the last time you were out there?"

Her expression drooped. "Too long," she said. "I honestly don't remember."

"See? I'm in the same boat."

"Hah."

"We make terrible landlubbers. We get grouchy if we
don't get on the water at least once a decade. Don't you
think?" He meant it, too. He hadn't realized until he came
back here how well he could think when he was on the
water.

She chewed the inside of her cheek. "I thought that
getting grouchy was just us . . . growing up. Becoming
responsible citizens."

"Nope. And the truth is, I need to write some songs.
Maybe being on the water will help. We can scratch each
other's backs, so to speak."

"*No.*" She was doing everything she could not to look
down at his exposed belly. Or his towel.

"You know what I mean. It's an expression." But he
was having trouble role-playing that he was Terence. All
he could think about was pulling her into his room, putting Honey's only tiara on her head, and having his way
with her.

She thought some more. "All right. But—"

"What? Are you worried about crabs? We're going at
high tide. If you fall off the paddleboard—which you
won't—your feet won't touch the bottom of the creek."

"It's not that," she said. "It's just"—she shook her head—"last night . . . we had an issue. So you have to move out. Not Gage, though. He can stay."

Harrison put the phone to his mouth. "Dan, I'll call you back." He hit the OFF button, but not before he heard Dan squawking like a chicken.

True's gorgeous baby blues were big and troubled.

"That was Patsy Cline's fault," Harrison said gently. "It's why she's a legend. You and I both know how hard we've worked the past ten years. We have plans. And we're not going to let anything stop us. Especially feeling sentimental about something that happened long ago."

True nodded. "Exactly. I'm glad you get that."

"Do I ever," he said with a self-deprecating grin. "So let's get this wedding going, shall we? We need a new checklist."

"I've made one up." She looked a little more chipper.

"And if you still want me to move out, I will." He meant it, too. "The last thing I want is for you to feel stress before the big day." Terence would say something just like that.

"Me, either." She headed to the bathroom. "I'll think about it," she said over her shoulder. "We've had some fun with you and Gage here. I think it's good for Weezie. It takes her mind off the wedding. She's not too keen on it, as you know."

"I can help her with that," Harrison volunteered with a sick feeling in his stomach. He hated the idea of True's marrying Dubose, too. Hated it so much he nearly told her then and there that no way, no how was he going to stand by while she married the biggest jackass Biscuit Creek had ever produced.

But then he remembered that she was a grown woman with a good head on her shoulders. She'd have chosen him if she'd wanted him.

And she hadn't.

Lord knows he was sending out vibes right now . . . if she went wild and pulled off his towel, he wouldn't object in the least.

"You already have helped with Weezie, and I thank you." Her face was too serious, poor thing. She really needed this paddleboarding excursion.

And a roll in the hay, his treacherous mind added. But that was none of his business.

"See?" he said. "We've got our priorities straight."

She granted him a small smile. "I'll join you in the kitchen in twenty minutes." She paused. "Are you wearing a bathing suit?"

"No. I don't have one. But I wouldn't anyway. I'm not gonna fall in."

"Then I won't wear one, either," she said.

Darn. He wondered if it would have been a one-piece or a bikini.

Her face brightened. "I forgot to tell you." She looked furtively around. "Gage and Carmela . . . are involved," she whispered. "I'm only telling you in case Gage needs support. Carmela said that he basically told her to go home, afterward"—she winced, probably because she was making it clear exactly how far they'd gone—"and said he'd never text or call her."

"You're kidding."

True shook her head. "I know he said that because he thinks he'll be overwhelming her. He didn't mean to hurt her feelings." She paused. "I might have said more than I should."

"No, I'm glad you told me." He liked how she assumed Gage was a good guy—which he was. "He told me he really likes her. He's not a kid, so I'm not gonna get in the way. I'll hint around, but if he doesn't bring it up himself, there's not much I can do."

"That's fair," she said.

Harrison sighed. "Carmela's a good girl. I hope this works out."

In his room, he flung off his towel and called Dan in the buff. "I'm naked," he said.

"Oh, gross. Put something on, will ya?"

Harrison chuckled. "Nope. It means you'll say what you have to say and then leave me alone. How can I write songs with you bugging me?"

He folded his free arm across his chest and peeked out his window at the tomato fields. An early-morning mist was already being burned off by the sun. It was going to be a hot one today.

"*This* is bugging you?" Dan said. "A few calls here and there?"

"Yes. Don't forget—I'm naked."

"All right, all right! They want you on that singing competition show as a judge. You know that one you especially like?"

"Yes," said Harrison, his wet hair dripping down his neck. "Is there some reason we're not using the name?"

"It's kind of like saying *Voldemort*. You just don't want to jinx things. Are you interested? This would catapult your career to the next level."

"I've been catapulting for ten years. How many levels are there?"

"More. I promise you. The exposure you'll get here will make you more mainstream than ever. That translates into a huge bump in sales. And hey—you'll be on a panel with some great stars in their own right. That should be fun for you. I know you like fun."

Harrison sighed. "Are you reading that off an index card?"

"Yes, but because you're naked, I edited out the entire middle about how much you'll love spending more time on the West Coast."

Harrison scratched his neck. "I'm interested," he said, and was surprised he didn't feel tremendously excited. "What does the studio say?"

"They're willing to go with it. As long as you honor your commitments to them in a timely fashion. Which means you'll be juggling a lot of balls."

"We'll talk about it soon. I'll stew on it for a few weeks."

"We don't have that luxury. The show producers need an answer this week."

"No, they don't. You know the pressure game deal makers play. Handle it."

"I *am* handling it. And I'm telling you that they're not messing around. The network honchos want to fill the slot *now* and get the PR campaign rolling. I can't take on the entire network, buddy. They've got plenty of people lined up to take your slot. Do you want to risk losing it?"

"I'll think it over. I gotta go. And Dan?"

"Yes?"

"I'll call *you*."

"For the love of—"

Harrison hung up again. *Focus on True*. At least for the next few hours. Now was not the time to think about his career. And after he helped True out, he was heading to the construction site to check on that. He made a quick call to Vince to give him a heads-up.

"We're making tremendous progress already," Vince said. "We've got the footings poured. The concrete columns are up, and brick masons are covering them today. The beams are in. We'll be framing the floor this afternoon and tomorrow."

"Great job. Can't wait to see it."

In the kitchen, Gage was in his running clothes and making pancakes for everyone. True and Weezie's mouths were full, and they were already slicing through their stacks to cram in another bite, just in case they disappeared somehow.

Which they might. The dogs were staring at their plates with devoted concentration.

"Want to head over to the house site with me this afternoon?" Harrison poured himself a cup of coffee and peered over Gage's shoulder.

"I'd be foolish not to," Gage replied, stiffer than ever, "as I'm investing in it."

Damn. He was obviously smarting from what had happened between him and Carmela. Either that, or Harrison had made a huge mistake interfering in his brother's life. "Hey—you don't have to spend a dime on this project. I'm happy to cover it."

Gage flipped over five pancakes in the pan. "No, thank you. I made a commitment."

Yeah, he did. And Harrison felt like shit about it. "All right," he said carefully. "Maybe when you see it, you'll get excited."

Gage didn't answer. Just walked to the table and laid a stack of pancakes on Harrison's plate. They looked beautiful: fluffy and steaming. With a nice dollop of butter and a swirl of Aunt Jemima syrup, they were the perfect breakfast.

They went down like cardboard.

Weezie told everyone she had plans for the day and would be back at dinner. Gage drifted off to his room to work on a puzzle.

"What kind of plans, Weezie?" True sat up on the alert.

"The driver who picked up a bushel of tomatoes for that restaurant in Charleston asked me out to lunch." Weezie giggled. "We have a lot in common."

"He did?" It was obvious from the level of panic in True's voice that her sister hadn't had a dating life up to this point.

Weezie nodded. "No big deal. We're going to stick around Biscuit Creek. I told him the Starfish was really good. And then we might shop on Main Street."

True's mouth hung half open. "I'd like to meet him first."

Weezie's brow furrowed. "It's too late for that."

"You should have thought of that before you said yes."

"He's not an ax murderer." Weezie picked up her plate and took it to the sink. She turned on the hot water in preparation to do the breakfast dishes. "He's just a guy. He's a sophomore at the College of Charleston."

"Does he have a major yet?" True asked.

"I think it's psychology." Weezie was breezy as she squirted some dishwashing liquid into the water.

"Just make sure you have your phone with you," Harrison said, "in case you need to touch base."

"But we won't be here," True said.

"Gage will." Harrison tried to sound calm and reasonable.

"I'll be fine." Weezie looked over her shoulder at True. "It had to happen someday."

"What?" True said, distractedly rubbing behind one of the Lab's ears.

"My dating." Weezie turned back to the sink. "When a woman blossoms, men take notice. She's like a flower. That's what this book on sex says. It was pretty good. I found it at the library."

True put her hand over her eyes. "Please, don't say that. Especially not to *him*. What's his name?"

"Stephen Tyler, like the rock star, but with a *PH*, not a *V*. And he's very nice. Please don't Google him."

"Well, we don't want Stephen Tyler," True said with all sorts of reluctance, "to get the idea that you're ready to be . . . plucked."

Harrison had to restrain a chuckle. "I agree with your

sister, Weezie. Let this date be a chance for you to evaluate Stephen and not the other way around. Let him do the work, okay? You just enjoy the compliment of being noticed."

Weezie wiped down her plate with gusto. "Good idea, Harrison. You'd make a great brother. I wish—"

Harrison sent her The Look. The don't-forget-what-we-talked-about look.

Weezie shut her mouth just as True stood, almost knocking her chair over, and brought her plate to the sink. "I know you'll be careful," True said. "Don't bring him in the house. And if he acts fresh in the car or starts driving you out of town—"

"He's not going to do that," Weezie said.

"Slap him," True went on doggedly, "and get the hell out of the car. I don't care if you have to stop, drop, and roll. Just—"

"True," Harrison said. "It's time to go."

She sighed, gave Weezie a big hug, and she and Harrison walked out the front door.

The woman needed this expedition. Boy, did she ever.

A few minutes later, they'd carried their paddleboards out to the dock to set them in the creek. Harrison wished he'd never eaten breakfast at all. It was like he had a rock in his stomach. This house issue was putting a barrier up between him and Gage. Maybe he should have stayed out of it. But that trailer . . . Gage had been in a definite rut, just as True had said the first night they arrived at Maybank Hall. And what were brothers for but to get you out of one?

"Don't worry about Gage," True said. "He'll come around."

As usual, she read him well. "I hope so."

"If he works things out with Carmela, she'll be a really good influence on him."

"Let's hope he does." Harrison slid her board in. "And don't you worry so much about Weezie. She's a smart girl."

"I know," True said weakly.

She lowered herself onto it in a crouching pose, and as he handed her a paddle, he couldn't help noticing that her thighs were sleek and toned.

"Thanks." She stood and wobbled a few seconds before gaining her balance. The water lapped at the edge of the board, but she was in control. Some of the strain left her face. "Wow. This is cool. It feels pretty stable." She was wearing Sperrys, some cute nylon hiking shorts, and a clingy little tank top. She looked hot without even trying.

"It should," he said. "It's three feet across and ten feet long. It can hold over three hundred pounds, and you're light as a feather." He took out his phone. "I gotta get a picture of this. But you have to smile."

She faked it at first until he said, "Come on! Don't be an overprotective sister! Now smile for real, or I'll knock you in the water."

"You wouldn't!"

"Yes, I would."

She laughed at that. "You're crazy."

"I know."

She smiled at him broadly, and his heart zinged around in his chest like a drunken dragonfly. She looked like the old True. Miss Adventurer. He *knew* this outing was going to be good for her.

He put his phone in a ziplook bag and stuck it in his shorts pocket. "All righty. We don't have long to go. The tide's slowing down, but it's taking us in the right direction."

She put her paddle in the water and moved slowly away from the dock. Harrison got on his board without a problem and followed. They floated down a small inlet that they'd follow out between borders of marsh grass on either side to the big water.

After a full minute of navigating their boards, she called back to him, "This is fun!"

"Isn't it?" he yelled up to her. He was glad she was taking the lead.

It was a miracle world, this place. Harrison soaked up the peace. The wind skittering across the top of the water. And there was an egret, poised on one leg, oblivious to their presence.

When they entered the main estuary that was Biscuit Creek, the wind picked up. The water wasn't smooth as glass anymore. It wore little ripples on its surface, like hammered silver.

True's stance got a little stiffer.

"You okay?" Harrison asked her.

"Fine," she said. "Just adjusting a bit."

He had to, as well.

But the paddleboards were an ideal mode of transportation. Neither he nor True had any problems controlling them. She relaxed her shoulders, looked back at him a few times, and commented on the beauty of the water. The sun. She wondered if they'd see dolphins. Harrison tried not to stare at her butt and to look where he was going—although he could have paddled with his eyes closed, and he'd still have floated down the middle of the creek toward Cornelius's house.

"I feel like singing," he said.

True laughed. "Go ahead."

So he sang "Here Comes the Sun." He and True both loved the Beatles. She even joined in on the chorus.

Good Lord above, this was a perfect morning. He wished he could trap it and keep it forever.

Ten minutes later, they were at Cornelius's rickety old dock. Landing there was a lesson in humility. First, True tried, and nearly toppled off her board. She shrieked, but then she laughed and he joined in. There was no real danger if either one of them landed in the water. Even so, if someone had to suffer the indignity of falling of the board, he'd rather it was him.

She clambered onto the dock—damn those short shorts of hers!—and held her paddleboard still so Harrison could come in. He had no problem until his board bumped a piling, and then he almost fell off the back.

"Noooo!" True cried.

But he saved himself—walking across stages for ten years had given him something of a cat's balance—and climbed up onto the silver-gray planks alongside her. He couldn't help liking that she yelled like a banshee on his behalf.

"I know it's no big deal if we land in the water," she said, almost apologetically. "But it still makes me scream when it's about to happen."

He knew something else that would make her scream, too, but a gentleman tried not to entertain those thoughts when the woman in question was smiling at him like Gidget in that old-timey surfer movie.

They got their boards up on the dock and went in search of Cornelius. No doubt he'd heard True yelling and should appear any second. His crazy little shack looked almost the same as it had ten years ago—it was tilting maybe ten degrees farther to the east, but it was upright.

Sure enough, a grizzled old black man appeared at the door.

"What the *hey*?" he called when he saw Harrison. "What you doin' back? I thought you was stayin' in Hollywood! Or Nashville! Not hangin' out here with the little people."

Harrison let out a belly laugh. When he and Cornelius met in the middle of his front yard, he slung his arm around the old man and pulled him into a tight embrace. "Good to see you, brother."

"You, too." Cornelius gave him a big slap on the back, testament to the fact that he was still in good shape. "Who's this pretty girl you got wid you?"

Harrison made the introductions.

"Oh, yes," Cornelius said, "I knew your daddy well. He was a good man. A very good man."

True's face lit up. "Thank you."

Cornelius beamed at her and gave her a hug. "No way you gettin' outta here without that."

When he released her, she smiled broadly. "I'm so glad to meet you."

"*Yeah*." Cornelius clapped his hands as if he was preaching the gospel, which he often did at a tiny church up the road. He looked Harrison up and down with those bright eyes of his. "What's this about? Purely social? Or you got a gig coming up nearby you needin' a fiddle player for?"

"Actually, it's my wedding," True jumped in.

Cornelius's eyes widened. "You two?" He pointed his finger back and forth.

"No, sir," Harrison said in jaunty fashion so he didn't look like he was pining away for True. Which he was, but he wasn't gonna be a whiner. He'd be nice and cheery if it killed him. "She's marrying Dubose Waring."

Cornelius crinkled up his face. "A Waring, eh?"

True nodded. "Yes, sir."

Cornelius didn't look too happy. "You'd be the first of the Maybanks and Warings to marry, you know that?"

"Yes." True's face turned a pale pink. "Are—are you interested in playing at the reception?"

Cornelius scratched the top of his head a few seconds.

Harrison sure as hell hoped he wasn't going to say no, for True's sake. She bit her thumb and waited.

"Why not?" Cornelius finally said. He grinned at True, then at Harrison. "If this boy brought you here, there must be something special about this wedding. Who am I to say no?"

True hugged him. "Thank you! Can you bring some fiddle-playing friends with you?"

He nodded. "I'll be happy to."

They worked out the details of the arrangement, and then Cornelius invited them to stay for lunch. "I got some catfish Mamie Howard fried up for me this morning. I think she's after me," he told True with a delighted grin. "Her and Lizzie Wilson both. Lizzie made me some corn bread. And I got some fresh green beans from the garden."

"It sounds wonderful," True said.

"Cornelius, anytime you and a friend want to come to a concert, you know you just have to let me know," Harrison told him. "I'll send a limo here to pick you up, the plane ticket will be at the airport, and I'll put you up in a nice hotel."

Cornelius winked at him. "Once I decide between Lizzie and Mamie, I'll let you know. But I don't know if that'll ever happen. They spur each other on. And I get all the spoils. Give all that up for one concert from a boy who used to sound like a frog? I dunno about *that*."

True giggled.

"My voice was changing," Harrison protested. "I was fifteen."

Cornelius cackled. "Me and the boys'll never forget it. Harrison came over and played his new guitar. He was so proud of himself."

"I got it on Craigslist," Harrison said. "It was a banged-up piece of junk, but I loved it."

"Even so, the guitar playin' was pretty good," said Cornelius. "But then he open his mouth to sing, and he scared all the dogs away. They haven't come back around to this day."

True looked around. "There really aren't any dogs!"

"That's because Cornelius is allergic to 'em," Harrison said. "And I'm honored that I'm the subject of one of his tall tales."

Cornelius laughed until he had to wipe away a tear. True joined in. Harrison took advantage and stole the last piece of catfish.

It was a great lunch.

"Come back again, True," their host told her at his front door when they were leaving. "When you become Mrs. Waring, you can bring your husband with you."

"I will," she promised in a very sweet, polite voice.

Harrison heard the slight strain. He knew—and she knew—that visiting old men in tiny shacks wasn't something Dubose Waring would ever go out of his way to do—not unless he had to collect a deposition.

"As for *you*"—Cornelius punched Harrison in the arm—"am I gonna see you at this wedding?"

There was a split-second pause.

"Of course you will," True said, then looked at Harrison. "He's been like a brother to me while Dubose is gone. It was his idea to seek you out, and I'll always be grateful that he did."

Dang. What a bummer. It looked as if he and True had officially gotten over their torrid past. He'd achieved brother status in her eyes.

Cornelius grinned at him. "Well, that's good you stickin' around. I won't have to wait another ten years."

God, that was a long time. Harrison had been a really bad friend. "It won't be so long next time."

And it wouldn't. He'd come to see Gage a lot more often. Although the prospect of being in the same town with the new Mrs. Waring held no appeal.

After one more hug, he turned his back on his favorite fiddle player and headed out with True to the dock.

"The tide's at a standstill," Cornelius called after them. "Enjoy!"

"We will!" Harrison threw him a little salute.

"Bye, Cornelius!" True waved wildly. She even jumped up and down, as if she couldn't get enough of seeing him one last time.

"Bye, young lady! Hey, Harrison?"

"Yes, sir?

"It's not too late to steal her away, you know. And I'd play at your wedding for *free*."

"You old dog!" Harrison yelled.

Cornelius let loose with his trademark cackle.

When Harrison looked at True a second later, she'd settled down quicker than bubbles in a can of flat ginger ale. She was standing with her board, ready to put it in the water.

"You ready?" he asked her.

"Sure," she said in a small, tight voice. She knew it. She knew marrying Dubose was all wrong for her.

She knew Harrison knew, too. But there was nothing he could do about it. Nothing at all.

CHAPTER TWENTY-FIVE

True thought the visit with Cornelius had gone really well, except for that little pause he'd made when she said she was marrying Dubose. And then at the end—sheesh! How embarrassing! She didn't hold it against him or anything, what he'd said about Harrison stealing her away. Older people had the privilege of speaking their minds. But the part that really dampened her spirits was when she realized that Dubose would have no interest in visiting the old man. It made her realize how unalike she and Dubose were—because she'd loved the visit.

She and her fiancé were different from each other—maybe too different.

She wouldn't show that she was upset, though. It was too nice a day. And it would be churlish of her to get moody when Harrison had gone to all this trouble to help her.

"Thanks so much for arranging the visit," she told him when they were back on their paddleboards.

"He's great, isn't he?" The wind picked up Harrison's hair and played with it.

True was a little jealous. She'd love to run her hands through his hair, just one more time. They were traveling side by side, and she couldn't help admiring his physique, too. She'd have to be blind not to appreciate his muscles.

Obviously, country music superstars worked out.

"He's a lovely man," she agreed, and pulled her paddle through the water. She had to put in more effort rowing back home because they had no current at all to help them. "So you went over to Pee Dee Island when you were in high school?"

"All the time," Harrison said. "I borrowed the same johnboat you and I used as kids—I just traveled farther afield. Cornelius treated me like family. After Mom died, he had me to supper at least once a week."

Regret sliced through True, sharp as the edge of an oyster. "I'm so sorry." She was mortified at the little catch in her voice and the way her eyes stung. But she deserved the embarrassment. "Our family never invited you to supper. You were alone almost through high school."

Harrison's oar streamed through the water. "It's what grew the songs in me. All that solitude. I don't regret it. So neither should you. Your dad helped me, too. He arranged it so DSS wouldn't place me in foster care."

"He did?"

"Yep. Said I was the best lawn boy he'd ever had. He pulled some strings."

"You're very kind to frame his selfish act so generously," she said quietly.

"Not really. He was thinking of me, too. I sensed it. But whatever his motive, the end result worked for me."

"I'm glad."

"Don't be hard on your dad. I think of myself a lot, too."

"Only because you've had to."

"Don't give me any breaks. I've arranged my life this way."

They paddled on a few more minutes in silence. The

day was hot. Really hot. The wind on the water wasn't enough to keep True from sweating. Harrison, too, had a sheen on his brow.

"You want to take a break and swim?" he asked her. "Cornelius is right. The tide is at a standstill. I wouldn't mind jumping in."

"Sure. I'd love that."

He sat on the board and took off his shoes. "I'm diving in."

"Good luck," she said.

He stood again, grinned at her, then did a perfect dive off the front of his board, propelling it backward. He came up with a swish of wet hair and whooped. "It feels great! Come on in!"

She laughed as he swam with strong, sure strokes to his board and hung from its edge. "Let's go, Miss Maybank. It's plenty deep. You won't encounter any crabs, I promise you. And we're in the middle of the channel, so you won't hit an oyster bed, either."

"All right." She refused to think about crabs. She took off her Sperrys and jumped in, holding her breath.

Ah, the sensation of landing in cool water! It was so refreshing. It made her downright giddy. Why hadn't she done this more since she was a kid playing at Sand Dollar Heaven? At the surface, she opened her eyes and laughed out loud. "You're right. It's awesome."

He'd already grabbed her board and placed the two side by side.

He swam up to her, and her heart raced. His eyelashes were covered in beads of water. "It's like the old days, isn't it?"

She nodded. "The really, *really* old days."

"Let's get away from the boards. We could use a little exercise."

"Okay."

They both swam about a hundred feet, then stopped and treaded water and looked at each other. He was only slightly out of breath. She was actually panting a little.

"Here we are," he said.

He might as well have said *Just we two*.

It hung in the air between them.

The boards bobbed not too far away, an easy escape anytime True wanted to take it. But something kept her there, her hands and feet swirling through the salty creek, which wended its way around them, supporting them from below, a benign presence.

"I really hope you'll be happy," Harrison said out of the blue.

True gulped. "Thanks." She ducked under the water to get away from him for a second, then came back up and brushed her hair off her face. He was lying on his back, looking up at the sky. He looked like the boy she remembered on the dock. She missed that boy. But what else was there for them to do but return to the boards?

"This was a great idea," she said. "You ready to get back?"

"Sure." He swam freestyle again.

She did the breaststroke this time, wanting to linger, feeling sad for some reason.

When she got back, he was waiting patiently in between the boards, holding on to them loosely, his chin still in the water.

She swam right up to him and accidentally kicked her left leg against his. "Sorry." She backed right up.

"It's all right." He smiled, and her sadness evaporated. His eyes were warm. Accepting.

Even when he'd seemed to hate her in high school, it wasn't her he scorned. It was the phony True. He'd always stayed loyal to the girl she really was beneath her mistakes and rationalizations. He'd never forgotten her. And that had helped her so much . . . there were still times she wasn't sure who she was. But he always seemed to know.

Always.

It was a cozy little space with the paddleboards penning them in. Only a few inches of cool water separated them as they bobbed gently, face-to-face. Birds cawed from the banks. The wind came in short, easy gusts.

And then it happened. Harrison leaned forward and kissed her, his mouth wet, salty, and warm. She kissed him back, and it was as natural as breathing. Her mouth was open and wanting. Wanting *him*.

He pulled her close with one arm, and she hung there, her legs tangled with his. They fit perfectly, their tongues clashing and exploring like familiar playmates reunited.

Nothing had changed.

Oh, God. Nothing had changed at all.

She moaned in her throat. He pressed his ready erection against her belly, and she reached down with a hand to caress it. *Old, old friend*, she thought. *My lover. My love*.

He ran his hand down her back, into her waistline, and grabbed her bare buttocks. "You're perfect," he said, over and over. "Perfect."

His words affected her as much as his kisses did. She hadn't realized how much she'd longed to hear him say them.

An airplane flew high overhead, but it was enough for True to open her eyes to gather her wits.

"Harrison," she whispered.

It was a plea. But how did you stop when the only man you wanted to kiss was kissing you? When he was saying things that you'd only dreamed you'd hear from him again?

"I'm sorry," he said between loud, increasingly passionate kisses that were teetering out of control. "I'm so, so sorry."

She ran her hand down the side of his face, over that sculpted cheekbone.

They stared at each other a few seconds. And then she hung from his shirt, literally, as she unbuttoned it. She even went under water and worked the buttons loose before laying kisses up his belly until she broke the surface again. Then she kissed his chest once more and helped him out of his shirt, throwing it on her paddleboard, where it landed with a splat.

Neither one of them said a word.

It was his turn now. He removed her camisole top, and while he did, she caressed him—wherever she could grab purchase—as he boldly peeled the fabric off her. It passed over her face so fast that she didn't have time even to close her eyes.

He kissed her deeply as he unhooked her bra.

Sweet heaven! Her naked breasts felt so good, especially with his hand cupping the right one, caressing it with his thumb.

"Uh-oh," he said.

They both looked down between them. There was a flash of pale gold, and then her bra was gone.

They laughed. He encircled her waist while she wrapped her arms around his neck, and they kissed and laughed.

Kissed.

And got quiet, except for the soft, smacking sound of mouth against mouth.

He extended his arms on either side of her and grasped the board behind her. She clung to his neck and wrapped her legs around his waist, tantalizingly above his erection. He lifted himself higher so they could meet at that sweet spot . . .

And it worked. They made love in their clothes, kissing all the while. True grew angry that she was trapped inside her stupid, evil shorts, but the frustration made her come hard—a rapturous, transcendent feeling, in water, no less—her moans swallowed by Harrison's mouth.

"There," he whispered, his mouth curved in a smile. He kissed her tenderly, then wiped her hair back off her forehead.

She floated, her legs uncurled from his torso, and started to cry. Just a little at first.

He gathered her head to his neck. "It's okay, sweetheart. It's *okay.*"

She cried harder. "No, it's not. I'm getting married. And all I can think of is that I just had an orgasm in Biscuit Creek. With you. And you didn't, which doesn't seem right. But you're not my fiancé, so why do I care? Why am I even here?"

She wouldn't tell him that it was the first satisfaction she'd found with a guy—Dubose being her only other lover—since prom night, all those years ago.

Harrison chuckled softly. "Hey, I'll survive. And I'm not sorry it happened. Don't you be, either. Think of it as a little release. You've had a lot going on. And it breaks my heart to see you go through it all on your own."

Panic made her tremble. The water seemed too vast now. Maybe a shark was lurking nearby, lured from the ocean by a shrimp trawler. Maybe it was exploring Biscuit Creek the way the dolphins did.

The current was beginning to move, ever so slightly.

"We have to get home." Weezie would be waiting. So would Gage. And she still had a lot to do for the wedding.

"Whoa," he said, "stay calm."

She swallowed. "I will." She didn't have a paper bag to breathe in out here. But she could cup her hands.

"Let me help you get your shirt on," he said, "and then I'll push you back up. Do you think you'll be able to paddle?"

"I'll have to."

He winked. "Good girl. The rhythm will help you settle down. And don't worry. The current's going with us. So even if you get into trouble, I gotcha."

"Okay." She let him help her with her shirt. And when she grabbed the side of her board to get on it, he pushed her from behind, help she accepted gratefully. Her wrists and hands were still trembling.

You're fine, she told herself. Harrison was acting so calm about what had happened. Her embarrassment had worn off, but her guilt remained.

He got himself in order, too, rebuttoning his sopping shirt, and when they stood and paddled off, a sense of normalcy returned to True. The V between her legs felt warm and heavy. But she focused on paddling. Harrison was right—rowing did help her feel better.

All the same, things had changed in a big way.

"I-I don't think you'd better come to the wedding, after all," she said eventually.

"Agreed." His tone was firm but friendly. "I'll tell Weezie I have to leave town."

True hurt inside for Weezie. And herself. But it couldn't be helped. "As for your staying at the house—"

"I'll move out tomorrow morning if that's okay," he said. "I need a little time to prepare Gage and Weezie both. I'll make something up about having to have more peace and quiet to write my music."

"Good idea." Neither sibling, as they both knew, was great with change. Even a little transition would help.

Harrison steered toward the entrance to the small, winding path they'd taken through a finger of the creek. True followed.

"This afternoon," he said, "while I'm at the construction site, I'll work on finding a place I can stay without a whole lot of fuss. Though, hell, I might as well stay in the trailer."

"You could do that." She looked over at him briefly and smiled. Just a little.

He chuckled. "What an irony. If I stay there, Gage is gonna want to come back. And then I'll never get him out."

As he spoke so cheerfully about being kicked out of her house, she couldn't help thinking how cute and sexy he was. What an upbeat, good man he was. And how skilled he was as a lover. The best she'd ever had. And she'd only been with him two times . . .

Maybe the second time hadn't even counted.

Oh, yes, it did, her body told her.

She was crazy to still be daydreaming about him—she must be totally out of her head, like millions of other women. He wove spells.

"Shoot," she said. "So maybe you should forget the trailer and find a discreet hotel. I'm really sorry it didn't work out at my house."

"You're the last person on earth who needs to apologize," he said. "I'll be out of the house almost all afternoon, unless you need more help with the wedding details."

"No. I'll be fine." Like hell she would. She was a total mess. But she'd never tell him so.

"All right."

A few minutes later, they glided up to the dock and had no trouble getting themselves off the boards or removing them from the water.

"You run up to the house and take a shower," Harrison said. "I got these."

"Are you sure?" They were being so polite to each other.

"Positive."

So she left him there, and while she ran, she wondered if she and Dubose would ever take out paddleboards, or make love in the waters of Biscuit Creek.

No, her gut told her. *No, it won't happen, and you know it.*

She thought of Honey with her goofy hats and outrageous glasses. Honey dancing and playing her ukulele to no audience beyond two little girls and a wary nephew who wished she'd stop so that his very proper wife would get off his back. Honey, desperate to be loved and admired for who she was. Brave—but spurned all the same.

True slowed to a walk and ascended the steps of the house.

Poor Honey.

She opened the screen door and walked over the threshold, shielding her breasts in her wet camisole in case Gage was downstairs. Weezie was on her date. True prayed it was going well and that Weezie wouldn't be stupid, the way True had, and forget all common sense.

But she also didn't want to risk being Honey all over again. She didn't want Weezie to, either. Somewhere there was a compromise, wasn't there? Being who you were, yet not getting ostracized? Or shamed?

True thought she'd found the answer, for her *and* for Weezie—just don't share everything with the world. Hold some of yourself back. Even Harrison said he held himself back. He had his stage persona, but then he also had his private life.

You didn't hold yourself back today, her stricken conscience reminded her.

No, she hadn't. She'd messed up. But she wasn't going to dwell on it. She'd start over. It was hard. But necessary. Look at Mama. She'd loudly proclaimed to the world through her words and actions that rules mattered—and then hurt Daddy so very much by breaking those rules and having an affair.

But she'd gone on. Her marriage to Daddy had survived.

The truth was, as much as True was tempted by Harrison, she was bound to Biscuit Creek. She had a sister to act as a pseudo-parent to—at least until Weezie got out of college—and no man was going to distract her from that duty. She had an estate to care for, too, and a town she loved. Mama and Daddy were buried here. So was Honey. So were all those other Maybanks that had come before her.

She had Carmela and her church friends, as well as neighbors who'd helped her the last ten years stay afloat with one kindness or another.

Harrison had his career. It would take him all over the world. He'd need to live in Nashville. New York. Los Angeles.

A relationship between them would never work.

By the time she was dressed again and ready to leave—she was stopping by the photographers, then visiting the manager of Booty Call, and after that, she needed to go wedding shoe shopping—Harrison was already gone. He'd merely washed himself down under the hose by the barn, according to a text he sent her. And then he'd helped an old lady who'd come to pick tomatoes—Mrs. Finch, the same one who'd told him all her ailments on another visit—and by the time he was done assisting her, he was dry enough to jump in his Maserati and go. He'd only come into the house long enough to pick up Gage, who'd been holed up in his room working on a puzzle.

True was glad. She hoped she didn't have to see Harrison the rest of the night. She might make up some wedding excuse and retreat to her room. She could come up with something reasonable. She didn't even know how she'd face Weezie. How could she ask her about her date with Stephen Tyler and not totally feel guilty for being a hypocrite herself?

Carmela was the only one she could talk to.

Those Gamble men, Carmela would say. What was a girl to do with them?

True didn't know. She really didn't. So she called Carmela to ask her, but her phone just kept ringing and ringing. Which was weird. She usually didn't have any customers and picked up on the first ring.

Maybe that was a good sign, True thought, and set off on her errands in her ancient car. Any day now, the potholes in the dirt road leading to Maybank Hall were going to shake the muffler right off. For the last couple of weeks, she'd been looking online and in the newspaper for a new one.

She slowed to a crawl and thought about how Dubose told her right before he left not to bother—that he was buying her a new car when they got married. "And I'm going to choose it," he'd told her. "My wife won't drive junk."

He was thinking of her when he'd said that, right? Thinking that he wanted to spoil her because he loved her . . . not because he cared about her making him look good.

She pressed on her brake and took out her phone.

Hope you're doing well, she texted him, even as her entire body flooded with guilt. She was a cheat and a traitor. *Thanks for the sweet offer to buy me a car, but I think I found the one I really, really want already, and I'm going to buy it myself. It's a used GMC Terrain. Just the right size for me. And good on dirt roads. If I can't get it, there's a Honda CR-V that looks cute, too.*

She waited a good minute. No answer. *You there?* she texted.

Finally, she got a reply.

"Crap," she said out loud, and took off again, the car body shuddering as she accelerated out of a pothole.

Crappity-crap-crap-crap, the tires answered her on the pitted drive.

She held both hands on the steering wheel—hard—and desperately tried to forget that Maybanks were born to play by the rules. But she wouldn't be able to for long. Dubose had just called a car broker in Charleston. She'd have a new BMW sedan at her front door that evening.

Wives of successful attorneys drive high-end cars, he'd chided her via text. *Enjoy the Beemer and see you soon.*

CHAPTER TWENTY-SIX

That afternoon Harrison noticed that Gage came back to
the trailer at Sand Dollar Heaven from a so-called errand
on Main Street looking mighty pleased with himself. He
had a light in his eye. And his hair combing didn't meet
his usually high standards.

"Are you involved with Carmela?" Harrison asked him
outright. To hell with hinting around.

"Yes, she's my girlfriend." That was it.

"No shit."

"*Yes* shit. As of today. I had to go apologize for . . .
well, for not understanding how to act last night. We—"
He hesitated. "She brought over that lasagna."

"I can guess the rest." Harrison slapped him on the
back. "Congratulations. This is why you need a new place
to stay, so Carmela can come over. You can cook her dinner. And you two can hang out in the hot tub."

"I'll accede that building the house was a good idea,
after all." But Gage still didn't sound like a happy camper.

"Is something bothering you?" Harrison asked him. "I
know it's scary to get into a relationship—"

"How would you know? When have you ever been in
one? If you have, you've never told me."

Well, dang. Harrison knew his brother wasn't trying to

be combative or insulting. He was just asking. "You're right. I've gone out with a lot of women, but I've never stuck with one for longer than a month or two." He'd never thought of it as a problem.

"So you're as stunted emotionally as I am," said Gage.

"Hey, wait a minute—"

"It's not Carmela. It's my crosswords. I haven't been able to come up with a single one since I moved out of here."

"That's not good." But Harrison refused to feel guilty. More than ever, Gage needed a house. "I'm having the same sort of block with my songwriting. Do you think you'll adjust soon?"

"I don't know."

"Maybe getting into the house will help." It sure as hell better. Harrison was spending a small fortune on it, and unless Gage took him down in a mud-wrestling fight, he wasn't going to let his brother help pay for it, after all. It was a gift. He hoped it would turn out to be a wedding gift, but he didn't want to act desperate and jump the gun in that department. So for now, he'd say nothing.

"Being at True and Weezie's house hasn't helped," Gage said. "It's too bad. I like it there."

They looked at each other, and as usual, there was a wall between them. Not a big one, but enough that Harrison felt a strong sense of regret. He and Gage weren't as comfortable as brothers as he wished they could be.

Would it ever happen? Or were they doomed to have an awkward relationship always? He hoped not. It wasn't like he had a whole lot of people to call family. Gage was it.

"Hey," he said. "I have to move out of Maybank Hall tomorrow morning."

"Girl trouble?"

"What?"

"You and True. You want her badly."

Harrison laughed nervously. "No, I'm not having girl trouble."

"Could have fooled me."

"Since when did you become so perceptive?"

"I may be slow to, sometimes, but I pick up on cues just like you. And you're attracted to her. Probably in love with her. And I suspect it's because you're comfortable enough with her to let your guard down, be your authentic self. You're more likely to reach self-actualization—according to Maslow's hierarchy—with her by your side."

"What did you just say?"

"Google it." Gage was dismissive. He picked up one of Vince's blueprints and started examining the corner.

"Damn." Harrison cocked his head. "You're a smart-ass now you got a girlfriend."

"Am I?" Gage chuckled.

Further proof.

"And you're outta your frickin' mind," Harrison said. "I can't focus on my songwriting at True's the same way you can't work on your puzzles because it's a little crazy over there. Lots of dogs. Lots of . . . tomatoes. I was going to check into a hotel. But we have this trailer right here, so—I don't know if I should ask this—you wanna come back with me?"

"Damned straight," Gage said right away.

Whoa. Carmela's feistiness was already rubbing off on him.

"My only worry"—Harrison had to tread carefully—"is that you won't be willing to give it up when the house is done."

Gage's mouth thinned. "It would be difficult."

"But maybe with Carmela in the picture . . ."

"She'll definitely help." Gage looked at the floor. "I

have to stay on track with my crosswords, though. I can't lose momentum. I'm not looking forward to having to leave the trailer again."

"I'm sorry," Harrison said. "I wish there was something I could do, man. But I don't know what to say, other than time marches on."

"A sentiment made popular by Westbrook Van Voorhis, narrator on the *March of Time* radio and newsreel series in the first half of the twentieth century."

"I was just gonna say that." Harrison punched his brother's arm.

Harrison brought Vince back with them to Maybank Hall for dinner—oyster stew, cheesy broccoli casserole, and corn bread from the Starfish Grill.

Roger the busboy brought it out to the curb. "Nice dress," he told Vince.

"Thanks," Vince said. "Nice paper hat. Could I have one, please?"

"This isn't Burger King," Roger replied.

"I know. But I'm from LA."

"That explains it." Roger went inside and brought him a hat.

Vince was fascinated by the whole southern experience. He wanted to stop at Southern Loot, but the NOPE sign was up in the window. That was Carmela no doubt recovering from wild monkey sex with his brother.

All Gage said was, "She's working on a new store concept."

"What's wrong with that one?" Vince's tone was wistful as they cruised by at ten miles an hour (the local police were hell on speeders).

"If we got a lot of tourists here, she'd do fine," Gage explained. "But we don't. Biscuit Creek isn't Disney World."

Vince whistled when he first caught sight of Maybank Hall. "Talk about authentic South. Am I on the set of

Gone With the Wind? Is this Twelve Oaks come back to life?"

"Twelve Oaks had imposing columns," Gage piped up from the backseat. "This house is in the Federalist style but with a whimsical southern bent, as evidenced by the preponderance of porches, rockers, and dogs."

"Right." Vince shot Harrison a discreet look.

"I told ya he was smart." Harrison decided to spin out his tires when he parked in front of the house as it was going to be his last time returning to Maybank Hall, and he was feeling distinctly pent up. Being with True in the water that day, messing around with her, and then not being able to find a little Marvin Gaye–style sexual healing himself—as much as he didn't mind; he was a gentleman, after all—was costing him his usual mellow state of mind.

Besides, there were two guys in the car. He had to show off.

But when he saw True in the kitchen, he was especially glad he was only one of a crowd. He'd called to let her know they were coming with supper, and he'd asked her to break the news to Weezie that the Gamble boys were moving out the next day.

"Hey," he said when True looked up from placing silverware on the table.

"Hey." She was cute as a button. Sexy, too, in a simple little white blouse and flimsy pink skirt with modest slits on each side that made him want to pull it up to see more gorgeous thigh. She smiled at Gage and Vince, not Harrison, which was entirely okay. They needed to keep those barriers going. "It's so nice to see you again," she told Vince.

"You, too." He gazed at her like he couldn't get enough of her. "Your accent is to die for. And I love how all of you say *hey* instead of *hi*. I thought *hey is for horses*, but obviously not around here."

"Everywhere but the South," Gage agreed. "Jonathan Swift used that phrase in *A Complete Collection of Genteel and Ingenious Conversation* in 1738."

There was a brief silence until one of the dogs burped. For real. Harrison couldn't believe it.

"*Striker.*" Weezie had obviously ID'd the offender.

True held out her arm to indicate her sister. "This is Weezie," she said gaily.

Weezie, who'd been folding napkins, tried her best not to stare at Vince's army-green dress, another athletic sort of garment with a wraparound belt that reminded Harrison of hostels and hiking.

"I hear you want to be a talk show host." Vince pumped her hand hard. "Sounds like a great goal. If you ever need a place to stay in LA, please consider my guest house."

"Thank you very much." Weezie sounded almost a little shy—or maybe it was that she was preoccupied. She'd had that date, after all.

"How'd it go today with Stephen Tyler?" Harrison asked.

Weezie's face lit up. "Great. I'm going to hang out with him again in Charleston in two days. I'm going shopping for some school clothes."

True met his eyes. They both could tell she was counting the hours.

Dinner was fun. It was as if nothing had happened between him and True at all. And a great side effect of Weezie's being distracted by this boy—and school—was the fact that she wasn't nearly as upset that Gage and Harrison were leaving the next day as he thought she'd be.

The only time it got awkward was when Gage and Vince went out on the porch to smoke cigars. Harrison couldn't. They affected his vocal cords too much. Weezie went upstairs to fill out some new paperwork from Trident Tech that came in the mail that day, and she was also probably sneaking off to text Stephen.

That left Harrison and True in the kitchen.

He brushed her elbow when he walked by her with a couple of plates. The lyrics to "Sexual Healing" flooded his brain.

Aw, hell. "Sorry," he said.

"No problem," she said back.

Yep. They were both pretty self-conscious.

"Any luck with Booty Call?" He picked up several wineglasses and set them by the sink.

"Lots of it," she said. "I booked them. Same with the tents, the tables and chairs, and the dance floor." She sounded satisfied. Not overjoyed, necessarily, but considering what had happened between them earlier in the day, he wasn't surprised.

He smiled at her the same way he smiled on PR junkets. "That's great."

"It is." She busied herself around the sink and looked back at him. "I can handle this. Thanks for helping clear the table."

"Are you sure?" He came up next to her and flipped over a butter knife on the counter to look busy, but he really wanted to smell her hair. "You've had a long day. Brides need their rest."

She pulled out a dish towel and put on one of Honey's aprons, the yellow one with dancing apples all over it. "I'll be done in no time."

Her voice. It was so . . . hollow. And seeing her so despondent in that cheerful but ridiculous apron just broke his heart.

"True." She wouldn't look up at him. He wanted to tilt up her chin—hell, he wanted to take her in his arms—but he didn't dare touch her. "You're *not* a bad person."

She stood quietly for a second, then gave a brief nod. "Thanks."

"Please stop torturing yourself by wearing tacky

aprons." He went to the drawer where they were kept and pulled out a white one with blue trim. "This one next time. Okay?" He lifted his brows comically high.

But she didn't laugh. "I haven't called Dubose. And the only texts we shared were about the car."

"Car?"

"It's in the barn. A Beemer. He bought it for me."

"Whoa. Nice gift." But so unlike True. He'd get her an SUV, if he had the choice. He folded the white apron back up in thirds, like a towel—his mother had taught him how; it was his one housekeeping skill—and shoved it to the back of the drawer. "He's on a business trip. You're fixing your wedding. You're both seriously occupied. The car was a nice gesture."

"No, it wasn't." She sounded bitter. "Not really."

He wouldn't ask. But he suspected. Dubose was prepping her to be Mrs. Fancy Lawyer's Wife.

"The wedding's in a week," she went on. It was like salt in an open wound, but Harrison maintained an easy expression. "We're supposed to be thinking of each other." She winced. "I wasn't thinking of him at all this morning. Obviously."

She'd been kissing the socks off Harrison. Pumping her pretty little pelvis against his like a female Elvis. Lord, have mercy, that woman was—

He slapped his sex drive down. "I take the blame for that, all right?" He did, too. He'd kissed her first. "Move on from this morning."

She stared out the back-door window, where the sun had set and left a streak of orange behind the oaks and pines.

"If you were in a fairy tale," he said, "maybe everything would be all hearts and flowers a hundred percent of the time. But this is real life. Real problems happen.

Sometimes big ones. If you love someone, you work them out. And that's all there is to it."

True sighed. "You're right, I guess." She sent him a small, worried smile. "I think after I'm done here I'm heading to bed. Could you please send Vince my best?"

"Will do."

"See you in the morning for breakfast."

Served up with a side of happiness.

How long ago that day seemed, when he'd first arrived in Biscuit Creek, and it hadn't even been a week ago.

"Good night," he said from the door.

"Good night," she called to him, but didn't look over her shoulder. She definitely wanted to do those dishes in peace.

He, Gage, and Vince hung out on the porch a long while before a limo came and picked the house designer up and took him back to his hotel in Charleston.

"He's a good guy," Gage said. "I can't tell if he's straight or gay. Not that I care. Just curious."

Harrison sat on the front porch steps. "I wondered, too, at first, but you forget about that really quick with him. I think it's because he's always about other people. Not himself."

Harrison was rich, successful, creative—to an extent— but he was hyper-focused on building his own career. Yes, he was floating other people's boats by doing so. That was a good thing. But who was he also leaving behind?

"You know, it's not your fault that Dad got taken to jail," Gage said.

"What the hell?" Harrison sat frozen. "Why are you bringing this up?"

Gage let Ed join him on the porch swing because Ed was that kind of dog. "I know you blame yourself. You hung out at the still when Dad wasn't there. I used to watch you from the trees."

"I know you did—"

"And I saw everything that day the sheriff came by. He followed you out into the woods straight to the still. He pulled everything out as evidence and arrested Dad when he got off the shrimp boat."

"Shut up, man. I know all that." Harrison took a deep, shaky breath. "Dad told me never to go there, and I went all the time. It *is* my fault. The sheriff was always telling me hello. Now I know why. I was the son of the criminal he wanted to catch. He was hoping I'd say something, do something, to help his cause."

"Dad made his choices. You shouldn't be held responsible."

"I know that in my head, but in my gut—"

"The day Dad got arrested wasn't the first time the sheriff had been out to the still."

"Wait a second." Harrison shook his head. "What're you talking about?"

"I was up in my favorite tree one day, and he came looking for Mrs. Nelson. Remember her? She lived a few trailers over?"

"Yeah. She had a steady stream of boyfriends."

"Exactly. I think the sheriff was one of them. I heard him on his cell phone talking to her. She was playing coy. Leading him on a wild goose chase through the woods. She used to go down to the boat landing on the edge of the woods where it met the marsh. She'd cast her shrimp net there. That's probably where she was when he called her."

"So?"

"She made the sheriff find her. Kind of like hide-and-seek with sex at the end. The sheriff found her, yes, but not before he stumbled upon the still in the process. I heard him talking on the phone about it. You had nothing to do with him discovering it."

"You're kidding."

"No. I wanted to tell Dad, but he was on the trawler for a whole week. And when he came back, he was home for only one day before he got caught. I blame myself for not warning him that day—but he was so happy to see Mom and us. I was trying to work up my nerve. So I'm more to blame than you."

"No. You can't take the blame."

"Why not?" Gage asked. "You are."

"God." Harrison rubbed his eyes. "Even if you'd told Dad, the sheriff would've got him anyway. He wouldn't have run. He wasn't the type to abandon us."

"No, he wouldn't have," Gage agreed. "And we're not to blame for the fact that he died in jail. He was in the wrong place at the wrong time. So were we, each in our own way."

Harrison bowed his head. So many lives had changed when Dad was taken away.

"He was just making hooch," he whispered. "Five years in jail was rough. I didn't agree with the law, but I understood. Even Daddy did. But to lose his life there—three weeks after he arrived?"

"I know." Gage sighed. "And what's so ironic is that micro-distilleries are popping up everywhere these days. Down in Charleston a guy's selling his own blend on King Street and making a pretty penny."

They sat quietly a minute. The locusts were loud, buzzing their evening song. And the moon—God, it was gorgeous. It hung high in the sky. The weatherman had said it was an especially luminous one—a super moon, he called it. Now Harrison knew that the moon he'd looked at with

True a long time ago on the Isle of Palms had been the same kind.

"Why didn't you tell me all this before?" Harrison eventually asked his brother.

"It never occurred to me that you might blame yourself," said Gage. "The truth is, I haven't thought much about what you were thinking. I'm usually thinking about me. Or words. But the last couple days I've noticed more about you. Being in the trailer with you today especially took me back. It made me wonder if you've ever been happy since Dad was arrested. That's why I'm telling you now what really happened. I don't think you're happy. And I can tell you feel guilty about me. Look at this house you're building for me."

"It's not from guilt, Gage. It's because I love you. Are you gonna make me keep saying mushy stuff like that? Because I'm about to kick your ass."

"Shut up a second." Ed whined on the swing, and Gage scratched his ears. "This isn't easy for me, either. You've always felt guilty about me. I hung around you and your friends because I never made my own. And—and I never tried to take that load off your back. Ever. I just took it for granted that you'd always be there."

"You should have taken it for granted. That's what brothers are for."

"Well, I want to be a brother to *you* now. I want to take this crazy burden off you. Dad and Mom would have wanted me to. I'm the big brother. And I'm going to try to act more like one from now on."

Harrison didn't say anything. He was filled with all sorts of emotions. It was like being in the dark and bumping into one thing after the other, and you had to reach out and feel it, whatever it was, and just hope it wasn't something really gross or scary with fangs.

"Well?" Gage waited.

"I don't know what to say." It was the story of his life lately—at least his songwriting life.

Gage chuckled. "You're usually the one running off at the mouth."

Harrison gulped. "I know." He stood.

Gage stood.

Ed didn't move. No way was he giving up his seat on the swing. But he was watching them both and panting his little heart out.

The two brothers hugged.

"Thanks," Harrison said over Gage's shoulder.

"One more thing," Gage told him when they broke apart. "True asked me what Dubose Waring's name was as an anagram. You know, there are so many combinations of letters, most of them nonsensical."

"No, I didn't know. Did they implant Einstein's brain in your head? That would make a cool movie."

"Out of all the combinations," Gage spoke over him, "one leapt to mind immediately. But I didn't tell her. I gave her one that was innocuous enough: *wagons buried*."

"What was the other one?"

"*Bad rogue wins*. I thought I'd pass that one on to you. Good night, little brother." He walked past Harrison without another word.

"Is this a setup?" Harrison asked him.

But Gage ignored him. He just walked into the house, the screen door slapping shut behind him. Harrison stood and looked at Ed, but in his head he was slashing through the letters in *bad rogue wins* one at a time. Sure as shootin', it spelled *Dubose Waring*.

That was weird. That was *really* weird.

"Let's go, Ed." He opened the door to the house, feeling weird for a lot of reasons. But weird in a good way. Lighter. "I think we're in the *Twilight Zone*."

Ed leapt from his seat and took the lead inside, his tail

high. It didn't take much to make a dog happy. And they had no compunctions about showing their butts or burping in public. No wonder. All of 'em had clear consciences.

Harrison walked up the stairs and thought about his family. About Dad, who worked like a Trojan on those shrimp boats and could never get ahead. Mom, too, cleaning houses so much that the skin on her hands was permanently cracked and red. Gage, the silent follower who also held his own, hanging out in those trees, building himself a world of words.

And then he had to look at himself. He'd been scared. Always. And he'd hid it by being a leader of the boys, and then when Dad got sent to jail and Mom got sick, he'd become this aloof guy with the dry wit and the I-don't-give-a-shit attitude.

Except when he was playing guitar. Music had saved him from becoming a total dropout from life. It was his lifeline—that and his memories of True.

Each one of the Gamble gang had tried to do their best. No one was to blame for any of their family story.

His eyes began to sting.

Not even him.

He couldn't see the super moon from his room. But in bed half an hour later, staring at the ceiling and thinking about True next door, he remembered the moon that glowed over the Isle of Palms that long-ago night. It had been a super moon—

To match their super love.

He chuckled to himself. Corny, yes. But he wrote songs about love. And maybe he did because he was meant to. Maybe he needed to embrace that truth more. He was an artist—not just a hack. Nor was he merely a cog in the giant moneymaking machine that was his studio label.

He didn't have to feel guilty. Out of place. Undeserving of his success.

He closed his eyes. Dreaming up songs had nothing to do with whether a body deserved anything or not. When it was good, it just came through a person, like moonlight through a window.

CHAPTER TWENTY-SEVEN

That night True tossed and turned—it was the kind of sleep that felt more like a wrestling match she couldn't win than actual slumber. At one thirty in the morning, she awoke with a start, her heart pounding.

Everything's fine, she told herself, and shut her eyes again.

But her heart . . . it was revving up, like a rollicking, fast-moving train with a wheel missing . . . *karump-a-thump-a-thump, karump-a-thump-a-thump*. She squeezed her eyes shut and burrowed deeper into the pillows.

But her heart wouldn't slow down. She was alone. She couldn't breathe.

No.

Not a panic attack. Not now. She was done with those.

Staying in bed wasn't working. So she got up, paced the room, inhaled slow, ragged breaths. She'd made the right decision. Marrying Dubose was exactly what she should do. The insecurity—it was all gone now. Life was looking up. The bad times were over.

Why wouldn't her heart slow down?

Her hands started trembling. A bath. She needed a distraction. Something to focus on . . . that's what the doctor said. Focus on one thing—focus on her breathing. Slow down . . . forget everything else.

She walked swiftly, quietly to the bathroom at the far end of the hall—the one she shared with Weezie while the guys were in residence. In detached emergency mode—because her heart was still jerking hard in her chest, strident, insistent—she turned on the taps and didn't even wait for her mother's claw-footed, cast-iron tub to fill. She got in, fully clothed in a tank top and little shorts. She crouched, her knees trembling, eyes filling. With a shaky hand, she poured in some bubble bath and watched the bubbles blossoming all around her, felt the warm water rise and hold her, like a mother's hug.

Stay calm, she told herself. *Watch the water.*

The panic attack hovered like a silent, hungry shark and then after another thirty seconds or so . . . disappeared.

Thank God.

She turned off the tap, lay back, and closed her eyes. The only sound was the drip of the faucet, the sizzling sound of tiny bubbles popping. Her heart was quiet, her breathing even, her mind at ease again. It unfolded quietly, like a flower, and revealed one thought only:

Harrison.

He was right down the hall.

The knowledge comforted her like nothing else.

She peeled off her tank and shorts and dropped them to the floor. But the velvety bubbles made her aware of her nakedness, and the heat of the water against her softest flesh reminded her of what he'd done to her in the creek. She spread her legs, let her head loll, and remembered.

God, she wanted him. And she wanted him to see her like this. She wished he were with her right now. But he was asleep, unaware that there was a woman in the tub down the hall fantasizing about him at that very moment.

She gave a little laugh. Probably every minute of every day, a woman somewhere in the world was fantasizing about Harrison.

In just a few hours, he'd be gone. And she'd never be alone with him again. She pressed her eyes shut. *Never.* The faucet dripped.

Never.

Maybe she shouldn't marry Dubose.

God.

Maybe she shouldn't.

The thought ripped through her mind like a bad car crash, demanding attention. She put her fingers in her ears and slipped all the way under the water.

No thinking allowed.

No thinking, True Maybank!

But when she came back up, she was crying.

She got out, her hair dripping down her back, toweled off just barely, tears streaming down her face. Everything sucked. Everything sucked so bad.

Blindly, she padded down the hall in a towel to go to her room, where she'd don another little T-shirt and shorts and . . . and what then? Go to sleep with sopping-wet hair, cry all night like a helpless fool, and pity herself for the rest of her life?

When she passed the attic door, she stopped.

This.

Inhaling a deep breath, she opened the door carefully, quietly. As she walked up the stairs, she gathered herself, step by step.

She'd marry Dubose.

But she wouldn't be a victim. She'd made her choice, and she'd kick ass at it.

Yes, she would.

Her studio would be command central. She'd come here to fill her well. To help her get up when she stumbled.

Yes. *Yes!*

Her hair was like wet rope, but she barely noticed. She dropped her towel. And from a hook on the wall, she pulled down an old buttondown cotton shirt of her father's and put it on. The laundry label sewn on the inside of the collar said COLLIER MAYBANK. Sometimes she came up here just to bury her face in it. Close her eyes and think about how strong those letters looked. How reliable and predictable in an unpredictable world.

A Maybank was loyal to the end. A Maybank never gave up.

She grabbed her sketch pad. Coolly selected a pencil. Dark silver.

She knew what she had in mind. A wedding collage for Dubose, something they could hang in their bedroom for only them to see. He'd see it every day and understand why she was up in her studio. He didn't know about it yet—she hadn't told him, and she wasn't sure why. She'd need to soon.

The pencil was poised over the paper. Where to begin? She waited patiently, but nothing came. With a small sigh, she put the pencil back in her cup and smoothed the paper out. Maybe right now she was too overwrought to work on that.

No problem. She'd wanted to do a birthday collage for Weezie. One for Carmela, too.

Two projects—two fun ones.

Weezie's first. She immediately picked out a pink pencil and bit the end of it. Put it back. Maybe that was the wrong color.

Her mind was blank.

Think.

No, no, she'd just work on Carmela's. She could do this. Just like she had the rest of her life under control. She was competent. She was a Maybank.

But twenty seconds later, she couldn't even figure out where to begin. A minute later, she started sketching with a black pencil, but she stopped. It was wrong. All wrong.

The paper loomed before her, empty. Taunting.

She blinked and looked around. Her studio was just an old attic with a bunch of junk in it left over from an old lady's life. And some bad art from a woman who was afraid.

True ripped the blank page out of the book and crumpled it into a ball. The more she worked it, the greater her anger grew. The greater her fear. What was going wrong? She threw the balled paper, a useless act that gave her no satisfaction. So she threw her cup of pencils. It bounced off the wall, hit the floor with a thunk, and the pencils scattered.

She didn't care about the mess *or* the noise.

Rifling through her canvases, she saw her life: pent up, confused, angry, afraid. Apart.

When would she get to beautiful? Happy? Where was the canvas of celebration? Inclusion? Peace?

The house was as quiet as ever. For no reason at all, she opened her shirt and looked down at her breasts. She wanted to get more use out of them. She craved touch.

But when she thought of Dubose, the feeling disintegrated.

That's because you're stressed, she told herself.

Huh. All she had to do was think of Harrison, and her body sparked to life.

She had to face it: She wanted sex with him. Badly.

Join the club, she could hear Carmela say. *The international Harrison Gamble fan club . . .*

She picked a random pencil off the floor—red—and went back to her sketch pad and made bold arcs and lines. Ideas bloomed in her head, came together. They fit not like puzzle pieces but with flow, which she always felt when she looked down a row of tomatoes or blueberries, the line slightly undulating, leaf crossing leaf, dirt clods stationed here and there like miniature abstract statues, the scene bursting with the mayhem of growth.

No sense. But such unity.

This was the collage about her and Harrison making desperate love between the paddleboards, her bra slipping down into the dark green-brown depths of Biscuit Creek . . .

It was going to be a celebratory canvas if it killed her.

But she was still angry . . . her hand movements slowed, then came to a stop. She bowed her head. It would never be a celebration, she realized. Because there was no happy ending to their story.

The attic door opened. The hinges didn't squeak, but a rush of air came up the stairs.

She knew it wasn't going to be a psycho killer. The dogs would have put up a fuss. No, it was someone from downstairs. She hoped it was Weezie.

But it was Harrison who appeared at the top of the stairs in a pair of duckie boxers and a T-shirt that read, FBI: FEMALE BODY INSPECTOR. His hair was shaggier than usual, a little flat on one side, which only made him more adorable than ever.

"You're kidding me," he said in a regular daytime voice.

She put her finger to her mouth. Though why she bothered after she was throwing pencils and tossing around canvases, she didn't know.

"Oops," he said without changing his volume, although his voice was also thick with sleep. "You'd make a great librarian. They're sexy. Smart. I've never met one that doesn't have a sparkle in her eye."

"You need to go." She sent him a small warning look. Nothing too mean. She liked librarians, too.

"It's four o'clock in the morning." He yawned and spread his arms wide. His shirt rose, exposing his washboard abs, and stretched tight over his pecs. "Aren't you gonna pick up all those pencils?"

Mercy. How was a girl to behave herself around such male magnificence? She felt an unwelcome heat in her lower belly. "No. They're there to keep intruders out. Walk across them at your peril."

Which he did without even wincing, all the while looking around, apparently fascinated.

Something in her was shocked that she didn't feel violated. This was her secret space. Maybe she felt she owed him. After all, he'd shown her his secret place when they were kids . . . the honeysuckle bower. Or maybe she was incredibly glad to see him.

That was it.

He stood just a foot away from her now. She lifted her chin at his shirt. "I see you made it to Goodwill, after all."

"Yep." He looked down at the naughty words. "It's the same one I used to shop in. I paid a visit for old times' sake. And I made a little donation."

Little? She doubted that. "Did you hear a thunk on your ceiling?"

"Yep. And so I lay in bed wondering if you had raccoons or rats in the attic. And then I heard a couple of creaks. I decided to check it out, although it took me a second to find the door. When I saw the light, I knew it had to be you or Weezie. Good thing, because if it had been a raccoon or rat, I woulda screamed like a girl and woken y'all up."

"No, you wouldn't have," she said. "You used to look for snakes under rotten logs. And I know you ate a spider."

And he was out of her life tomorrow.

"Only once. Remember I had a thing for alligators, too? At least until I found out the Crocodile Hunter was dead. I kinda lost my gator joy after that."

It was intimate up here. "This was Honey's special room. I made it into a studio."

"It's awesome."

No, it wasn't. He was out of her life tomorrow.

"How come I didn't know you were still doing art?" He scratched the stubble on his jaw, which wasn't exactly polite, but it was four in the morning. Rules were different then. And she liked the sound anyway. *Beast*, is what she thought. And wanted him to ravish her.

"I don't tell anyone," she said. "Only Weezie and Carmela know."

"Why not Dubose?"

She shrugged and had to look away.

He went to the window. "There's a big moon."

"I know. It's beautiful, isn't it?"

He turned around, his face in shadows. "It's a super moon. They don't come around a lot. I saw it tonight and I recognized it. It's the same moon we had."

The night they lost their virginity to each other and declared their love, was the understood end to that statement.

She padded over, her arms folded over her chest. "It *is* a special moon."

He was looking at it so earnestly, his profile strong and brave, that of a Sewee warrior who'd conquered the world.

All on his own.

They watched a cloud slowly move across the moon's face. She didn't want him to go. This was the last time they'd be together like this. Friends. Old lovers. Sharing their own, private space in the world—an enchanted space—for the last time.

"I'll miss you," she whispered. "For ten years I've

been hiding out in the open. My version of Terence Jones. I was too embarrassed to contact you. And ashamed. You came to get me the day after the prom, and I betrayed you."

"No, you didn't." He turned toward her. "I put you in the corner. Tried to force your hand. I'm smarter now. That's not the way to love. Or be loved."

"We were kids."

"Yeah." He wiped a tear off her cheek with his thumb.

She took a step toward him, and he wrapped his arms around her. Put his chin on her head.

"You're a good egg," he said.

She half laughed, half sobbed into his T-shirt. He stroked her hair. She laid her palm on his chest to absorb his heat.

"You'll keep getting more successful," she said, "until someday you achieve legendary status. Like Johnny Cash."

"No one can rival Johnny."

"Okay, then Tim McGraw."

"I wish."

She closed her eyes, sighing. She didn't want to leave the circle of his arms.

He rubbed her back. "It's not as if I'll never see you. Especially if this thing with Gage and Carmela works out."

"That's true," she said hopefully.

But they both knew it wouldn't be the same. She'd be with Dubose. Harrison might be with another woman. Who knew?

And once she was married, Dubose would be the one man she'd give access to her innermost heart. That was only right. It was what marriage was about: two people becoming one. She wouldn't disrespect it by yearning after someone other than her husband. Else why get married at all?

Snack on this, girlfriend. She remembered those words had run through her head the day Harrison dropped her off at Maybank Hall.

"True?"

"Hmmm?"

"Maybe you'd better stop caressing my chest."

"Oh." She pulled back, flustered at how curt he suddenly sounded. "Sorry."

He stared at her a long moment. The sweet intimacy between them was gone. "You knew what you were doing," he said carefully.

"I said I'm sorry." She felt guilty. But angry, too. She ran her hand through her hair, suddenly self-conscious. Being in her father's shirt didn't help. "I wasn't thinking."

"I know," he said low. "You were playing games. Maybe I've been, too, since I got back here. But that moon's convinced me. I'm not gonna play games with you anymore."

There was a beat of silence. She didn't know what to say.

"You're with the wrong man," he said, "and we both know it."

The anger flared up high. "You don't have any right to say that to me."

"I can say anything I want. And so can you. You seem to have forgotten that. Or maybe you never learned."

"I don't need a lecture. You have no idea what I've been through—" Tonight in the tub. This past year. The past *ten* years.

"You're still with the wrong man."

Her fingers trembled. "And you're the right one? Is that what you're saying?"

"You know damned well I am."

She reached up and twisted his shirt with her fist. "I've had just about enough of your showing off, Mr. Country

Music Star. You don't like not being number one, do you? That's all this is."

"You and I both wish."

The snarky bastard.

But he was right. Neither one of them needed this . . . this thing between them. She pulled his shirt tighter. "Prove it to me then. Prove to me I'm with the wrong man."

"Looks like you've got something to prove first."

"Maybe I do." She reached up and kissed him, boldly exploring his mouth with her tongue. He tasted of wood smoke and sex. "You may be hot. You may have an official Twitter page and a fan club that holds conventions. But I can live without you and your charm, cowboy."

"Are you sure about that?" Before she knew it, he'd turned her around and was holding the hand that had gripped his shirt behind her back. Then he palmed her belly and hauled her right up against him.

A deep thrill shot through her. She was trapped against him, her bottom pressed up to an erection worthy of a porno. "Yes, I'm sure," she lied.

He laughed and kissed her neck—soft, sexy, loud kisses—and lifted his mouth a fraction of an inch. "God, you taste good."

"Mmmm" was all she could manage, and arched back to give him better access. "Don't think this means anything."

"No, this is all a big test. You got something to prove."

"That's right."

While she lay back against him, he unbuttoned her shirt. It landed on the floor, and he turned her back around and went right to her breasts, his tongue hot on her nipples.

The shock and pleasure went straight to her core. She gave a little moan, and her hips thrust forward in response. But she was still in charge of herself. She excelled at staying in control. He might have her body, but he didn't have her heart.

Nosirree.

"Sexy," he murmured, and put a hand in the space between her thighs.

She clenched around his palm while he suckled her breasts and she held on to his hair.

"Why is it so good with you?" She was desperately trying to be furious. "We've barely started."

He lifted his head and kissed her, a bold kiss that promised fantastic sex. "I don't try to understand it. It's like trying to understand a pretty tree. Or really good pizza. It just damned *is*. And you're glad for it."

"Come up here." She ran her hands up his chest to encourage him to straighten so she could tug off his shirt. "Wow." She pulled back to admire him. "How often are you in the gym?"

"A lot. I have to stay in shape for the road."

"You look good."

"It's lonely"—he pulled her close—"having no one to look good for." He reminded her of his hand. "Ride it, baby. If you dare."

Unable to resist the pure pleasure the heel of his palm afforded her, she did just that.

"Sweet Jesus, this is my lucky day." He watched her through half-slitted eyes. "Admit it. It's yours, too."

She was about to come to a rip-roaring climax. "No," she whispered.

"Too proud for your own good. You always have been."

She moaned. He was doing everything he could with his hands, and now his mouth, to make her capitulate. "Don't stop," she heard herself begging, almost over the edge.

But in one swift move, he turned her around, buckled the backs of her knees with his own, and lowered her to the floor with his he-man grip. Next thing she knew, he was hunched over her. Boxer-less. "Got any condoms?"

She didn't *care*. She wanted his hands back on her, playing her like a fiddle.

"My little hedonist." He chuckled. "You're annoyed, aren't you?"

"Yes," she admitted.

"You won't be for long," he said silkily.

She inhaled a shaky breath. "Look in the closet. I bought some for Weezie and stored them in a bag up here—in case I ever need to give some to her."

"Don't move." A second later, he was back with a tin-foil package. "You do need to give them to her. Before she starts school."

"Really?" True closed her eyes.

"It doesn't mean she'll use them." He spanked her lightly. "But she needs them."

"You're right."

"You're hell on a man." She sensed him moving around, readying himself. "But you're a good sister."

"Thanks . . . I think."

He straddled her, one muscled arm holding his weight up, the other running up and down her belly, his fingers finally settling at the nubbin that was the center of her pleasure—and frustration. "You have to make a decision," he said into her ear. "It's me or him."

"No." She drew in a quivery breath and pulsed her bottom against his hand. She couldn't help herself. He brought out the heathen in her.

His erection pressed relentlessly against her flesh. "You're the only one who's ever made me crazy. Ever." One hand on her breast, he entered her from behind.

Sweet mercy. The fullness of him inside her! She rolled her head in a circle and moaned with the sheer wonder of it.

"Choose," he said, stroking her slowly.

"Later." She was panting, for goodness' sake. Couldn't a girl enjoy the moment?

"*Now.* You can see all the good turning away from me does for you. I'm still the one. And I always will be."

In. Out. A sweet pinch of her nipple. A slow roll of his hips. He was torturing her.

"Make me come," she said. "*Please.*"

"You're a stubborn woman."

She didn't deny it.

He quickened the pace of his ministrations. "Say you choose me."

"I—"

She was coming. She was on the brink.

"Say it."

"I choose—" He was pumping now, the eroticism so great she was getting lost in it, the sweet, heady prelude to utter bliss.

But then he withdrew, pushed himself off the floor. She felt him behind her, but she was cold. Oh, so cold.

"Make a decision, True."

"Come back," she whimpered.

"No more chances. I walked away from you once, and I can do it again. Can you?"

God, she felt empty. Cold. A shell without him. She bowed her head. "No," she whispered to the floor. She'd lost her little game.

But it felt so good to admit it.

Finally.

She gave a little sob. "I choose you. I do."

She felt him over her again, his solid, comforting presence. "It's all right, baby," he murmured into her ear. Then he kissed her shoulder and entered her once more, showing no mercy until she climaxed with a roar.

At least, it felt like a roar. She was a tigress on a high

rock, proclaiming that this was her territory—this man, this time, this place, this love.

"Oh, God. Just like the Katy Perry song." She gave a little laugh, and wilted against his hand on her belly.

He chuckled and lowered her down so that her cheek pressed against the floor and her arms splayed out. Only then did he take his own pleasure, supporting her lower body weight and caressing her flank as he entered her again from behind. She came again with him, a wild woman dangling from his arms.

A woman who'd chosen.

CHAPTER TWENTY-EIGHT

Harrison lay down beside her and they kissed, a long, luxurious kiss, a let's-not-let-this-end kind. She laid her head on the crook of his arm. He was a sated version of da Vinci's Vitruvian Man. She was his. *His.* He didn't know how they'd work things out. But she wasn't going to marry Dubose.

No way. No how.

"Let's go outside," she said eventually, "to really catch this moon in all its glory."

"I like how you said that." He sprang to his feet without making any noise, fully alert.

"Don't tell me you take ninja classes, too," she said with a chuckle.

"Nope. I *teach* them. Superhero classes, too." He helped her into her father's shirt, then pulled on his own T-shirt and boxers. "What about the dogs?"

"They'll try to get up and ask us what's going on, but if we give them a quick head rub, they'll go right back to sleep. We'll go out the back door."

"Gage sleeps hard," he said.

"So does Weezie."

Their plan went off without a hitch, and they stepped into a friendly darkness. The earth was sleeping off a heady day. They held hands and walked into the tomato field.

"Everything looks so different at night." He enjoyed the feel of the cold dirt between his toes and the green vegetation smell of the ripened crop. His heart rate was still a little elevated from the hot sex and True's nearness.

She crouched between the rows, looking like a stealthy cat in the jungle. And then she sat with her palms back and lifted her gaze to the moon.

God, now she was a she-wolf.

He'd waited so long for this. Too long.

He sat at her feet and leaned on her shins. "We're good together," he said simply.

"I know." She stroked his long, silky hair.

She let her legs fall open, and he landed on her belly. Then she lay on her back in the dirt and they both laughed.

"This dirt feels amazing." She wrapped her legs around his chest. "I'm not letting you go."

Dang. He was so overwhelmed, he wanted to have sex again. It came the closest to expressing how he felt about her. He caressed her shins with his hands, and then he twisted around and cradled her in his arms.

They started kissing. Before long, they were naked between the tomato plants, his shirt and boxers laid in chivalrous fashion beneath her bottom. He had a hard-on that was begging for release.

"I didn't bring anything," he said.

"Check Daddy's shirt pocket." She grinned. "I slipped a condom in there. Why do you think I wanted us to come outside?"

"Ah," he said. "She a hot tamale *and* a vixen, all rolled into one luscious, vanilla-scented package."

But he took his time, kissing the whole length of her. She threw her arms out to the side—a silent invitation for him to storm her castle. He lifted one of her legs over his neck. "Gorgeous," he said, and brushed his lips across her inner thigh.

Her fingers uselessly clutched the dirt.

And then his tongue went to work. She bucked and moaned, and his fingers joined the action. All the while, he murmured against her skin how beautiful she was, how much he wanted to be inside her. When his mouth took full possession of her, she arched her back like a bow about to let fly an arrow. And when she came, she cried out loud, her legs wrapped tight around his neck.

He was smothered in sex. And he loved it.

When she was done, she lay spread-eagled in the dirt.

"I've never felt better," she told him with a smile.

"I'm glad." He pulled her up and kissed her lazily, rubbing his hands in little circles on her back.

But very quickly, she insisted on pleasuring him.

"I won't fight you." He leaned back on his palms, his knees propped wide apart.

"You have to lose the boxers," she told him.

"Make me." He pulled his legs in and sat cross-legged.

"You do yoga, too, don't you?"

"All the time."

It was easy enough to gain his cooperation. All she did was rub him between the thighs with her palm while she told him what she was going to do to him. And then she stood tall and stretched, her back to him, her face raised to the moon, her sweet bobbed hair now a mess curling on her shoulders.

"Aphrodite," he said.

She giggled, and when she turned around, the boxers were off.

Now it was her turn to take her time. She teased. She licked. She stroked. He moaned. He told her that she was

the most beautiful fairy creature he'd ever seen. When
she took the length of him in her mouth, she took him
down like a sacked quarterback.

Almost.

He had another play in him. Oh, yes, he did.

He chased her across a few rows of tomatoes, and
when he tackled her, they lay and laughed a long minute.
Then sheltered by the plants, cradled in the dirt, and shel-
lacked by a silver moon, she let him all the way in, rocking him between her legs while the world sang its night
song, a lullaby of love.

CHAPTER TWENTY-NINE

Half an hour later, they were back in the house heading upstairs to return to their separate bedrooms.

"Can you show me some of your art?" He thought it was a simple question. But judging from True's face, he'd asked her to scale Mount Everest.

"Sure." She didn't look too happy about sharing. But he didn't give her any slack.

In the attic, he followed her to the wardrobe where she stacked her canvases. Man, there were a lot of them . . . some big, some tiny.

All freakin' awesome.

When he was done looking through them, he shook his head. "These shouldn't be in a closet."

She bowed her head.

"Why haven't you shown anyone?"

She shrugged.

He took her by the shoulders. "They're beautiful. You're *good*. You should have an art show. Why haven't you taken them to a gallery?"

She started to laugh but held it in. "I don't know."

He sighed. "You and I both know who you really are. Let the rest of the world know, too. You can still be your buttoned-up, prissy Maybank self when it suits you. But there's so much more to you than that. You're not honoring any dusty old ancestors by hiding."

"I'll have to think about it." Her mama was written all over her face.

"I'm out there stripped naked for the world to see in my songs, aren't I? There are some nuisances that come with that kind of exposure, but the payoff outweighs any pain-in-the-ass factor. I get to share my songs. I even get paid for it. It's a great feeling."

"I'm sure it is."

"Don't give me lip service."

She didn't deny it.

"Tell you what," he said. "Let's try a little Weezie-style interviewing. If you weren't afraid, what would be your next step as an artist?"

"I'm not an artist—"

"Yes, you damned well are."

"Okay, I'd—"

"You'd what?"

And she told him about the big copier machine she wanted, the kind that could copy and magnify fabric patterns, leaf veins, product labels, postcards. It would give her so many new options. "I love working with 3D textiles, but I'm really excited about trying something new with a two-dimensional surface. A flat canvas is so much easier to transport and sell, too."

"See?" He chuckled. "You lit up like a Christmas tree. You even talked about selling! You can't *not* do this. You're an artist. Follow through."

She pushed her hair off her face with both hands. "I-I'll work on it."

He pulled her close. "I hope you do, baby. You won't be totally happy until you do."

She was stiff in his arms, but he held her anyway. "I work with an art broker. She helps me find great pieces for my houses. Anytime you want me to show her your work, she's a call away."

She didn't say anything, but her fingers uncurled on his chest. "Thanks," she whispered.

But something was wrong. It took him five more minutes to get it out of her. Five minutes in which she cried softly, nonstop.

"Come on, True," he urged her gently. "What's going on? How can we do what we just did together and you leave me out? Again?"

"Okay," she finally said, wiping her nose with her arm. "I'm ready to tell you. I *have* to tell you."

Shit. Her tone didn't sound good. The room was still dark, but nighttime was sliding away. "What is it?" He braced himself. It obviously was going to be bad news, whatever it was.

"I told you I chose you." She pushed some hair off his brow. "And I meant it." She paused for a long time, her eyes bleak. "But let's get real. We can't happen as a couple."

A sick feeling fell over him. It was happening—again. "Come on, now. We can work this out somehow."

"Listen to me." She took his upper arms and squeezed. "You want me to be an artist. You tell me I *need* to be. Otherwise, I won't be happy. Harrison, don't you see? You were talking about yourself, too! I don't want to be the woman who keeps you from your art. I refuse to be country music's Yoko Ono, you hear?"

"Yoko didn't deserve that rap. And I'm not a Beatle."

"It doesn't matter. I'm in your way."

"Stop saying that. Let's *think*." He was desperate to find the right answer. It was there, on the tip of his tongue, but he couldn't speak. The old numbness was on him, the same one that accompanied him to Nashville after the last time she rejected him ten years earlier. And when Dad had died. Mom, too.

He knew no other way. You just kept going. You didn't stop.

"You know we don't need to think about this," she insisted. "We both know. Some things are meant *not* to be." Her eyes filled with tears. "When we put on our thinking caps, we're pretty smart people, and I'm calling it, for the last time. I'm going to marry Dubose, and you're getting back to your career."

"No." But it was like watching a wreck happen on TV. He couldn't get to it—to her. His wires were cut. "No," he said again.

It was the most he could come up with. But he heard the feebleness of it. The pain. The fear. The giving in.

Her face was grim. "I'll see you in the morning, and please—let's say good-bye on good terms this time."

And she slipped away.

CHAPTER THIRTY

Being a mature man sucked, Harrison thought the next morning at breakfast. Gage was making everyone fried-egg-and-bacon sandwiches. He even had fake bacon for Weezie. What a guy.

Harrison sat in the chair next to True, which was tough. But he soaked up every second of being near her while he ate his sandwich, a puny distraction but pretty damned good. He felt like shit, but for Weezie and Gage's sake, he was determined to go out on a good note. Let True see what she was missing.

Damn that girl. But damn him for not knowing what to do about her. Again.

He could pull it off. He'd done a concert once with a 103-degree fever and vomiting between songs. Leaving behind a heartbreaker with a penchant for wearing pearls at breakfast would be a piece of cake.

Gage joined them at the table with his own sandwich.

"I've got some news," Harrison said.

True's eyes widened. And he understood why. If he had news, why hadn't he told her during their middle-of-the-night tryst-turned-relationship? Or afterward, during their almost instantaneous breakup?

"News?" Weezie sat up super straight. "Is it like . . . a secret, maybe?"

"Sorry, Barbara Walters," he said. "Nothing like that." Her expression dropped just a tad. "It's still news."

"With any luck, good news," Gage said warily.

"I hope you'll think so." Harrison was actually sweating bullets. "This is gonna sound a little strange. But if anyone can pull it off, Vince can. I actually got the idea from an artist friend of mine. She reuses materials—all kinds of things. Fabric, bottle caps, string, shells, paper . . . and she makes them into something new and beautiful."

True's face went beet red.

He took a leisurely sip of coffee, enjoying her acute discomfort.

"Wait." Weezie looked around the table. "That's my sister."

True took a big bite from her egg-and-bacon sandwich.

"Well, maybe it is," Harrison said, and put his cup down. "I'm not telling. It's not my place. But have you ever noticed that taking big bites out of a sandwich is a good speech-avoidance strategy? I'll have to use that tip in my next interview."

True swallowed. "Your brother's a troublemaker, Gage."

"I know," he said, a glimmer of a smile playing about his lips.

"Is anyone gonna listen?" Harrison asked. But he looked only at Gage and Weezie.

"I am," said Weezie. She actually had her cell phone out, her fingers poised on the keys.

"No," Harrison told her. "This doesn't go on Facebook."

"I was gonna send it to AP's Twitterfeed," she said.

"Uh-uh," he told her. "This is family talk. It doesn't go anywhere else."

Only slightly abashed, Weezie put her phone away. He knew True must have heard him say *family*, but she didn't even flinch. Too bad. He wanted her to feel guilty. Because they had become a little family in a way.

Ed butted his knee, looking for bacon.

And that included the dogs.

He scratched Ed's muzzle. "Vince has done some consulting work on Hollywood movie sets. He's got an expert—a close friend of his who needs a vacation—flying out here today to help us. The plan is to take the trailer"—he looked at Gage—"and put it *inside* the new house. It'll be Gage's retreat. It can even be a cool guest area. Vince is calling it 'the trailer pad.'"

"I love it!" Weezie clapped.

True's mouth dropped open.

Gage pushed his chair back and stood up. "That's ludicrous. It'll cost a fortune, too." The color on his cheeks was high.

"Nothing I can't afford," Harrison assured him calmly. "And whatever I spend on this house, I'm matching that amount and donating it to the Biscuit Creek United Way. So get off that high horse of yours and sit back down."

Slowly, Gage sat. True reached over and squeezed his hand real quick then put her hands in her lap and looked at Harrison, her gaze excited but afraid, too.

He appreciated her seeing to his brother. And he was glad she was giving him a chance to explain his dastardly genius idea without pooh-poohing the whole thing right away. But he'd never tell her so. They were done. Over. Kaput. And he couldn't wait to get the hell outta Dodge.

"Now, when I say we're putting the mobile home inside the house," he started up again, refusing to look her way, "I don't mean the undercarriage or the outside. Vince is going to dismantle and recycle as much of the parts we don't use as he can. His goal is to re-create the interior as accurately as possible. Gage, you'll remember that only one side of our trailer had windows. That side will look out on the backyard from the first floor of the house. The front door, on the same side, will face a porch."

Gage was taking it in . . . taking it in . . . So were True and Weezie.

Harrison just kept hoping they would.

"You or your guests," he went on to Gage, "who might like privacy, can access the trailer pad from that backyard staircase. But to meet code and for convenience, Vince is going to scatter a discreet couple of doors—one in each bedroom, and one in the living room area—on the other side so you can enter from the interior of the big house if you'd rather."

Gage was chewing hard on his cheek.

"The fun part for Vince's friend and an interior designer friend of mine coming in this afternoon from Nashville," said Harrison, "will be salvaging what they can from the interior of the original trailer. And if they can't do that—they're going to find exact or close copies so that when you walk in, Gage, it's our old homestead. Down to the vinyl flooring, the tacky ceilings, and the fake wood paneling on the walls. Your guests will think it's kitschy fun. And you can write your crosswords up there knowing that both Mama's and Daddy's memories are being honored through this special project."

He heard a sniffle. It was True crying. Dammit, so was Weezie. And Gage—his eyes were watering up, too.

"Stop it, everyone," he said, his own eyes burning all of a sudden. "I got one more thing. Gage and I aren't moving back to the trailer now, obviously. So if you don't mind"—he was forced to glance at True—"and if Gage is amenable to unpacking his bag again, he'll stay here."

"Of course!" she piped up right away, damn chipper for a woman who'd just ended their future. Again.

"Thanks," Gage told her. "You two ladies are great hostesses."

"We like having you," Weezie said. "You're a good cook. And most of the time, you're not boring anymore."

"Thanks," Gage said. "Neither are you. Sometimes."

Harrison was dying to share a secret glance of amusement with True, but those days were over. "I hope you'll have better luck with your puzzles," he told Gage, "now you know what's gonna be waiting for you in the new house."

"I sense my stress levels plummeting already," said Gage, "a sure sign that my productivity will not only increase but be of a higher quality."

"Yeah, whatever," Weezie said with a chuckle.

"Weezie," said True.

"He can take it," she said airily and glanced back at Gage, who was scrolling through his messages, oblivious.

Here came the part Harrison really dreaded. "I'm heading back to Nashville today," he said quietly. "I've got to stop by the construction site first to talk to Vince. But then I'm outta here. I'll come back when the house is done. So maybe three weeks."

"No!" Weezie cried. "The wedding! You'll miss the wedding!"

Harrison put his hand on her shoulder and gave it a squeeze. "You'll have to email me pictures." Which he would promptly delete before opening.

Weezie was really crying now. True's face was pale. She looked at the floor, her expression pained.

"I don't want you to go, Harrison." Weezie wiped at her eyes. "Stay here. Move back. You can live with Gage, and everyone will be happy."

If only life were that simple. Harrison shook his head. "I wish I could, Weezie. But my life is too complicated to be able to do that. Don't forget I told you that anytime you want to fly out and see me, you can. We won't be losing touch this time. I promise." He stood. "I'm going. I could use some hugs."

Weezie jumped up from her chair and tried to make it to the back door, but Harrison was fast on his feet and caught her. "Come here."

She sobbed into his shirt. "I can't believe you're leaving again. I can't believe it."

She was a mess. And if she kept this up, soon he'd be, too. He closed his eyes and held her tight. "I'm gonna miss you. And every time you drive that car I promised you at the end of your first semester, I want you to think of me. Okay, little sister?"

"Car? What car?" True stood and came over.

Weezie pulled it together long enough to look up and say, "The one he's going to get me if I get good grades and act socially correct."

"Oh," True said softly.

And then Weezie started crying again, but softer this time, poor girl.

"Why don't you run out and feed the chickens," her sister suggested in a calm, gentle voice.

"All right," Weezie whispered, and was about to open the door when she turned back around. "At least we still have Gage," she said hopefully.

Aw. She sure knew how to pull at a guy's heartstrings.

But Harrison's brother just stood there. Was Gage thinking about what to say? Or was he just gonna ignore her? Because that would suck.

True was opening her mouth to do her usual save when Gage spoke up. "Can I be your big brother, too?" he asked Weezie. "I'm not going anywhere, so I hope you'll come over to my new place and hang out a lot. Your friends can come with you."

Hallelujah. Too bad Harrison couldn't share his happiness about this little Kodak moment with True.

Weezie wiped a hand across her eyes. "Sure," she told Gage with a trembly little smile.

And then she was gone.

A little bit of Harrison's heart went with her.

Thankfully, the farewell with True was surprisingly easy. Gage was there. So Harrison thanked her for her hospitality the same way he'd thank a hotel manager for a nice stay. She, gracious southern belle that she was, said it had been entirely her pleasure.

On the porch, he hugged Gage first, who fortunately went back inside. Now Harrison wouldn't have to give True a mock hug. Too bad, because her soft little body was the one thing in the world he loved to hold more than his guitar.

She followed him down to the car.

He turned the key in the ignition and looked at her from his window. What the hell to say? "It's been crazy, huh?"

"Sure has." She nodded tightly.

"You really don't have to be out here."

"I know."

"Have a good wedding." Saying that was hard.

"I will," she squeaked back. "Good luck with those songs."

He was going to say, *I hope the bow ties are a hit*, but he'd had enough of the bullshit-southern-manners stuff. So he took off, waving from the window, refusing to look at her in the rearview mirror. He didn't want to remember her that way, getting smaller and smaller until she disappeared.

At the construction site, Harrison had one last consultation with Vince, who assured him that he had everything under control.

"Forget about all of this until I call and tell you it's done," Vince said over the noise of the construction crew pounding nails. They were framing the floor. "You go back home and take care of business."

"Thanks." He looked at the view of the creek that Gage would have and thought, *Lucky man.*

"Did you know there's a guitar without a case in the master bedroom closet of the trailer?" Vince asked him as he headed to his car. "You should rescue it."

Harrison's chest tightened. "That's my father's. I'll pick it up before I go."

He'd never touched that guitar and had forgotten all about it. He'd always felt too guilty, thinking he'd landed his father in jail, so he'd bought his own. But it was Dad's guitar that had gotten him interested in playing.

"One more thing." Vince grinned. "Weezie Maybank's coming over to interview me. She wants the story behind the dresses. Says she has a human-interest class coming up, and she wants to get a head start on her assignments."

Harrison pulled at his ear. "You don't have to help her out, you know."

"I'm looking forward to it. She's got get-up-and-go. I suspect this might be her way of trying to get reassurance, too, before she heads off to college with her funky outfits and semi-outrageous personality. You can be different . . . and still make a difference."

Whoa. Awkward silence. They looked at each other, and then they both burst into laughter.

"Now that was plain purty," Harrison said.

"Shut up, you cave man."

They exchanged a bro hug, and Vince headed back to the construction site, whistling "Dixie" as he walked.

Harrison retrieved his father's guitar and put it carefully in the car trunk. His emotions were already tied in huge knots, and now they were practically strangling him.

Road trips—even road trips from hell, as this one would surely be—called for MoonPies and Twinkies from the gas station and the Eagles on his iPod. Maybe while he was stuffing his face and singing "Take It Easy," he'd forget about the empty seat next to him, the one that still smelled a little bit like a vanilla ice cream cone dipped in sass.

Maybe he'd finally move on.

CHAPTER THIRTY-ONE

"It's called The Damn Yankee!" Carmela crowed. Then she thumped her fist on the table for good measure. "What do you think?"

True stopped chewing, embarrassed that the only thing on her mind was an image of Harrison naked above her, his hot, adoring gaze on hers.

She and Carmela were at the Starfish Grill. Harrison had left three days ago, time enough for her to recover from their insanely memorable coupling and focus on the fact that any day now, she'd be a bride.

Mrs. *Dubose* Waring. *Mrs.* Dubose Waring. Mrs. Dubose *Waring*. She said it it in her head all the time now, including with every bite of her lunch, to avoid thinking of Harrison. Reading didn't help, either. She'd tried but got nowhere. And of course, she couldn't get anywhere near her studio without thinking of him.

"I think . . ." She looked up at the ceiling, over at Roger, the busboy, working diligently to clean a table, and then back to Carmela, who was biting the side of her hand, waiting for her response. She was thinking of Harrison's face when he'd told them his genius plan for Gage's trailer. "I think it's a *genius* idea."

"I do, too!" Carmela grinned broadly.

True felt guilty, but what could she do?

"Gage is brilliant," Carmela said. "No one around here wants any more Pat Conroy bobbleheads or Charleston dish towels, right? But they might want something 'from off.' And who knows 'from off' better than I do? I'm the town's resident damn Yankee, and now I can say 'you guys' whenever I want! I'll have Boston brown bread kits, New England clam chowder, soy candles from Cape Cod, and a whole travel book section on New York."

Mrs. Dubose Waring, True said in her head, to help her put aside that image of Harrison's profile looking at the super moon. "It's going to be so great." She took her friend's hand and squeezed. "And do you think it's time, 'Mela?"

Carmela's happy expression disappeared. "No," she whispered.

"I think you should," True said softly. "It's not exploit-ative. It would tie in with your shop's theme. Your father would be really proud of you for including him in your plans this way. He was a hero. All the guys from his fire station in Queens were. Maybe . . . just maybe, if you let go of being afraid, you could honor them in some way at the store."

Carmela stared at their laced hands. "I know." She looked up. "But it's so hard to talk about 9/11 to people these days. I'm not looking for pity."

True chuckled. "No one could ever pity a strong per-son like you. They might come up and thank you for your father's sacrifice, however."

Carmela smiled. "That would be incredible."

"Yes, it would." True released her hand. *Mrs. Dubose Waring.* "Have you told Gage about your dad?"

"No. Not yet."

"Well, I hope you do. Soon. Things going well there?"

"Really great. It's so weird how we click. I get him. And he gets me."

True put her fork down and leaned forward. "I'm so happy for you both."

Carmela took *her* hand this time and squeezed it. "And I'm happy for *you*. Are *you* happy for you?"

True hadn't talked to her about Harrison. It still felt too raw. "I'm doing well," she answered carefully.

Mrs.DuboseWaringMrs.DuboseWaringMrs.Dubose-Waring.

"Oh, hon."

Tears instantly sprang to True's eyes at Carmela's tender tone, but she wouldn't look up. "I'm doing the right thing," she said, blinking them back. "That other situation—it can't happen. It won't happen. So I have to get on with my life." She took a discreet sip of water to get rid of the lump in her throat.

"Okay," said Carmela. "I won't push. But just know this. I'm here for you, no matter what. It's too soon to say what'll unfold between Gage and me, but I have to tell you—there's something different about this relationship. It feels deep and honest already. I feel like a grown-up. I think—"

She looked carefully around, and they both caught Roger listening.

"Go away, please, Roger," True chided him gently.

"All right." He glowered. "But don't expect any refills on water or tea."

Carmela waited for him to shuffle away, then they both giggled.

"I think I'm falling in love," Carmela whispered. "And it's made me see that nothing is bigger than love is. Not Gage's quirkiness, or his OCD, or my trust issues with any man who's not my father, or my Yankee accent. *Nothing.* It truly frickin' does conquer all." She stood and tapped the table with her index finger. "You remember that, True Maybank."

"I will." True forced herself to smile. "Where are you going?"

Carmela lifted and dropped her shoulders. "Nowhere, actually." She laughed and sat down again. "I just got so inspired."

"I appreciate that," said True, chuckling.

And she really did.

Pre-wedding jitters. Pre-wedding fling. She knew all about both. She could write an informative, tell-all article— anonymous, of course—for one of the bridal magazines. She clung to the hope that when she saw Dubose again, her love for him—because that had to be what it was—would smack her in the face as an obvious truth, and she'd come out of this silly, worried mode.

Love conquered all.

Over the next day or so, she kept recalling that speech of Carmela's. Whenever she thought about Harrison— which was night and day —she'd replace his face with Dubose's. And whenever she looked at her new BMW sedan, which she hadn't driven yet—not until she was married—she thought about how Dubose had so thoughtfully purchased it for her. And if she looked at the tomato fields, she'd remember how Dubose had promised to help her keep Maybank Hall's U-pick operation thriving even after they got married.

She wouldn't think about what she and Harrison had done in that field.

The only problem with her strategy was that it didn't *work*. So by the time Dubose called, she was a wreck.

"Mom and I are arriving on the same afternoon flight from LaGuardia to Charleston," he told True on the phone.

"That's convenient."

"Yeah, well, she asked me to delay coming home a day so I could sit on the plane with her."

"You're a devoted son." Although a devoted fiancé pining after his woman would have taken a flight yesterday, especially as Penn was a seasoned traveler.

"I'll drive her home first," he went on. "She'll be pretty jet-lagged. And then"—his tone got distinctly amorous—"I'll come see you."

"I can't wait!" True said. "Although—"

"What?"

"Remember our promise."

"Damn. You're really going to make me wait? I've been working my ass off here in New York, barely stopping to eat and sleep. Some TLC will do me good."

"Sorry. But I have to ask, Dubose, have you thought about whether some TLC would do *me* good? Does that matter at all?"

"Of course it does. What's gotten into you? Wedding stress? Maybe you need some Xanax. Lots of the partners' wives take it."

"No, thanks." She ran her hand over her hair. "I just wish—"

"What?"

"That we wouldn't fight." Her heart felt sore. And vulnerable. She wanted a bubble bath and chocolate. And she wanted her mother. Yes, Helen Maybank had been selfish and too worried about appearances, but she'd still been her mother.

"It's pre-wedding jitters," Dubose said. "That's all. Hey, since we're sticking to these rules, I'll wait to see you tonight at Mom's."

"Dubose, I made you supper. I've got so much to tell you about the wedding."

"Save all that girlie stuff for tonight. Mom will want to

hear it. Her housekeeper is making us an early supper. We're eating at six."

"But I baked your favorite chicken-and-wild-rice dish. I was hoping we'd watch a movie."

"Tomorrow night, maybe. Although, wait—that's my bachelor party."

"Tonight was going to be our only chance to really hang out together—"

"Freeze the casserole, True. We'll eat it after we're married. Problem solved. Now stop fretting."

That was exactly what she'd been doing, ever since Harrison came back into her life.

Before she left for Penn's, she heated up the casserole for Gage, Weezie, and Carmela. She'd done a lot of thinking that afternoon. Her infatuation with Harrison had been just that. She'd forgive herself her romantic nature, which was intertwined with her artistic one, and let the memory slip away. Dubose was real. Here. In Biscuit Creek. She could make a life with him, and she'd make sure it was a good one.

The UPS man knocked on her door just as she was about to run out and buy Penn a nice bottle of wine.

"What is *that*?" A massive oblong box sat on her doorstep.

"Not sure," the man in brown said. "It looks like it came from a local business supply company in Charleston."

"Are you sure it came to *me*? I never ordered anything."

He double-checked his screen. "Yes, ma'am." He helped her get it inside the front parlor and left.

She struggled a few minutes to open it, truly baffled. But when she finally saw what it was—a deluxe, state-of-the-art tabletop copier machine, complete with a coupon for free installation and maintenance, an hour-long, in-person tutorial, a DVD tutorial, and a certificate for free ink cartridges for life—she burst into tears.

Of course it was from Harrison.

It was such a generous gesture, but she knew he was also taunting her. Would she spread her wings and fly as an artist? Or would she keep hiding in the attic?

"You got me this time," she whispered out loud. The artist in her was absolutely seduced by the beauty of that machine. She'd never forgive herself for giving it up. But she'd also never be able to forget Harrison if she kept it.

That was probably his diabolical plan.

A short while later, she knocked at Penn's door. When she stepped over the threshold, she remembered doing the same thing all those years ago, when she'd been late for the post-prom brunch because she'd slept with Harrison the night before on the beach. An amazing night—up until then, the best of her life—followed by that disaster of a morning.

The housekeeper led her to the living room.

"A bit underdressed, are we?" Penn said, a gin-and-tonic in hand. "But what does it matter? You're glowing like a woman in love. Dubose would find you enchanting in a paper sack."

True had kept it simple in one of Honey's homemade poplin skirts and a sleeveless summer sweater. "I'm not sure if I should thank you or not." She kept her tone light. "But you look lovely yourself, Penn."

Her mother-in-law was a real fashionista. She wore a chic brown sheath and a silk scarf in the traditional Burberry pattern, probably in honor of her trip to England.

Where was Dubose? True was almost frantic to see him. But she couldn't show it. So she sat carefully on the edge of the sofa and smiled at Penn. "How was your trip?"

"It was interesting enough. I called Neville Barker from London to ask him to escort me to the wedding." He was a wealthy Charlestonian known for his charitable work, like Penn. "Would you like a drink?"

A drink always meant a gin-and-tonic in Penn's house. "Yes, thanks." She needed one.

The housekeeper swiftly prepared it, and True managed a few large swallows when Dubose walked into the room.

"Hey, beautiful." He seemed genuinely happy to see her.

She, thank God, felt a genuine stirring of gladness. Now she could get on with her life again, surely.

"You're a breath of fresh air." He kissed her cheek.

And her entire world stopped on its axis. Oh, God. She couldn't bear the feel of his lips on her skin and had to try not to flinch.

"Thanks," she said faintly. "You look great."

Her reaction was a fluke, she told herself. She was nervous. Penn was watching. Reunions in front of judgmental mothers-in-law were never fun.

They made agonizing small talk for ten minutes. And then they adjourned to the dining room. Dubose showed her no particular attention—didn't pull out her chair. But then again, he didn't pull out his mother's, either.

Over their appetizer course of Lowcountry she-crab soup, True gathered her courage.

"We had some glitches in the wedding plans," she told him. It was surprisingly easy to say. "But the good news is that I've been able to get us back on track."

Penn didn't bat an eye.

Dubose paused with his spoon poised in the air. "Glitches?"

"Yes, as in losing our caterer and reception site," True said.

He put down his spoon. "You're kidding, right? How in hell did this happen?"

True glanced at Penn, who blithely continued eating her soup. "The caterer double-booked."

Dubose looked back and forth between them. "So what are the plans?"

"Don't look at me," Penn said. "I was in England."

"We're having the reception at Maybank Hall," True told him. "I couldn't get a high-end caterer. It was too late in the game. We're having a barbecue, fiddle playing, and Booty Call. You know them, Dubose. They're a good rock-and-roll cover band."

There was massive silence at the table.

Dubose cocked his head at her. "Booty Call? *Really?*"

True's chest tightened. "If you don't like the plans I came up with, we can always elope."

"Warings don't *do* redneck weddings," said Penn. "Nor do we elope."

True refused to acknowledge Penn's rude remark. "You like Booty Call," she reminded Dubose. "You and I danced to them for hours last time we heard them."

"Yes, but that was at an oyster roast. This is our *wedding.*" His face registered shock. Distaste.

"And it'll be *fun.*" True pushed down the lump in her throat. "We're supposed to celebrate."

"But the partners will be there, and Maybank Hall—"

"What? What about Maybank Hall?" True's heart thumped against her ribs.

"I can't see it working." Dubose had his lawyer face on.

"My family home is a beautiful place for a wedding reception. It's charming. Real. Not some rental space with party props."

"But it's not spectacular," he said with some heat, then seemed to sink in his chair. "At least not now. You've got shutters hanging sideways—"

"I get it," she said, her throat tight.

"No, you don't." He shook his head wearily. "I want our wedding to be the talk of the town for months."

"Why?" Her heart was full of anguish, and it hurt. It hurt so very much. "To impress everyone at work and all your society friends in Charleston?"

A beat of heavy silence went by.

"This is about *us*." Her voice quivered. "This isn't some business function. And real friends don't care about one-upping each other."

Penn injected an unfeeling laugh. "You poor, naive girl."

Dubose threw his mother a quelling look, then reached across the table to True and took her hand.

No, no, no! His touch was foreign. Unwelcome. Inside, her soul cried at her folly. But doggedly, she persisted. She was a Maybank. She would let him hold her hand because he was her fiancé and they needed to work this out.

"Don't you want me to become partner one day?" He spoke as if she were a child who needed soothing.

Maybe she was. Maybe she'd lost perspective, stayed too long on a country property and done nothing with her life. "Only if that's what makes you happy," she whispered.

Penn gave a dramatic sigh. "Bosey's job is what will keep you in BMWs and diamonds and trips to the islands."

"I don't care about those things." True found her voice again. She had plenty to say to Penn, and she didn't care anymore what her future mother-in-law thought.

Penn cocked her eyebrow at Dubose.

"I want to know something," True said to Dubose. "Do you care about what makes *me* happy? Is that why you bought me that car?"

"We're talking about the wedding," he said. "Let's not get sidetracked."

"By the really important questions?" True stood, her knees like jelly. "Thanks for the car, but I'm sending it back. I chose a used one I prefer. As for the wedding plans, they're a done deal. Even if you wanted chandeliers and a fancy party room with finger canapés, you can't have them. It's not that important anyway. It's all the years that come after the wedding that really matter. Right, Dubose?"

He wouldn't look at her.

"This is all very hurtful, Gertrude." Penn's lips were pursed.

"My name is True," she said evenly. "I have a right to assert my opinion about what car I drive. And I worked hard to fix our wedding problem." She folded her arms over her chest and stared at Dubose until he made eye contact with her again. "It makes me happy to hold our wedding reception at Maybank Hall. And that should be reason enough to do so."

Dubose tossed aside his napkin. "Fine. Drive the car you want. Reject my well-intentioned gift."

"I'm sure it was," True said, "and I'm sorry, but—"

"As for the wedding"—he interrupted her coldly, but she refused to feel guilty—"we have no other choice at this point." He frowned at his mother. "You really screwed this one up. You should have stayed an extra day or two here to help."

"I assumed she'd handle it." Penn's tone was cool. "I'll call someone tonight. We'll get everything back on track."

"Are you kidding me?" Dubose's anger was palpable. "Why didn't you fix it earlier?"

"I had a *conference*." Penn gave a light shrug.

Dubose narrowed his eyes. "I think you set her up, Mother."

Penn tossed her head. "That's ridiculous. But I can fix the matter. You should show a little appreciation."

"I don't believe you," her son declared.

True didn't believe her, either! Though why it had never occurred to her that Penn had orchestrated the whole thing . . .

She was naive, that was why.

Penn looked away from Dubose, her silence speaking volumes.

"You threw a wrench in the works," he said. "I know it. How could you do that? True is my fiancée. Not one of your personal assistants or nurses to browbeat."

True was grateful he was supporting her. He might be used to calling the shots—and she might have been too willing to give in to him, up to this point in their relationship—but he always propped her up in the end.

The problem she had with him touching her? She'd get past it. She'd simply need time. And she would no longer kowtow to his wishes. This reception was the first step toward her asserting herself. In a strange way, she was glad the wedding fiasco had happened.

"I had nothing to do with this snafu," Penn lied brazenly, "but it only proves that Warings shouldn't marry Maybanks. You, in particular, should know better than to try. Look what happened to you on prom night."

"That's ancient history," Dubose said. True was so glad he thought so. "What other complaints do you have about True, Mother? You'd better get it out of your system now. Because she's going to be my wife, and I'm not going to have you making her life hell."

"All right, then." Penn stuck out her chin. "If you want to know the truth, Helen and I never got along."

"Helen?" Dubose raised a brow.

"I thought you played bridge together for years," True said.

"We did." Penn's tone was icy.

"Why would you bring her up?" Dubose asked. "Did y'all get in a fight?"

"Never. We merely stopped speaking."

"I-I had no idea," True said. "What happened? Did Mama insult you somehow?"

Penn gave a short laugh. "You could say that."

Dubose was still in courtroom mode, watching his mother's expression and listening to her answers closely. He put his palms on the table. "Does this have anything to do with Dad?"

"No." Penn was adamant. "Why would it?"

Dubose angled his head. "Why is it you never liked Helen? She was a lot like you. The perfect wife. Dressed nicely. Followed the rules."

Penn flushed. "Not *every* rule."

Dubose pulled back and nodded. "So that's it."

"What?" True said.

Penn sucked in her cheeks.

And then True got it. "Oh, no. My mother and"—she swallowed and looked at Dubose—"*your* father?"

"Is that it, Mother?" Dubose's face was like granite.

Penn pushed back her chair. "I don't like discussing crass topics. I'm going to bed."

Well. There was their answer.

"That explains a lot." True sank into a chair.

Dubose sat next to her. "I think I need a drink. How about you?"

"Yes." For years and years she'd wondered what the truth was. *It's okay, Mama and Daddy*, she thought, her eyes stinging. Their secret didn't matter anymore. They could rest in peace. She and Weezie were more a family than ever.

In the living room Dubose poured himself a single-malt whiskey. She had a Baileys Irish Cream. They sat side by side, not touching—True's subtle doing—in front of the empty fireplace, which Penn had filled with candles.

"I guess Dad and I have similar taste in women," Dubose said eventually.

"I don't think I'm much like my mother." True took a sip of her drink and knew that she really couldn't say that anymore. She was very much like her mother, repressed in her own way, harboring secrets.

Mama, was it this hard for you, too? Is that why you held back so much of yourself? Did it hurt too much to feel?

"Sure you're like your mother," Dubose said. "You're both refined southern ladies, born and bred."

"But I'm a farmer now, kind of." Maybe Mama would be proud of her for that. She'd gardened, hadn't she? Maybe getting earth under her fingernails had been Mama's private form of rebellion.

"Not for long, you're not," said Dubose.

True's heart sped up. "You know I want to keep my U-pick operation."

"Let's talk about that later, okay? I'm still pretty shocked by tonight's revelations."

"All right." She ignored the hurt and straightened her spine. "When I was younger, I heard Mama and Daddy talking about her affair. It didn't last long. Less than a month. I didn't know who her lover was, though. I always wondered."

Dubose drained his glass. "Biscuit Creek is like Peyton Place."

"Yes, it is." She paused a beat. "Can you take a little more news?"

"Another scandal?"

"I don't think of it that way. Because the consequences were . . . beautiful."

"I'm not sure about this."

"You need to know."

"Then let's get it over with." His crankiness was perfectly understandable.

"Weezie"—she focused on his eyes—"is your half sister."

His pupils enlarged. "You're kidding."

"No. The affair with your dad lasted only a month, but she was the product of it."

"Is there proof?"

She flinched. "Of course not. And it doesn't matter anyway. She's becoming your sister through our marriage vows."

He stood and went straight to the old mahogany bar table. "Dad really did a number on us." He poured himself another drink. "Your mother wasn't his first affair. Mom and I never know if someday someone's going to come knocking on our door with paternity papers and expecting a third of his assets."

"That must be hard." True tried to be sympathetic. "But we're not the types who would, of course."

"You're not?"

Wow. *That* hurt.

"You're talking to your future wife," she said coolly. "And that's my sister you're also wondering about. Come on."

"Geez"—he shook his head—"I'm sorry." He came back to sit beside her. "What a jerky thing to say."

"I forgive you. I know this is a shock."

He held her hand tight. She ignored her discomfort and focused on the fact that he seemed humble, for the first time since she'd known him.

"I'm glad I have you, True. You're not like the other women I know. You honestly don't give a shit about money, do you?"

"Of course not! I mean, it's great to have. But we've

both lost family. We know what's most important—being with the people you love."

He kissed her, and it was warm. Tolerable, when she thought about everything he'd ever done for her.

She felt a surge of hope. Marriage wasn't meant to be easy, was it? She'd make sure theirs worked, the same way Mama and Daddy had made theirs work, even though Mama had strayed . . .

"You'll always ask me why I care so much about making partner," Dubose said. "And then when I'm partner, you'll tell me having supper with the family is more important than my next big deal."

She smiled. "You're right."

"Every man on the path to greatness has a weak spot." He pulled a strand of hair off her face. "And you're mine. I've just learned to accept it."

She sat there for a few seconds, processing what he'd just said. And while she did, streams of images flowed through her head, past and present, like thread in a needle cinching together the worn calico quilt that was her life. She thought of Weezie. Carmela. Her studio. Gage. Tomatoes. Roger at the Starfish. Her dogs. Paddleboards. The moon. Maybank Hall and the people who'd lived there before her.

Harrison . . .

Oh, Harrison!

What had she done? Why was she perpetually such a fool? When would it end, her enslavement to her parents' worldview? And when would fear stop guiding all her decisions?

"Dubose?"

"Yes?"

She put her drink down on a small coffee table and stood. "I'm not interested in being your weak spot. As a matter of fact"—she couldn't believe she'd taken so long to see this—"I'm tired of trying to be good enough for you and your mother. I'm more than good enough."

"Come on." He gave a short laugh. "I was saying that I *want* you, no matter what."

"No matter what? As if I present a lot of obstacles to be overcome?"

"You're upset about what my mother did," he said in his assertive yet soothing attorney's voice, "and the wedding stress has been enormous." He stood. "Don't forget that I was there when no one else was, when you were alone and suffering."

She backed away from him. "I'm grateful for that. Really. But I don't want to spend the rest of my life thanking you for the privilege of being your Achilles' heel. I have better things to do with my time."

She grabbed her purse. "I'm an artist. I'm a farmer. I'm also a fantastic girlfriend and sister. I would have made you an amazing wife, but I'm no longer interested. The wedding's off."

"An artist? What're you talking about?" He stood in front of her at the door. "Rethink this, please, True. Just take a couple hours to calm down, all right?"

"Dubose?"

"What?"

"If I were any calmer right now, I'd be dead." She pushed by him and didn't look back.

CHAPTER THIRTY-TWO

Harrison got a call from True's number at ten PM. He didn't want to answer it. But what if something was wrong? He blew out a breath and clicked the ON button on his cell phone. "Hello?"

"Harrison?" She sounded awful.

"Yes?" He imagined Weezie missing. The barn burned down. Something wrong with Gage.

"I was stupid," she said. "I made a huge mistake telling you to go. Please come back and talk to me about how we can work things out."

"You're getting married."

"No. No, I'm not. I told Dubose tonight we're over."

"You're just having cold feet."

"No, I'm *not*." Her voice cracked.

"Sure, you are. I've seen you in action, True, and I told you I was done." His pride could take no more beatings. "You were right. We'll hold each other back. Now go marry your rich boyfriend. I wish you both well."

He hung up the phone.

It didn't ring again.

CHAPTER THIRTY-THREE

Busted.

Harrison looked up from the floor and saw Dan standing over him, a disturbing leer on his face.

"What'd I tell you I'd do if you get drunk again?" Dan asked him.

Harrison closed his eyes. "Kick my ass."

"Exactly."

"I've been waiting for you to do that for ten years." His mouth tasted like a garbage dump somewhere in the Sahara Desert. "It ain't never gonna happen."

"Watch the double negatives."

Harrison rolled over onto a bottle and put an arm over his eyes. "I can talk any way I want. I'm a country music superstar."

"That may be, but I'm your manager. And if you don't get up in ten seconds, I'm pouring this glass of water on your face." Dan held up a cup.

"Not a Big Gulp."

"Yes. It's the king of cups." Dan laughed a miserable little laugh. "Ten, nine, eight, seven—"

Harrison lifted up on his elbows, and it was like his brain slammed into a giant wall.

"Six, five, four—"

He grabbed Dan's ankle and pulled. But he didn't budge. Maybe because Harrison felt weak. The last thing he remembered eating was a couple of Moon Pies in the car on the way back from Biscuit Creek. But that seemed like weeks ago.

"Three, two, one, and—"

Hell, he needed a shower anyway. He closed his eyes and tried to enjoy the cold water bath.

"You dumbass," Dan whined because he was already feeling guilty. "It's getting on your Rolex."

"*Your* Rolex. I was gonna re-gift it to you for Christmas."

Hah.

When the shower ended, Harrison took a deep breath, rubbed his hand down his face, and grabbed Dan's leg again.

Success.

Dan went down, his butt landing in the pool of water that sure didn't belong in the middle of Harrison's living room floor. But neither did all the video games and beer bottles.

Why a bicycle was there, Harrison had no idea. And then had a vague recollection of riding it down the grassy hill outside his house and screaming "Whoopee!" like he was a kid.

But it didn't work. It was no fun. No fun at all. He needed another person there to have fun. Person, for him, also included dogs.

"My job sucks," he said. "I got a trillion dollars, but I can't have a dog. Will you hurry up and marry a sweet girl who likes dogs so when I have to travel, she'll watch it for me? No way is my dog going to a doggy hotel. I hear the service is awful. No TV. Dogs love football."

"You're out of your mind."

"He already has a name. Sam."

"Good name."

"Get me a dog collar with that name on it, please."

"Not until you sober up. This is ridiculous." Dan stood up and held out his hand. "Come on."

"I got it." No way was he gonna let his manager lift him off the floor. He groaned and pretended he was Rocky. After a good twenty seconds of extreme effort, he was standing upright, wincing so bad he could hardly see.

"Advil," he rasped, and started walking like Franken-stein toward his bedroom.

"I got it right here." Dan caught up with him and gave him the pills.

Harrison swallowed them down with no water.

"That's bad for you." Dan filled only the bottom of the Big Gulp with water and handed it to him.

Harrison drank. And drank. "That thing's like a bot-tomless pit." He finally finished and handed it back.

"I'll give you one hour to pull it together," Dan said. "And then I need your answer about LA. If you say yes, you have to fly out tomorrow for a photo shoot."

"What's today?"

"Sunday."

Shit. It was done. True was married. Last night was her honeymoon. Harrison wished he could cry like a baby, but he was a manly man. He didn't cry. He wrote hit songs instead.

He felt a huge one coming on. "Gimme my guitar." He paused a beat. "Please," he added politely.

No sense making Dan really hate him. Pretend hate was okay. Even fun. But Harrison sensed that maybe, just maybe, he'd been pushing his manager too far. He looked down.

"I'm begging you, man." Dan was on his knees, hold-ing on to Harrison's legs. "Write something great. And I'll come back in an hour and ask you about LA."

Harrison shook him off gently. "I can tell you right now. I'll do it, so go home and relax. And don't worry about the hit song. This one's gonna go straight to number one."

He already had a little bit happening right now, and it was hick hop all the way:

*So I'm shooting up the charts, and you're breaking
    lots of hearts.*
Wh-wh-whoopee for me, wh-wh-whoopee for you.
*My Grammy shelf is growing, and your confidence
    is showing.*
Wh-wh-whoopee for me, wh-wh-whoopee for you.
*My boots are by Lucchese and your Bordelle bras
    are racy.*
Wh-wh-whoopee for me, wh-wh-whoopee for you.
*You might not know it, and I'm probably gonna
    blow it,*
*But I gotta have the answer from my favorite
    moonlight dancer,*
*Would you join me in the attic for some kinky
    acrobatics,*
*I want nothing more to do . . . than to make
    whoopee with you!*

So True might guess he was talking about her, but he doubted she had Bordelle bras. That would throw her off. They used to run him around a thousand bucks a pop anytime he'd buy them for one of his exes.

Should he change *attic* to *kitchen*? They'd never done it in the kitchen. Then she could sing it when she heard it on the radio and not be embarrassed.

*Would you join me in the kitchen for some lovin'
    and bewitchin' . . .*

He wished he could ask someone. Someone who was good with words.

Gage.

He called him up. "I got this song," he said, "and I was hoping you could tell me which line is better."

Gage listened, then said, "I prefer, *Would you join me in the store, we can do it on the floor.*"

"Wait. That's you and Carmela! You dog."

"You never heard it from me."

There was an awkward silence. But Harrison was too hung over to fill it. He looked at the hands on his wet watch.

"Hey, you missed a great event," Gage jumped in a long twenty seconds later.

Yes! Harrison pumped his fist in the air. His brother was getting more socially comfortable by the day. Sure, most people would have said *You missed a great time.* Or, *You missed a great party.* But it was a good start.

"I hate events," Harrison said, remembering he was in a very bad mood.

"True had an art show. One hundred thirty-six people came. She put out the word at the Starfish Grill. Your friend Cornelius and his buddies played for a while, and then Booty Call took over. Man, Carmela can dance."

"What the hell are you talking about?"

"True even sold a few collages and got enough to pay the bands."

"Wait a second. She got Booty Call for the wedding. When was this so-called *event*?"

"It was last night. She didn't have a wedding."

Everything in Harrison's house went strangely red and out of focus, and he heard an odd buzzing noise. Then everything went back to normal except for his heartbeat, which was going crazy. "Oh, so they're gonna elope next week or something? She told me Dubose and Penn might not go for the down-home wedding reception idea."

"No, that's not it at all. She told Carmela that she told Dubose she didn't want to marry him. She called off the wedding."

"Damn." Harrison had to sit down. She'd really followed through. "Why didn't you call me?"

"Why should I call you?"

"I'm your brother. And you know damned well I'm in love with her."

Shit. He'd been trying so hard not to be.

"Oh, that's right. And you did nothing about it. Even when I told you *Bad Rogue Wins*. That was a sign. So why should I call you? You blew it. You don't deserve her. You should have fought for her."

"I asked her to marry me once, and she said no. And it would be foolish to ask her again. I can't hunker down in Biscuit Creek and hit the top of the country music charts all at the same time. And she can't travel the world. She has an estate to tend, collages to make, and a sister to overprotect. I'll be living a lot on the West Coast, especially this coming year. I'm going to be a judge on that singing competition show. I'm heading to LA tomorrow to get that ball rolling."

He kicked a beer bottle and watched it spin across the room. They really ought to come with an extra warning label, something like, CAUTION: DOES JACK SQUAT TO MEND A BROKEN HEART.

"Your loss," said Gage.

"That's it?"

"What do you mean?"

"That's all the comfort I get?"

"Oh. I wasn't trying to comfort you. It was a literal observation. Today the girls are at the store getting it ready."

"Appreciate the random change of subject. Who are the girls?"

"Carmela, Weezie, and True, of course. The store's opening as The Damn Yankee tomorrow."

"Hey. I like that."

"Three firefighters from the Queens fire station where Carmela's dad worked before 9/11 are coming down for the ribbon cutting."

Gage gave him a quick explanation.

"I had no idea about her dad," Harrison said.

"She never talked about him. But now she does. And I can see a difference in her. She's still affable and gregarious, but she's also serene somehow."

"Wow," Harrison said. "Is that your fancy way of saying she's pretty much perfect?"

"For me, she is."

"I'm glad. For both of you." He paused. "I have to go. But it was great talking to you. Oh, and I hope the house building's progressing well."

"It is. Quite well. Good luck in LA tomorrow."

"Thanks."

When he hung up, Harrison wrote down the lyrics and chords he had come up with for "Whoopee." He picked up all the beer bottles and righted the bike, then wheeled it out onto his porch. A housekeeper would come tomorrow to get things spiffy again.

It was time to pack for LA.

If Sam the Dog were real and with him on the porch, Harrison would scratch his ears and say, *I'm glad the bad rogue didn't win, aren't you?*

He was really, *really* glad.

Good for True for dumping Dubose. And, man—she'd even held an art show.

"'This girl is on fire,'" he managed to sing, even though his head still ached, all through his shower. As long as she was thriving, he could bear his own misery.

When he looked civilized again, he pulled out his fa-

vorite leather bag from his closet to pack for LA and saw
his dad's guitar, which he hadn't touched since he'd gotten back. His mouth crooked up, which surprised him.
There was no guilt anymore. Just regret. And love.

He ran his hand over the instrument's smooth surface.
Dad.

He'd only been able to visit his father in jail once.
Mama had scrounged the gas money together to get them
to Columbia. Dad had told him through the window to
learn how to play it.

Now Harrison sat down on the edge of the bed and
strummed a chord. It was hopelessly out of tune, but with
new strings and a good cleaning it would be just fine.
He'd use it, too, in honor of Dad, for an acoustic number
at his next concert.

Huh. He heard a noise inside the body and gently
shook it. A piece of wood must have come loose from the
inner frame, so he shook the guitar again, tilting it in the
hope that the fragment would fall out.

A football-shaped piece of paper dropped onto the bed
instead.

What the hell?

And then he remembered. He and Gage, when they
were little, used their father's guitar like a secret post office. They left each other notes. But that had stopped
when Gage was ten and he was seven and their dad had
caught them and said he didn't want them using his guitar
as a toy.

The paper was yellowed looseleaf, and as he unfolded
it, he wondered what it could possibly say. Was it one he'd
written? Or Gage?

His astonishment grew when he smoothed it out and
recognized a young girl's scrawl. He'd seen it often enough at school. And the signature at the bottom confirmed it.

This was a note from True Maybank, age twelve.

Not Gage or Harrison. Why was it in the guitar?

He put that question aside for later, and read the note, his eyes burning. And then he read it again.

And again.

She told him how her birthday was terrible and she couldn't play at Sand Dollar Heaven anymore. She had responsibilities at home:

> *I hope you'll understand. My family needs me to grow up.*
>
> *But I love you, Harrison. I'll love you forever, and when I move away from Mama and Daddy, I'll look for you again. I won't stop until I find you, either. Friends like you come around only once a lifetime. Your Sewee princess, True XOXO*

This was weirder than Bad Rogue Wins. He looked around the room, half expecting Rod Serling to appear.

Dan called a few minutes later. "Any luck with the song?"

"Yep." Harrison was folding a few of his favorite T-shirts into three sections and then in half again and putting them in his bag. "I should be able to send the studio some samples this week."

"Fantastic. The producers in LA are going to be treating you like a king. They're really excited. And here's the best part. Hold on to your suspenders."

When Harrison heard how much money they were paying him, he sat on the edge of the bed again. "That's ridiculous."

"They think you're worth it."

"Thanks for pulling that off, Dan."

"It was my pleasure."

Harrison scratched the top of his head. "There's only one problem."

"Name it. They'll fix it. That's how much they want you."

"I've changed my mind," he said gently. "I'm really sorry."

There was a long pause on the other end.

"Why?" Dan croaked.

"I have to stay on the East Coast." It felt exactly right to say that. "I've got people over here. And I don't want to leave 'em."

"Your brother?"

"Yes."

"Anyone else? Maybe that blond? The one with the crappy car?"

"Her, too," Harrison said. "Especially her."

"Congratulations. It's about time. I was about to buy you a stuffed dog and call him Sam. You're getting a little insane on your own."

Harrison laughed, and it felt good. "I don't know if she'll have me. I don't know how we can be together and still do what we each have to do."

"This is big," said Dan.

"Yeah, it is."

"Big and wonderful. My job is to help you do what you want to do in this business. So I'm here. I'll go to bat for you, my friend. We can get as creative as you want. We can't teleport people yet, but we have Skype and laptops, and pretty much every major city has great recording studios."

"Thanks, Dan. Hey, you've been such a sport, I'm going to let you hang up first from now on, okay?"

"What a perk."

The dial tone sounded.

Ah, Dan. He was a good guy.

Harrison whistled to himself as he finished packing. He'd fly commercial to Charleston tonight and write songs in the Francis Marion Hotel, then in the morning he'd drive up to Biscuit Creek in time for the opening of The Damn Yankee.

You know you're going to True's first.

A huge rock lodged in his stomach. He was nervous. He remembered the last time he'd declared his intentions in front of a whole roomful of their peers. The silence, the scorn, the shame of being rejected, and the pain of seeing what he'd done to True—she'd sobbed into her hands, her delicate shoulders quaking . . .

To this day, thinking about it made him a little sick. And it could happen all over again. It made sense that it would happen all over again! He wasn't sure he should put her through it another time. Was he selfish? Was he naive? Did he need to stop playing games with people who led happy, normal lives and accept that he never could?

He didn't know.

But there was one thing he could do that would alleviate some of his stress. He'd try to catch her at home before she got to the store and talk to her in private. If he got there early enough, he could sit at the table with her and Weezie and eat breakfast. He hoped True would make that oatmeal again, the kind she got all excited about. And maybe he could ask to see her copy machine, and when they were in the attic, he'd . . .

He didn't know.

Add new toner to her copier machine? Jump her bones? Get down on one knee and declare his love? Sing her a song called "Miss Priss," which he hadn't even written yet?

It wasn't much of a plan. But at least he'd gotten her as

far as the attic. Although maybe he should do some be-witchin' in the kitchen instead . . .

"Damn," he said out loud when he locked the house behind him and threw his bag in the car. He had a revela-tion. He'd do all of the above, starting with the toner and ending with the song.

Because being in love wasn't for sissies.

CHAPTER THIRTY-FOUR

"So are we going to look for a boarder again?" Weezie asked True two days after the wedding was supposed to take place. They were outside collecting eggs.

"I guess so," True said. "Why not?"

Weezie stood straight. "We'll be fine without Dubose."

"Of course we will." And in her heart, True believed it. They had their U-pick operation. And if she could sell a collage here and there, that would supplement their income. Of course, her big hope was that she'd be able to sell a lot of copies of one great print to an art broker . . . something that would hang in hospitals or hotels or offices around the country.

"You act happier when you're not around Dubose," Weezie said.

"I am." True closed her hand over a warm brown egg and put it in her basket. She missed Harrison, but she felt good. She'd decided to stop chasing security so much and take more risks. She was an artist out in the open now. She had Weezie, Carmela, and Maybank Hall. She even had the town of Biscuit Creek behind her. At the impromptu art show party she'd thrown, she'd learned that very few people could tolerate Penn, which was understandable. But she was shocked to hear that an awful lot

of folks never managed to get excited about her and Dubose as a couple.

"He's town and you're country" was the general con-
sensus.

Only one person appeared truly regretful that they
didn't marry: Mr. York, a local developer. "It's a shame,
darlin'. We coulda made a fine neighborhood on your back
property. But if you're still interested, let me know. I'll
bring the plans right over."

"Mr. York"—her hands were shaking—"I didn't know
a thing about this plan of Dubose's."

Great balls of fire, did Mr. York's face turn red!

"And I'll never sell," True had told him, "so please don't
get your hopes up."

The day was going to be gorgeous, perfect for the ribbon cutting of The Damn Yankee. She found another egg.
And then another. "The chickens are happier, too," she
told Weezie. "They're laying more eggs."

Her life wasn't over, not by a long shot. That feeling of
sadness about Harrison would dissipate someday, she
hoped. Maybe when she was fifty? Or sixty? Surely by
then, she'd lose her longing for him.

Which meant she only had twenty or thirty years to go.

Sweet grandmother's spatula. Who was she kidding?
He was the love of her life. She'd never get over him. At
least she could Google him to see what he was doing.
There were women out there who weren't as lucky, who
lost track of the "one who got away." True could watch
tapes of him, listen to him sing . . .

It would be utter torture. Her vision got a little blurry,
and she sighed. "I'm going in now to cook the oatmeal."

"I'll be there in a little while," Weezie said. "I'm going
to clean out the coop."

"But it's my turn."

"I know."

True smiled at her sister. "Thanks." She'd grown up so much. "Weezie—"

"Yes?"

True inhaled a deep breath. "I think you should move into that apartment this semester, after all. Get the real going-away-from-home experience from the start."

Her sister's eyes widened. "Are you serious?"

"Yes." True clenched the egg basket. "You're ready. I'm going to be so proud to see you thrive."

"Oh. My. Gosh." Weezie had tears in her eyes.

So did True. "Don't drop the eggs!" She walked over and kissed her sister's cheek. "See you in a few."

She had just finished stirring the oatmeal when the front doorbell rang. Maybe it was Carmela or Gage come to get the treat bags of Coney Island saltwater taffy that she and Weezie had made up the night before for the ribbon cutting. Gage still had his stuff here, but the last two nights he'd spent at Carmela's. True turned off the burner and put down her spoon.

When she saw who the visitor was, her face flamed, and her hands instantly began to sweat. She opened the screen door only partially.

"True." Dubose's smile didn't reach his eyes. "You're looking well."

She wouldn't acknowledge his compliment. "Hello, Dubose." She held tight to the door handle. "Why are you here?"

"If you don't mind, I'd like to talk to you inside."

Hmmm. She *did* mind. But she didn't want to be rude, either. The Warings and Maybanks were still neighbors. And she and Dubose had a long history together. They didn't need to turn this into something ugly. "Come on in."

She gave him a small, polite smile, but she absolutely would not invite him to breakfast. They headed to the kitchen, and she sat at the table. "Please take a seat."

He did, stiffly.

Something in his eyes scared her. He didn't look like the Dubose she'd been engaged to. This was the attorney before her.

"I have a favor to ask," he said.

She felt the need to gain the upper hand. "I'll be happy to entertain it, but first I have to tell you that I don't appreciate your going behind my back to Mr. York and discussing a sale of my back property."

He did flinch, but just barely. "He approached me. It was only a chat over coffee."

"He'd drawn up plans."

"Overeager, I'd say. That's not my fault."

"I don't care how informal the discussion was," she said. "It was wrong to hold it without me. That's all I want to say on that matter." She folded her arms across her chest. "What's this favor you need?"

He smiled again.

Phony, was what she thought. And not just the smile. How could she not have recognized that before?

"We talked about Weezie the other night," he said, "the fact that she's likely my half sister."

"Wait." True stood and looked out the window. Weezie was still out at the coop, thank goodness, so she resumed her seat. "She doesn't know anything about that, and for now I'd rather it stay that way. She's about to go off to college. She doesn't need any shocking news."

"That's an extremely wise judgment," said Dubose.

"It suits our situation, anyway." She felt a little uncomfortable with the effusive praise.

From his back pocket he pulled out a sheaf of papers. She hadn't realized he was carrying any.

"In fact," he said, "I'd be really grateful if you could sign these. Feel free to look them over. It's pretty straightforward. All they are is a promise that you Maybanks"—wow, already she was part of the "other" family—"won't try to sue my mother and me to gain a portion of my father's estate."

True felt ill. "You're kidding, aren't you?"

"No." He shrugged. "I'm protecting the family. I would have done the same for you had we married. So don't go casting judgment, please."

"But you don't need to protect yourself against me or Weezie. That's . . . that's crazy!"

His mouth thinned. "It's why I'm an attorney and you're not. It's not crazy at all. Plenty of people would try."

"But we're not plenty of people. We are still your neighbors and friends. We're not interested in your money."

"You're not?" He drew in his chin. "You sure seemed willing to use it to fix up Maybank Hall when you were going to marry me."

True colored. "That's different. You'd have lived here, too."

But it was too late. He'd thrown it out there . . . that she'd been after his money.

"I obviously wasn't a gold digger, if that's what you're implying." She strove for patience. "I broke off the engagement, didn't I?" She pushed away from the table. "I'm not interested in signing your papers, but you have my word. We will never sue your father's estate. Let's live in harmony, Dubose. Biscuit Creek's a small town."

He stood, too, and tossed the papers on the table. "You're forcing me to play hardball. I'll give you ten minutes to look them over. And if they're not signed, I'm going outside to tell Weezie she's my half sister."

True's temples pounded. "That's so needlessly cruel. If and when I tell her, it will be at a time I decide is appropriate. And quite frankly, with the way you're behaving right now, I don't know that I want her to find out she's related to you."

"You have nine minutes," he said.

"All right." True grabbed the papers, her hands shaking, and sat back down. "I can't believe you're doing this."

"Here's a pen." He sat back down, too.

She grabbed the writing instrument unceremoniously from his hand and kept reading. It was all gobbledygook legalese. She had to pray he wasn't going to cheat her somehow. "How do I know you won't try to blackmail me again?"

"I'm not interested in anything else from you. I can have my pick of Charleston's beauties anytime." He paused. "New York ones, too."

She nearly gasped. "What do you mean by that?"

"You'll never know, will you?" His eyes were hard. But amused.

Bastard. All those late nights he'd texted her about? Those long silences on the phone when she thought he'd been watching sports?

"Boy," she said, not taking her eyes off his, "did I ever make the right decision. I guess you're right. The apple doesn't fall far from the tree, after all."

"Touché." He looked at his elegant watch. "Six minutes," he reminded her coolly.

True read faster. She wanted to cry, but she didn't dare.

"Stop it, Sister." Weezie's angry voice came from the entrance to the hallway. "Throw those papers away."

True looked up and saw her sister, her face white and stricken. She must have circled the house to drop a bucket off near the barn and come in through the front door.

"Shit," Dubose muttered.

"Weezie, honey—" True began.

But Weezie was on fire. She pointed to the back door.

"Get out of my house, Dubose Waring. I don't care if I'm related to you or not. You're mean. You're fake. And you took advantage of my sister when she was scared and lonely. I never want to see you on our property again."

The dogs must have gotten her message because suddenly they all started to bark.

"Now settle down, Weezie." Dubose pushed George's and Ed's heads away. But as soon as he did, Striker, Skeeter, and Boo barked at his feet. "I only wanted to make sure you wouldn't sue—"

"Shut up," Weezie said. "Just shut up and leave right now before you make me really mad!"

"Goddammit, True." Dubose's face was beet red, his mouth an ugly snarl. "Talk some sense into her."

"Leave now," True said quietly. "You've only come here to cause tremendous strife. I'll forgive you someday, Dubose, if you remain a polite neighbor, but for right now, I'm seriously irritated with you, to the point that"—she grabbed her egg basket from the kitchen table—"I just might start throwing eggs."

"You're crazy."

Weezie came up to her and grabbed two.

"Back door, please. Not the front," True said pleasantly. "You can take the long way around, escorted by the dogs. And maybe Phred, the rooster. He's in an ornery mood today. We let him out of the coop to work it off. Watch out—he loves grabbing ahold of people's calves with his spurs."

Dubose narrowed his eyes at them. "Thank God I didn't get saddled with you two."

Weezie pulled back to throw the egg, and he ran out the back door.

"Hahaha!" she called after him. "Coward!"

They watched him skedaddle out of there, and then

True drew her sister back into the kitchen. "Give me those eggs," she said.

Weezie obeyed.

True put them in the basket, and before she'd even turned back around, Weezie was sobbing hysterically.

"Daddy's not my father?"

"Of course he is." True hugged her tight. "In all ways that matter."

Weezie cried.

And cried.

True soothed her as best she could. "Who took you on his knee every day? Who bought you that red bicycle you wanted?"

"But another man slept with Mama," Weezie wailed.

"Daddy knew all about it"—True rubbed her back—"and he forgave her. You were his daughter. He was your father. You were precious to him and Mama both. Nothing will ever change that."

She reached over to grab a kitchen towel and wiped Weezie's nose.

For the first time in three minutes, Weezie took a break from sobbing. "There was a secret about me. A really big one." She inhaled a shaky breath.

True smiled gently. "I know—crazy, huh? And you've been trying to find out everyone else's."

Fresh tears came.

"I thought about telling you later," True said, "but I wanted to think about it first. I didn't want *this* to happen, right when you're going off to school."

Weezie used the towel on her eyes. "I'm glad I know."

True pulled a lock of hair from her face. "Are you going to be okay? I know it's a shock."

Weezie didn't answer, then she said, "How long have you known?"

"Since I was about eight. I didn't know all the details, however."

"And you kept that secret *all these years*?"

True nodded.

"Wow." Weezie shook her head. "I had no idea we had secrets in this house."

"Well, it didn't change a thing about how anyone felt about you. Look at us. We're sisters forever. We're May-banks. And no one can take that away." She led her to the kitchen table and kissed the top of her head. "Sit here, and I'll make you some cocoa. I don't care that it's hot outside. It's your favorite drink."

They spent half an hour together. True hoped Weezie wouldn't suffer much adapting to her new reality. She hated change more than most people. But nothing *had* changed. Not really.

Damned Dubose.

They laughed together about threatening to throw eggs at him.

"If only Harrison had been here." Weezie she started to cry again.

True's throat tightened. "You can tell him all about it on the phone."

"He'd have kicked Dubose's ass." Weezie sounded wistful. "Don't you miss him?"

True looked into her now empty cocoa cup. "I do."

"Do you love him? Tell me the truth, please. No more secrets, okay?"

True sighed. "All right. I do." It was sad, but she couldn't afford to get that way. She grinned and added, " 'I love him like crazy, Ma.' "

"*Moonstruck.*"

"Yep."

"I love him, too," said Weezie. "Like a brother."

"I'm glad. He loves you, too." True looked at her watch and tried to forget that Harrison had rebuffed her on the phone. It was too painful to think about. "You think you'll be up to going to the party? We'd need to leave in forty-five minutes so we can help set up."

Weezie nodded. It was shaky, but she was a real trouper. And she remained that way when they got to The Damned Yankee. Gage was arranging Reubens on several large platters, lining them up just so.

"Great job, Gage." True's heart quickened when she saw him. He was her friend. But he was also Harrison's brother.

"Thanks." He barely looked up, but his tone was warm.

Carmela hugged her. "We're making Vermont floats, too."

"Is that what Roger's doing?" True asked. He was setting up some kind of station beneath a tree on the sidewalk in front of the store. "Weezie's out there helping."

"Yes," Carmela said. "It's milk, real Vermont maple syrup, and a scoop of vanilla ice cream."

"That sounds fabulous." True looked around at all the new merchandise. "I have a great feeling about this, 'Mela."

"Me, too. I put a big ad in the Charleston paper. I dedicated the opening to Dad and his friends. And I mentioned that we had three special guests coming for the ribbon cutting from the same station. So maybe we'll get a few people in. And look at this." Carmela took her to a wall and pointed.

"Oh, my gosh. Who did this?"

Carmela had tears in her eyes. "Gage did. It's perfect, isn't it?"

"Yes." It was a beautiful plaque naming the firemen from Mr. Sherman's station who'd been lost on 9/11 at the World Trade Center. On one side of the plaque was a picture of all the guys from that time, and on the other side was a picture of Carmela with her father on their apartment house doorstep. She was about eight or nine.

True hugged her. "This is so special."

"Thanks." Carmela smiled. "The guys from the station are supposed to be here any minute. They're so young, their early twenties. Isn't that sweet that they came all the way down here?"

"So sweet." True wasn't going to tell her anything about her morning. That was news for another day.

Carmela squeezed her hand. "You okay in general?"

"Sure." True squeezed back. "I'm so excited about your store."

"Me, too." Carmela's gaze softened. "But being with Gage all the time now makes me think about Harrison. And you. I'm glad you told me what happened between you two. You're single now. You should contact him."

True's heart was still bruised. "I told you . . . our lives are too different."

"Remember I said love conquers all?" Carmela turned to Gage, who was arranging napkins in a perfect fan shape. "When's Harrison coming back again?"

"I don't know. He was planning to be here when the house is done. But he just got signed as a judge on that big singing competition reality show. He'll be on the West Coast a lot this year. He's heading to LA today to get the publicity going."

"And you didn't tell me?" Carmela threw out her arms and stared at Gage with her wide cat eyes.

Of course he'd be a judge on that show! True was happy for him.

So why did she feel so miserable?

"I just found out yesterday," Gage said. "We were busy here . . . I forgot."

"Gage"—Carmela's cheeks were flushed—"you have

to promise never to be too busy to tell me about family, all right? He's your only brother."

"All right." Gage looked momentarily unnerved by Carmela's strong admonition, but she followed it up with a big kiss on his cheek. So all was well again.

"I'm so sorry," Carmela came back to True and wrapped an arm through hers.

"Don't be," True said. "You see what I mean. A relationship with Harrison is impossible. Look at you and Gage. You have to be together. One kiss can make all the difference between a good day and a bad day. Talking face-to-face matters."

Carmela's forehead wrinkled. "I know what you mean, but I'm still not convinced you two can't have the same thing. Let's focus on the store opening right now. But I promise you, I'll be thinking."

People in love always wanted other people to be happy, didn't they? True appreciated her friend's concern, but she had to live in the real world.

Half an hour later, everything was ready, and the opening was officially under way.

"Wow," said Carmela. "This is it!"

"You did a great job." Gage readjusted some jars of mustard from a Brooklyn deli.

"It's perfect." True tried not to be worried that no one had shown up yet. "Let's go outside and look."

The door to the store was flung wide open. On the sidewalk, True took in the enchanting view and squeezed Carmela's hand. "I am *so* proud of you."

Carmela smiled. "Thanks."

She'd painted the words THE DAMN YANKEE in an old Colonial font above the shop, and True felt that the beautifully rendered name alone was enough to draw people in. To the right of the stairs, an American flag flew in the breeze from a bracket that Gage installed on the brick storefront. Roger and Weezie were poised behind a bar table with ice cream scoops, ready to make Vermont floats. A cooler behind them brimmed with vanilla ice cream and gallon jugs of milk. On the table itself, glass containers of maple syrup stood at the ready, along with red-white-and-blue straws and plastic beer mugs with the store name emblazoned on them. Strains of patriotic flute-and-drum music floated out from the interior of the shop, welcoming one and all to visit.

Carmela did a 360. There wasn't a soul on the street. "I hope someone comes." She peered across at the Starfish Grill. It was open, but only a few people sat in the window. "Where is everyone? It's like a ghost town."

"I don't know," True said, "but they'll come."

Carmela wrung her hands. "My three firemen aren't here, either. Do you think they got lost? Maybe I should call them."

Gage put his arm on her shoulder. "Give them a few more minutes."

"You advertised it as noon to two," Roger said. "It's already twelve fifteen. This ice cream's gonna melt. Maybe I'd better take it back to the freezer at the Starfish."

"No, Roger," said True. "Let's be patient."

Carmela's face was pale, but she walked back into the shop and waited.

Six people trickled in over the next ten minutes. But all of them were shopkeepers on Main Street, doing the polite thing, wishing Carmela well on her new venture.

She was happy about that—but where were her firemen? Where were the customers?

At twelve thirty, two old ladies came in, enjoyed the sandwiches and floats, then left with their plastic mugs and a promise to return someday to buy something.

"Maybe at Christmas, dear," one of them said.

"Thank you." Carmela sent them off with a cheerful smile.

"See?" Gage rubbed her back. "They were very happy eating those Reubens. And I'll bet they come back way before Christmas."

"That would be nice," said Carmela, but her sad expression broke True's heart.

Weezie came inside. "Hey, where *is* everyone?"

True widened her eyes at her, and Weezie froze.

"I'm sorry, Carmela," Weezie whispered. "I'm sure they'll come soon."

"It's okay, hon." Carmela reached for a box of tissues and wiped her eyes. "It's not your fault. I was sure this idea was going to work. I don't know what to do now."

"It's *my* fault," said Gage. "I thought of it."

"It's not a mistake," True said. "I feel it in my bones— this is the right store for you, Carmela, and we'll make it work. No matter what. So everyone buck up, okay? Maybe there's a big event going on somewhere that we don't know about. As for the three firefighters, go ahead and call them now, 'Mela. Maybe they need directions."

Carmela picked up her phone, tapped out their number, and waited.

"No answer," she whispered.

"We're not quitting." Some of True's old Maybank spirit kicked in. "Did the Americans quit when the British came to Lexington and Concord? No."

"Okay." Carmela took a deep breath. "Let's keep hoping."

It was twelve forty.

From far away, a siren sounded. They could barely hear it above the flute-and-drum music. But then another one sounded. And another.

True's heart sped up. It was always scary to hear a lot of sirens at one time.

"There must be a big fire somewhere," said Gage. "Or an accident on Highway 17."

"Oh, God, I hope it's not my three firefighters." Carmela crossed herself.

The sirens came closer and closer. And now there were many more.

Weezie came in again. "What's going on?" She sounded a little frightened. "They're getting so loud. But I don't see a fire anywhere."

"We don't know." True felt alarmed herself. She took her sister's hand, and they went outside to stand with Roger.

Gage and Carmela followed behind.

At the end of Main Street, a fire engine came into view. It was rolling slowly, its lights flashing, almost as if it were in a parade.

Carmela's face scrunched up. "What's going on?" She sounded afraid.

"Look!" Weezie pointed. "There's another one behind it! And another one behind that one!"

"Oh, my God." Carmela's hands, resting on her cheekbones, were shaking. "The first truck is from Queens!"

Her three firefighters poked their heads out the window and waved. "Hi, Carmela!! We're so glad to be here!"

Carmela started sobbing. "I didn't know they were bringing the truck. Oh—my—God. What's happening?" She was clinging to Gage for dear life. "Why are all these other trucks here, too?"

"I think they're here to honor your father and his friends from the station." Gage's voice was a tad rough. "And to see *you*." He wrapped his arm tight around her shoulder.

The procession came on . . . and on . . . and on . . . from all over South Carolina.

Roger stood with his Starfish Grill hat over his heart.

True linked arms with Weezie. She was so overcome, she couldn't say a word.

The trucks took up all of Main Street. Behind them came a huge crowd waving little American flags—the people of Biscuit Creek, and at least a hundred others True didn't recognize.

It was truly overwhelming.

She went to Carmela, who couldn't stop crying, and kissed her cheek. "See, you damn Yankee? You belong here, after all."

They hugged each other tight.

"Oh, True," Carmela whispered. "Dad would be so proud."

"I know," True said. "And I'm proud—on his behalf—of you."

"Oh, I knew all about this plan." Roger, the king of interrupting tête-à-têtes, handed Carmela a tissue.

"You did?" Carmela was still wildly emotional, but she was one of those lucky people who looked beautiful when they cried. Today the tears magnified the happiness that shone in her eyes.

"I wasn't supposed to tell," Roger said. "When your ad came out, the Charleston fire chief got on the line to stations all over the state. Everyone was supposed to meet up by Sand Dollar Heaven. I guess it took a long time to get the crowd organized and moving. A lot of these people are families of firefighters. And there's a big crowd from Charleston—regular shoppers who want to show their appreciation."

"They can have everything in the store," Carmela said between hiccups.

True laughed. "You can't give all your stock away."

"I'm just so glad everyone's here." Carmela blew her nose.

"So am I," said Gage. "Roger and Weezie, back to your

station. True, can you help me inside? Carmela, you stand out here and greet everyone."

Everyone did as Gage told them, and for an hour they were so busy that True couldn't think straight. The line to get into the store went down the entire length of Main Street. A lot of the crowd was composed of firemen or their families, so crowd control came naturally, as did making sure the legal number of people in the store wasn't exceeded. Everyone understood the issues and tried to go through The Damn Yankee as swiftly as possible so the customers behind them would have a chance.

"Wow," Gage said at one point, when a man stood aside to let a woman who had to get back to work go ahead of him. "This is what small towns are all about."

"Yes, they are," said True, and knew in her heart that she belonged here in Biscuit Creek. It was small comfort when she'd lost Harrison. But it *was* a comfort.

Weezie and Roger dispensed as many Vermont floats as they could. A couple of kindly souls helped them out. Another good person—the owner at the Starfish—kept a steady stream of hot dogs coming after Carmela ran out of Reubens. The other business owners were prepared, too, passing out bottles of water and candy—Carmela's treat bags of saltwater taffy had gone in a flash.

True did the best she could to ring up customers and answer questions.

At one point, she looked up and saw a man gazing at a calendar of New York City sights on a nearby shelf. He was shoulder-to-shoulder with the crowd, but something about him was familiar.

It was his Indiana Jones hat.

True felt a searing pain near her heart. *Harrison.* She missed him so much. This man didn't have the long hair, but he had the same build. She pretended for a moment that Harrison was here. He'd have loved seeing this triumph for Carmela. He'd have been so touched by the presence of all those firefighters, their trucks, and families. And he'd have been proud of Biscuit Creek.

True was.

"Thank you, sir," she said to a customer who'd just bought a big shopping bag of gifts. She smiled at him, then glanced over at the Indiana Jones man again. He'd turned slightly sideways, and she nearly fainted.

She'd recognize that chin anywhere.

"Ma'am?" A woman at the register eyes her with concern. "You look ill."

Probably a third of the people in the crowd were qualified emergency responders, so True had to be careful.

"Oh, I'm fine," she said lightly.

"It's stuffy in here," the woman said. "Maybe you should get outside and sit down."

True couldn't move. "I'm okay," she whispered.

"No, you're *not*," the woman insisted. "Everyone, back up," she barked. "And get this woman some water. Stat!"

Harrison turned around. He was wearing those god-awful '80s sunglasses.

True couldn't stop staring at him. "What are you doing here? And where's your hair?"

Someone shoved a water bottle in front of True, the cap already off.

"Drink it," the helpful woman said.

True kept her eyes on Harrison, and dutifully drank a few sips.

"Feel any better?" the woman asked.

"I think so," said True.

"She needs to be outside!" True's new guardian angel came behind the counter and took her arm.

"I got her, ma'am." Yes, it was most definitely Harrison's voice.

"And I've got the register." Gage was working his way over. "Are you okay, True?"

"Sure." She wouldn't admit she felt a little loopy.

Then Gage saw Harrison. "*You're* here?"

"Hi." Harrison stuck out his hand. "Terence Jones. This is a great place."

No, he wasn't Terence Jones, True wanted to say out loud. Terence wore John Lennon glasses. This was merely Harrison's dorky tourist disguise.

But Gage got it. Harrison didn't want to steal any thunder from Carmela's opening.

"I gotta ask you a question, man," Harrison said to his brother.

"What?"

"Did you leave a note from True in a certain person's guitar when you were in high school?"

Gage looked blank for a moment. "Yeah," he said slowly. "She gave it to me to give to . . . someone . . . and I found it in my book bag a couple weeks later. I felt guilty about it, and instead of 'fessing up, I threw it in the guitar. Like an idiot."

"Yeah. You were an idiot," Harrison concurred. "But I forgive you. I was one, too." He brushed past him and exchanged places with the kind stranger who'd tried to help.

True's heart was slamming against her ribs, and she truly *was* about to faint.

"I came by your house this morning," he said.

"You did?"

"Yeah, but I drove off. I saw Dubose's car out front. I wondered if maybe you two were working out your issues. So I left you to it, mainly because I didn't want to cause a scene in front of Weezie. But I decided then and there that I ain't quittin'. I came to the store to tell you that if I have to fight Mr. High and Mighty for you, I will. And I'm gonna win this time."

She smiled. "You don't need to fight him. He was coming over to be a jerk and throw something in my face. We are well and truly over."

"Makes my job all that much easier." People were looking at them, so he took her by the elbow. "Let's go, little lady. Outside in the fresh air."

She was like the worst kind of fan; she was so thrilled at his touch, she made a little sound in her throat. A joy sound. Totally primal.

"You're used to that, aren't you?" she said for his ears only.

"What?"

"Women losing it with you around. You know, whimpering, moaning. Fainting."

"Oh, sure." He kept his cool as they descended the steps of the store. "Happens all the time."

The day was beautiful. People were talking and smiling. Laughing. Carmela was in the middle of a pack of firefighters, hugging each and every one of them.

True felt much better outside.

"What I'm *not* used to," Harrison said, "is being in love with the person who's doing the whimpering."

"Oh." True's heart flooded with a happiness so big and bright, she blinked back tears.

He kissed her then—a long, sweet kiss. "You're stuck with me, babe. I'm gonna make you whimper, moan, and faint every day." His intentions were very clear.

"I can't wait." She was thrilled to the core. But she was scared, too. "Harrison, this is a great daydream, but you can't not be a country music star. I *want* you to be one. And I can't leave Biscuit Creek."

"Hey! That's Harrison Gamble!" someone shouted.

"Shoot." Harrison adjusted his hat lower. "I was trying to avoid this happening."

"It's okay," True assured him. "Carmela will be so happy you're here. We all missed you this morning when we were getting ready."

The Italian bombshell caught sight of him then and ran over. "Oh, my gosh! Harrison!" She wrapped her arms around his neck, and the fan squealing started.

True backed up and watched him handle the crowds.

She was so very proud of him. He smiled at everyone, scribbled out autographs, and cracked funny jokes.

He was such a good man.

But he was also a wanted man. A beloved star.

She sighed, afraid that her presence in his life would pull him away from what he was meant to be.

Finally, he was able to take a breath. When she saw him looking for her, her whole body flushed at the knowledge that she was the object of his search. She was talking to some older ladies down the street who couldn't wait for Harrison to improve the library's inventory.

He caught up with her—first giving the other women a thrill by complimenting each of them in turn—and then said, "Do you mind if I take True for a walk?"

"Go ahead," they all exclaimed, knowing looks on their faces.

True could hardly breathe, she was so excited. And so in love.

"Don't forget she's young and single!" Mrs. Finch called after them.

Harrison laced his fingers through True's, and she'd never felt so happy . . . and worried.

"Where are we going?" she asked.

"To get a Cheerwine," he said. "And maybe a candy bar."

"Sounds good." She grinned at him.

They reached the end of Main Street and turned toward the wharf. The shrimp trawlers were out to sea, all but one, the *Miss Mary*, which was in for repairs. The canvas awning on Wyatt's Pharmacy had been changed out a long time ago. There was now a permanent copper-covered awning in place. Wyatt's had been fancied up.

"Good for him," Harrison said outside the shop window.

"Mr. Wyatt's gone now," True told him gently.

"Aw." Harrison's face softened.

"But his daughter's great." True kissed his cheek to cheer him up. "Remember Jane? She runs it now, and she's as nice to the kids from Sand Dollar Heaven as ever."

"I'm glad." Harrison pulled her close. "I don't know what I would have done without this place. Without Mr. Wyatt making me feel like I belonged." His expression was tender, which only increased his hotness by infinity times sixty-nine. "And then I met you here. After that, I knew exactly where I belonged. For the rest of my life." He paused a millisecond, just long enough for a wisp of a sea breeze to lift their hair. "I love you, True."

True's eyes filled with tears. "I love you, too. Will you faint if I kiss you, Mr. Gamble? Maybe moan and whimper? You're looking pretty wobbly right now. Kind of how I was inside The Damn Yankee."

"I think I can handle your star power, Miss Maybank."

"But you'll need to take off those dorky sunglasses first," she advised him. "And maybe lose the hat. I'm pretty choosy about whom I kiss among my fan base."

"Oh, yeah?" He'd tucked his gorgeous lion's mane inside that hat, and now it came tumbling down. "Do you always say *whom*? You sound like a librarian. It kinda turns me on."

She laughed, and before she could take outrageous advantage of him, he gathered her in his arms and kissed her senseless.

"Wow," she whispered when they took a break.

He looked at her long and hard. "I'm staying here. You matter more to me than my dang career. I can still keep it up. I write better songs when I'm with you than any I could write apart from you. I'll work out the rest. Love'll find a way."

Just like Carmela had assured her in the Starfish Grill. Love had found a way for True and Weezie to make it through their hard times. It had brought Gage to Carmela— and Carmela to Gage. Today it had united hundreds of strangers at The Damn Yankee.

Boundaries, roadblocks . . . none of them mattered.

"We belong together," Harrison said. "Maybank Hall and Biscuit Creek—Weezie and Gage and Carmela—me and you." He held her close. "Will you marry me *again*, my Sewee princess?"

True looked up into those warm brown eyes, the same ones that had shone with quiet pride and happiness when he'd shown her his secret honeysuckle bower for the first time. He'd made a drum from a coffee can and a flower wreath for her hair. They'd done the limbo under a low oak tree branch and pretended it was a ceremonial dance. "Yes, you dear, dear man." She smiled. "I'll marry you again."

The *Miss Mary* bobbed in the creek behind them. Her shrimp nets were out for repair, and her hull was about to get a fresh coat of paint. Her new owner figured that paying quadruple what the boat was worth was the least he could do to help the previous owner retire. He already had three new co-captains, too, young men from Sand Dollar Heaven. Among them they had seven kids, and two of their wives had babies on the way.

"Wanna go swimming to celebrate?" Harrison asked True.

"Yes," she said with a grin. "A dip in the creek would feel wonderful."

"This way." He took her hand. Just like the old days. "I got something to show you."

They walked along the wharf beneath a blue bowl of a sky. And he sang her a love song called "Miss Priss," which he'd written for her that same morning. Conveniently, the very last line ended with the words *wedded bliss.*

"It's perfect." She squeezed his hand. "I love how you got 'sexy kiss' in there, too."

"You do?" His boyish look of surprise made her laugh out loud.

"I love everything about it." She gave him the sexiest kiss she could muster.

He gave it right back.

Her bones must have evaporated. She was pure Jell-O. "I can't believe you wrote another song for me."

"They're all about you, True. I look back now, and I see that so clearly. It's because you're the one I love. You're the one I feel all the emotion about."

"You mean, I really *am* MoonPie fine?"

"Hell, yes, you are."

Not ten minutes later, True's left hand had a diamond ring on it from Croghan's Jewel Box in Charleston. She and Harrison stood on the stern of the *Miss Mary*, an open bottle of champagne and two half-drunk glasses behind them in the cockpit.

"Ready?" Harrison asked her.

"*So* ready," she answered him.

They jumped into Biscuit Creek together.

"Whoopee!" Harrison yelled in midair, his hand clutched tightly around hers.

True laughed under water, and they came up kissing.

HE'S SO
Fine

CHAPTER ONE

Blackballed Hollywood bombshell Lacey Clark was one of those GRITS people—a Girl Raised In The South—and knew all about Scarlett O'Hara and Tara and how to hang on during rough times. Out in L.A. she thought she'd escaped a bottom-of-the-barrel existence, but she was right back where she started, home again—the same way she'd left it, too, with only a few dollars in her pocket. But she did have Henry, her five-year-old son. In his tiny cubby of a room, she dutifully got him into bed and tucked him in tight with a threadbare quilt, her heart squeezing with a love so strong she knew she could take whatever craziness life threw at her because she had something bigger and better—the love of this little man. His hand curled in hers, and his lips, puffy and dry from keeping the car window down for three thousand miles, curved like a slice of watermelon, sweet and pink.

"Tell me a story, Mama." Henry's husky boy voice sounded like snakes and snails and puppy dog tails—

along with jellyfish and horseshoe crab carcasses, his new favorite things.

The South Carolina rain came down something fierce, but the weatherman said it'd all clear out by morning, which was a good thing. Lacey had a life to build from scratch. "How about the story of the brave little boy who crossed the country in an old ambulance and survived on white-powdered doughnuts and hot dogs?"

"Hey!" Henry grinned. "That's me!"

"Yeah, well"—she smoothed his hair back—"you'd think it was you. But this boy was named George. And he was a secret spy."

"He *was*?"

"Uh huh." She wished *she'd* had spy skills in L.A. She'd never have allowed herself to get caught up in the easy life she'd lived the past three years. She should have known it was all a mirage, a silly game she'd been playing, too good to be true. What kind of mother let her life implode like that?

Never again.

Even above the rain she heard a car door slam shut.

"What was that?" Henry's brow creased. "I thought no one was coming here for a while."

No one was supposed to.

Lacey stood, her heart pounding like the dance floor at a honky-tonk on a Saturday night. "It's probably the pizza man delivering to the wrong address," she said smoothly, but no one came out this way and in this kind of weather unless they had a reason. "Don't you worry a *thing*. Just close your eyes and I'll take care of this." She leaned down and blew out the candle which stood sentinel in front of the solitary window. "'Night. I promise I'll finish George's story tomorrow."

"Yeah." Henry already sounded sleepy. "'Night, Mama."

She shut the door, walked briskly through her own

connecting bedroom, then raced down the spiral stairs, glad for the loud downpour and her bare feet. *Dear God, let him sleep and dream, lulled by the rain. The sea.*

At the bottom of the stairs, a cozy lamp on the kitchen counter glowed yellow behind its old paper shade. She strode past the plank table and heard a grunt, a clattering of metal against metal. Visions of axe murderers made her turn back and grab the flashlight lying on the counter. A second later she was at the thick wooden arched door, which lacked a window or a peephole. On the other side was a small portico, but it wouldn't provide much cover for whoever stood out there.

She felt very much like the Cowardly Lion until she thought of Henry. And then she was Dirty Harry and Indiana Jones, all rolled into one. "Who's there?" she called coolly.

"Can you give me a hand with this door?" a male voice boomed.

The keyhole rattled, but the door stayed shut.

She knew that voice. She did. And she wasn't scared of it. Annoyed, yes. But . . .

How did she know that voice?

Adrenaline made her throat tight. "You're at the wrong place," she called. "This is a private residence."

"Yeah, I know. Hurry it up, please. The rain's coming down sideways, and this Louis Vuitton bag ain't cheap."

He said *ain't* with all the insouciance of a true Southern male. Whether gentleman or redneck, they knew a guy's worth had nothing to do with his grammar, how much money he had in the bank, or what his ancestors' names were. It was about how well he could hold a rifle, drink his bourbon, and tell a good story.

Her guard went up another notch. "I'm sorry you're miserable, but I'm not letting you in. Only a fool would open the door to a stranger these days."

Especially when you're a woman alone with a precious child upstairs.

She held tighter onto the flashlight. If he stormed the door, she'd clonk him on the head with it if she had to.

"You think a psycho killer would bother having this conversation? If you're the Molly Maid people, you're gonna regret leaving me out here. I'll be tracking in sand and—"

"I'm not the cleaning service." Her heart hammered against her ribs. "I'm telling you again, sir. I'm not letting you in. I'm about to call the police. So you'd better skedaddle."

"Skedaddle, my ass!" He gave a good thunk on the door. "But hey, what's a little more water? And a little more humiliation? I've endured plenty the last couple days. Oh, yes, indeedy."

She was the one with the sob story, so she wasn't going to feel sorry for him. But somehow she did. All Southern men could hold TED talks about how to charm the ladies.

Don't go soft on him.

"You should get back in your car," she said. "I don't care how wet you and your luggage are. When are you men gonna take responsibility for your own choices? I'm so sick of y'all expecting women to be your mothers. Honestly."

She was breathing a little hard, and her accent was coming back thicker than a Dagwood sandwich.

"Don't take your man woes out on me, girlfriend. And you can keep my mother out of this discussion, if you don't mind." There was a flash of lightning and an almost instantaneous clap of thunder. "Now open the damned *door.*"

She swallowed hard and ignored her wobbly knees. Lightning didn't sit well with her. Neither did being responsible for a man getting fried on her doorstep. But she wouldn't panic. She couldn't afford to.

"Your key"—she said in her best no-nonsense voice—
"doesn't work because you're at the wrong place. *I* have
the lease here." Monica did, actually, but Lacey was the
double-crossed former employee with no place to go. That
had to count for something.

"That's it," the stranger said. "I'm calling Callum."

Lacey's eyes widened. "You know Callum?"

"Of course I know him. *You* know him?"

"Yes, but—" Callum lived on the West Coast. A local
wouldn't know him. Unless—shoot. Unless he was somehow involved with the movie. Lacey's heart sank. She
was hoping to steer clear of the movie and all the hoopla
associated with it.

"Lady?"

"Yes?" She bit her thumbnail, wondering what he
would say next to coax her to open the door.

"I'm telling you now." The man's tone was softer now,
a little menacing. "I'm not going to drive to that crappy
Beach Bum Inn and deal with this tomorrow. I have to get
to work early in the morning, and I need my sleep. Callum said no one was here and to make myself at home. I
intend to do that. With or without your permission. And
with or without a key."

Lacey drew a breath. "I'm going to let you in," she said
slowly. "But only for a minute."

"About damned time."

With shaking hands—but ready to do battle—she
opened the door. A huge crack of thunder split the air.

"You're in my lighthouse," he said in toneless greeting
and strode past her—*whoosh*—like a freight train. He
wore old jeans, Red Wing boots, and a brown quail jacket
with the corduroy brim popped up, not for show, it appeared, but to keep off the rain. Beneath the coat was a
ratty mustard-brown sweater vest with braided leather

buttons, and underneath that, a faded red Henley open at the neck.

He was about her age, with hard cheekbones and a distinctly pissed-off demeanor which intensified when he turned to look directly at her, water streaming off his high-crowned, wide-brimmed sable fedora.

Her heart nearly stopped in her chest.

It was Beau Wilder. *The* Beau Wilder. International superstar. He'd won the People's Choice award for Favorite Movie Actor the past three years. He excelled in action adventure, rose to heroic heights in detective or police stories, and kept the audience on the edge of their seats in thrillers.

"Holy bejeezus." Even as a Hollywood insider of sorts, she was gobsmacked.

"Uh huh, I know," he said dismissively.

He hadn't shaved for days—typical behavior for your average macho male celebrity—but he was Ralph Lauren handsome, too, tall and broad-shouldered. A man's man, for sure, but distinguished—elegant, even—in the way that a sweaty, mud-laden horse with highly muscled flanks is when it wins the Kentucky Derby.

Shock and—she had to admit it—*awe* were quickly replaced by indignation. His eyes were bloodshot, and he reeked of alcohol. Henry was upstairs, for goodness' sake. "I've got some bad news for you, Mr. Wilder." Her voice shook just a little, but he was only a man—and an actor at that. "This isn't your lighthouse."

"For the next two months it is," he shot back and dropped his bag with a thunk, managing to avoid the puddle forming at his feet. "I traded Callum four front-row seats to a Lakers game to get this place. That's a business transaction. I have rights."

His tone was deliberate, gritty, as if he were facing a Bad Guy. A Bad Guy who was gonna lose.

"You don't really expect me to buy that," she said.
"What?"

She laced her right arm over her left. "You're in a *light-house*. Not a courthouse. I'm not your perp, and *you're* drunk."

He scowled at an invisible audience first, then looked her up and down, taking his time. She was used to that—but he was getting off on the wrong foot with her in a big way.

"Hey," she warned him. "Mind your manners."

She shifted on her feet, nervous again because suddenly he exuded unholy joy, his eyes glowing the same green golden-brown as the tips of marsh grass caught in a beam of sunlight.

"Well, I'll be," he said. "You're the hot tamale who starred in *Hell on Wheels*."

Released online-only, five years ago. It had gone viral, too, but in a bad way. Which was why Lacey was no longer a natural blond. She tossed her head. "Don't get sexist with me, Mr. Stud Muffin."

"Oh, for crying out loud. It was a compliment." He lifted a *very* suggestive brow. "Greta."

He might be a pain in her backside right now, but, Lord, he drew the eye. And he'd seen her movie. She couldn't believe it! Her whole body responded to the new energy he put out—at her expense, yes, but she'd always liked bad people. Really bad people. Not pretend ones like Sheena who rebelled because they needed attention but people who bucked the system because they were too smart to stay bored—too selfish to sacrifice fun.

Like her.

But she was done. Done with bad people and the excitement they brought into her life. For Henry's sake, she was willing to learn bored. There had to be something to it.

"You look like *I Love Lucy* now," he said. "But you're still Greta Gildensturm. You can't hide those eyes, or that—that—"

Despite her warnings, he gazed at her as if she were Cool Whip and he was the spoon—which considering the source, she knew she should find flattering. But she was over all that malarkey and over all the men who did it, even one-in-a-billion men like Mr. Beau Hot Stuff Wilder. And because he must have valued his life, he didn't finish the sentence.

"Her name was Lucy Ricardo, not *I Love Lucy*." She made a *duh* face. "That was the name of the show." And she refused to acknowledge her character's name in *Hell on Wheels*. She'd refuse to her dying day. She'd refuse even after death, if that were possible. She'd come and haunt anyone who tried to put her and Greta Gildensturm together.

"She'll always be *I Love Lucy* to me." Smug. Still a little drunk. But damned cute. And bad clear through.

Oh, God. The worst kind of man.

And the best kind of movie star.

She crossed her arms over her ample breasts, which she'd declined to have reduced. Her back didn't hurt. So why should she? Was it her fault God made her that way? And she was scared of doctors and knives and, oh, anything that had to do with medicine, including Band-Aids and Luden's Cherry Cough Drops, which she'd choked on once when she was five.

So it would be a cold day in hell when she got a breast reduction.

"Let me get this straight," she said. "If you meet someone who looks like Theodore Cleaver, you're gonna say, you look like *Leave It to Beaver*? Does that make sense?"

He didn't seem to be listening. "And you were just in the news. You spilled a whole pitcher of margaritas over

Callum's head at a West Hollywood restaurant with Monica Lowry sitting right next to him. Don't tell me you wanted to break up those two lovebirds. They deserve each other." He lifted a wet cigar to his mouth and clamped down on it, grinning. "Yep, *Hell on Wheels* and Greta Gildensturm both trended on Twitter that day."

But not Lacey Clark. No one knew her real name because she wasn't a memorable enough actress, was she? She wasn't even memorable enough to get on *Survivor* or any B-list Hollywood reality show. She was on the F list. F for failure. And there was a much worse F word to apply to her acting career, but she was a lady, and she wouldn't use it, much less think it.

Which might explain why she liked fudge so much. And they made a lot of it on Indigo Beach. That was one good thing about being here.

"You can go to hell." Lacey angled her chin at the open door. "And lose the cigar while you're at it."

His grin disappeared, and he threw the cigar outside. "Wow. You really *are* a buzzkill."

"Apparently guys like you have nothing better to do than point that out."

"Guys like me?"

He might think he was one of a kind. But he wasn't. There were plenty of spoiled, rich, handsome, charming men—many of them *actors*, a word she could barely say anymore without seeing red—who'd been blessed with a confidence they hadn't earned. But she wouldn't bother to explain. His kind was too cocky to get it.

"Callum's a jackass," he said. "But I'm not Callum. So lay off the I-hate-men routine, please, until you see the guy—or guys—who've actually done you wrong. 'Kay?"

"Fine." She felt a small stab of guilt—but not on his behalf. Oh, no. He'd merely reminded her that she'd let Callum off too easy. "I'll overlook your general lack of sensitivity and make you a cup of coffee." Maybe she'd find out how he knew Callum. "But then you're leaving. If you're not sober enough to drive thirty minutes from now, I'll call the sheriff to pick you up. Now that's a Tweet that would trend! Why don't you get on there right now and let everyone know you were driving under the influence?"

The rain fell steadily but with less force. It had wimped out, something she wasn't going to do anymore.

"I didn't drive," he said, "and I'm not going anywhere. Nor do I Tweet. My assistant does." He went to the door. "Thanks, doll," he called to someone and blew a kiss.

There was the honk of a horn, and then the loud, sputtering sound of a car engine starting up.

"Wait!" Lacey pushed past him. "Was that your assistant?" From the light of the small sconce on the portico, she caught a glimpse of a silhouette of big pageant hair in the driver's seat of a white Ford pickup truck. It spun up some sand and took off, its oversized tires and raised chassis rocking like mad over the uneven surface of the drive as it sped away. Lacey recognized monster truck rally mania when she saw it.

Over her shoulder, Beau Wilder murmured, "You could call her that. Just for the past twenty-four hours."

"Ewww."

He shook his head, a ghost of a smile on his lips as he watched her go. "I love a woman who can drive like a bat outta hell. Cooks up a storm, too. Homemade biscuits and ham this morning, along with her mama's own peach jam. Suh-weet."

And he didn't mean about the jam, either. That much was obvious.

Lacey had had enough. "You'll have to walk or call your one-day assistant back for a ride. If she's not here in half an hour, I'm calling the police."

He pulled out his phone. "I don't think so. *You're*

trespassing. Not me." He dialed a number and held the phone to his ear.

"Who are you calling?" Her heart pounded.

"Sheriff's office." His face was serene.

"*No.*" She swiped at his phone.

But he swiftly lifted his arm. "Why not? You're about to call them anyway."

"We can solve this," she said, realizing too late that he'd never dialed, "without contacting the authorities."

Dammit, she'd messed up. So she tossed her head and stared him down like a viper hypnotizing its prey.

Mr. Wilder cocked his head. "Whoa."

She put her hand on her right hip and turned her left foot out to intensify the effect.

But all he did was send her a searing look—he was good at that—and tuck the phone back in his pocket. "Were you ever an evil first-grade teacher in another life? Because I swear you're channeling Mrs. Biddle right now. She's why I hate naps and milk in little cartons to this day."

"You were the non-stop talker, weren't you? Or the sly boy who hid on the playground at the end of recess when you had a substitute teacher?"

"Don't change the subject. I thought you were all about getting the police involved."

A flush of heat spread across her chest and up her neck. "Why should I? I've got a lease. You don't. Your consolation prize is that cup of coffee, and then you're outta here. Deal with it."

"Little lady"—he opened his jacket and pulled out a plastic grocery bag with an oblong square shape inside—"since I'm actually where I'm supposed to be, and you might be kinda cute when you're not frowning—I'll try to be patient. I've got a steak, and I'm about to cook it. And then I'm going to sit back and enjoy my new place, me

and Jim Beam, since the liquor store was all out of Jack."
He tossed the steak on the table, pulled a silver flask out of
another pocket, twisted off the cap, and took a swig. "Sorry,
but you're not invited, although I could be persuaded to
change my mind." He cocked that famous brow at her.

Damn him for being so good at that. "Forget it."

"Are you sure?"

"Yes."

Their eyes met, and for a split second, she thought he
saw everything she'd been trying to hide.

He advanced toward her, his tread slow, careful. She
wasn't in physical danger. That she knew. His was the
careful walk of a man who was either still drunk or
hungover—hardly aggressive. But it was more than that.
He approached her the way he'd done that horse with the
broken leg in the last war movie he'd made.

She stuck her chin up. No need to feel sorry for her.
She was A-okay. She had a head on her shoulders, and
she'd been through the wringer in the craziest town on the
West Coast and come out the other side not totally
crushed. And, man, had she seen some people out in L.A.
plowed over, innocents like her who'd gone out there to
find themselves and lost themselves instead.

But Hollywood crazy had nothing on Southern crazy.
Therefore, she told herself as she exhaled through her
nose, *I can handle anything, including this man*.

When he was a mere foot away, he stopped.

"If you're hoping Callum's gonna show," he said in
that velvety-rough voice that had melted millions of
women's hearts, "I hate to tell you this—he's not coming.
But you can keep me company for a couple hours instead.
If your heart's broken, that is." He chucked her chin
softly. "Maybe that accounts for your ornery attitude."

She pushed past him, her hands trembling, and straightened the placemats on one side of the table. Dancing blue

crab and shrimp. Henry loved them. "I'm not heartbroken." She looked up. "And you're obviously a womanizer, a trait I find a complete turn-off. How do you know Callum anyway?"

"We go way back."

"Why'd he give you a key to this place?"

"I'm doing the movie. And seeing as he jumped ship with Monica, he handed over his key."

"His?" She gave a short laugh. "It wasn't his to give."

"Maybe it wasn't yours to take. Why are you in Monica's rental?"

He had her there. "She owes me."

"A likely story."

"You know what?" She sent him her best withering look. "I really don't need any actors around here."

Understatement of the century.

She needed sleep, salt air, wind, and Henry. She needed a job, too.

"It's a moot point," he replied. "You're not staying."

"Yes, I am." Her words might as well have been hammered into rock by a big, sweaty hand gripping a chisel, they were so solid. "You may be a big star, but I got here first. That counts for something under the law. You'll have to pry me outta here by my fingernails, you hear? Or spend weeks trying to evict me. Your publicist won't appreciate the news stories that'll come out of that."

The corner of his mouth crooked. "Here's your problem, Greta. You overact. All Southerners do. It's in our blood to live larger than life. Doesn't matter if we come from a trailer park or a mansion. It's our thing. But here's a secret: if you want to make it big in Hollywood, you gotta bury your own heart. It's easy for me. I don't have one."

"Talk about overacting." She almost rolled her eyes but then decided to show him she could do *restrained* and *mature* with the best of them. "What'd you do? Sell it to the devil? Or did some woman rip it out?"

He sent her a look, stood still and tall. Dignified. She felt vaguely embarrassed, but then she remembered she'd seen that same look on him on the big screen when he'd played a hero attorney who sued a big, bad company on behalf of an entire town of poor coal miners.

"All I'm saying," she said, "is that you're throwing drama right back at me. Of course you have a heart. You couldn't have played all those roles without one."

"You saying I'm good?"

"*No.*" She gave another short laugh. Was he kidding? She wasn't going to say that, not when he was trying to throw her out on her ear! "I'm just saying I see why maybe you make the big bucks. *Maybe.*"

She winced. It was not intended to be a smile in any way, shape, or form, so it annoyed her when he chuckled.

He pulled down a frying pan hanging over the sink, released it with a quick twirling motion through the air, then caught it right above the stovetop, and set it down on a burner. "I'm not used to sharing, Miz Greta."

Big baby. Which didn't jibe with his knowing his way around a kitchen, but that was probably a fluke.

He flicked on the gas, and a bright blue flame appeared beneath the pan. Over his shoulder, he said, "This lighthouse is out of the way, and it's big enough for just one person—me. Now in Casa Wilder, I fry up a steak the night before I start work on a movie set. I also give damsels in distress breaks if they cooperate, at least until morning. You'll be packed and ready to go."

He sprinkled salt in the pan. Then he unwrapped the steak—just held one end of the paper and let it roll out into the pan. It was probably the way women unwrapped themselves for him all the time.

The sizzling smell made Lacey hungry. She'd been

going light lately to save her food money for Henry. To-night she'd made him scrambled eggs, but there were only two left, so she'd saved them for tomorrow and had eaten a peanut butter and jelly sandwich instead.

"Well," she huffed. "I can tell you think the sun comes up just to hear you crow, Mr. Wilder. But I've had enough of your talk. If you insist on staying, I'm going up. But don't you *dare* smoke inside, leave the stovetop on, abandon dirty dishes in the sink, or walk around naked. I'm armed with a Colt .45, and I'm not afraid to use it."

She turned on her heel, hoping he believed her lie about the gun. She wouldn't tell him about the Heinz 57 sauce she'd found in the cupboard yesterday, either. He could eat his dad-blasted steak without it.